# *Tuesday's* CHILD

## LINDA CHAIKIN

**HARVEST HOUSE PUBLISHERS**
Eugene, Oregon 97402

*Cover by Koechel Peterson & Associates, Minneapolis, Minnesota*

**TUESDAY'S CHILD**
Copyright © 2000 by Linda Chaikin
Published by Harvest House Publishers
Eugene, Oregon 97402

Library of Congress Cataloging-in-Publication Data
Chaikin, L. L.,
    Tuesday's Child / Linda Chaikin.
        p. cm. — (A day to remember series)
    ISBN 0-7369-0068-3
    1. World War, 1939-1945—France—Fiction. 2. World War,
1939-1945—Morocco—Fiction. 3. Ballet dancers—France—Paris—Fiction.
4. Sisters—Morocco—Fiction. I. Title.
PS3553.H2427 T83   2000
813′ .54—dc21                                    99-057069
                                                     CIP

**Printed in the United States of America.**

        00 01 02 03 04 05 06 07 / BC / 10 9 8 7 6 5 4 3 2 1

**LINDA CHAIKIN**
is an award-winning writer
of more than 17 books. Her
recent Trade Winds series
includes *Captive Heart, Silver Dreams,*
and *Island Bride.*
*Tuesday's Child* is the
second book in the popular
A Day to Remember series.
Linda and her husband, Steve,
make their home
in California.

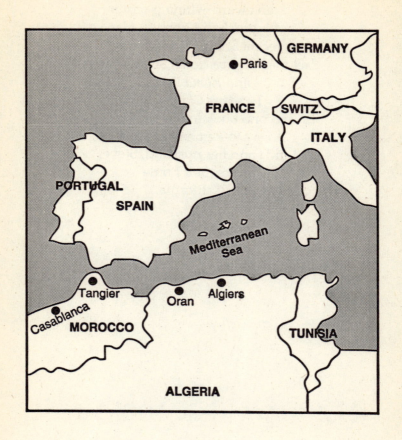

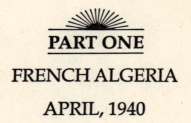

# PART ONE

## FRENCH ALGERIA

### APRIL, 1940

# 1

The West Algerian Company train chugged across a desolate expanse of obscure dunes that were constantly shifting in the wind, and now and then a remote date palmerie appeared beneath a blue marble sky.

Valli Chattaine removed her sun hat and fanned herself in a futile attempt to keep cool. The long, airy sleeves of her practical blue cotton traveling dress hung limp, the cloth sticking to her perspiring skin like a bandage. *Don't complain, you knew what you were getting into when you made the decision to come,* she thought, looking about the ramshackle interior. A few other passengers had melted into the hot enclosure, and opposite her was an amiable but talkative Englishman who had boarded at the last junction near the Port of Oran where the French war fleet was anchored. He was fast asleep, his floppy snow-white mustache quavering as he snored. He'd been "waylaid by a bunch of Mussolini's Italians" during his trip home from Cairo, he had told her indignantly, and had been forced into this indirect and "tedious" route to reach Casablanca, in the hopes of getting to neutral Lisbon.

For some reason his explanation seemed rather odd to her.

She looked out the dusty window—just scorching heat, the sunbeams blazing down, reflecting off white sand without mercy. Her feet felt swollen in her tan sandals, and her wavy, blue-black waist-length hair was casually formed into a French twist that in the heat felt too heavy for her slender neck. When she shut her eyes against the glare she could almost envision Tangier Bay. She allowed herself to sink into the memory of Great-Aunt Calanthe's palatial house in Tangier, and of its jasmine-scented garden that sheltered rustling palms and lucid pools of still water. She sighed.

Tangier was home, and the years she'd spent in Paris pursuing a career in ballet had done little to extinguish the happy memory of her teenage years. She'd grown up in the French quarter of the International Zone in French Morocco and she still had melancholy days in Paris when she would recall Tangier with longing. Ah, to be sixteen again, standing on the veranda of her bedroom in Great-Aunt's house.

*Dear Calanthe. She had been so proud of me.* At seventy-five she had boarded a plane alone and flown all the way from Tangier to watch Valli graduate ballerina school. *If only she could come next month,* she thought. *My first starring role in the Paris Opera Ballet Theater, and I'm dancing with her favorite, the ballet master, Rodolphe Gaillard!*

But there was no chance of Calanthe coming to Paris in May. Great-Aunt had disowned her four years ago when Valli's sister Giselle had—

*No, don't start that again,* she lectured herself. She wanted to forgive Giselle, to forget the shattered past and go on with her life. She had even written her sister telling her so, and Giselle had written back with bubbling emotion, telling her how "Christian" Valli was, and how she would never forgive herself for what had happened. Giselle was even getting married, she had written Valli, to a wonderful man, a Colonel Sebastien Ransier who served under General Charles de Gaulle in North Africa, and she wanted Valli to attend her wedding.

Valli had reached out in reconciliation and gone to Casablanca for the gala wedding. Giselle had kissed her and shed tears, and Valli had hugged her in return and stayed the weekend before flying back to Paris. But as far as she knew, Giselle had never explained the truth to Great-Aunt Calanthe, who had ignored her at the wedding and reception following.

All that was three years ago. Now, after what seemed like hours of listening to the monotonous clacking of the wheels, she realized her mouth was dry. Valli lifted her canteen and discovered she'd forgotten to fill it at the last stop. So much for independence and preparedness. She might be courageous enough to come all the way from Paris to the Sahara, but she'd forgotten water. She laughed at herself and glanced at the Englishman, Sir Edward Blystone. It made her feel a little better that a man heavily into Egyptian archaeology, as he told her he was, also had shortcomings when it came to preparedness—she recalled how out of sorts he had been over misplacing his hat just before boarding. She looked back out the window.

So much had changed since she'd first left Tangier for ballet school nearly seven years ago. And now she was moving constantly forward. Valli had come from the port of Oran on the Mediterranean and was on route to Sidi-bel-Abbes, a romantic military outpost belonging to the famed

French Foreign Legion. Bel-Abbes was a mere fifty miles inland from the port of Oran, but by the amount of time it was taking the train to get there, the distance might well have been five hundred miles.

*I shouldn't have taken the train,* she thought, as the old brakes squealed, and once again they were slowing down. Once again they were coming to another frequent stop along the route. She should have hired a driver at Oran when she arrived from Marseille. *I would have been there by now.* She wouldn't arrive until sunset. Would Davide be waiting to pick her up? She'd written her missionary brother weeks ago letting him know she was coming, but upon leaving Marseille there had not yet been a reply at the French Consul.

She frowned. In his last letter, Davide told her he'd been ill. He was also undergoing opposition in his work from the Berber Muslims living in the mountains. He hadn't told her what his health problem was, but she knew he'd suffered from dysentery and fever the year before. With no one except an Arab friend to care for him, he'd dwindled down to a hundred and thirty pounds!

For Davide, who stood six feet, such a weight loss had made him look emaciated. This time, Valli was determined to care for him herself. She had brought medications from Paris just in case the supplies were limited at Bel-Abbes.

Valli had always been close to her brother. They held in common their deepest spiritual values. In fact, it was Davide who like an undershepherd led her to the Great Shepherd of wayward sheep. He had come all the way to Paris to be with her during her "heart's crisis" after losing Kraig Gestler to Giselle just weeks before the wedding. It was during that painful ordeal of betrayal and loss that Valli had opened her heart to God.

"The love of God is different than a man's love. He will never betray your trust, never mislead you," Davide had told her. "Jesus will never seek to take from you selfishly. God is the greatest Giver. The greatest Lover of souls. The greatest Friend a woman will ever have."

Valli's heart had melted. In her third year of ballet school she had placed her faith in Christ as her one and only Savior. Nearly five years had slipped by since then and she had never regretted that decision. God indeed was the greatest Lover of souls.

Now she had come rushing to Davide. It was her time to help him. But why hadn't he answered her letter? Worried, she had even sent a letter to Great-Aunt Calanthe. A response arrived in Paris two weeks before (not from Calanthe, but from her secretary, Madame Viole) that no one had heard from Davide in the past two months. That news, along with her own wish to see his work, had been enough to send Valli on the lone, adventurous trip into French Algeria.

The train jerked, screeched, and came to a stop on the narrow gauged rail. "Eh? What's this...have we arrived, m'dear?" Sir Blystone awoke, rubbing a hand across his chin.

Valli looked out the window. "Just one more of the many small red stations scattered along the route to Sidi-bel-Abbes," she said with a smile.

"Oops, here they come," Blystone said. "Like a swooping flock of vultures." He tried his canteen. "Maybe I can buy some water if it's drinkable. You can catch dysentery, you know."

The crowd of Arab vendors robed in dusty *djellabas*, their brown faces as baked and cracked as dried mud in the sun, gathered beneath the window selling their wares.

Competing voices shouted in a hodgepodge of Arabic, French, and Spanish. They pushed and shoved, waving baskets and trays of green sweet figs, ripe oranges, lush dates, and bright melons. Everywhere there were big, lazy flies that clung to the cut fruit, and the smell of Arab tobacco, along with *champoraux*, an Algerian drink of strong syrupy coffee with gobs of sugar and throat-scalding brandy, was strong. Drugs were sold boldly—cannabis, mixed with tobacco, and hashish. The train passengers were in a consuming mood, and French francs and Spanish lira were passed back and forth through the windows as fast and loose as chips on a gambling table.

There were still more passengers jamming the aisle hoping to get off the train to stretch and find the lavatory. Valli clutched her empty canteen. In spite of the confusion, she thought perhaps she could hail a waterboy once she escaped into the station cabana. Patience, she lectured to no avail. At last Valli got into position in the aisle to disembark. She had just found a spot when—

"Oh!" she said as someone clumsily bumped into her, pushing her forward into the next passenger, jarring the canteen and handbag loose from her hand. The canteen landed on the floor with a tinny clatter.

"Posh! Dreadfully awkward of me, m'dear—" Blystone mumbled. "Heat's getting to me, I think. Most sorry about this—"

She smiled. "Oh it's quite all right, Monsieur Blystone. Are *you* all right?" she asked as she steadied him. "This heat, monsieur, it's not beneficial to you at all." He had told her of his heart ailment back at the last station when he arrived.

"Yes, quite so. So clumsy of me, Miss Chattaine, but I'd vow someone pushed me." And he turned around with a scowl, mopping his heavy florid face with a large dangling handkerchief. Valli, too, looked behind them protectively, looping her arm through his. The impatient passengers were paying them little attention, except that some cast glances, anxious to get off the train. "Monsieur, you are blocking the aisle," someone said from behind them.

"Oh. Great Scot—so I am. So sorry, old man." Sir Blystone, half as wide as he was tall, stooped and picked up Valli's canteen and purse, groaning as he did. "Crotchety knees, I'm afraid," he explained apologetically. It took him a moment to straighten, but he looked proud of himself when he presented them to her. "There you go m'dear. Dry, hot weather good for arthritis, indeed! Ho, I've had more trouble in the Sahara than I ever had in foggy London."

She smiled sympathetically, aware that people were trying to squeeze past them. She stepped back toward her seat, waiting for him to hand over her canteen, which he held as he chatted.

"I'm widely traveled you know, writing articles about archaeological sites, taking photographs. Interesting work, it brought me everywhere, till these blasted Nazis and Italians decided to muddy the international playground. Like mean army ants, they're everywhere. I collect postcards from the places I've been—a silly habit, perhaps, but I enjoy going over them later when the winter rains keep me indoors." He showed her a stack of cards with a rubber band around them. "This is Ezbekiah Gardens in Cairo...lovely spot. Roses, you know."

"It's very lovely," she said politely, looking back toward the aisle, anxious to disembark.

"Oh, go ahead, take a look at them at your leisure, m'dear. We've plenty of time between now and Bel-Abbes." At the same time, he removed a cigar from his watered-silk vest, bit the end, and pulled a cluster of several white roses from under his jacket. He sniffed it, chuckling.

At first she thought they were real and wondered where he'd bought them in the desert, but a moment later she could see they were paper. "Lovely, aren't they?" He winked and leaned toward her. "And they never die. Best part about 'em. My granddaughter made these for me. She sells them in London. 'Everlasting,' she calls them."

"They're realistic looking." Valli smiled.

"For you, m'dear." He pinned one to her handbag. "Egypt, interesting, mysterious. Many ancient secrets. Do you have an interest in ancient history?"

"Well, actually no—"

"No, you wouldn't, nearly forgot, a ballerina, you told me, and with the famous Paris Opera Ballet Theater. Most charming. And you're on your way to visit your missionary brother in Bel-Abbes. What was his name? Davide Chattaine, that was it. By golly, I'm holding you up, aren't I? Allow me to fill your canteen for you—"

"Oh no, Sir Blystone, please don't trouble yourself—"

"No trouble at all, 'tis the least I can do. You've been most patient with me. I need a bit of exercise, you know. You just hold onto my seat, and if you wouldn't mind, my canvas bag. No need to carry any extra weight around with me." He chuckled. "I'll just take my umbrella. Works wonders for shade, you know. You can try it if you like. Posh! I wish I hadn't misplaced my hat. Well, no matter, I'll pick up another."

"You must not trouble yourself over me, monsieur—"

He glanced out the window. "I say—" he leaned over, squinting, trying to peer out. He placed a round glass spectacle in his right eye. "Isn't that a waterboy coming now?"

She followed his glance, trying to swish away a persistent fly. Her eyes, the rich, warm color of brown velvet, surveyed the area. Yes, it was a waterboy, and he balanced two jugs, skillfully maneuvering his way through the throng. She pointed. "We're in luck."

"Marvelous, call him over."

The hot, dry wind tossed loose strands of her silky black hair as she leaned out the window. Valli noted with casual interest that some international mercenary soldiers were also arriving, from another direction in the station. This particular junction was a deployment area for new recruits of the French Foreign Legion, and before she had boarded at Oran she'd been warned by a disapproving fatherly conductor that a dozen civilians had signed up in Marseille and were aboard. They would be collected further up the line by a transport officer and brought to another Algerian training camp. She knew that the recruits were already seated in the back of the train. Valli had thanked him for his concern but assured him she would be quite safe, that in these dangerous days she wouldn't think of going on such an adventurous journey without bringing a small revolver.

She waved her hat for the waterboy and called, but he didn't appear to notice. However, she seemed to have caught the glance of a mercenary soldier walking toward the train.

His legionnaire hat was tipped forward against the sun's glare so as to partially shadow his face. Even so, she could see he was quite good-looking. He wore the uniform well, and he appeared well-trained for the demanding life in the harsh environs of North Africa. Although she couldn't say for certain, she thought he was a captain.

Foreign legionaires were not new to her. She had grown up seeing them on the streets in Tangier, but their reputation for being some of the worst romantic rogues in the world had kept her at a safe distance. She wondered about this one, for he was either watching her or the train. What was he up to?

Captain Marc Louis Durell of the French Foreign Legion looked up at the West Algerian train and wondered if the German agent named Dietrich Gestler had been wise enough to color his blond hair brown, or was he overconfident? He had heard that Dietrich was a boaster.

The hot gust that rippled the sand and blew it against the wheels of the train cooled Marc's perspiring face. A face that was handsomely sculpted and tanned from the Algerian sun. The tan enhanced a pair of crystal blue eyes, ridged with thick lashes, that gazed out from under straight dark brows. It was to his benefit that he had inherited the elegance and tender heart of his mother, Josephine Jacqueline Ransier, to temper the bold, roguish ways of his father, Sergeant Louis Durell. His father, when young, had escaped Paris by night to avoid the guillotine before joining the legion. The tale had little effect, however, on the devotion Marc felt for his father, who was killed in the Rif War in Tangier.

The shoulder-length white scarf attached to the back of Marc's pillbox-shaped hat fluttered in contrasting color to his legionnaire jacket. His white trousers were bloused into calf-length boots, and he wore the customary uniform sash of blue tied at his waist, where a revolver was sheathed in leather. By all outward accounts he appeared as his father before him: a soldier who, either willingly or due to extenuating circumstance, was willing to break bonds and ties with family and, sometimes, country to serve as a mercenary.

But things are rarely as they first appear. Few of his comrades at Sidi-bel-Abbes knew that his five-year "duration" in the legion had ended several years ago and that he was now a member of the Surete, an elite group within French Intelligence headquartered in Paris, serving in Morocco and Algeria under his mother's cousin, Colonel Sebastien Ransier.

"Your assignment is simple," Sebastien had told him two days ago when they had met in a deserted area of the sandy expanse. "The stand-in for British agent Hartley is in trouble. He's a novice, so you'll need to play the game as he hands the cards. His name is Blystone. He's passing through on the West Algerian Company Railroad. He carries crucial information that must be delivered to the Surete in Paris. You are to see that it does not pass into the wrong hands."

Marc had accompanied Captain Renault as he prepared to leave the post to collect recruits. Marc worried knowing that Blystone was a novice who would be under surveillance. But he had to respect the man for lifting the fallen flag and carrying on. How Blystone had ended up on the West Algerian train was unclear to Marc, though he'd learned he had been foiled from leaving Oran for Lisbon. In desperation, Blystone was trying to reach Colonel Ransier, the top man in North Africa. However, the Surete was afraid that Blystone, by doing so, would end up leading an agent from Berlin straight to him. Marc's own identity was also to be guarded.

Marc walked toward the train. But where had Captain Renault disappeared to? He was to board the train and gather the new legionnaire recruits while Marc met with Blystone. Then, in the window, he glimpsed the Englishman. With relief, Marc saw that he was still alive. Even that was a success for the poor professor with someone like Gestler after him. Next to Blystone, Marc noticed a striking demoiselle—Valli Chattaine. He had seen her recently on a lovely oil painting hanging on one of the walls of Colonel Sebastien's residence in Tangier. His wife, Giselle, had placed it there. The painting had been of a striking young woman with large velvet brown eyes and almost blue-black hair posing in a white ballerina costume. Her modesty had also caught his attention. Instead of the typical tutu, she had posed in a longer white chiffon skirt that swirled as softly as butterfly wings.

*Don't tell me Blystone will use her as the courier?*

The station was crowded. Some camels grumbled beneath their loads. Thin donkeys flickered their pointed ears to chase away flies.

"Your absence began to worry me," came a taut but relieved voice near his elbow. "I would not care to find you somewhere on the railroad track, a bullet in your back."

Marc showed no recognition as he turned toward the voice he knew so well. Rue Jacquette stood in an Arab woman's *haik*, a long, hooded robe of dark cloth. Jacquette began unloading oranges and melons from the back of a donkey.

"You wish to buy, oui?" Jacquette's shrewd black eyes above the section of cloth he wore across the lower portion of his face, called an *itham*, were laughing at his own disguise. He held out an old wine jug.

Marc took the bottle and uncorked the lid. Even through the cloth covering the lower part of his face, Marc could make out Jacquette's masculine jaw line and his grin. Marc tossed him a French franc as though paying *her* for use of the jug.

Jacquette murmured: "How do I look as a member of the mysterious female clan?"

"Mysterious perhaps, but about as feminine as a camel in ballet slippers." Marc glanced back to the train window, scanning the face of the demoiselle he remembered from earlier years in Tangier. She was looking in his direction, but he didn't think she recognized him from this distance. He had known she was coming to visit Davide, but even if he hadn't, he would have recognized her. Such grace was not often seen in the scorching Sahara.

Marc handed the wine bottle back to Jacquette, making sure his friend with the drinking problem put it far out of reach. Marc kept his eye on the scene and waited. He gestured to the lush fruit. "What poor mademoiselle did you rob this time?"

"You underrate my talents, Captain. Good old Jacquette does not need to 'rob' women. They are always willing to help one so handsome and talented." He grinned. "It so happens I have many and varied friends, though not all are so fair of character as you and Davide."

Marc knew all about Jacquette's raffish friends. His father, a legionnaire now dead like his own, had been a sturdy Frenchman who joined the legion because he was hounded by debt. Jacquette's mother, who was still alive, had originally come from Spain where once she had been a famous flamenco dancer. After a serious leg injury years ago she had come to Algeria and opened a seamy tavern in a dangerous district of Bel-Abbes catering to legionnaires.

Called Rue by his father, but Tomas by his mother, he compromised and called himself by his last name, Jacquette. Marc saw him slip comfortably into either culture, "like a snake shedding its skin," he liked to tease him. He'd been bringing Jacquette to listen to Davide Chattaine, a self-appointed chaplain to the legionnaires at Bel-Abbes. Recently, Jacquette had begun to show some spiritual interest, and Marc hoped it was genuine.

Jacquette had been Marc's childhood friend after he had arrived from Paris at the age of nine to join his father at the legionnaire outpost. He had remained a loyal friend throughout the years, even though in many ways they were as far apart now as snow was from the Sahara.

Jacquette's ties to family in fascist Spain were also an important commodity to Colonel Ransier. Because of that, the Surete in Paris was more than willing to use Jacquette with Marc as the go-between.

Marc noticed nothing unusual in the station, but he gave his enemies as much credit for subterfuge as he did Jacquette and himself. Marc was certain he was under watch, but fortunately there was nothing linking him to Blystone.

An old Arab walked past them leading a donkey loaded down with fruits and vegetables. The animal halted and the Arab stopped, stooped down, and examined its right rear hoof.

*Very convenient,* Marc thought. *Was he spying?*

"Do you have any almonds?" Marc asked Jacquette, pretending an interest in produce.

Jacquette wisely kept his masculine voice silent and searched among his own goods, taking his time to arrange them on the ground. He produced some almonds, followed by several pouches of tobacco. Marc stooped to have a look, debating Jacquette's prices, insisting they were too high. At last the old Arab moved on.

"Anything on Ahmed?" Marc asked of their own Berber agent.

"He's posing as a waterboy. Blystone will approach him and pretend to fill his canteen."

Then, somewhere in that brief meeting the information would be exchanged between Blystone and Ahmed. Marc would then make a brief exchange with Ahmed.

Jacquette reached for a melon among his goods, drew a long Berber knife from under his robe, and sliced it in one slick swipe. The juice ran. He scooped out the seeds and the flies swarmed to check it out like a band of marauders attacking a caravan. The sun beat down. He handed Marc a chunk of the orange fruit and glanced toward the train. "What's keeping Blystone aboard?"

The melon was warm and sweet. The pesky flies buzzed persistently. "The same could be said for Captain Renault. He should have been here by now," Marc said worriedly. "Blystone may be waiting for Renault to board. If he's not here in another minute I'm going on the train myself. He needs a distraction to get off without drawing attention. It will be up to you to get the information from Ahmed." He looked at Jacquette. "Did anyone think to check the new recruits boarding at Oran?"

Jacquette's knife ceased its carving. "A German would fit in well, wouldn't he? You think Dietrich Gestler is posing as one of them?"

"I wonder." Marc tried to remain relaxed while the moments ticked by. The longer the delay, the more chances for failure. He glanced again toward the train window. "I'm going aboard. Be ready for anything."

"Wait—Renault is coming."

And so was Ahmed, carrying two jugs of water on the ends of a pole across his shoulders. At the same moment Marc joined Renault, who whispered: "I had trouble, monsieur. There is more than one Nazi agent here. Use caution."

Aboard the train, Valli leaned out the window to wave her sun hat once more at the waterboy. An unknown vehicle came tearing into the station. A tall, straight-shouldered man with dark sunglasses and golden hair got out quickly. There was something unpleasantly familiar about him, but she didn't want to consider the familiarity. He disappeared into the shade near the side of the train platform. Her tension began to mount. Sir Blystone had seen the man as well, and she felt the clasp of his fingers tighten on her arm. He said in a low voice quite unlike his previous manner: "Never mind about the waterboy."

Valli turned her head and glanced at the Englishman. The lines had deepened in his face. "Anything wrong?" she whispered.

"Yes. Colonel Sebastien Ransier is your brother-in-law, is he not?"

"Yes," she whispered. "He has a post in Tangier. Why, what is it?"

"Tell me, your eyes are better than mine, that man who got out of the vehicle just now, the one with the blond hair, did he have a bandage on his hand?"

"I didn't notice." She searched his face. "Is it important?"

"For an old man, I'm wading in deep waters, my dear."

"I'm sorry. Can I help?"

"We haven't much time. If I do not return in ten minutes, can you bring the canvas bag to me?"

"Why—yes—of course I can, but—where will you be?"

"See that cabana behind the *souk*?" he said of the Arab bazaar. "There's a hat stand. If I don't return in ten minutes, look for me there. Ten minutes," he repeated, leaving.

Without warning, gunfire broke out. Blystone pushed his way toward the back exit. Valli ducked in the seat, her fingers tightening around the canvas bag.

What was happening?

As Marc and Renault had neared the side of the train, an open vehicle, tires screeching, had come to a stop with three men inside. Marc caught a glimpse of a tall, fair-haired man in sunglasses who jumped out and disappeared into the crowd of vendors. Gestler! Marc wanted to go after him, but his disciplined nature told him to keep his eye on Blystone. It was the Englishman who had the information. Nothing else mattered.

The driver remained behind the wheel while a third man jumped out and swiftly intercepted Ahmed, who was posing as a waterboy.

Marc glanced back at Jacquette to signal him to go to Ahmed's defense, but the old Arab man who had earlier stopped to check his donkey's hoof had also reappeared, and he was shrieking at Jacquette: "Thief! Thief!"

*A diversion. Ignore him, Jacquette.*

Jacquette understood as well, and he pushed past the man and began to run toward Ahmed, but the man with the donkey jumped him, bringing him down, displaying youthful strength.

Captain Renault ran toward the vehicle to help Ahmed, who was being dragged into the back seat. Renault fired at the front wheel as the vehicle was pulling away.

Where was Blystone? Marc moved toward the back exit of the train car just as the door opened and a pudgy man stepped out with a white paper rose in his lapel.


Inside the train, Valli sat up. The gunfire had ceased as quickly as it had begun so she cautiously looked out the window. It was pandemonium out there, and inside the train, passengers huddled together in the aisle.

"Is it a robbery?" someone shouted.

Had a recruit changed his mind about joining the legion and tried to escape? she wondered. She had heard often enough that punishment was severe. Firing a gun at the poor fellow wouldn't surprise her at all. She looked at her watch. Her heart was thudding. Blystone's entire demeanor had changed when that vehicle pulled up. What did it mean? Who was he, really? He had been quite friendly ever since she had met him—yes, come to think of it, he had literally bumped into her when they were first boarding at Oran.

She looked at the time again. Five minutes had passed since Blystone left. It seemed like twenty. She moved restlessly in her seat and then looked out the window again, but she didn't see Blystone anywhere.


Marc felt a wave of sympathy as he looked at the man with the white rose in his lapel. Why, Blystone must have been over sixty, yet he was doing the job of a young man in a life-threatening situation. Any criticism he had previously felt for the novice dissipated.

Blystone's gaze darted about looking for Marc. Marc stepped forward, but the Englishman shook his head slightly, looked back at the train door, then touched the paper rose. The message to Marc was clear, and he now knew exactly what to do.

Blystone made the ultimate sacrifice; he walked down to the train steps and then turned and hurried off carrying a small handbag, deliberately trying to catch the attention of the Nazi agent in sunglasses who was waiting somewhere in the shadows.

All this had happened in just a few minutes.

Marc boarded the train to make certain the man in sunglasses hadn't entered. He didn't think the German agent knew about Valli, and by now he should be after Blystone, but Marc took no chances. He saw Valli seated by the window, but she didn't see him. It was safer for her if he didn't explain about Blystone. If he could get the information without her knowing…

Just then a French policeman entered the front of the train. Marc kept toward the back, out of view.

Valli thought of Blystone. She might as well admit it to herself; he had behaved oddly over the waterboy—no, not the waterboy, the man in dark glasses. Her fingers were clamped around the canvas bag. She loosened her grip, rubbing her hand. Near the front of the train, by the door, someone sharply blew a police whistle. Her spine stiffened. With the rest of the passengers she looked up to see the entry of the French policeman.

"Messieurs, clear the aisle! Sit down at once. Please! No one shall be allowed to proceed with his journey until your passports and papers are checked."

There was a murmur.

"Why? What is wrong, monsieur?" someone called.

"A man has been murdered, monsieur."

"Murdered!" came the echo.

Valli pulled herself together. She looked at the canvas bag on her lap. For a moment her mind refused to think.

"We have found a waterboy dead on the far end of the track," the policeman said.

The waterboy, not Sir Blystone.

"A robbery, señor?" a Spaniard asked.

"For water?" someone snorted.

"He sold a lot of water today," the Spaniard said defensively. "Why would someone murder a waterboy otherwise, eh? It had to be money."

"I must ask you all to be silent," the policeman ordered. He turned as a legionnaire entered, short, squarely built, with a wide, black mustache slightly curled at the tips, who introduced himself as Captain Renault. His anxious gaze took in each and every passenger. Valli thought he was checking to see if someone in particular was on board. Who? Her instincts told her it was the man in sunglasses. Did this have something to do with Blystone as well?

"Légionnaires à moi!" the mustached officer was calling out. The men in civilian clothes at the back of the train moved forward uneasily to form a line. When they began marching toward the front exit, Captain Renault looked at the face of each man carefully. Valli reached down and gathered Blystone's heavy canvas bag and her handbag into her arms. What did he have inside, rocks? She left her overnight case on her seat, hoping it would be there when she reboarded.

As the recruits filed past her and down the aisle, coming between her and the officer with the mustache, she calmly stood and moved in the opposite direction toward the back exit. There was another legionnaire there who turned his back, writing something on a small slip of paper. Valli glanced at him. She must be imagining things. He too looked rather familiar, just as the man with sunglasses who had stepped out of the past did. She paused by the legionnaire, but he obviously didn't want to turn and look at her, so she shrugged and went down the train steps. She'd better find Sir Blystone.

Slipping the strap of the canvas bag over her shoulder, she merged swiftly into the throng of Berber merchants. Something odd was happening, but what?

# 2

Outside the train, the brightness and heat were stifling. A withering gust whipped at Valli's hair and blew her full skirt. *What if the legionnaire captain saw me leave? I don't think he did, but if he follows and tries to stop me from delivering the canvas bag—what shall I say?* Her brow furrowed. *But he couldn't possibly know Blystone entrusted his bag to me, and why do I even think it might matter?*

She knew why: Valli was becoming convinced that she was being followed and that Blystone might be in trouble.

She walked casually but swiftly through the vendors that were still crowding near the train exit and pushed her way through the sluggish throng toward the small *souk*, or market, located to one side of the junction.

She paused in the *souk* when she saw a French policeman standing just ahead questioning some uncooperative Arabs who were seated on the ground. A few women stood by, stony-faced. Why would anyone murder the waterboy? The Spaniard aboard the train had been right when he asked the question of the policeman.

Valli turned her head away and kept walking.

Near the whitewashed walls at the edge of the *souk* some Berber women sat in the dust wearing striped blankets and straw hats adorned with black pompons—a little touch of old Spain that had once ruled the Sahara before France. The women were guarding their piles of eggs and dried medejual dates. She paused, dug into her handbag for some French francs, and handed them to one of the women in exchange for the dates, but she was too thirsty to eat them now.

She walked forward, glancing in all directions for Blystone, hoping beyond hope that he might somehow materialize.

She stood in the dusty square, her concerns becoming as heavy as the bag slung over her shoulder. She tried to assure herself there was no lasting reason for alarm. But why had Blystone said he might not return? And if he did not, what should she do with his canvas bag?

An Arab walked by hawking his drinking pitcher and a tin cup. Water! If she didn't get some soon she'd begin seeing mirages! She called for him to stop. "How many francs?"

The stoic-faced trader held up five fingers.

"Five francs!" She didn't have that much change.

"For you, two francs," he said.

"One franc—and these dates." She pushed both toward him.

"Allah will reward you."

"Have you seen a heavy Englishman with a very white mustache come through here? He wanted to buy a hat." She pointed to her own.

He touched his left ear and shook his head as if he couldn't understand. He poured the trickling water into the tin cup used by all his customers. *I don't care if a camel drank from it, I'm thirsty,* she thought.

Valli took the cup with a sigh and was about to drink—

"Bonjour, mademoiselle," came a richly masculine French voice.

She paused, turned her head, and glanced from beneath her lashes. A legionnaire was standing a few feet away leaning against the *hanootz,* a bazaar stall, watching her. He was a formidable entity in dashing uniform with the luck (or ill luck) of being remarkably good looking, and she grew cautious.

"Bonjour," she replied, collecting herself.

"Drink that water, and by tonight you will be sick enough to stay in bed for a week."

Her disappointment sweltered with the sun beating upon her. Not drink it! She'd been thinking of water all afternoon.

He walked up. Somewhere in her mind she recognized him from the far distant past—perhaps in Tangier? Paris? Then she remembered. But...it couldn't be Marc Durell.

His damp hair below the hat was dark and wavy, and as his eyes came to hers, they were like a plunge into a light blue sea. Yes, it was Marc, the roguish scamp she had met at Great-Aunt Calanthe's house in Tangier. He'd been about eighteen then, and she, sixteen. That would make him twenty-five, and if possible more handsome, and therefore more dangerous and roguish than ever. He seemed to exude some untamed quality, or was it a contrast to the harsh and blistering surroundings?

As their gaze held she felt oddly embarrassed. Did he remember her? There was no reason why he should since she had snubbed him on the rest of that day and evening of nearly seven years ago after finding her sister Giselle wrapped in his hearty embrace on the lawn. She didn't know who had taken the initiative, Marc or Giselle, but it didn't matter; he had cooperated.

Realizing she was staring, she pulled her glance away to look back at the cup.

He removed his canteen and unstopped it. He handed it to her. "I wouldn't want you to think mercenary soldiers are totally without genteel civility, Mademoiselle Chattaine."

She looked back quickly. "So you do remember me, Captain Durell?"

He smiled. "I'm not likely to forget."

She glanced away.

"Your painting in ballerina costume graces the ballroom wall of Colonel Ransier's house in Tangier," he explained. "Giselle placed it there."

She was shocked that Giselle would want such a reminder of her on the wall. Of course, Marc wouldn't know why she felt this way about Giselle. She hoped Giselle hadn't hired someone to paint her photograph and put her in a flimsy bit of chiffon. "I have not seen it," she said a little uneasily.

"It does you very well, mademoiselle." He briefly took her in. "I hardly expected you to remember *me*, however."

He was a rogue all right. Was he suggesting she hadn't forgotten him because she had been attracted to him? Nevertheless she was thirsty. She handed the tin cup back to the Arab. He accepted it with a shrug and faded back into the crowd. She accepted the canteen from Marc. "Merci, Captain." She tipped it and drank while watching him under her lashes. Strange that Davide had never mentioned him. Was it his reputation? Probably.

He watched her drink as casually as one might watch a bird flitting about in a birdbath. She drew out a handkerchief and wet it, dabbing her face and throat, meeting his gaze as evenly as he met hers.

"Do you often go to my sister's house in Tangier, monsieur?" she asked meaningfully, the image of Marc and Giselle stamped and sizzling on her mind.

The blue eyes grew laconic as though he followed her thoughts.

"Your brother-in-law, Colonel Ransier, is my superior officer. One must obey orders, demoiselle," he said silkily.

Yes, she thought. One must. And how convenient to be posted in Tangier to obey those orders, or was she being unfair? She knew so little about Marc except for that single incident. She knew he had attended Saint Cyr, the War College in Paris, and she had even seen him once at a social gathering that she had attended with Kraig. She and Marc had pretended not to notice one another.

It was shameful to admit, but Giselle's weakness for handsome men would give her trouble leaving this one alone. Was he Sebastien's attaché?

He appeared calm, yet she detected some underlying sense of restlessness under his polite manner. She saw him glance at the canvas bag. She tensed. A gust of wind was tugging at the white canvas attached to the back of his hat. He held out his hand. "May I see your passport, please."

She was taken by surprise. Now why was he doing this? "Is it really necessary, Captain Durell?"

His face was inscrutable. "Pardonne, demoiselle, but the Foreign Legion is very precise about following orders."

Maybe, she thought, but she wasn't exactly convinced of any order to see *her* passport. She thought of Blystone and was anxious to be on her way.

"It is very inconvenient to stop now," she cajoled. "I'm afraid it's at the bottom of my bag." He managed to look grave and gallantly apologetic, but he remained adamant, arousing her suspicion that he was affecting both the need and the apology. He gestured to a deserted booth, his keen blue eyes looking directly now at Blystone's bag. "Your burden does appear heavy. Allow me to assist you."

"Oh, Captain, that really isn't necessary."

"But please, mademoiselle, I insist. And I would like to speak with you a moment after so long a time." Marc offered her a charming smile as he gestured to some precious shade under a small, conveniently abandoned cabana.

He was hard to resist and his manners were disciplined and gallant. She dragged her gaze from his warm blue eyes. "Very well, monsieur," she said too casually, "if you insist."

"Ah, but I do. A very warm day for one used to Paris in the spring. Are you rooming at the Ransier estate in Paris?" he inquired.

"How did you know?"

"I assumed."

She glanced at him curiously, but not so definitely that he would notice. What else did he "assume" about her beside the painting and the Ransier mansion? She knew that his mother, Josephine Jacqueline Ransier, had been born and raised on that estate and that Marc had spent the first early years of his life there as well. "Monsieur Claude Ransier is your great-uncle, isn't he?"

His expression yielded no family secrets. "Claude is my mother's uncle. I haven't seen him since I was at Saint Cyr."

"I don't mean to pry. I'm sorry."

He smiled. "Don't be. Is he still as dour as he used to be?"

Dour was the precise word for Monsieur Claude and she covered a smile. "Yes, to be truthful. Not that I mean to speak against your mother's uncle."

He laughed. "As a boy I thought worse. He had a thundering bad temper, just don't tell him I said so. I may yet visit him one day soon." His mood altered. "Before war starts with Germany I'd like to urge him to leave Paris, but I doubt if he'll go."

"He is quite set in his ways," she admitted. "And you might like to know he is very patriotic."

His smile was faint, with a touch of thoughtful cynicism. "Isn't all of my family, mademoiselle?"

She wondered what he meant by that, but she made no response. She didn't think he expected an answer.

"Monsieur Ransier has been very kind to me."

He looked pleased. "Has he? I'm glad." He seemed to be remembering something. "He was kind to my mother as well."

Valli was thinking of his remark about Germany. A chill inched up her back. "Surely you do not think Berlin will attack France?"

"I do. And soon." He looked at her, musing. "You should not go back to Paris, but instead return to your great-aunt in Tangier. Calanthe, isn't it? Calanthe Malaret. A sweet elderly lady if I recall. You'll be safer there, at least for a while. The Nazis have an appetite for North Africa as well."

"Oh, but I must go back to Paris. I have the starring role in the main ballet of the spring season," she said happily. "I'll only be here at Bel-Abbes a short time, and then I've got to return."

He watched her thoughtfully, saying nothing, but she had a vague notion that he did not fault her convictions, but rather held them in admiration. Was it her sensitivity to the contents of the canvas bag, or did he look there again?

"Well, I've always admired a woman with courage," he said. He promptly led her to the indigo shade, dusted a large white rock with his handkerchief, and bowed her to place. He was so handsome that she was cautiously on guard. She sat on the large smooth stone.

He was still displaying his best manners as he smiled and reached for the canvas bag. "I'll just hold your satchel while you search your handbag for the passport."

"No," she said too quickly. "I mean, I shall hold it, merci."

"You're certain?"

"Yes, it's quite all right." She tried to unbuckle the catch on her large handbag, but there wasn't enough room on her lap to hold both her oversized purse and Blystone's bag.

He smiled. "I'm sorry to trouble you like this. Shall I look for you?"

She noted his glance at the canvas bag again. He mustn't look inside. Better to hand him her purse. "Yes, please, Captain Durell, if you wouldn't mind. The passport is in there somewhere."

She sat in the shade watching as he removed the paper rose from her purse and searched.

"Do you have any idea who harmed that poor waterboy?" she asked thoughtfully.

"An unfortunate incident. We're investigating now."

We? She took in his legionnaire uniform. Did the French Foreign Legion investigate crimes?

"You didn't happen to see anything unusual from the train window?" he asked, still fishing about in her over-crowded purse for the passport.

"The window?" she repeated, bidding for time.

His gaze came to hers briefly. "Yes, I saw you there."

"Oh. I see." That was no answer at all. It wasn't meant to be. He seemed to know it, and a restrained look of amusement showed in his glance. He turned back to her handbag. "It looked as though you were about to call the waterboy to fill your canteen."

"I was, actually." Had he noticed Sir Blystone as well?

"See anything out of the ordinary?" he repeated.

"What is considered out of the ordinary?"

His gaze searched hers. "Maybe the man in the white jacket with blond hair and sunglasses. Ever see him before?"

"Was there such a man?"

His gaze caught and held hers until she felt a touch of heat flare up in her cheeks. She looked away, feeling a jab of guilt. She was embarrassed by her unexplained lack of honesty. *Now why did I do that?*

"He wasn't on the train from Oran," she said truthfully. "At least I didn't notice him. No, I'm sure I've never seen him before."

She wondered at her defensive mood. Surely she could trust a French captain? Especially Monsieur Claude Ransier's great-nephew? Marc's romantic reputation might be called into question, but surely not his allegiance to France. But what could she say? It was true that she could not recognize the man from the distance of the window. And Blystone had asked her not to mention anything to anyone. She couldn't very well break her word to one gentleman just to please Marc, she thought.

A gust of wind ruffled her silky hair and the hem of her green dress. His gaze left hers, scanned her, then briefly came back to the canvas bag.

Afraid he would ask what was inside, and too aware of him, she stood quickly. "Monsieur Durell," she said stiffly,

"I have nothing more to tell you, and I have a friend to meet before the train leaves." She looked at her watch. "I am afraid I am already running late, and—"

Unexpectedly an Arab woman in a *haik* came running toward them following a runaway goat. It darted past the *hanootz*, kicking up dust as it ran; the woman was yelling at it with exasperation. Valli backed out of the way, fanning dust from her face.

Marc picked up her sun hat, which she'd dropped, and shook it off.

Valli laughed. "A goat is very precious here. I would dash after it too if it got spooked and ran off on me."

He smiled. "It will only take me a minute more and I promise to let you go in peace." Marc flipped through her passport and read.

After dusting her dress and straightening her hat, she glanced at him, watching him memorize the information. She said uneasily: "Is all in order, Captain?"

"Yes. All is in fine order, mademoiselle. I suppose this is your correct address when you're away from my great-uncle's estate?"

"Yes..." she admitted slowly. "I have a small flat in downtown Paris. The hour is often late after a ballet performance and I'm sometimes too exhausted to take a taxi all the way across town to the estate. As you probably remember, it is perhaps ten kilometers outside town."

He did seem to remember. "Do you have a telephone at the flat?"

She hesitated, glancing at him from under her lashes. Why did he need to know that?

"Yes. I have a telephone."

"What is the number?"

Their eyes held for a moment. She was nearly sure his request was not official. She looked away first. "You don't have a pencil, Captain."

"I have an excellent memory."

He waited, closing the passport and placing it back into her handbag. He left the rose off and snapped the latch.

Her eyes narrowed thoughtfully and dropped over him. Was he a rogue? She had to admit he appeared to be on his best behavior, but a French legionnaire—

The train whistle screeched a warning.

His eyes came to hers again. She was surprised to hear herself calmly giving him the number. She was almost disappointed with herself for giving in to his gaze, but would she have been more disappointed later if she hadn't? After all, she told herself again, he was Monsieur Claude's nephew. That made up for everything, didn't it?

Valli took her handbag, avoiding looking at him. "Is that all, Monsieur Durell?"

"Yes, that is everything, for now." He bowed lightly.

For now? Her gaze swerved to his, but his expression was inscrutable.

"Au revoir, Demoiselle Chattaine."

"Yes, goodbye, Captain."

Valli left quickly, passing the crowded stands selling fruit, and took a sharp turn into a more secluded area of the *souk*. Here, the blazing sunlight came through a lattice roof in the form of speckled shadows, dark splotches against vivid light. The enclosure was airless and hot, crowded with merchant stalls that were now empty. Where has everyone gone, she wondered uneasily, glancing about. She noticed, then. These *hanootz* were extras, rented out perhaps at busier festival times than this Tuesday afternoon.

Why had Blystone asked her to meet him here? She shuddered and walked ahead. Where was he? She turned about full circle. Was he a magician? She shaded her eyes and looked in all directions.

There was a *hanootz* with several dilapidated straw hats and faded black pompons. A growing feeling of unease troubled her confidence.

She walked on, her sandals making stilted clicking sounds on the stone floor. A tiny gust of wind came from somewhere and the black pompons on the hats gently swayed. Sounds from tiny bells filled her ears with lyrical notes.

She stopped, her spine stiffening with an unnerving sensation of being watched from the darkness. Her gaze peered intently into the shadows nearest the walls, her fears telling her she might see poor Sir Blystone slumped there on the floor, murdered like the waterboy.

"Sir Blystone? Are you here?"

Stony silence enveloped her. Only the wind stirred, creaking the dilapidated roof. Her hand automatically went to her throat as she looked up. *Please, don't let him be there dangling on a rope—*

A desert bird hopped on the beam and looked down at her with a cocked head. Her breath released.

Valli took command of her courage and walked around behind the booth, approaching precariously. A quick movement brought a muffled cry from her lips and she jumped back as a lizard sped across the stone floor and disappeared.

She laughed, releasing nervous tension. If she had expected to find him lying on the floor like the waterboy, she was happily wrong. He was probably waiting for her now in the train, prepared to apologize for her inconvenience, and proudly displaying a hat he had bought from one of the vendors. Nevertheless, to make sure, she calmed herself and made a quick search of the rest of the cabana, thankfully with no unpleasant surprises in the shadows.

The shrill warning blast from the train whistle alerted her that if she did not hurry it would pull out without her. She went scurrying into the sunshine, leaving the salient enclosure behind.

Strange, she thought, walking briskly through the *souk* toward the platform. She stopped and looked at the train. Oh no. Was she imagining it? The wheels were beginning to churn, the boxcars were inching along. Yes, it was pulling out. "Oh wait, Monsieur Conductor, wait!" She began to run, and for the first time she thanked God the old train was sluggish. At last she reached its weathered side, where the conductor stood on the narrow step with his hand outstretched. "Here, mademoiselle, faster!"

Valli finally came running beside the conductor and reached to catch the Frenchman's strong hand. In another moment she stepped up as he pulled her to safety.

"Merci, monsieur!" she gasped, hand at heart as he steadied her. He took the canteen from her shoulder, unstopped it, and handed it to her.

Again, she quenched her thirst on Marc's water. She leaned there against the side of the train, strangely enjoying the warm wind as she watched the red station recede. As it did, she thought of Marc and Blystone.

She lifted the canteen and her eyes read: Captain Marc Durell, 1st Etranger, Sidi-bel-Abbes. Should she have told him about Sir Blystone after all? A few minutes later, flushed with heat, she made her way down the aisle, still carrying his canteen of water. Hardly anyone bothered to notice her as she sank into the same seat where she'd left her overnight bag. It was still there.

The train was gaining speed toward Sidi-bel-Abbes. She glanced at the faces of the passengers, almost expecting to awaken from a strange dream and see Sir Blystone, head back, mouth open, mustache quavering contentedly as he snored. His seat remained coldly empty.

She sank down and peered out the side window, thinking of the strange events. For now, at least, she would leave the mysteries surrounding Blystone behind in the shifting dunes.

How refreshing it will be to see Davide, to sit in his small, cozy kitchen eating sausage and fried eggs, and hearing again about the Lord's great plans instead of the "vaunted, vain, and vaporous" boasts of mankind.

Exhausted, Valli leaned her head back against the seat and closed her eyes. Even so, she couldn't get Marc's warning of Nazi soldiers out of her mind. Her skin turned clammy even in the heat. Would they enter Paris? It was too painful to dwell on. "Never," she whispered aloud. The song had gone out of Paris, perhaps out of all Europe. Had it gone out of her own future as well?

She must have fallen asleep, for she envisioned the horizon of the city she loved, with its Eiffel Tower and the Ballet Theater, dark with war clouds and crimson with blood. Out of the devilish flames the swastika arose, threatening evil in a burning sky.

Valli's eyes blinked open to white sand and stunted palms. But now the train lurked with malignant shadows and the rumble and squeal of the wheels took on a menace all their own that followed her into tomorrow.

Thinking of Marc, she didn't remember him putting her passport back into her handbag. Valli quickly opened the snap and breathed a sigh of relief. Yes, it was there, and satisfied, she began to snap it shut when she noticed a small folded piece of paper poking out of one corner of the passport. She removed it and read:

> *Bonjour! I wouldn't want you to needlessly worry over the canvas bag. It is what our Englishman called a "red herring." My humble apology, mademoiselle. Thank you for the rose and postcards.*
>
> M. Durell

Valli stared at Marc's message. She was remembering how Blystone had given her a set of postcards before he entrusted the canvas bag to her care. She had placed the postcards inside her handbag... and Blystone had placed the paper rose on the strap. A sign for Marc? Undoubtedly! *Why, I'll wager Marc's subtle interest in Blystone's bag had been deliberate too, just to take my attention away from what he really wanted, my handbag. How could he have lifted the postcards without my noticing? The woman chasing the goat! If it had been a woman—she had run terribly fast, and she was rather masculine at that. Probably some friend of Marc's.* Despite herself she smiled ruefully.

She looked at the heavy canvas bag she had been protecting, lugging about for what seemed like an hour. She had even run with it to catch the train. And the skin was raw on her shoulder. A red herring! When all along it was the postcards that were important.

Her curiosity was kindled. What information did they contain, and why did Blystone want Marc to have them? Well, she wasn't likely to find out. With the war enlarging there could be any number of reasons. She was mollified when remembering that he had taken extra time to memorize her address and telephone number. He could have allowed her to go on thinking the contents of the bag were important, but he hadn't.

Valli used her foot to push the canvas bag out of her sight and to give herself more leg room; then she settled back comfortably in the seat. Well, so much for her bizarre adventure. She might as well try to nap before reaching Sidi-bel-Abbes. There would be new things to think about when she saw Davide.

Her thoughts trailed back to Captain Marc Durell. He had said he would be coming to Paris to see Monsieur Claude Ransier. If he came to his great-uncle's house she was bound to see him again.

Was that the reason he had left her the little note? He may have wanted to make amends when she discovered the postcards and rose were missing, or was she making too much of his memorizing her telephone number? And the white paper rose, why had he taken that? She had so many questions to ask him—*if* he showed up again.

# 3

Davide's independent "station" was unlike any mission compound Valli had seen before. He had used his own resources, along with the help and strength of several friends, to build it. And it was rather grand, though it didn't come close to Great-Aunt Calanthe's palatial house in Tangier, which once belonged to an emir.

Davide's house, five minutes from Sidi-bel-Abbes, was built all of rocks painted a glistening white, and it had a blue roof. He'd chosen blue because of the Arab superstitious belief that a blue stone they wore could keep away "the evil eye," whatever that was. He hoped the blue roof would give the Christian compound more acceptance by the locals. There had already been several rock-throwing incidents, and Davide bore a scar on his leg from a dog bite.

The house had a cluster of rooms, mostly small, that were kept close to the average daily temperature by the massive walls. Davide's study was the largest, where he was working on translating the Gospel of John into Berber with the linguistic help of his elderly cook and housekeeper, Haroun, and Haroun's wife, Saidah. Davide had mentioned in one of his letters that he worried less about stone throwers and snarling dogs than a fire since his roof was vulnerable.

There were also times when Valli believed she needed to be part of the team in Bel-Abbes, but that would mean giving up ballet. After a day's practice in the theater she would go home to read from the Psalms. It was during those times that she felt the need to invest some special prayer time in the Bel-Abbes work. Now that illness had struck Davide, she felt even more convicted. Thereafter, Valli remembered to uphold her brother in prayer.

A second structure shaped like a horseshoe formed the living quarters behind the main house. Here, individual Berbers disowned by family and friends for converting to Christianity from Islam took up their unobtrusive lives. There was also a Spanish woman who'd escaped a life of harlotry. Valli counted seven children ranging in age from six months to about eight years.

Around the entire property were date palms for shade and bougainvillea vines with dense crimson flowers sprawling along the stone wall. The Berbers were self-reliant and Valli saw a host of well-established fruit trees and a flourishing vegetable garden irrigated by a well. There were some donkeys, two horses, chickens, and a few sheep.

A white-haired Berber with smiling chocolate-brown eyes greeted her warmly when she arrived. He remembered her from past visits.

"It is with regret I tell you Davide is not here. He is in Morocco," he explained, helping to carry her bags. "He left a month ago for Sefrou and El Hajeb."

Morocco, she thought, disappointed. She could have missed the entire Bel-Abbes experience and gone directly to Tangier had she known he was there. Well, no wonder he hadn't responded to her letter, but why hadn't he contacted Calanthe to let her know where he was? The two mission outposts that Haroun had mentioned were less than 300 kilometers from Tangier, and even closer to Casablanca.

"Then he must not have received my last letter telling him I was coming."

"I sent it to him in Morocco soon as it came. Do not worry, for he will be home in three weeks."

Three weeks. She sighed. "I'm afraid three weeks is too long, Haroun. I must be back in Paris in early May for the new ballet season."

She entered the cool, dim house that was beautifully clean and fragrant with the cooking smells of Mediterranean spices: cumin, onions, and olive oil.

His eyes brightened. "If he received your letter, he could come sooner. We will hope. Or you could go to Tangier. I will take you, Miss Valli. Me and Saidah both. We could leave early tomorrow, yes?"

She noted an anxious look in his eyes. Was he worried about Davide, or something in Bel-Abbes?

"I came to visit him here to see the work," she explained. "We'll hope he surprises us with an early return, but if he doesn't, I'll need to be content to see the work on my own. My ship from Oran leaves in ten days."

He nodded with understanding and didn't say anything more about Tangier. Valli asked: "Is everything going well here? Do you have everything you need until Davide returns?"

"Oh yes. Everything is well." He turned toward the hall. "Saidah! Miss Valli has come. Bring refreshments."

A nice way to change subjects, Valli noticed. The older woman, Saidah, appeared in the doorway, wearing a traditional *haik*. She smiled shyly, then moved noiselessly on bare feet to the kitchen.

"Tell me about Sefrou and El Hajeb," she told him. "Why did he go there now?"

Haroun told her that there were four unmarried missionary women struggling to keep open the other two mission stations in Morocco and that because of the imminent threat of war, they were being counseled by some on the board to return home before they were trapped and unable to get out. Valli didn't know all the women, but she did know the leader of the group, an older woman named Miss Maude Cary, who had spent the last twenty-some years laboring in Morocco to plant churches and establish a school among the Berbers—a tribe that had inhabited North Africa long before the Arabs. There had been trouble from the beginning with infighting among the handful of missionaries and opposition from the Moroccans, but Miss Cary continued to labor on, at times alone.

There had been a time when Valli planned to emulate the stalwart Miss Cary, but life's journey had taken her on another route, and the love of ballet had brought her from the sands of Morocco to the floor of the Paris Opera Ballet Theater. There, she'd met Kraig, who had graduated ballet school some years ahead of her and was already working as an assistant director at the theater when she graduated and sought a position. His enthusiasm had soon led her into a career in classical dance.

Davide had heard the lonely call of the blowing hot sands. He too had known Miss Cary, and he had come with her blessing to Algeria to try to reach the legionnaires at the fort, as well as the local Berbers.

Valli was pleased. God's little desert flock had increased from the last time she was here. It was clear that He was blessing Davide's sowing, even in what appeared to be "rocky and sandy soil."

"But there is trouble," Haroun said when she mentioned having seen the women and children. "Only a week ago on my way back from Bel-Abbes, those opposing us sent their dogs against me." He proudly displayed his bandaged leg while Saidah made clucking noises, shaking her head worriedly.

Valli was concerned that the wound was infected despite Saidah's use of Berber emollients to hasten healing, and she rummaged through her bag for the medicines she had brought from Paris for Davide. She prescribed the dosage for a skeptical Haroun.

He told her that every family kept several dogs that didn't hesitate to bite, and even when they didn't, they barked so ferociously that sharing the Christian message of eternal life in their homes was impossible. "Spiritual warfare, Davide says. The women listen more than the proud men. Davide goes down to the river where the women wash clothes and tells them about Jesus. They ask many questions until the men show up, then the women are afraid and leave."

"Tell me about Miss Cary," Valli said to Haroun as Saidah served tiny cups of thick coffee and a plate of home-dried dates and almonds. Saidah couldn't speak French, so Valli couldn't commune with her as freely as she did Haroun, and while Valli could speak some Berber, she wasn't as proficient as Davide. Haroun could converse in both languages.

Valli sat wearily at the round wooden table as Saidah smiled on and Haroun explained about the plight at the stations in Sefrou and El Hajeb.

The "Christian friends," as Haroun called the missionaries, were being told to leave before war cut off any hope of their return. "But Miss Maude won't leave. Morocco *is* her home, she says."

Valli remembered that two years ago, in 1938, Miss Cary found herself with only one other woman to keep the Moroccan station open. Two more single women had arrived, but they were still without men.

"So Davide thinks and prays about what to do. Should he help in Morocco? Or should he stay in Bel-Abbes with us? We desire the words of God in the Berber language, and Davide is needed here to work on the translation of Saint John, so we pray he will not leave for Morocco." He looked at his wife and said something in Berber and she nodded eagerly.

Yes, Valli thought. Not everyone could work on the translation of Scripture, but they could work at El Hajeb or Safrou in order to keep the witness alive during the war in spite of the shortage of missionaries—not that there had ever been enough missionaries in Morocco or Algeria.

The thought crossed her mind: *If it wasn't for the starring role in* Giselle, *I could offer to take one of the stations and free Davide to stay in Bel-Abbes.*

Doing so would be full of adventurous risks, however. Was she capable enough? Did she know what she was getting into? No one knew how long the war would last, or what would be the outcome. And what of her weakness with the Berber language? If she did stay, she would need to study.

After sleeping soundly, Valli awoke the next morning to voices outside, from the backyard. Her mind still sluggish from sleep, she thought: *Davide has returned sooner than expected*. It was promptly evident that the voices were not happy, but urgent. What was happening? Trouble with wild dogs again?

She put on her cool cotton duster and went to the screened window.

Outside near the horseshoe structure where the Berbers were living, it appeared as though a small disaster was in the making. The women were running, shooing the children indoors like a hen with chicks at the approach of wolves. The younger children were alarmed and crying. Haroun and a Berber lad of around fifteen were in a discussion as they hurried toward the front of the house.

Valli frowned. The two men looked grim, and the women appeared concerned with apparently hiding the children. Wild dogs? Valli wondered. Stone throwers?

"Safia," someone was calling in a hissing voice. "Come!"

That sounded like Saidah's voice. A movement below Valli's window caused her to look there. A small child not yet school age was hiding behind a large pottery urn where bougainvillea grew and climbed up a lattice to block the sun from shining in the window.

"Are you Safia?" Valli asked her through the screen, smiling.

The child looked up startled. Her wide eyes suddenly filled with tears. She looked pale and sickly in the dark, child-sized *haik* covering her from head to toe.

"Saidah is calling you," Valli told her in Berber.

The child merely stared up at her without answering.

"Why are you hiding?" Valli asked gently, trying to sound happy. "Are you hiding from your mama? Oh, but you mustn't do that. You will make her worry."

"Safia!"

"She's over here," Valli called cheerfully, "below my window."

A moment later Saidah came hurrying, gathered the girl into her arms and, making clucking noises, hurried away.

Valli dressed swiftly in slacks and blouse and was weaving her hair into a French twist when she paused. She listened as a motor grew louder, coming to a stop in the front. A motorcycle? She pinned her hair in place, then left her room.

As she entered the living room she heard bootsteps in the courtyard coming up to the front door. There came a rap.

She waited, thinking Haroun may have come inside and would answer. Had he left with the boy for some reason? The house was silent. She walked to the front window and glanced out. She couldn't see the area in front of the door, but the dusty motorcycle was parked in the courtyard. Again, the rap on the door, this time more persistent.

How silent the compound had become. No voices, no movement. Why? She looked out the window, trying to see the door.

"Hello! Anyone there?"

Valli's throat tightened. That voice!

A man stepped back from the door and looked up at the top window. All at once her heart was thumping with dread. She knew that face, the arrogant jawline, those well-defined cheekbones—the fair, close-clipped hair—

Her fingers tightened on the front of her blouse as she stepped away from the window. Then, there was little doubt left. The man in the sunglasses at the train was Kraig's brother, Dietrich!

Dietrich. She had never liked him. It didn't surprise her that he would now be dedicated to the Nazi party. Even before Hitler came to full power in Berlin, when she had known Dietrich in Paris, he had accompanied her and Kraig to cafés where they would sit after a ballet performance to unwind and talk the night away. Dietrich had always controlled the conversation. He controlled everything, even Kraig. Back then, in 1935-36, Dietrich talked by the hour of the future glories of the Third Reich. His radical racism, his belief that Germany had some preordained destiny to rule Europe, in which every German had a calling, had troubled Kraig even as it had her.

"I can't do anything with him," Kraig had told her. "His mind is made up. If I resist, he becomes angry with me."

"If he's wrong in what he believes, are we obligated to allow his irrational anger to control us?"

Valli's reasoning had done little good. Kraig was not a fighter, but a pacifist, more consumed with the arts than with politics or the military. "I owe him so much, Valli. When Maman died," he spoke with a French dialect, while Dietrich preferred German, "it was my brother who finished putting me through ballet school. Dietrich has his faults, but he means well. Please, for my sake, darling, endure him, will you?"

Valli was remembering this painfully as she looked at Dietrich through the window. He had changed since that last meeting in Paris a month before she was to have married Kraig. Dietrich now wore a pair of small rimless glasses, but his self-possessed manner and icy gaze remained. Even his voice sounded sharper, as though he had plenty of practice giving orders in Berlin. He expected any "inferior" to immediately carry them out.

A ripple of alarm found its way through her like a chilling breeze. If she had noticed Dietrich at the train, there was a remote chance that he had also seen her. Did he associate her with Sir Blystone? And if he did, what of the canvas bag? That bag! It had caused nothing but trouble since Blystone had entrusted it to her. It didn't matter that Marc insisted it contained nothing important, what if the Nazis believed it did? Was Dietrich involved in espionage? What else could it all be? Blystone was still missing—and the waterboy was dead—

And she had the canvas bag!

Did Dietrich know she was here? If he had seen her on the train he must. Why else would he come?

He rapped again. She glanced toward the back door, then thought of the bag sitting on the floor in her room. She'd been too tired last night to do anything about it, and there hadn't seemed to be any reason to worry. Now, a disturbing thought came crashing into her mind. If Blystone's name was anywhere on that bag, or in his books, or magazines, Dietrich would know that he had trusted her. And why would Blystone trust her unless she supported his cause?

Heart slamming, she ran to her room. Still barefoot, she fumbled to slip on shoes, grabbed the bag from the floor and rushed with it toward the back door. She hadn't yet reached it when the front door opened. Haroun must have unlocked it earlier that morning when he arrived to fix the meal—

She froze, hearing footsteps in the living room. Her eyes swerved around the room and saw a large canister of dried rice. She drew back the lid, dropped the bag inside, and closed it. She turned around and moved across the kitchen to the stove, picking up the coffeepot and a cup. Her hand shook as she poured, but she kept her pose as she heard him coming.

It would be unwise to show alarm now. She must pretend surprise and meet him head-on without showing fear, as she always had in the past in Paris when he had tried to come between her and Kraig. All must appear normal.

He stopped in the doorway, a look of surprise on his face when he saw her standing there.

Then he hadn't known she was here...

He recovered. "Demoiselle Valli, a surprise, and as lovely as ever!" He was smiling, smirking, actually, tugging on one black glove as his eyes dropped over her, unconcerned with showing unconcealed interest. "How long has it been since our last tête-á-tête in Paris, five years? Much too long."

This was no time to portray kitten-like weakness, not in front of the drooling wolf. If perchance Kraig were also somewhere in Algeria, she wanted him to know through Dietrich that nothing remained of the past except ashes. As for Dietrich—there had never been even a spark, although his pride wouldn't permit him to believe that. He was handsome, ruthlessly so.

"Didn't you hear me knocking?"

"I did, but I didn't hear Haroun let you in."

"Well, I didn't know you were here. You will excuse the interruption I am sure. I was in a hurry."

Valli raised the coffee cup and sipped. So far, so good. She looked at him with all the poise she had learned at the ballet theater, then smiled pleasantly, even while her heart still raced. "Whatever are you doing in the middle of Algeria?" She even managed a light, tinkling laugh. "Don't tell me you've decided to run from Berlin too. Have you come to join the Foreign Legion?" She smiled sweetly and lowered her voice. "Do you think they'll let you in?"

For a moment he was taken aback, then he threw back his proud golden head and enjoyed his own laughter. "That's what I adore about you. You are not afraid of me." He walked into the kitchen, took the pot from her hand, meeting her gaze, and poured himself a cup. "Do you know I've been looking everywhere for you since we last met?"

He was close enough for her to see the dueling scar on his chin that gave his Germanic looks a formidable quality. He was deliberately in civilian clothes, but she suspected his Nazi uniform was spotless and intimidating. She masked a shudder. How wrong he was. His savage interest in her had always frightened her, even when he finally went along with her engagement to Kraig. "Looking for me? But, why?"

"Ah, Valli, how typical of your charms to say such innocent things. I suppose that's why I have remembered you so well these years. You amuse me. You know I always thought your beauty was wasted on that dreamy brother of mine. And to think I have found you, still unattached. What luck." His light gray eyes mocked her. He drank the coffee, then leaned against the sink. Reaching into his pocket, he removed a gold cigarette case and lighter.

*Money,* she thought, glancing at the gold. *Where had he gotten money to waste on gold cigarette cases?*

"Has Kraig been in touch with you yet?"

Her heart lay as heavy as a rock in her chest. She ignored the question. "Is my suggestion of your joining the legion amusing? I didn't realize." She moved back from him. Her voice became honey-sweet. "I've heard there are so many young German men trying to escape Berlin to join the legion that your fuhrer—what was his name?—ah yes, Hitler, well, I heard Monsieur Hitler had to begin arresting them and having the SS beat them up as only the SS know how—or was it those Brownshirts kicking them on the street?"

He flicked a bit of ash and looked at her for a long moment, his eyes turning chillier as they seemed to rummage through her mind. Then he smiled. "You naturally have heard wrong. Not that I blame your ignorance. One can expect nothing except lies from the French press. These melodramatic journalists are experts with their propaganda, inflaming the French and British people. Berlin is at peace. Hitler desires peace."

"Then why don't we have peace?"

"Your government does not wish peace."

"It isn't French soldiers invading Poland and Czechoslovakia. It is German soldiers."

"You misunderstand our motives. The leaders of these countries, faced with the internal rebellion from the Communists, have pleaded to the fuhrer for help. They cheer the German soldiers as they enter to restore civility."

Valli laughed at him.

"There! You see? You misunderstand. I can see you don't believe me. You must come to Berlin again and see for yourself. There are jobs for everyone, prosperity for the first time since the Great War, and everyone loves their fuhrer, even the smiling school children."

"Has God's Kingdom now arrived? One thing worries me: In place of the true Master you Nazis practically worship Hitler. The people don't seem to recognize the difference. That, I think, is Germany's worst danger."

"Oh come, Valli, you echo the hysterical Christian ministers—like Dietrich Bonhoeffer! They've arrested him, finally. He is a radical. The German people know the difference between God and the fuhrer."

"Do they? I'm beginning to wonder. Why have both the educators and the press been silenced in only a few short weeks...The only organization in Germany that has the courage and persistence to speak out for intellectual and moral truth is the Christian Church, and it is suffering from its stand. Hitler has imprisoned over two hundred thousand Christians behind barbed wire in frozen Nazi concentration camps. I admire the two imprisoned pastors Bonhoeffer and Niemoller for refusing to pray for the success of the Nazi military."

He had become angry, but his smile persisted. "Oh Valli, can't you see how you're being deceived—probably by listening to the BBC." He smirked and changed the subject. "Really though, how good to see you again. I am serious. I have kept up with your fame in the Paris Ballet. Congratulations on your role in the *Black Swan*. I was told you were magnificent." His eyes drifted down her throat. "I must see you dance. When is the next ballet of the season?"

Her smile was frozen. "May. The ballet is..." she hesitated over the ironic name. "*Giselle*."

He laughed. "Dear sister Giselle. How fitting. But I am sure you will be outstanding. I will look forward to being in the audience."

She tensed. "You will come to Paris?" The audacity of it!

"That is my plan."

"I'm surprised you knew of the *Black Swan*. I didn't think my reviews would reach as far as Berlin."

He smiled. "They did not. Kraig mentioned that he saw the performance. I saw him recently."

Her hands went cold. She hoped her expression was closed to his prying eyes. When had Kraig been in Paris? She refused the bait and did not ask.

He seemed to read her thoughts and it afforded him amusement. "You mean he did not come backstage? That is not like him. He was so dedicated to you and your career," he said with smooth savagery, his words cutting her heart. "I would have expected him to send you two dozen red roses." He blew smoke rings toward the ceiling.

She would not give him the satisfaction of seeing her pain. Kraig had always sent red roses after a performance.

"Or was it white roses?"

White—her eyes looked into his. The sound of the wind about the window broke the growing silence.

At last he smiled and stubbed out his cigarette. "Then I shall send red roses in his place next time."

"And you, Dietrich," she said hurriedly, "what sort of work brings you to Algeria? Business for the Third Reich?"

"Your mind is made up against me. I suppose you think we have plans to come to North Africa to aid the bumbling Italian army under Mussolini. You see how unfair you are with my government? I am here on leave—visiting a friend, an American who owns a plantation not far from here. He believes he has found oil. As I drove by I remembered how in Paris you spoke of your brother, Davide. I thought I would stop by and say hello."

"You're on leave? You mean holiday?"

"The fuhrer rewards his followers. That is more than your foolish Reynaud has done for his French soldiers."

"Reynaud is an honorable leader."

"When your government sells out France for a treaty with Hitler, you will see what nonsense you speak."

"Sell out France? Never."

"German soldiers will one day march freely down Paris streets. When they do, you can turn to me for kindness."

She would as soon turn to a desert viper. "Nazi soldiers will never march the streets of Paris! Our soldiers will fight."

"Ah, such brave French soldiers. Do not believe it. Neither France nor England will fight. They are all pacifists. They know it is time for the rise of the German Reich. Do not worry, Valli. France has nothing to fear if it submits to the fuhrer. You will find us kind and benevolent masters."

Masters! Her anger sizzled. "You are wrong, Dietrich. We *will* fight. As Churchill has said—we will fight in our streets, we will fight in our homes, we will fight until the last man, the last woman, the last—" she stopped, corralling her outburst, feeling the warmth in her cheeks.

Dietrich was watching her steadily, his smile having all but faded. He shook his head sadly. "I fear I was right about you all along. Such patriotic passion is beyond reason."

"Hello, am I interrupting?" It was Davide who walked into the kitchen, casually dressed in an open shirt and jeans. He threw an arm around Valli's shoulders, kissing her cheek.

"Davide," she cried, an excited, relieved squeak in her voice, and throwing both arms around him, she hugged her brother tightly. She felt the steadying pressure of his fingers on her arm, as though he understood about Dietrich and was asking her to remain calm.

His amber eyes and wavy walnut-colored hair were a welcome sight. His wide, warm smile made her feel as though everything were all right again with the bleak world. Even the presence of Dietrich no longer seemed as chilling. She forgot him and turned her attention to her brother.

"Davide," she held him from her, searching. "You're skinny!" She felt his tanned forehead. "You have a fever, too."

"Hello, ma petite," he said with a grin. "So you came at last to help me. I've been flat on my back for a month. I got nothing done except some work on the Gospel of John. Then, Maude Cary wrote me about El Hajeb and I forced myself to travel. What did you bring me? Medicine for fever, I hope?"

"Yes—but what are you doing here now? Haroun said you wouldn't return from Morocco for three more weeks. I was fearful I'd have to go back to Paris without seeing you."

"You mean you didn't get my letter in Paris? I promised to be here. I intended to get here last night to meet you at the depot, but the car had a blowout outside Algiers." He shook his head. "A catastrophe out here," he laughed. "I had to wait until dawn for Oman to hike in and arrange for the legionnaires to locate a tire. Quite an ordeal!"

Davide then turned toward Dietrich.

Valli spoke with a note of lightness in her voice: "Davide, you remember Kraig's brother, Dietrich Gestler?"

"Hello, Dietrich. Sorry, can't say that I do."

Dietrich had stood back, watching and listening to their meeting.

"Dietrich, my brother, Davide. He's chaplain at the legionnaire post."

Dietrich was now all pleasure again, smiling and congenial. His composure was intact as he shook hands with Davide and politely explained his presence. "Chaplain? Somehow I thought you ran a charity hostel for women and orphans."

"Whatever gave you that idea?"

"I noticed your hostel out back."

"Oh that. We have a few Berber families helping out."

"Very commendable of you." He changed the subject, declaring that he must now go. "I hope we meet again," he told Davide, looking at Valli. "Goodbye, Fraulein Chattaine. If all goes well with my itinerary, I may yet get to Paris before taking up my new post in Casablanca."

Valli managed a smile. Davide asked: "What business are you in, if I may ask?"

"I'll be working in the German embassy this summer."

"A diplomat? Interesting work, especially now."

"You mean the war? Casablanca will remain neutral, I'm told."

"I hope we manage to stay out of it altogether," Davide said.

He smiled knowingly. "Oh, I am sure you will. France is now full of pacifists." He bowed his head toward Valli. "Enjoy your visit." He handed her a small card. "My number in Casablanca. Auf Wiedersehen."

Valli watched him leave, then placed the card in her pocket. Calling on Dietrich Gestler was the last thing she wanted to do. It was troubling to learn he knew so much of her plans. "Annoying man," she murmured.

"I must be dim," Davide said after the roar of the motorcycle faded away. "I didn't know Kraig had a brother, or that he was interested in you until last night when Marc told me."

"Marc? You saw him last night?"

"He and Jacquette delivered the tire. Tell me about Dietrich."

"You needn't worry, I have no interest in him. I doubt he is as friendly toward me as he pretends. We were debating when you came up."

"He is a Nazi, isn't he?"

"Yes, dyed-in-the-wool. Did Captain Durell tell you that?"

Davide shoved his hands in his trouser pockets. "Yes. He said you were here and that I should keep an eye on you. That there was some trouble with a Nazi agent earlier on the train from Oran. He suspects it was Dietrich."

"Well, you didn't seem to show your concerns about his Nazism," she said. "But I'm afraid he knows exactly where I stand."

Davide frowned. "Be more careful next time, will you? Marc asked us to befriend him."

"He *what*?" She searched his lean, tanned face. "Why would he ask us to do that? A Nazi?" She lowered her voice. "One that is suspect as an agent?"

"And one about to take on a job at the embassy. Interesting, isn't it? Marc thinks more can be learned from Dietrich through friendly interaction. Needless to say it goes both ways. That's probably why he was here. Did he say what brought him? Besides you, that is."

"He didn't, not really. Oh, he gave some lame excuse about wanting to meet you, but I don't believe it. And yet, he was genuinely surprised when he saw me. I can't think why he would come here, can you?"

Davide walked over to the table and began munching the dried dates and almonds. "There could be a number of possibilities, and all of them could be wrong."

"That isn't very brilliant, Davide," she said wryly.

"I don't feel very brilliant. He doesn't have business here. He's a bit out of his route, especially if he's on his way to Casablanca. You seem to have his interest, though."

*But for what reason?* she thought uneasily.

Davide looked tired and sat down, stretching his legs out in front of him. With head in hand he looked at her thoughtfully. "Seen Kraig?"

She turned away to rinse her cup in the sink. "No. How much did Captain Durell tell you about our meeting?"

"If you're asking whether or not he mentioned Blystone, yes he did. They haven't heard from him."

"I hope he's alive," she said softly. There was a window above the sink and she gazed out across the empty space toward Bel-Abbes. "I found him to be an old dear."

"The 'old dear' also plunged you into some very hot water, I'm told."

She turned, masking her curiosity. "Marc told you?"

"According to him, we may not have seen the end of it yet."

"Can he be trusted? Completely?"

"Marc? I've known him for years now." He waved an arm. "He and I practically built this house together. He lived here for a year and was the first to help as a linguist with the Berber language. That room you're staying in, dear, is his. He stays here whenever he gets a few days away from the post, or between assignments. I won't tell you any more of what he does. He'll need to do that. But you can trust him. When he's worried about something, I take it seriously."

She mulled all that over and looked back out the window.

"And what did he say that worried you?" she asked after a minute of silence.

Davide looked a little gloomy. "He's asked me to wait and allow him to explain. He'll be in touch with you, but he doesn't know when. There is one thing, though."

She turned, her gaze questioning him.

"You're *sure* there is nothing between you and Dietrich Gestler?"

Valli was shocked that he would need to ask the second time. What had Marc told him?

"I thought you knew me better."

"I know you very well, but it has been a long time, hasn't it," he said gently. "I've been in the sand dunes battling fever, and you've been in the bright lights of Paris."

"And anything can happen there, is that it?"

He smiled. "Most anything, I'm told. It's been so long since I was there I don't remember."

"Well, worry no longer. And if Captain Durell is also worried, you can tell him for me that my allegiance in this coming war is not up for grabs by someone like that odious Dietrich Gestler. My heart belongs to France." She smiled.

"That's what I told Marc."

"Did you?" *And did he believe you?* She had the uneasy notion that Marc wasn't sure. She remembered that he asked her about the man in sunglasses. She insisted she had never seen him before.

"I told Marc you are a committed Christian now. You wouldn't become involved with a man if he didn't share those beliefs."

"That definitely leaves out Dietrich, doesn't it?" she said with a rueful smile.

"I don't know where the man stands in the Faith, but he is on the wrong side in this conflict. Anyway, Marc will appreciate your patriotism. I have the idea he and Sebastien both need you in the war. Whatever you decide, you'll think about it carefully won't you? And pray about it first?"

"You know I will."

Valli felt cheered by his trust. But the foreboding presence of Dietrich lingered, as did the death of the waterboy and the missing Sir Blystone. The compound was empty and still, and tomorrow promised uncertainty as well as hope in the dry wind that moaned overhead.

She stood studying Davide, hardly seven years her senior, yet worn out in health. The trip to Morocco had drained him, and there was little in his future that could quickly bring him back to his feet except a long rest and the proper medical care. *If anyone should return to Paris, it's Davide,* she thought worriedly. *Yet, he would be the very last to leave or put himself first above the need here at Bel-Abbes. And now he has the added burden of sharing the concerns of Sefrou and El Hajeb. How can I leave it all on his shoulders?*

"You're going straight to bed," she announced suddenly, and she knew her fears were genuine when instead of protesting he meekly allowed her to lead him to his room.

She removed his shoes and covered him with a blanket. "You have chills," she said.

"It's nothing. Don't worry about me."

Easier said than done. She went back to the kitchen for water and the bottle of medicine that the doctor had prescribed.

When at last he was asleep she walked to his desk and gazed thoughtfully at the piles of papers and books. His Bible was open to the Gospel of John, chapter 15. Verse 16 was underlined. She read: Ye have not chosen me, but I have chosen you, and ordained you, that ye should go and bring forth fruit, and that your fruit should remain...

# 4

The rest of the week passed quickly as Valli was busy caring for Davide and learning the operations of the station. Chapel was held each morning, and she nervously filled his vacancy, taking the familiar Psalm 23 for her text, while Haroun translated for her. The inadequacy she felt as a teacher went unnoticed since the women and Haroun were less skilled in the Scriptures than she. She also became acquainted with the women and was an instant success with the older children, who wanted to know about "ballet."

By Wednesday, Davide was again on his feet, and on Friday he taught chapel. Saidah returned on Friday and Valli asked Davide about the incident with the little girl.

"Oh yes, Safia. A sweet child. She's without her mother, poor thing, and Saidah is doing her 'grandmotherly' best to cheer her." He grinned suddenly. "You're not thinking of adopting Safia for your own?"

Valli laughed, realizing she had shown more interest in the child than she had the others. "I might," she said. "But she'll either need to learn French, or I'll need to speak better Berber. I tried to communicate with her when I first arrived and didn't get very far."

"How did you speak to her?"

"Berber. I guess I'm worse at it than I thought. She didn't seem to understand me."

"Cheer up, ma petite. The longer you stay here, the more proficient you'll become."

"Oh Davide, there are times when I wish I could."

"But that time hasn't come yet," he said gently.

She shook her head no. He smiled. "Don't feel badly. We'll leave it all with the Lord." They both knew that the day of her departure was drawing near. Even so, they heard nothing from Captain Marc Durell.

On Friday, Davide said confidently: "Well, if he doesn't come tonight, he must be on an assignment."

Valli touched her mussed hair. "Don't tell me you asked him to supper without telling me?"

"I don't need to invite him. Marc always drops by on Friday unless he's away from Bel-Abbes. He's at home here. However, he did make a point of inquiring whether you'd still be here."

"Did he?"

"And that's notable, considering his wish to avoid feminine entanglements."

She smiled ruefully. "No wonder you two are friends. I know another young man who thinks along those same lines."

He laughed. But Valli's care in dressing that night for supper reaped no interesting benefits as far as Captain Marc Durell went. By six o'clock there came a knock on the door and a message delivered to Davide.

"So much for a threesome. Marc's on assignment in the Sahara. He sends his regrets."

"Maybe I frightened him away," she said with a laugh.

"He doesn't frighten. He wanted to come. He's been asking questions about you long before you arrived. Before you got mixed up with Blystone."

That caught her interest. Just what had her brother told his best friend about his sister? "What kind of questions?"

"Oh—just whether you were over Kraig—and about your career in Paris."

Valli was flattered by Marc's interest. She decided he must know more about her personal life than she thought if Davide had been the source of information. However, even if he showed up next Friday she would be on her way to Paris.

"Well," she said, glancing at the pretty table she had helped to arrange. "It's not all in vain, we at least have an extra helping of Haroun's special lamb kabobs. And I've a few questions of my own to ask you." Two could play at that game, she thought. And now that she knew how friendly Davide was with Marc, he could provide her with the answers she wanted.

"I see I'm caught in the middle," Davide said with a smile. "There's nothing I like better than being a bridge builder between two very special people."

Valli already knew that Marc had spent his early years in his Great-Uncle Claude's home, but she didn't know that he had been sent away from the Ransier estate in Paris when he was only nine years old.

"Just two weeks after Josephine died."

She looked at Davide, surprised. "So soon?"

"Yes. He was sent to live with his father, Louis Durell. Though he has chosen to follow in his father's footsteps, a great deal of his mother's gentle blood flows in his veins."

"I've never even heard Josephine's name mentioned by Claude. I wonder what she was like." She was curious about Josephine now and hoped to find a photograph or painting of her at the estate. But how had such a woman ever married Louis Durell? A scoundrel from what she had heard. Davide had an answer for that as well.

"During the Great War Josephine had volunteered as a nurse, helping the French soldiers at Verdun. That's when she fell in love with Louis. They were married within a month."

Though Valli thought it romantic, she raised a brow. "Not very long to know one another is it?"

"No, and Great-Uncle Claude was so furious when she returned a year later married to Louis and expecting a child that, though he took her in, he disowned her. Louis was unemployed after the war and still recovering from a wound. Marc didn't learn about the enmity between Claude and his father until Josephine died. It seems Claude sent for Marc to come to his bedroom and announced that he was being sent to his father, a soldier in the French Foreign Legion. Not that Marc minded. He was anxious to leave and join Louis."

"How did Louis Durell become a legionnaire?"

Davide rubbed his chin, looking at her thoughtfully, as if wondering if he should tell her. "Louis was forced to leave Paris."

"Then Marc was brought up by his father as a soldier," she said thoughtfully.

"He arrived in Morocco just as the bloody Rif War in Tangier was at its height."

Valli had heard about the war but was too young to remember it. She knew the legionnaires had fought the leader of the Arab independence movement, a tough and determined bedouin named Abd el-Krim. Krim had made one of many fierce attacks upon the French civilians living in the International Zone of Tangier, and the legionnaires had been sent in to defeat him.

"Marc was still a boy when he'd seen numerous soldiers die in the fighting. He served as a waterboy for the wounded and as a courier, bringing military dispatches back and forth between officers. He's spoken of legionnaires who'd been his friends dying right before him. The war went on for several years, as you know, and by the time he'd turned thirteen Louis Durell was also killed."

Valli felt a surge of sympathy. "Then he'd only known his father for four years," she said quietly.

"True, but Marc says they had a good relationship. Louis had proudly hailed him as a 'magnificent son.' Marc stayed with him after his death, guarding his body for hours until the fighting ceased and the legionnaires under Louis Durell's command were able to return him for burial at Quarzazate."

Quarzazate—the desert outpost in Morocco near the Atlas Mountains, she thought. With such a harsh background, no wonder she had imagined him a rogue. She was quickly altering her perception of Marc, though she could see that he was an adventurer, a man without family ties.

Davide shook his head. "We both know the emptiness of not having parents alive. Marc once told me that after his father died he had nightmares of the battle for days afterward, with the sound of the legionnaires' song 'Artilleur de Metz' haunting his dreams."

Valli sat looking off into space, her chin cupped in her palms, her elbows on the table. She too could hear the trumpets blaring while the legionnaire's unit flag waved in the desert expanse. She looked at Davide. "Are you suggesting Marc just grew up in the legion?"

"Something like that, at least for a time. Of course, the other soldiers took him in as their mascot."

"Mascot!" she said rather indignantly. "A boy?"

"They're legionnaires. It's a whole different world than ours. They live isolated lives. They're reckless, yes, scoundrels to be honest. That's the reason I came as a chaplain. So many of them have no one except their comrades. That's around the time I met him. I'd just come from Morocco, after visiting Miss Maude Cary, and I was trying to get this mission station started."

Valli had known years ago that Davide had become friends with Marc Durell, but she hadn't known the circumstances. Little by little Davide told how he had broken down the tough walls that Marc had erected to protect his emotions. Davide had spoken of Christ as a loving friend and a personal redeemer who had given His life as a ransom for sinners.

"Marc started reading the Scriptures and eventually became convinced of their authenticity." Davide smiled, satisfied. "Once he realized the Bible wasn't simply a religious book conceived by men, he studied it for himself. But he also supported my dream of translating some of the New Testament into Berber. We built this house; he put in as much time here as his off-duty hours permitted. By the end of that year he had come to faith in Christ. I consider the change in him to be conquered territory through the intervention of God. He'd been headed for a life of sin and corruption, but the Lord rescued him by His grace. His favorite verse is in Psalm 40, which he wrote in the front of his Bible. 'He brought me up also out of an horrible pit, out of the miry clay, and set my feet upon a rock, and established my goings.'"

Valli sat, listening, as her interest in Marc grew by leaps and bounds.

"After that, Sebastien arrived, and Marc's circumstances changed for the better. So when he was ready he enrolled at the War College in France. You remember that?"

Valli did, and she was sorry now that she hadn't answered the two letters he had written her from college when she was at the ballet school in the same city, Paris. At the time she hadn't known any of this and had thought him a rascal with too many girlfriends. She had been afraid to get to know him. She had even seen him at that party in Paris and snubbed him for Kraig.

"Marc spent four difficult years at War College, or so he told me in his letters," Davide was saying. "He followed graduation with a year of advance study in foreign languages and in Secret Intelligence."

Secret Intelligence. So. Her suspicions were right. Her heart pounded. This seemed even more intriguing. Did the assignment which had kept him from dinner involve espionage?

"He graduated with honors, didn't he?" she said.

"Yes, how did you know?"

"From an article I saw in the Paris paper."

"After graduation he sailed to Morocco and worked in an administrative capacity under Sebastien's tutorage. But Marc felt restless sitting at a desk and he told me he longed for action and adventure. Reluctantly Sebastien yielded, and Marc volunteered for regiment duty, serving for a time in Madagascar, then at the garrisons in the Sud Oranasis area of southwestern Algeria."

"How did he become involved in Secret Intelligence?" she asked in a low voice.

"He fought in Algeria with 'legionnaire valor and distinction.' He was promoted to lieutenant. But after three years of fighting, he decided Sebastien was right after all. Marc had worked hard for his education and deserved better. I think it was around 1938, with the Nazis on the move, that he was placed in the sensitive area of French Intelligence here in North Africa. He caught the attention of General Nogues, an ally of Charles de Gaulle, and Marc was placed on staff. After only a few months, Marc discovered the false loyalties of one of the men on staff. Soon after that his abilities were recognized and he was promoted to Captain Marc Durell."

"Are you saying he works with the Surete?" she whispered.

Davide searched her face. "I wouldn't think you'd know about that."

"I heard it mentioned somewhere in Paris. It's the French Security, isn't it?"

He nodded. "Centered in Paris, but their men are everywhere, especially now. The Surete ordered the legion to formally organize the Intelligence Service, which also included the Bureau des Statistiques de la Legion Etrangere (BSLE) at Sidi-bel-Abbes. Marc was chosen from the general's staff to work with the inner circle that was linked to Casablanca, and that's why he's presently reporting to Sebastien."

"How is it you know all this?"

Davide smiled and said nothing. Her lashes narrowed, and she scanned him. Was it possible that he belonged to the Surete as well? She knew that people from every walk of life served as agents, and she supposed Davide could operate an independent mission *and* serve his country at the same time. War did strange things to peoples and cultures. And the evils of Nazism brought out a passionate desire in many to defeat Hitler at any cost.

"I'll probably be in hot water with Marc for telling you all this," Davide said gravely, "but I want you to trust him. You'll need a friend you can turn to after what's happened with Blystone. And Dietrich Gestler worries me."

He worried her as well. Davide added: "He claims he heard about my work as chaplain here and stopped by to see the mission, but I don't accept that. And if he didn't know you were here, why did he come?"

"Are you helping Marc?" she whispered.

Davide rubbed his chin and glanced casually toward the other room where Haroun was cleaning the kitchen. "Yes, but don't be alarmed. It's nothing that important or dangerous."

"You mean it wasn't—until Dietrich showed up."

"I don't know why he came, but I'll mention it to Marc when I see him. And please don't think that my helping him out in any way diminishes my commitment to the Christian work here."

She smiled and quickly placed her hand over his. "I hadn't thought that, I'm just concerned is all."

"Looks like we'll worry about each other, doesn't it?"

She now wished she were able to see Marc before her return to Paris, but she doubted there'd be an opportunity. If he were on some assignment in the Sahara there was no guessing when he would return. By then she might run into Dietrich again in Paris. The thought was enough to keep her awake at night. Just why had he come to the station?

A few days later Valli's visit had come to an end. She left Davide standing on the bustling dock at Oran, in the warm Mediterranean wind, with the formidable French war fleet quietly looking on. She waved goodbye as minutes later the passenger and cargo ship *le Fleur* slipped away from the North African coast. Soon, Valli settled in for the voyage across the Mediterranean toward the crowded streets, the cool spring rains, and the ballet theater of Paris.

# 5

## NEAR SIDI-BEL-ABBES

Three weeks had passed since Marc delivered the information contained in the postcards to his superior, Colonel Sebastien Ransier. Though no one had heard from Blystone, and Ahmed was dead, the colonel and the Surete considered the mission a success.

Marc would miss Ahmed. He kept wondering if there hadn't been something left undone that would have secured his life. The "rescue mission" to safeguard Blystone's information had been hastily arranged, and he remained concerned that Blystone had needlessly involved Valli Chattaine. Although Jacquette had informed him of her safe arrival at Davide's station house after Marc quietly sent him ahead to make sure, he remained concerned about the display of the rose on her handbag. If the German agent had realized the white rose identified the courier, Valli could face future danger.

Not that the Englishman had much choice at the time except to use her. Blystone had known Valli was Sebastien's sister-in-law, and she was the one person on the train he could trust to bring the information to Sebastien. How could you fault a dead man who had given his life for his country?

Blystone was just the beginning of a long list of men and women who would end up making the supreme sacrifice in this coming war. He really had no reason to single out Valli Chattaine as a patriot any more than the other women he knew who were in dangerous positions. From the short time he had spent with her, he already suspected she would agree. If she hadn't felt patriotic she wouldn't have agreed so readily to help Blystone.

Marc scowled. For while Sebastien rejoiced over such women, Marc was hoping that the Surete colonel didn't cast an eye in Valli's direction for future assistance.

In the thirsty moonlight, the arid wind rippled the endless sea of sand dunes and sent a cluster of stunted date palms dancing, as though in tune to some ancient bedouin music.

Above, the black Sahara sky was smothered with a dazzling array of jewel-like stars and planets. Marc walked the still smoldering white sand, on a new assignment. With France edging toward all-out war with Germany, the regular army officers in Paris were apprehensive about their colonies in North Africa. One of their misgivings concerned the loyalty of German officers serving within the Foreign Legion itself. With Italian troops entering North Africa in support of Hitler, French control of Algeria and Morocco stood at risk in the shifting political scene where the Fascist Italians and Nazis were taking advantage of Arab unrest. German espionage was as thick as desert scorpions. With the help of any German-born collaborators within the Foreign Legion, Morocco and Algeria could be a powder keg.

While in Tangier, Sebastien had received orders to send Marc here to discover if there was secret support for Hitler's

Third Reich. Captain Zimmer was of primary interest since he had family in Germany heartily committed to Hitler. Marc had arrived here two weeks ago when Zimmer's regiment was beginning a month of training for possible duty in France. Already he'd learned that Zimmer was receiving fiery letters from the "home front" telling of the glories of the Third Reich. Then, tonight, Captain Zimmer had sent for him. Was he suspicious?

He walked toward the meeting, the brilliant full moon reflecting upon the sand, which stretched before him as an endless horizon. After a few minutes he neared the command tent. Trained to notice anything out of the ordinary, he wondered about the jeep parked near some silhouetted date palms. The driver had to have come from Bel-Abbes, the nearest garrison within a radius of fifty miles. Who would send a driver from Bel-Abbes?

The tent swelled like a bloated toad with a gust of parched wind. The regiment flag snapped, as if coming to attention. Marc's footfall alerted Zimmer's guard. He stepped forward saluting energetically. "Monsieur le Captaine!"

Marc returned an easy salute. "At ease, Corporal. Captain Zimmer wishes to see me?"

"Oui, monsieur, he waits," and he stepped back from the sandy path lined with rock markers.

Marc pushed aside the tent flap, ducking under the opening. He let the canvas fall into place.

A lantern swung from a hook in the pinnacle of the roof, flinging enlarged images on the tent wall. Zimmer stood from behind his desk, unsmiling. Nothing unusual there; he rarely cracked a grin. He was a brawny, rawboned man with pink skin that refused to tan, producing instead half-cooked splotches on his nose and ears. His pale gray eyes were filmy from years of staring at endless sand dunes. He really belonged in the Austrian Alps where he'd been born.

Zimmer waved him toward a patched canvas chair that looked as though it had survived a half century. Marc sat near the open tent flap where gusty winds stirred memos pinned up on a board. He noticed a faded magazine picture of American movie star Betty Grable in shorts.

"So, Durell! You leave me so quickly." Zimmer pulled a rumpled pack of red and white Lucky Strike cigarettes from his shirt pocket.

Leave? Marc studied his face. Zimmer struck a match and watched it flare before holding it to his cigarette. He seemed attracted by the flame, thought Marc.

He puffed several times to get it burning before deeply inhaling the gray smoke.

"You come and go like the desert wind. A wily desert fox I should call you."

Marc lifted a brow. "A compliment, I hope?"

"One month here, six weeks there. Then a month off to enjoy Casablanca." His lower lip went up. "Who do you know at headquarters that I don't?"

"A good many people so it seems." Marc smiled easily and refused the crumpled pack of cigarettes.

"Once again you are called away." Zimmer poured two tins of coffee and handed one to Marc.

Cautious, but keeping his expression inscrutable, Marc drank the burnt coffee, trying to outguess fast-moving events before they overtook him. He had nothing on Zimmer, nothing but the letter, and it wasn't a crime to receive mail from family in Berlin. Marc had lifted the letter, copying names and addresses before replacing it, but there had been nothing incriminating. Zimmer displayed no rantings of racial superiority in the treatment of his troops. He had Poles and Czechoslovakians as well as one Jew, who had escaped Austria. His record in the legion was clean, his service in the Rif War in Tangier from 1921-26 had been one of valor. It was a policy that a legionnaire's nationalism was not promoted, since the primary merit for the hired mercenary was his valor wherever he fought.

"Called where?" Marc inquired.

"Nowhere far. Bel-Abbes."

Marc found it unusual that his assignment should be called off before he could come up with the information the Surete wanted for their report. He was just now becoming friendly with Zimmer and the handful of Germans in his regiment.

"Bel-Abbes? By whose order?"

Zimmer exhaled, watching him blandly. "Colonel Ransier."

He felt Zimmer's scrutiny. He was curious about his relationship with Sebastien.

Marc retained a blasé expression, which hid his rising doubts. Sebastien was not supposed to be in Algeria. He had left Tangier for Paris with Blystone's information, and by now he should be arriving. His wife, Giselle, Valli Chattaine's sister, was already visiting Paris, and Sebastien was soon to depart the military for a civilian post in Prime Minister Reynaud's government. This was a change that Giselle had been encouraging her husband to make for the last two years. Giselle refused to believe Germany would try to invade France, and when she talked of Paris, she spoke glibly of its past.

Marc glanced at the desk where Zimmer pushed a dispatch toward him. "This arrived a short time ago, brought by Jacquette."

He hadn't noticed Jacquette standing at the jeep, who would normally have called out to him. If his friend was here, then the dispatch must be from Sebastien. What had gone wrong? Why hadn't he left for Paris?

Marc read the colonel's brief message, but the change in his assignment was ambiguous. He was told to meet Sebastien tonight at Bel-Abbes. A trip to Paris was also in his future, and it appeared as if Great-Uncle Claude Ransier was ill and requesting to see Marc.

Was it true? He considered the request to be part of Sebastien's efforts to prevent Zimmer from suspecting the purpose of his mission. Marc wasn't convinced the great-uncle who had sent him away when he was a boy would wish to see him now.

"You are lucky," Zimmer said, crushing out his cigarette. He made a sweeping gesture to the sand on his desk that invariably found its way into everything. "It has been many years since I visited France. I went to see a cousin there after the Great War. She was looking for work to put her two boys through the best schools." He shrugged his heavy shoulders. "She died of the influenza epidemic that followed the war." He shook his head sadly, as if remembering. "She worked too hard. She killed herself off so her younger son could wear white silk tights and leap on his toes about a stage. He always reminded me of a girl," he said with a trace of thoughtful scorn. "A man ought to be a soldier, like Dietrich."

Marc was suddenly paying attention. Dietrich. *Don't rush to conclusions,* he thought. *Dietrich is a common enough name in Germany. There's no reason why this Dietrich could also have the last name of Gestler.*

Marc, attempting to draw him out, spoke absurdly: "Oh I don't know... I always liked the ballet...I wouldn't have minded becoming a lead dancer."

Zimmer looked at him, his pale eyes bulging. "You're crazying me, Durell, *you*?"

"Sure, mon ami, why not?"

"Why not!" He lit another cigarette. "A legionnaire—a ballet dancer!"

Marc shrugged, keeping a straight face. "Well, how did your cousin's youngest son turn out?"

Zimmer dragged on his cigarette, walking away restlessly from the desk as Marc glanced down at the dispatch. "Kraig," he said, "ah, he's really of no account."

Stay calm. Then it *was* the same Dietrich—and a brother to Kraig the ballet conductor. Kraig, who at one time had been engaged to marry Valli Chattaine. Something had gone wrong in their relationship, and Kraig had left Paris for Spain. Marc remembered hearing about it some four years ago but had never learned why the romance was terminated. Since meeting her again at the train junction two weeks ago, however, he found that he personally was curious.

"Dietrich is different," Zimmer was saying. "Discipline and strong measure make a man. But we all have our Achilles' heel they say. He is due in Paris soon. He is interested in a woman there, and she is available again. He insists on finding her."

Marc affected detachment. And just why should this French woman make such an impression on Dietrich?

Zimmer came back to the desk. "I think he's out of his mind. He should forget her. He'll be a rich businessman after the war. He could have anyone then."

If Dietrich were to become a businessman after the war it would probably stem from his dabbling in the black market now. There had been talk at the last Surete meeting of some smuggling going on in Tangier. Could Dietrich be the agent in the sunglasses trailing Blystone?

"I would not worry," Marc suggested easily. "He sounds too smart to ruin his future. There are plenty of women in Paris. All beautiful in their own way," he said to draw him out.

"Yes, but his problem is that there's only one Valli Chattaine."

Marc could agree to that. Her demure smile with the provocative dimple came to mind. He set his empty cup down and stood. How did Dietrich's interest in her coincide with Kraig's? Had a romantic triangle broken things up? What could Valli tell him about Dietrich Gestler? If he had been the man following Blystone then she hadn't told him the truth when she said she didn't recognize him.

For a moment his disappointment was acute. Then he realized that even at the station he hadn't fully believed her. Why hadn't she mentioned Dietrich? Could there be something between them?

"Valli Chattaine? The ballerina from Paris?" Marc asked innocently.

Zimmer merely nodded. "Dietrich will get burned yet. Just like Kraig."

Valli didn't seem the sort of woman to play romantic games, even though her sister was an outrageous flirt. But Zimmer seemed to blame Valli for the failed engagement. Marc knew this information about Valli raised a caution flag. If for some reason she cared for Dietrich Gestler, then Blystone had blundered badly by trusting her—*and so have I*, he thought.

A glimmer of irony shone in Zimmer's pale eyes. "I see you have heard of her—a talented lady." Marc made no comment. Zimmer changed the subject. "Do you think Hitler will give his generals the order to attack France this year?"

Marc refused to allow the words to unsettle him. He did not think Zimmer approved of the idea, but was curious and perhaps even awed by the success of the German Wehrmacht.

Marc folded the dispatch and put it in his pocket. "If he does, we must deter him."

Zimmer looked grim. "Yes," he agreed thoughtfully, "if we can."

If we can...a reminder that none had been able to stop the German thrust into the heart of Europe.

Zimmer momentarily appeared candid, and Marc, aware that his work sometimes called him to act on his instincts, took a risk. "Is Dietrich expecting to enter Paris on his own or as a part of the German army?"

Zimmer was rubbing his chin, looking over at the frayed picture of Betty Grable. "If he knows, he won't discuss it in my presence. He despises the legion and scorns me. Imagine if he knew that I want to emigrate to America. He thinks I'm a coward for not returning to Berlin to enlist. Knowing Dietrich, I think he will go to Paris alone. He expects Hitler to enter Paris victoriously and for the ballerina to welcome the Nazis' arrival."

Marc tried to cool his glowing temper. Was it possible the gracious ballerina was a Nazi collaborator? Possibly, but not likely. He couldn't believe it of her, but he had to remind himself that he'd been wrong before. He only had to be wrong once to lose his life as well as the lives of his colleagues.

Zimmer came back to his desk, shuffling papers around to signal his impatience. His expression was strained as if he knew he had said too much.

"Well, Durell, you're out of my camp now. Jacquette's been waiting for you. Stay out of trouble in Paris."

Marc smiled. "I'll try hard. See you when I get back."

They exchanged bland salutes, then Marc turned and left the tent.

Standing outside, Marc frowned. The gusty hot wind blew grains of sand against the side of the tent. The vast Sahara was silent, but stars and planets spoke volumes from the deep blackness above.

He would need to inform Sebastien that Zimmer's second cousin was none other than Dietrich Gestler. This wouldn't look good for Zimmer. The Surete would assume that any enthusiastic Nazi might solicit his cooperation, and they were probably right. If Zimmer was able to inform him about French troop movements in North Africa, or about the fleet anchored at Oran, Dietrich would force the matter even if Zimmer refused. It was time to get Zimmer transferred to Mexico. Twenty minutes later, Marc tossed his baggage into the back of the vehicle as Jacquette started the motor. Marc settled into the seat, resting his arm on the door as they drove away, scattering sand.

"What do you know about the colonel's change in plans?"

"Very little, mon ami. I have been sniffing about all day. Nothing except he will not be going now to Paris as he thought."

This was news. "What about Blystone's information?"

Jacquette shook his head dubiously and shrugged. "The change in plans might have something to do with Madame Giselle's sister."

Marc wondered, *could Sebastien have found out that Valli knew Dietrich?*

Sidi-bel-Abbes had been incorporated by Napoleon Bonaparte into the French Republic in 1849. Soon thereafter the conquest of what was to become French North Africa was completed from the blue Mediterranean to the white dunes of the Sahara.

Now, in 1940, Algeria continued as the main "home" of the Foreign Legion, and Sidi-bel-Abbes remained the outpost most familiar to Marc. It was here among strong, rugged men "without a past" that Marc had spent his younger years. Only later did he learn that it was not a crooked twist of fate that determined his path in life but a personal God who was good.

Marc had arrived in Morocco nearly sixteen years previous at the tender age of nine, just two weeks after the funeral of his mother, Josephine Jacqueline Ransier Durell. By the time he turned thirteen he had become familiar with death, including that of his father, Sergeant Louis Durell. On that occasion Marc had managed to break through the enemy line with the help of an Arab friend, but the first-aid he brought was too little and too late. The last memory he had of his father was holding his head in his arms while he died of multiple wounds. The years spent with his father were fewer than he would have chosen, although more than many boys received.

A year after the funeral, his life took another unexpected turn as Providence guided his path. Marc met up with Davide Chattaine, a young man with strong Christian ideals who became a self-appointed chaplain in the lone outpost near Tangier. Davide had taken a great deal of rousting from the legionnaires, and Marc respected his courage. Marc once rescued Davide from an empty well that several of the rogues had placed him in. "Ah mon ami," Davide said joyfully, "I feel like the Prophet Jeremiah after being drawn up from the mud pit by the Ethiopian who warned the king that the prophet might starve. So I prayed for a friend and the Lord has sent you."

Marc had smiled wryly. "You think so, do you? And what makes you think I am any more interested in your meddlesome preaching than the others?"

Davide had grinned up at him, a winsome lad only five years his senior. "You would not otherwise have cared about me being left here. You came back. That tells me much. God has sent you, of that I am convinced."

Marc had pondered, hands on hips, scanning him. He had made no reply and tossed Davide a canteen of water. From then on Marc had simply scrutinized Davide's life. Little by little Davide had broken down the tough walls that Marc had erected to protect his emotions from pain. Davide had laughed a lot. Like Marc, he had very little, yet he appeared to have everything that was important. What made Davide special was that he was a Chattaine. He could have lived in Great-Aunt Calanthe's palatial house overlooking Tangier Bay—yet Davide had preferred to tell the scoundrels at Sidi-bel-Abbes that God loved them. That amazed Marc.

Thereafter, Marc had left the barracks at Bel-Abbes where he worked as the cook's helper and went with Davide. At the end of a year he had come to personal faith in Christ and was helping Davide build bridges to the Berber men.

Marc was still thinking of Davide as Jacquette steered the jeep over the bumpy road toward Bel-Abbes. Soon they

climbed steadily through a desiccated countryside sprin-
kled with dwarf palms and other stunted bushes. When the
narrow unpaved road leveled off, they drove onto a dusty
plain. Here, in the middle of irrigated palmeries, emerged
the familiar walls of the town of Sidi-bel-Abbes and the
environs of the public garden, where he had spent many
hours through the years until beginning his military
schooling in Paris. There was also a tree-lined street, but it
was crowded with cantinas run by the Spaniards. At least
half the town's population was people from Madrid, who
made their living catering to the unwholesome off-duty
desires of the legionnaires.

But the dark-eyed Spaniards were not the only ones
who made a living preying on the sinful desires of soldiers.
Across from the legionnaire parade ground lay the "village
negre," the Arab district, which was more of a shanty. It was
off-limits to the soldiers, but Marc knew of only a few who
kept the military rules. But while most of the Spaniards and
Arabs preyed on the legionnaires, Davide had become a
caring shepherd. Marc always thought of what Saint Paul
had written in Romans: "Where sin abounded, grace did
much more abound." God's grace had not left sinners
without a witness.

"Home sweet home," Marc said dryly, looking at the village negre.

Jacquette laughed.

Here, the air was heavy with the smell of Arab tobacco.
Legionnaires wandered the narrow alleys illuminated by
torches, some buying lamb kabobs grilled over braziers on
the dirt street, or if the mercenary soldier had it in mind to
desert, he would exchange his uniform for old civilian
clothes and make for the train that ran to Oran. In his earlier
days Marc had been among the patrols making sweeps,

sometimes arresting the soldiers who scattered down dark alleys to hide. Even now he knew of certain legionnaires who had retired and formed minor businesses here. There was even a small Jewish quarter that converted the banknotes of most countries of Europe, sent to the legionnaires by their families, into French francs.

Jacquette drove to the legion fort that housed unadorned barracks with empty windows. How familiar it seemed. Marc remembered those early years after his father's death but before Sebastien had taken him in, when he was a fifteen-year-old bent for trouble. Sebastien had sent him off to a strict military school in France. He never wanted to go back to those early days as a legionnaire, which sometimes required marching and jogging up to forty miles with a heavy pack.

Jacquette stopped the jeep and looked at his watch. "We are on time, Captaine." He pointed across the gravel-colored barracks yard. "The colonel waits."

"Wait for me in the yard. Don't let anyone else claim this truck. We may need it tonight."

Jacquette groaned as he guessed they might not be getting much sleep. Marc smiled. "See if you can scrounge up some coffee and sandwiches, will you?" Jacquette gave a salute.

Marc walked across the barracks square toward the "salle d'honneur," which was a separate building, this one suitably impressive with a grand entrance.

Marc entered the large room. The inside walls were covered with imposing portraits of earlier valorous legionnaires and large canvas paintings of glorious battle scenes in which the legion was either victorious or had died to the last man to safeguard the regiment standard. Sebastien was studying the paintings on the wall. What awaited him, Marc wondered, something troubling, or even dangerous?

# 6

Colonel Sebastien Ransier stood gazing at a large canvas painting glorifying the third company of the French Legion regiment that had fought the battle of Camerone with such valor. At fifty, the straightness of his uniform and the carriage of his shoulders spoke of the disciplined character that won him the silver cross for action in the Great War of 1914-1918.

Marc often thought Sebastien would fit well into one of the scenes depicted in the paintings. He wore the military "pillbox" hat, like General Charles de Gaulle, and beneath it, though it could not be seen, his hair was light brown and graying at the temples.

Also like de Gaulle, Ransier was tall, agile, lean, and tough. He smoked a pipe that he was rarely without, and his tanned, rather craggy face was pleasant to behold, with a haughty aquiline nose and midnight blue eyes that were much darker than Marc's sky-blue ones. While he had an unrelenting gaze that could make an opponent uneasy, he had mellowed since his surprising marriage to Giselle three years ago.

Sebastien turned away from the paintings at the sound of the door shutting behind Marc.

Marc smiled at the man who years ago had kindly stepped into a place of responsibility left vacant by the death of his father. His smile vanished and he saluted smartly. "Captain Marc Durell reporting as requested, Colonel!"

Sebastien chuckled and walked across the room toward him, one hand grasping Marc's solid shoulder. "Is this legionnaire formality the way to greet your cousin?"

There was a touch of a smile in Marc's eyes as he gestured his dark head toward the unsmiling portraits of heroes weighted down with medals on the fronts of their jackets. "In this hallowed hall? You have left me small choice. Such a meeting place you have chosen, Monsieur Cousin!"

Sebastien caught the glimmer of humor in his tone and followed his glance. "Ah, yes, a hallowed hall. Instead of Roman Church saints, we have soldiers. Many of them rascals, to be sure." He grew serious and thoughtful. "I tell you, Marc, we could use a few of these valiant old wolves in Paris at this time. I respect Reynaud," he said of the present leader in the government, "but I fear many surrounding him are leaning unsteadily toward compromise with Germany. They are not determined enough to oppose the diabolically clever Nazis at the Reichstag in Berlin."

"Paris is still exhausted from the Great War, which we won against Germany," Marc reminded him. "Our soldiers came home from the trenches expecting to be rewarded as victors. Instead, they returned to indebted farms and cities without employment. We Frenchmen have fared little better

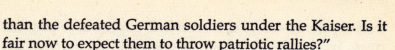

than the defeated German soldiers under the Kaiser. Is it fair now to expect them to throw patriotic rallies?"

"Yes, yes, I know." Sebastien paced. "Yet it's also true we do not see such weariness of spirit in the Foreign Legion."

Marc thought of Zimmer. "It is there, under the surface. For the right price, some would collaborate with the Nazis."

"Still, I blame the French generals who are failing to galvanize both soldier and citizen for what is ahead. It is the worst act of treason to keep the people blind to the danger awaiting them."

Marc could empathize with his military frustration. "You know the generals," he explained lazily. "They have staked everything, including the security of Paris, on the invincibility of the Maginot Line."

Sebastien looked pained. "General de Gaulle is not one of them. He has argued for years of the need to update the fighting tactics of the French army. Many of our techniques are outdated. He does not think the Maginot Line will hold against a German offensive of tanks and bombers."

Marc too had studied the Nazi tactics. Everything was hurled as quickly as possible against an unprepared opponent. Once the line was broken, armored tanks thundered ahead, protected by the low flying Luftwaffe using the Stuka dive bomber that also attacked ground forces. The army would soon be widely scattered and leaderless. Exactly what Hitler planned.

Marc noted the anguish in Sebastien's tired face. He too felt frustrated. The grandeur of France was disintegrating. The people were without a moral compass. The majority did not appear to care. Her leaders were weak and compromising. The Church seemed to have given up. France was dying needlessly, and who would listen? It was frustrating because there was time to alter the direction, to stop the death knoll from ringing out over the land, but he was only one voice. Sebastien, another. Still—one man here, another there, and if they could gather together under a true leader they could form a strong French resistance to Nazi Germany, but—the will to resist, to fight, to believe, must be present in every heart before they could stand against such diabolical oppression.

Marc knew better than to try to spare Sebastien discouragement by pretending that victory would somehow materialize like a genie out of a bottle.

"Unless things change soon, Hitler is likely to march into Paris. Occupation will be far worse than the citizens of Paris dare to think. But England will fight. We have at least one bulldog alongside of us."

"Yes..." Sebastien murmured thoughtfully. "Leaders with ramrods in their backs, that is what we need. And a people willing to sacrifice their ease for something that matters. France needs such a leader to take to the airwaves."

Marc's light-blue eyes flickered like ice in the sun. "General de Gaulle."

Sebastien rammed his hands into his pockets and walked to gaze once more at the paintings on the wall. "Yes, but try to convince the other generals to listen to him. While some trust the Maginot Line to protect us, others are defeatists. Hitler can't be stopped, they say."

Sebastien turned and stared at him. A disdainful twitch appeared in his tanned cheek. "Do they actually believe we can fight with military maneuvers as old as Napoleon?"

"The history of France is a proud history," Marc said quietly. "The generals have no wish to change the tactics that won the Great War or wars before that. They expect them to still be effective. It seems the generals will not be convinced until jackboots are goosestepping through Paris streets."

They stood looking at one another, the silence growing, then Sebastien scowled grimly. "I did not mean to launch us on such a dark and precarious topic so soon after meeting..."

"I've already been thinking about it—for months."

Sebastien drew in a breath as if to clear his mind of mocking demons with swastikas. "Well! A change of subject and a walk is called for."

Marc too smiled grimly and went to the door, opening it for his cousin. They left the salle d'honneur and stepped into the desert winds.

"Look at those stars!" Sebastien breathed. "Billions! And here we are sick to death over Berlin. He knows, does He not?" he asked almost wistfully.

"You can be sure He does. 'The Most High rules in the kingdom of men.'"

"Where is that written?"

"Daniel, to a very proud king named Nebuchadnezzar. 'He puts kings on thrones, and takes them down. And places there the basest of men to rule.'"

"Meaning?" Sebastien cocked a brow.

"Meaning," said Marc, "we sometimes get the kind of ruler we deserve."

Sebastien sighed in thoughtful agreement. "That worries me."

"With good cause."

They walked in silence, looking at the stars and planets. The heavens declare the glory of God, and the great expanse shows His handiwork. Marc soaked in the revelation of God's sovereignty. When everything fell apart, you at least had that to hold onto in Scripture.

They had loosened their collars and the buttons at their necks while the warm breeze whinnied about the buildings and barracks. Their spirits cooled and their tensions calmed. Hitler had plans to conquer Europe, but he hadn't won yet.

Marc glanced at his wristwatch, it was nine o'clock. "The 'bewitching' hour," he said with a smile and nodded toward the gates. Nine meant "all in" for the legionnaires. Groups of them were making their way back to the barracks now before the sergeant of the guard closed the gates, leaving only a small sally port open.

The two men walked toward the training ground, called a chateau because it was on a slight mound. By six in the morning it would be filled with running recruits.

Marc looked at Sebastien. "I had expected you to be in Paris by now, reporting Blystone's information to the Surete."

Sebastien did not appear worried by the delay. "I was targeted."

"You!" Marc worried. "By Dietrich Gestler?"

"We're not sure yet. Don't worry, the information was sent by someone else. The Surete will have it by now. I imagine the lights are burning late tonight in Paris and London." He frowned. "At least I hope they burn later. I don't trust Prime Minister Neville Chamberlain," he said of England's minister. "Nor do I feel all that comfortable with those surrounding our Reynaud."

Marc didn't know all of the information that the postcards conveyed and it was likely he wouldn't find out, but he knew that it concerned an all-out attack by the German Wehrmacht against the Western Front. There were postcards of France, Belgium, Denmark, Norway, Holland, and England. There had also been a snapshot of the French fleet anchored at Oran.

"What of you?" Marc asked. "If you're a target the Nazis won't let up."

"They won't be as blatant as they were. They knew about Blystone, and he's taking the heat, poor fellow. Still no word from him. I'll soon be in a 'quieter' role. New orders arrived at Oran for both of us." He looked at Marc, as if wondering how he was going to take the next bit of news. "Looks as though my military career is winding down. I'm being sent to Tangier for the duration of the war."

Marc managed his surprise. The military was Sebastien's total occupation. Perhaps Marc should have expected such a change. Giselle wanted civilian life. Great-Uncle Claude Ransier's death would also produce a sizable inheritance for Sebastien, that is—as long as Great-Uncle's son, Aubert, didn't end up controlling the will. Aubert had always been a jealous sort, criticizing anyone in the family that Claude might praise or wish to be generous with. Aubert, because he lived in the Ransier house with his father, seemed to expect favored treatment in regard to the will. Marc was thankful that this kind of greediness had never been a temptation for him. He was learning that when your greatest expectations are from God, you are less likely to be disappointed by people. He remembered what God had told Abraham: "I am your shield and your exceeding great reward." In the end, all true blessings, at least those of eternal value, came from God. Marc knew he had more than Aubert. He could depend on God as Father, but Cousin Aubert had all his treasures upon earth, which was not a very safe place under the present circumstances.

"A post in Tangier? I thought the Surete wanted you in Paris, serving in Reynaud's government." Though the location might offer more security, all of North Africa had its own brand of danger and intrigue.

A small frown formed above Sebastien's eyes as he appeared to be considering the path he trod. "They're now convinced I'm more useful in Tangier, heading up the French embassy—just in time to cheer the arrival of the Third Reich's new ambassador. Cozy, isn't it?"

"Cozy *and* dangerous." So the French embassy too would be used for espionage purposes. Marc smiled. "You're too humble. Congratulations, 'Ambassador' Ransier!"

"Better reserve your congratulations for the end of the war," he said wryly. "I may end up tripping over my own shoelaces. I've never seen myself as a polished, glib-tongued diplomat."

Marc smiled. "You'll do all right."

"I wouldn't have taken the position if the Surete hadn't convinced me they expect a Nazi invasion in North Africa. A great deal of information will be sneaking in and out of this location. That's the reason for the new German ambassador and his henchmen crew. They're a pack of desert jackals, all SS agents, I'm told." He shot Marc a glance. "One of my responsibilities will be to find out what they have their eye on in this area."

Marc was silent, considering the news. He suspected that Dietrich Gestler would be one of those SS agents.

Sebastien paused on the night-darkened chateau, a small smile on his mouth. "You might as well be told now. After Paris, you will also be posted in the Tangier embassy. You'll continue to report to me."

Embassy! "You know I don't like to get bogged down behind a desk. I prefer field work."

Sebastien smiled. "Yes, I know, it's more adventurous, more risky. You don't mind being a target, it suits you. But one day some woman will look into your eyes and beg you to take a desk job. Then you'll have no choice."

Marc smiled. "We'll see about that. Anyway, that day hasn't arrived."

"Believe me, Marc, this is no pencil-pushing promotion, if that's what you're afraid of. You'll see risk aplenty before it's over. You'll also still report here at Bel-Abbes, to General Nouges, at least for the next six months. We intend to keep you busy," he said with a smile.

The position was a promotion? He glanced uneasily at Sebastien. "Whose idea was it?"

"Now it is you who are being too humble. It wasn't at my request. The order came from Danjou himself." He smiled. "Does that make a difference?"

It did, in an important way. Marc wanted to be counted worthy of any promotions, not receive favored treatment due to a relative's influence. The mention of Gaston Danjou, however, the head of French Intelligence in Paris, brought Marc's appropriate silence.

"I hope Giselle will be pleased about Tangier when she finds out," Sebastien said a moment later. "Becoming the right-hand lady of the new ambassador suits her disposition, don't you think?"

Marc looked away toward the stars. It suited her all right. It would give Sebastien's wife more opportunity than ever to try to alleviate her spiritual emptiness and bouts of boredom with secret flirtations. Giselle was skilled at filling her ballroom with military officers in dress uniform and making herself one of the few attractive women in a group of lonely men, far from home, without spiritual convictions. Now, as the wife of the new French ambassador, there would be ample opportunity for her to linger over cocktails among important officials.

Marc avoided a direct answer to Sebastien's question. He couldn't hurt him. In actuality he thought his wife would make a good Mata Hari.

Marc was always a little curious about the blindness that settled over Sebastien when he discussed his young wife. That he trusted Giselle so completely when she had already cheated behind his back in Tangier provoked Marc's pity. Sebastien deserved so much better. What did he ever see in her? Beauty, naturally, and while she was an attractive woman, her spiritual discernment appeared to be absent.

"She'll be an asset to me," Sebastien was saying. "I'm no good at this entertaining. Sipping cocktails with a roomful of spies and pretending friendship boggles my mind. I much prefer to meet the enemy on the battlefield."

Marc might agree to that. But something could also be said for keeping your enemies rounded up in the dining room where you could keep an eye on them as they feasted on crêpes suzette.

"Giselle has a knack for mixing with the other ambassadors and their wives that far exceeds mine. You'd be surprised at the amount of information she overhears at parties and gatherings. It still amazes me what she can divulge while informally discussing her musings at the end of the day," Sebastien said ruefully.

Marc stood casually with a bland expression on his face.

"Giselle is thoughtful, though. She's concerned that she do nothing to injure my reputation." Sebastien chuckled. "It's likely to be the other way around. I don't know what I'd do without her, Marc. Especially these last months with so many worries on my mind."

Giselle had been as bright and carefree as a butterfly when she'd left for Paris. Her mood might change once she found out that Paris was out and Tangier was in. Marc had wondered recently how much she knew of Sebastien's real work in the Surete.

"Will you tell her the reason for going to Tangier?"

"I must keep most of the details from her. It's safer for her that way."

*For you as well,* thought Marc, *and for all in the Surete.*

"I know she'll be disappointed when she learns I won't be serving in Reynaud's government. You know Giselle. She's an optimist, refusing to believe the Nazis will come to Paris." Sebastien frowned. "We had a disagreement before she left for Paris. I wanted her to wait in Oran at the hotel until I finished my business here, then we could go on to Paris together. She didn't want to stay in Oran alone. Strange, that's never troubled her before."

"Maybe it's the new responsibilities," Marc suggested to ease Sebastien's concerns. Was he worried about Giselle in "gay Paree" without him? Marriage to Sebastien required maturity, especially from a wife who enjoyed doing impulsive things. Giselle would need to change if Sebastien were to perform his work with the carefulness it demanded.

"Well...my personal dilemmas are not why I arranged the meeting with you here tonight," Sebastien said with a half smile. "I've new orders for you." He clasped his hands behind his back and they walked slowly on, keeping in the open, away from the trees. "First, what did you learn from Zimmer's regiment? Anything worthy to report to Paris? In so short a time I'd be surprised if you gathered much."

Marc had been waiting for this, wanting to find out about Valli. "The German soldiers were close-mouthed, hard to know. There was no discussion of the fuhrer. But I did learn something tonight from Zimmer. I admit it was a stroke of luck, since I wouldn't have guessed."

Sebastien became attentive.

"Zimmer had a cousin in Paris with two sons after the Great War. Nothing unusual there, except one of them happens to be Dietrich Gestler. He's going to Paris to search for an old romantic flame. A French girl." He went easy, not mentioning Valli's name yet. First he wanted to see Sebastien's response. "Dietrich must have met her a couple of years ago."

Marc expected Sebastien to react as strongly as he had when first hearing the news.

"We already knew about the girl," Sebastien admitted. "And about Gestler's plans to meet up with her again in Paris. That's one of the reasons we're sending you there, to protect her."

Marc bridled in his surprise. He still needed to master that reaction whenever the Surete pulled the rabbit out of the hat before he did. At such times he wondered why they even needed him.

"No use asking how you knew about her I suppose?"

"No use asking. But I'd be interested in knowing if Zimmer told you who this woman is?"

Marc could see that Sebastien watched him alertly. "Your expression tells me you know it's Valli Chattaine," Marc said. "You're not thinking Blystone made a mistake trusting her?"

Sebastien's eyebrows shot up. "It never entered my mind. The Surete has plans for Valli. And since she happens to be my sister-in-law, I wholeheartedly agree. She's a smart young lady and loyal."

Marc stopped on the sand and faced him in the bright moonlight. "Look, Sebastien, I wish I could say I trusted her completely, but is it wise to jump into this?"

"Davide trusts her," Sebastien reminded him quietly.

"Yes, I know." Marc remained vaguely troubled. "Keep in mind he's her brother."

Sebastien looked dubious. "I was under the impression you believed in just about everything Davide stands for, including that mission station not far from here."

"I do. That's the difficulty," Marc admitted, frowning. "Davide would never feed us false information deliberately."

"Deliberately," Sebastien repeated meaningfully. "So you think he misunderstands his sister?"

"I didn't say that, either. It's a fact, however, that Valli was once about to marry Kraig Gestler. Now, unexpectedly, Dietrich shows up with plans to find her in Paris. It all troubles me somehow." He didn't mention that Valli had failed to admit she recognized Dietrich at the train junction.

"As well it should trouble you, Marc. But I'll never believe Valli is cooperating with Dietrich. She's too fine a girl for that."

Marc was inclined to agree that Valli was a rarity, but it was also true that fine girls made errors in judgment and sometimes fell prey to deception. She had turned her back to him when he was at War College in Paris, yet trusted Kraig Gestler. Maybe there was some vanity in his suspicions now, but his doubts persisted. "His interest in her is actually a boon for us," Sebastien was arguing. "That's the other reason you're being sent to Paris."

Marc looked at him sharply. "You *want* him interested in Valli?"

"Only for a time," Sebastien said, glancing at him. "After that..." he shrugged, smiling. "You can move in with her brother-in-law's blessing. Right now we'd prefer that she played along with Gestler to see what he's up to in Paris. Danjou is also for this. We don't think she's the only reason Gestler is going there. If he's there to collaborate with a traitor, we'd also like very much to know who he is."

"Traitor? You mean French?"

"We think so. Maybe in Reynaud's cabinet. We're not completely certain of that. Valli could do a great deal to help us out."

"Now wait a minute—"

Sebastien lifted a brow, and Marc lapsed into stiff silence.

"Is Gestler following orders from someone in Paris or Tangier? Valli may be able to find out for us."

That explained Sebastien taking up residence in the Tangier embassy and why Marc was being sent to Paris, but Valli Chattaine was another matter entirely.

"I can see two things wrong with that," Marc insisted. "You're asking her to deliberately risk herself. Secondly, if we're wrong and she does have feelings for Dietrich, she's not likely to turn information over to me. She'll mislead me."

"She was never in love with Dietrich. It was Kraig."

"That was four years ago. Kraig betrayed her. This is now. Jacquette has learned that Dietrich paid her a visit at Davide's mission station before she returned to Paris."

"Oh?" Sebastien looked at him sharply.

Then he hadn't known. That was at least one fresh morsel he had come up with.

"Davide told you this?" Sebastien asked quietly.

"Yes. Davide walked in on them in the kitchen. Dietrich quickly made an excuse about having come to see the charity work. Small chance of that! Demoiselle Chattaine also recognized him at the train, but she looked me straight in the eye and said she hadn't."

Sebastien rubbed his chin. "She may have been afraid to say anything. We all make mistakes."

Marc laughed softly. "Oh come on, Sebastien. She's not dumb. You said so yourself."

"Precisely my point." He smiled. "The Surete needs her on the case, Marc. In fact, Danjou has specifically requested it."

Marc paused. "That settles it I suppose. All right, suppose she's loyal. Suppose she doesn't care for Gestler. She's still a novice."

"Is that the *real* reason you're hedging on this?" his eyes twinkled in the moonlight.

Marc ignored the suggestion because it was a good deal closer to the truth than he wanted to admit. "Blystone pinned a white rose on her handbag. If anyone knew that signal—including Gestler—the Nazis may already suspect her of working with us."

Sebastien frowned and walked on in silence. Marc continued in a low voice, "Or, maybe we have it all wrong. Maybe there's another way to look at this."

Sebastien looked at him. "Such as?"

"Just this. Maybe Dietrich showed up at the station for some reason other than romantic passion for Valli. Maybe his behavior is a front. Maybe Dietrich wanted something from Blystone other than the postcards?"

Sebastien shoved his hands in his jacket pockets and his stride increased. "You didn't tell me about the white rose."

"Is it wise to put her out front now with someone as clever as Gestler? This isn't very fair to her. If he does go to Paris, you know he isn't going to lay all his cards on the table at once. Of necessity there will be more suppers in candlelight until he accomplishes his task, whatever it is, in Paris or Tangier."

"You have a point there."

"Davide has met with Jacquette. Dietrich will be working as a diplomat at the German embassy in Tangier. That proves to me he's an SS agent."

"Yes, the Surete informed me of Gestler's new job. But that's just another reason we want you in Paris, Marc." He stopped abruptly and faced him. "You'll be there to bring Valli and Giselle back to Tangier before war closes the door."

Marc's jaw flexed.

"Look, I understand your concerns. You may very well be right in your assumptions about Gestler suspecting Valli even now. I worry too. About you, about all of us. But the hour demands the risk. Valli won't be the first to make sacrifices in this war, nor will she be the last. And it will get worse before it gets better."

Marc placed his hands on his hips. "Your optimism cheers me."

"Only a short time ago you faced the hard, biting facts of the future yourself. What has changed?"

Even Marc didn't know. His boot kicked at a small rock in his way. "I just prefer to pass up this assignment," he admitted grimly. "Can't you find someone else?"

Sebastien sighed. "I would, Marc, except you're the best man for the job. You can't expect us to settle for anyone else when it's a fact. You're a Ransier. At least your mother was. We've reason to suspect a double trail to all this that leads to the family in Paris. It may have something to do with Dietrich, we're not clear on that. But you can find out. You have an open invitation from Uncle Claude to call on him at the estate."

"I don't understand. What's Claude Ransier to do with this?"

"You will. And with Giselle staying there, you've even more justification for visiting. That will give you a chance to speak alone with Claude."

Marc felt the trap closing behind him.

Sebastien took a pipe from his pocket and looked at it. "Useless habit," he murmured to himself, putting it between his teeth unlit. Marc waited to hear about Claude Ransier.

"Claude telephoned me last week requesting you come to France. He says it's somewhat urgent that he talk with you."

Marc just looked at him.

"He wouldn't explain to me on the telephone, but he gave the impression neither Aubert nor anyone else at the estate knows he's contacted me. I believe I understand your take on that. I too think it's odd he's asked to see you now. It's been a long time. He could just as easily have communicated his concerns to me. He refused and insists you come." Sebastien raised both brows and bit on the stem of his pipe. "Interesting, don't you think? What's he up to after all these years?"

"He gave no hints?"

"None. You know Claude. He's a bulldog when he settles on an issue. And on this one, his mind is made up. His patriotism is sterling, and that's what prods me to send you there. Between bringing Giselle back to Tangier, and this important business with Valli, you can see that your assignment is fully justified."

And full of headaches, Marc mused. And what could Claude possibly have to discuss after years of silence? Personal regrets perhaps, or was there something more? Claude wasn't inclined towards sentimentality, not even in his elder years, and he was not emotionally erratic. Claude was practical.

There must be something definite on his mind. Something that troubled him as he lay awake at night with illness, most likely listening to the BBC's day by day account of the Third Reich army making its way through Europe.

Something Sebastien had said earlier came once more to mind: "We've reason to suspect a trail that leads to the family in Paris." Meaning...did Dietrich Gestler have contacts with anyone in the Ransier family? Valli, of course, but she wasn't actually related, except by a distant bloodline joining Claude to her Great-Aunt Calanthe Malaret in Tangier. Giselle? Aubert? Someone else?

Could Claude, then, know something about Gestler?

Sebastien's thoughtful tone brought Marc back to the present. "Valli's already proven she can handle the job when patriotism prompted her to help Blystone on the train."

That was debatable, but Marc let it go.

"Believe me, Marc, we've taken risk into consideration. We want to keep her as safe as we can. Sending you will help. It's going to be a difficult job."

An impossible one? That depends upon Demoiselle Valli Chattaine. Marc looked toward the barracks. The lights were going out.

"What worries me," Sebastien said, "is that blasted white rose. Blystone was a fool to pin it on her bag."

"Yes, but in fairness, what choice did he have? I'd otherwise not have known she had the postcards. I would have followed Blystone."

"No use my complaining now. The old boy was a novice and that's the way it goes sometimes. There is even a suspicion that Blystone could not be fully trusted. Thank God it turned out as well as it did. I'd feel better, though, if I could hear from him."

By now, Marc had little hope of hearing from Blystone. "Dietrich may have killed him. And when he didn't find what he wanted he may have remembered seeing Valli on the train. They were together at the window. If I saw them, why not Gestler? That could account for his unexpected presence at the mission station."

"Maybe. All the more reason to meet with Valli in Paris and discover what he may have said to her before Davide arrived."

"Davide says they were arguing politics when he entered the house."

"Yes...but what else did they talk about?"

Perhaps the debate had been staged for Davide's benefit, to make him think they were at odds? Marc couldn't see Valli Chattaine supporting the Nazis, but how well did he know her, really? He hadn't seen her since his youthful days before War College.

"Did Dietrich see you at the train?" Sebastien asked.

"I'm nearly certain he didn't. I was keeping my cover and Jacquette was dressed as a woman. Renault took the full glare."

Sebastien smiled approvingly. "Good. You'll both need to keep your cover in Paris. Better take Jacquette with you. And you'll need your legionnaire role since you're bound to run into Dietrich."

Marc looked at him. Did he expect Dietrich to call on Valli at the estate?

Sebastien removed an envelope from under his jacket. "This will help you, for now you've a good reason to see Valli."

Marc took the envelope, but it was too dark to read the address. "Who is it from, or is it, as the Brits say, a red herring?"

"No, it's genuine all right. It's a letter for Valli from her Great-Aunt Calanthe. The dear old mademoiselle wants her to return to Tangier before the war. Sentimentality has moved her at last. I'm glad to see it, really. There's been an alienation between the two for years. Maybe the war is good for something after all. It may bring reconciliation."

Marc remained thoughtful, looking off toward Bel-Abbes. He had hoped to evade the assignment but Sebastien wasn't letting him off. "Then, Valli left Davide's mission station?"

"Yes, a week ago. Your passage is also booked. You leave tonight." Sebastien tapped his pipe stem on his teeth and raised a questioning eyebrow. "Well?" he inquired at last.

Marc smiled briefly. "Do I have a choice, Colonel?"

Sebastien grinned. "No. But I knew you'd see it the right way in the end, or should I say, the Surete's way?"

Great-Uncle Claude wasn't the only bulldog in the family, Marc thought and smiled as he placed Calanthe's letter to Valli inside his jacket with resignation. They turned and walked in the wind back toward the barracks. The issue was settled. Marc was on his way to Paris.

Marc left Sebastien and was walking back toward the gate where Jacquette was waiting to drive him to the depot. The sand, the trees, the barracks, all were colorless in the milky light of the late-setting moon. Black velvet shade softly lurked near the fort walls. Marc's footsteps were inaudible in the barracks yard. His white trousers and the cloth on the back of his hat matched the moonlight, while his dark jacket faded into the shadows.

Jacquette started the engine and drove slowly toward him. As they met, Jacquette reached over and flung open the passenger door. Marc hopped in, tossing his bag behind his seat.

"Well, mon Captaine, how did it go, good, oui?" His dark eyes flashed and he tossed the lock of black hair from his tanned forehead.

"Depends on how you see a trip to Paris."

Jacquette laid a brown hand across his heart. "To see the ballet with the lovely mademoiselle?"

Marc did not return the smile. "You would never appreciate such refined culture, Jacquette. So I'll attend the ballet at the Paris Opera Ballet Theater, and you'll be watching the German agent Dietrich Gestler."

Jacquette grimaced. "The killer of the Englishman?"

Marc drummed his fingers on the side of the car. "Very likely."

Jacquette's eyes hardened. "And what is the Gestapo doing in Paris?"

"That's exactly what we want to discover."

"Ah, but the ballet..." he sighed. "The demoiselle is not a woman I can easily forget."

"You'd better learn, Romeo."

Jacquette's eyes danced as he looked at him. "You know my heart when it comes to the security of a desperate young thing."

"This 'desperate young thing,' as you call her, is going to befriend Gestler, with the blessing of the Surete."

Jacquette groaned and shook his head in disbelief. "One wonders if the monsieurs at Surete should not resign and let us two take over."

Marc smiled, and Jacquette drove toward the gate.

Marc looked at his watch. "We'll need to hurry to catch the boat at Oran." They would travel until late in the night. "Did you remember to fill the thermos?"

Jacquette reached behind the seat, pulling out a bag. "Voila. Would I forget?" He produced a beat-up thermos of hot coffee and some sandwiches.

Marc relaxed. "Ah, I haven't eaten since lunch, mon ami." As they neared the gate Marc gestured for the guard to let them pass. The legionnaire recognized Marc, saluted, then gave a signal to open the gate.

Minutes later he and Jacquette were traveling the narrow, sandy road toward the sea, with Marc balancing his tin of coffee and eating a sandwich. The wind felt good on his face and in his hair. The velvet domed sky was alive with stars raining down their glittering light. Even the difficulties ahead receded into the deep silence of the vast Sahara. For a time he thought of nothing, then it all rushed back like the desert winds. He would be spending days, perhaps weeks, watching Valli while Gestler pursued her. They would be facing some unknown dangers. He had better be prepared to look into those velvet-brown eyes again...and stay detached.

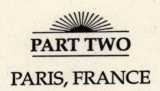

# PART TWO

## PARIS, FRANCE

# 7

It was dawn when Marc and Jacquette arrived at the garrison in Oran, where they left the truck with French soldiers. They were by the Mediterranean coast, two hundred miles east of Gibraltar, where much of France's sea power was anchored at Mers-el-Kebir. Marc felt a sense of pride and security as he viewed the great French warships—perhaps a false sense of security. Without incident they boarded *le Valient*, and by 10:00 A.M. they were crossing the Mediterranean for the coast of Marseille, France.

That foggy night, the hour late, Marc was standing at the rail looking out into the misty swirls, the ship making slow headway. The captain had taken relief from the steerage on deck. He saw Marc, and recognizing him, joined him at the rail.

"The weather is a concern, Monsieur Durell. The longer we run at reduced speed, the more danger of Nazi U-boats. They are thick in this area and think nothing of sinking civilian vessels."

"Ever suspect them of prowling near Oran?"

The captain guessed his mind and drew on his cigarette, the smoke mingling with the gray wispy tendrils. "Like sharks smelling blood, monsieur. If they smell French weakness they won't hesitate to attack."

Surely the French military was prepared for such attacks and would be alert, Marc thought, but he frowned into the eerie fog when he envisioned the warships sitting comfortably in the warm-water Mediterranean seaport like ducks for a shoot.

"I am not a navy man," he told the captain. "But if I have noticed our precarious situation, surely Paris will be on the alert."

The sage captain nodded thoughtfully, but did not look convinced. His anxious eyes scanned the dark, rolling ocean. "Let us hope so, monsieur. Let us hope so. But with so many doves in Reynaud's government, who knows? My definite opinion, monsieur, is that we need to have de Gaulle in command of our fighting force."

Days later, when *le Valient* docked at Marseille, Marc and Jacquette parted company according to plan. As soon as the Surete contacted Marc, letting him know that Dietrich had arrived, he would set his young friend on the Nazi's trail. Jacquette had a friend in Paris, an old mercenary soldier who once served in the legion during the Great War. Now retired and playing an accordion on the streets of Paris for a living, Jacquette would make quiet arrangements to stay with him out of sight until needed. "I play an excellent harmonica," he said. He whipped one from his bag and began a French rendition of an American popular tune: "You made me love you, I didn't want do it, I didn't want do it!"

At Marseille, Marc boarded the train at an hour that would bring him into the Paris station at dark. When he arrived, it was 7:43 P.M. and he used a public telephone to call his "cousin Aubert," thereby letting the Surete know he had arrived and was checking in at the Marquis Hotel. From the train station he caught a taxi downtown and signed in at the front desk.

Plagued by questions that kept barging into his mind, he entered his suite and was removing his jacket and loosening his tie when the door buzzer rang persistently. He hesitated. The Surete, so soon? Must be someone from the hotel.

Cautious, Marc replaced his jacket to cover his shoulder holster, his foot ready to slam the door shut if needed. He partially opened it.

"'Mon Cousin Marc, but how joyous to see you are here in Paris!" Giselle Chattaine Ransier smiled sweetly.

Marc sighed. This was the last thing he needed. "You shouldn't have troubled yourself to come to welcome me, Madame Ransier."

"How blasé! You always were so charming. Le heartbreaker," she sighed. "May I come in?"

When he hesitated, she lifted a carefully plucked brow.

Marc sighed to himself and opened the door.

"Merci," and she swept past, leaving a whiff of French perfume in her wake, her brown hair loose to her bare shoulders, her blue-gray eyes teasing. She dropped her handbag and fur stole on a chair and turned to him, pulling off her gloves. She persistently wore full-skirted dresses cinched at the waist and precariously high heels—even back in scorpion-infested Bel-Abbes, where feet could sink into hot sand ankle deep. Her fashion spoke of what kind of woman she was. Even in Tangier she had told him that her dresses were all shipped from Paris—as though it mattered to him—and made of silky looking cloth, almost always pink or white, always off the shoulder.

Marc felt a predictable rise of irritation. After a long day of travel and the concerns of his mission he was in no mood for Giselle.

She looked about. "What a charming suite. A perfect place for a cozy supper." She turned, still smiling, but had changed perceptibly and now showed tension, even fear?

Marc closed the door and leaned there, watching her curiously.

"Lock it, please," she whispered.

He did so, still watching her, wondering.

With relief she glanced about the room again, then apparently satisfied, faced him. "I've got to talk to you, Marc."

"About what?"

"Don't be so cavalier."

His eyes narrowed. "What's wrong?"

"Wrong?" she shrugged expressively. "So many, many things. And now, it's Monsieur Claude. Your great-uncle grows weaker and wishes to see you. Sebastien would have told you. You'd best come to the estate in the morning."

This was Friday and he had intended to drive out on Sunday. He wanted to talk to Valli first. "Sebastien sent you?"

"No, no, I came on my own."

"How did you know I was here?"

"Sebastien wired me your train schedule from Marseille," she explained, but the gaiety in her voice now sounded forced. Her eyes too, he noticed, looked worried.

She was lying. Sebastien didn't know his schedule, nor the name of the hotel. Exact schedules were dangerous when arranged too far in advance. Marc was doing most everything by the hour.

"Sebastien didn't know," he said.

She glanced at him. "All right, I've been watching the station all evening and I followed you here."

And he had thought he was being careful! "Why lie about it?"

She shrugged. "I thought you wouldn't like it if you knew I had followed you. As I said, dearest, Monsieur Claude is ill and wishes to see you as soon as possible."

"Don't call me 'dearest.'" He was almost sure that she hadn't driven out from the Ransier estate tonight to tell him about Claude. Whatever was on her mind, she didn't care to explain immediately.

His impatience was compounded when she said with stiff gaiety: "Oh, I just could not *think* of permitting my husband's cousin to spend his first evening in Paris all by his lonesome. We must have supper together. I want to know all about when I can expect Sebastien to arrive."

He remembered Sebastien's letter in his luggage, but he didn't care to provide the shoulder she would lament on after learning the Paris post had been exchanged for Tangier. He would give her the envelope after she got in the taxi. If there were any tantrums, he didn't want them in his hotel room. "Oh, the food here is par excellence," she continued. "Afterward, there's a divine little orchestra playing American music in the ballroom. It will help you unwind." She almost always included the word "Oh" somewhere in her speech pattern, and she had a habit of intertwining her fingers with painted red nails into a clasp at her heart when she spoke, as though the information she shared was so wonderful that it would simply break one's heart.

His wry silence at long last caught her attention, and she turned to look at him inquiringly. Both brows lifted this time.

"Oh my goodness," she breathed in false surprise, "why, I do believe you're still upset with me over that little incident in Tangier when last we met. Oh Marc! I'm so sorry about that."

"Forget it," he said laconically. He looked at his watch. "Look, Giselle, it's good to see you again, but it's late, and I had supper on the way. Why don't I call you tomorrow instead?"

She looked at him with exasperation. "Oh you. So maddeningly handsome, and gallant. I love you for it, I really do." She dug into her handbag for her gold cigarette case, found it along with her monogrammed lighter, and walked toward him, where he leaned against the door. "So, I can trust you, can't I?"

"You ought to know." He flipped the lighter and held the flame. She bent toward it, blowing smoke nervously. She glanced toward the window, walked there briskly, and looked out. "Raining," she stated. She turned energetically. "Oh Marc, at least send down for a little wine. I've got to talk to you."

He folded his arms. "About what? Misleading me about knowing the train schedule?"

"Oh dear, I see I've offended you." She drew back as if he were a cobra, fingers at her throat.

*Cute*, he thought dourly. *I'm supposed to assure her otherwise.*

"I keep forgetting...Captain Marc Louis Durell does not approve of bold women who know what they want."

"I wouldn't say that at all. What I disapprove of is married women with amnesia." He walked over to where she stood by the lamp.

"Amnesia?"

He smiled. Lifting her hand, he turned it over in the lamplight until the diamonds on the wedding ring sparkled.

"Nice ring," he commented. "So full of promise and commitment. I was at the church in Tangier when Sebastien placed it there with God's blessing."

Her mouth hardened and she pulled her hand away. "Stinker." She walked away, drawing nervously on her cigarette. "I've been perfectly good since I married, and you know it." She glanced at him quickly, caught his expression, and hastened: "Except for that one time before you left for Bel-Abbes. That was careless of me, wasn't it?"

"Rather," he said dryly.

"But you were a perfect gentlemen the way you covered for me when Sebastien caught us in the garden."

"He didn't 'catch' us in the garden. He came out looking for you."

"And found us together."

"My mistake," he said crisply.

"You were so gallant to shield my terrible behavior—"

He walked toward the door. "Look, Giselle, I've had a long, hot, tiring day. I'll call you a taxi, and out of respect for Sebastien, see you safely home. I might as well bring my bags and spend the night at the estate. I can drive into Paris tomorrow morning to see your sister." He went to the telephone.

"No, Marc, wait, please."

He paused, scrutinizing her. Was she ready to say what was on her mind?

But Giselle dropped into a chair, holding tightly to her handbag. She sighed, rubbing a hand across her forehead. "Marc, do me a favor. Just call down for me for a small drink?"

"No, that won't help you. I saw my father waste many nights, not on classy French wine, but with a cheap drug called *majoun*. It led him downhill to ruin."

She groaned, shaking her head. "Oh, I didn't know... "

"Until I met Davide I grew up in Bel-Abbes on my own, running around with Jacquette. I've seen it all. Before I came to Christ, Jacquette showed me the worst of it: kif, hashish, booze. Now, things have changed for me, and I'm trying to teach him where that bleak path finally leads."

"Oh, I didn't know," she repeated.

"Why? I told you in the garden."

She stopped and looked at him as though trying to understand him. "Oh yes, you told me." She shook her long hair away from her shoulders and checked her face in a gold colored compact mirror that glittered like a hunk of the real stuff, evidently satisfied her pink lipstick was in place.

That did it. Marc walked up to her. "Get up, you're going home. Sebastien ought to wring your pretty neck."

"Marc! What have I done? Oh, I know what you're thinking—but it isn't so. I'm sorry about what happened that last night you were in Tangier. I didn't mean—"

"If Sebastien hadn't trusted both of us he could have had me court-martialed. I try to respect you because you're his wife, but your behavior is making it difficult."

She jumped to her feet. "Marc, *please*. I'm sorry. I'd sipped too much wine that night in Tangier. I knew you were leaving for that forsaken place, Sidi-bel-Abbes."

"You shouldn't have come here tonight."

"What was worse, I'd just found out from Sebastien you had asked for the transfer, and that made it unbearable. I felt so guilty, I was afraid I was to blame, as though I had chased you away—"

"Forget all that. It was my decision. And now, you're leaving."

"But all I want to do is talk." She was unexpectedly subdued, and Marc waited, watching her thoughtfully. How could she be so different than Valli and Davide? Davide was like a source of light. He knew why: because Davide had a desire to please Christ. As Marc thought of Valli, he hoped that she was walking toward the light, rather than with Dietrich.

Marc thought back to his past with his father, Louis Durell, remembering the Saturday nights when Marc had to go looking for him in Bel-Abbes, hauling him out of the kif joints, messed up on drugs. His own wayward feet might also have led him to the very edge of a slippery cliff. He began to feel sympathetic toward Giselle; perhaps he needed to be more patient with her weakness.

He didn't realize he was looking at her with kindness until she actually blushed. He had never seen her embarrassed before. Her boldness usually embarrassed others.

"You have Davide's expression," she said. "I'd have given so much for a man to look at me like that when I was eighteen, in Paris."

"You have Sebastien," he reminded her gently. "He looks at you with love enough to break any woman's heart. Don't throw it away, Giselle. It doesn't come that often. If you're lucky enough to have it, protect it, cherish it. You may never see it again. You'll see lust, but not love and respect. He thinks you're wonderful. He's proud of you. Can you throw all that away?"

Unexpectedly her eyes moistened. "I don't want to throw it away. And I won't. Oh Marc, you may not believe this about me, but I do love Sebastien and I want our marriage to work. I came here because—because I *knew* I could trust you." She got up from the chair and walked away, head in hands. "I know, I behaved as if I didn't. Sometimes I just can't help myself." She turned and looked at him. "Whether you believe me or not, I want to preserve my marriage with Sebastien. He's been good to me, better than I deserve, but I'm afraid something—" she stopped.

Marc was watching her curiously. "Afraid something or *someone* could ruin it?"

She swallowed. "Yes, that's it."

"Who, Giselle? Who would want to ruin it?"

She shook her head and walked back to the chair, running her hand through the mink stole thoughtfully, but her mind seemed far away. "I don't know..."

"Don't know?" he looked at her dubiously.

"I've done nothing wrong in Paris. Nothing," she repeated, looking at him desperately.

"All right," he said kindly. "I believe you."

Her eyes searched his. "Do you, Marc?"

"Yes." He smiled. "Just keep it that way. Anything else will ruin you and Sebastien."

"Yes, I know..."

"Cultivate your marriage like a precious garden. It's worth protecting and saving. You'll never find a man who'll love you as Sebastien does. He may not be young and handsome, but he's all honor and fidelity."

She smiled wanly. "Coming from you, that means a lot. If it weren't so, I'm sure you would know."

She claimed she loved Sebastien, and Marc was hoping she meant it. But if she didn't wake up soon, she would lose him along with everything else she seemed willing to gamble away. Sebastien had not asked his opinion of Giselle before suddenly marrying her, and since then Marc had been shielding him from hurt, but he couldn't remain his armor bearer for very long.

"Sometimes I wish I were more like Valli," she said, but then she appeared to remember something. She looked at him soberly. "But she didn't extend much grace to you years ago at that picnic in Tangier, did she? I suppose none of us are perfect. How old were you?"

"Eighteen." He would just as soon have forgotten the picnic. He remembered it only too well.

Her voice lowered. "After it was over I realized it wasn't very fair of me. I wanted to get even with Valli about something, but now I can't even recall what it was, probably something petty."

Marc was remembering back to that day of the picnic. Davide had brought him home for the first time that weekend to Great-Aunt Calanthe's by Tangier Bay. He'd been lounging on the front lawn talking with Davide and waiting for Valli and Giselle to come out to the barbecue that Giselle was giving. Davide had left for some reason, and as Marc was looking up at the blue sky with his arms behind his head, Giselle had crept up, knelt down beside him, and wrapped her arms around him, giving him a kiss. Taken by surprise, he had responded by taking hold of her shoulders and looking into her face. Giselle seemed to have timed the "embrace" to coincide with Valli's appearance from the house. Although he hadn't known Valli well at the time, he had honorable intentions toward her that he thought might develop with Davide's help. Needless to say, he had not made a good impression.

Marc wondered why Cousin Sebastien, who was so serious and sane, would fall in love with Giselle, a woman so different than himself. But then she didn't seem to behave frivolously when she was around him, and when she wanted to, she could rival Marc's most serious acquaintances. It was remarkable, sometimes she reminded him of a chameleon that changed colors to match the background. Sebastien had once told him: "You underestimate Giselle. She is a vivacious and intelligent woman. It's too easy to

mistake her affection for people and her good cheer as recklessness, though admittedly some of her youthful expectations seem to have gone awry."

Sebastien's defense of Giselle showed their marriage
was holding together. He defended her like a warrior.

All frivolity now had left her face. "Marc, believe it or
not, I am sorry about being so mean when the three of us
were younger. I could tell you liked Valli, and I was jealous,
so I did the only thing I knew to ruin it."

"You were indeed a brat," he said with a faint smile,
"and I was caught completely off guard, but there was no
relationship to ruin. Valli wanted a ballet career more than
she wanted anything else. By the time I saw her again here
in Paris, she was already serious about Kraig. I next saw her
only a month ago when she visited Davide."

She smiled sadly. "Yes, you're so much like Davide.
Whatever woman captures your heart should thank God
every day."

He arched a brow. Giselle could overflow with too much
sentiment.

She looked bewildered. "I don't know why I brought all
this up. I didn't come here for all that. I'm terrible, aren't I?
Sometimes I don't even understand or like myself."

Marc backed off. Playing a counselor could easily
become a trap in which she might begin appealing to his so-
called "masculine wisdom." "Oh poor me, I just need your
help so badly, Marc. What do you think I should do?" He
smiled in spite of himself. In many ways she was still a little
girl. He found himself easily frustrated and even angry with
her, but it was difficult not to like her. She was both clever
and dumb. She had even given a large sum of money to
Davide to help support some of the women and children at

the mission station, as well as the construction of an orphanage near Casablanca.

"Cheer up. Sebastien thinks you're wonderful."

She brightened. "Yes, he does, doesn't he? And I'm going to make things up to him. I'm going to make him proud of me once he takes his position in the Reynaud government. No more partying for me." She looked at him, her eyes sober. "I'm glad you're here, Marc. We need you. We both do."

He looked at her oddly. Both? Meaning Sebastien or Valli?

"And since we're being so honest with each other tonight, I didn't intend to start out my life like this. I guess none of us do. When I was younger I was jealous of Valli because she had the ability to stick things out to the very end—and I didn't. Great-Aunt Calanthe was always praising her. Valli deserved it, I guess. She did go on to master the ballet, something I thought I wanted to do but didn't have the discipline to stay with. I quit in my second year. I was always quitting. Anytime anything was hard or unpleasant I dropped it and went in another direction. Anyway, I worked here in Paris for a year at the theater, helping the ballet director."

"Kraig?" he asked quietly.

She walked over to the window but didn't open the curtain. "Yes," she said quietly. "Kraig."

Marc tried to imagine what the inevitable triangle must have been like.

"Valli was in love with him, and I—well, it was one of the first times in my life that I could take something away from her that she wanted. Yes, I know...it was dreadfully wrong and selfish. But I did it."

Marc said nothing. It was best to let Giselle confess.

"But Valli? She just struggled on through her disappointments, full of grace—she even forgave me—" her voice cracked. "I didn't deserve it, but she forgave me anyway."

The silence seemed to enclose them, then after a moment passed, Giselle continued: "Valli went on to become the prima donna of the Paris Opera Ballet Theater. Whereas I—" she shrugged.

"Whereas you found grace, as well, in a second chance with Sebastien."

She turned and her cheeks were damp. She smiled and nodded. "That's just what I was going to say. I married a sane, dedicated, wonderful man who puts up with all my nonsense and tries to strengthen me. It's time I settled down, isn't it?"

Marc looked at her. "What do you think?"

"Past the time."

As though something unexpectedly disturbed her, she turned away. "Yes,...hopefully, it's not too late. Sebastien's post in Paris will give us a second chance to rebuild relationships." She looked off thoughtfully into space. "As long as the war doesn't destroy everything—"

Marc thought of Sebastien's letter again. It was obvious that Giselle didn't have a clue about the unexpected change in her husband's orders. He walked over to his luggage and opened it, removing the envelope and placing it inside his jacket. As he picked up her mink stole, intending to place it around her shoulders and escort her down to the lobby, her bag slipped off the chair and fell to the carpet. Reaching to retrieve it, he saw a small, shiny revolver lying at his feet. He didn't think much of it until Giselle gave a startled cry and dove for it. Marc picked it up first. It was loaded. His gaze came to hers and he saw the sudden fear in her eyes.

"I'll explain everything. I came here because of Dietrich—and Valli."

# 8

Marc held the pistol in his hand and looked gravely at her. "What about Valli?"

Giselle's face was tense. "Dietrich Gestler is in Paris. I saw him a week ago at a party where he asked me about Valli's visit to Algeria. I don't trust him. And tonight, I was followed again."

Marc thought back to the Englishman, Blystone. Maybe Dietrich had noticed the rose on Valli's bag after all.

"Why didn't you tell me at once?" he half-scolded.

She turned away, fingers intertwined. "Because I wasn't sure it was the best thing to do. I came here uncertain about whether I should tell you."

"Why, if there's danger?"

"Because this could be more involved than Dietrich's romantic interest in Valli. I must be careful too."

So, she also thought Gestler was inclined toward her sister. "Is it Gestler who's following you?"

She shook her head. "No, I think he's watching Valli. Someone else is following me—that's the reason for the gun. When I first married Sebastien he taught me to use it."

"Do you have any idea who it is?"

She turned, her face strained. "No, I've never seen him before, but he looks French."

"Then you saw his face?"

"I saw his face, yes. He might pass for a chauffeur type. A man around forty, brown hair, medium height, average build. You wouldn't notice him in a crowd. He's been following me for the last week. At first I thought Sebastien might have someone watching me."

Giselle walked away, obviously upset. Marc began to feel sorry for her. Maybe he'd been a little too rough on her. "Come and sit down," he said. "I'll ring for coffee. You can explain to me what's been going on." He picked up the receiver and called down to the front desk for coffee and sandwiches since she probably hadn't eaten.

Then Dietrich had arrived before him. He must have come as soon as he left the mission station. Why had he even gone there? To see Valli? And if he was asking Giselle about her now, didn't that behavior contradict Marc's first thought that Valli was working with Dietrich? What reason would he need to question Giselle, unless he thought she knew something incriminating or helpful?

When the food arrived, Marc poured two cups of coffee, handing one to Giselle. She drank quickly, taking several pills, but refused the food.

Marc drew up his chair. "All right. From the beginning."

"The beginning? There isn't enough time for that. I'll begin a week ago, the day I first noticed the man. I was backing the car out of the drive at the Ransier estate when I drove out the gate onto the lane. A car emerged from behind some trees and followed me all the way into Paris, keeping a good distance behind."

"Did you notice the make?"

"I'm not good at things like that...all I could tell is that it was a big dark sedan. I'd say American."

"That was the first time you noticed him?"

She looked at him as though alerted. "I hadn't thought of it that way. He may have been following me ever since I arrived from Tangier and I just hadn't noticed."

"The first time you noticed him did you have something special you wanted to do in Paris? Someone to see?"

"I had a luncheon date with Valli."

Marc didn't like the sound of it. "Anything happen when you two were together?"

"No, we just had luncheon at the le Fleur restaurant near the ballet theater. The man didn't come inside, but I noticed him through the window by our table. He hung about the sidewalk, going in and out of shops until we left. Then he followed again."

"Did Valli return with you?"

"No, she walked back to the theater with Rodolphe so they could get some ballet practice in."

"Rodolphe? Her partner?"

"Yes, he's a ballet star. They walked back together."

"Did he have lunch with you?"

"No, he arrived as we were leaving. He was still in his ballet habit."

"Did Valli notice the man following you?"

"No. I didn't mention him. I didn't want to frighten her. She's been so tense recently."

"Has she?" He tried to mask his concern. "Over the ballet?"

"Yes, she's been working late hours and staying over in Paris during the weekends—" she paused and looked up from her cup. "She seems concerned about something else, but she hasn't shared it with me." She turned her hands over, looking at her fingernails for chips in the polish. "We've been getting along together, but our relationship is far from close."

What was Valli concerned about beside the ballet? Marc had put a note in her purse thanking her for the postcards. Thinking back, he was irritated with himself for leaving it. If she was interested in Dietrich...He tapped his chin, thinking. Maybe she was still worried about Blystone...

"I drove home, and the sedan followed me again. It's been that way for a week." She set her cup down. "He may have followed me here tonight."

*Followed her straight to my hotel*, thought Marc. No real danger though, since the Nazis didn't suspect him. He also had a good excuse for being in Paris, and even in meeting Giselle tonight since she had come from his ailing great-uncle. But how had Dietrich gotten into Paris? The Surete could have easily informed the Reynaud government that he was a Gestapo agent out of uniform.

But, there was a slim possibility that the man following her was not an enemy at all, but someone Sebastien had requested to watch his wife because he worried about her safety. Hadn't he said at Bel-Abbes that he was a target?

Even if the man was friendly, Marc couldn't relieve Giselle's fears by telling her without receiving clearance first. It was still reasonably safe to use the phone in his room to ask for permission, since not enough time had elapsed for anyone to tap it. But his orders had been clear: Make contact only if an emergency develops. Someone would contact Marc.

On the other hand, if the man were a Nazi agent, what could he expect to discover by following Giselle? Perhaps nothing. Marc took note of how nervous she was becoming, which raised a different question altogether. "Why would Gestler want to frighten you?"

She looked at him, wide-eyed. "Me? There's no reason at all."

"Think again. Your husband is a colonel in the intelligence division of the French army. You know that is a sensitive position."

Her mouth tightened.

Marc watched her carefully. "French and German troops are fighting in several places in Europe...including Dunkirk and portions of France. North Africa is a powder keg. Neither Reynaud nor de Gaulle have the influence needed to galvanize the pacifists into action; many seem convinced there is no hope of winning. Paris is full of spies, and as you and I fully know, they're not all wearing Nazi uniforms. Maybe someone thinks you know something."

She turned a sickly pallor and stared at him. "That's crazy! I don't know a thing that could benefit the Nazis."

He watched her hands as they nervously plucked at her handkerchief.

"Sebastien was offered a position in the Reynaud government."

She jumped to her feet. "Just because I'm his wife doesn't mean that I know anything, not a thing, understand? If the Nazis think they can get information from *me* about Sebastien, or North Africa, they're wrong. I'd never tell them, even if I knew something, which I don't." Her face flushed. "They'll need to kill me first."

Marc stood and moved to calm her, watching her thoughtfully. He was rather surprised to see her patriotism come bounding to the forefront. It was the first time he noticed a similarity between Giselle and Valli. It was about the only thing they did seem to share. Now, a new worry sprouted in his mind. He thought about Sebastien's new position in Tangier, about Giselle being at his side. Giselle, whose shady past made her a perfect target for blackmail.

"Here," he said, refilling her cup. "Calm down, dear, it's all right. You'll soon be with Sebastien."

"He's coming soon?" she asked hopefully.

Marc frowned. He reached inside his jacket and touched the envelope. Her eyes searched his. "You'll soon be with him," he repeated. Marc walked over to the window and looked out at the drizzling rain, thinking.

He hadn't realized how long he had paused until Giselle became impatient. "What is it, Marc? What's bothering you? Is Sebastien in trouble? Is that it?"

He looked at her. "No, Sebastien was fine when I left him in Bel-Abbes." He looked at his watch. "I'd better get you back to the estate."

"Come with me, Marc. Let's go pick up Valli at her flat and bring her with us. We can all be together at Claude's. I'd feel better that way."

"She has the ballet performance soon, doesn't she? She'll not leave Paris yet is my guess."

"Oh no," she turned from him, hand at forehead. "I forgot. You're right. Then we'll go together. Claude wants to see you. He wants you to stay at the house while you're here. You are going to, aren't you?" she asked when he made no answer.

He had come for the purpose of seeing his mother's uncle, but he didn't know if Sebastien had clued her in about the Ransier family's dissensions. She had mentioned building bridges and reconnecting family relationships, but she'd been speaking of Valli. Marc also found himself wondering if Giselle intended to mend the misunderstanding she had caused between Madame Calanthe Malaret in Tangier and Valli. He had heard that Giselle was mostly to blame for that unhappy disunion.

"I'm aware of the distance between you and Monsieur Claude," she said sadly. "Do you think he's out to mend fences, too? Leave you as his heir?"

"Claude won't disinherit Sebastien or Aubert in favor of me, if that worries you. When his mind is made up, he doesn't crack easily."

"Oh I didn't mean to sound—" she stopped. "I only was curious about what he wanted."

"I'm here, as Claude requested," was all he admitted.

"You don't know what he wants?"

Even if he did, he wouldn't tell her, not with that too curious gleam in her eyes. He began to wonder again if she had told him everything she knew about Dietrich and about the man following her in the sedan. There remained so much about Giselle that lingered in the shadows.

"You do know, don't you, that Valli is rooming with us, especially during weekends?"

Marc was composed. "Yes. Who arranged it with Claude?"

"Monsieur Claude's son, Aubert—or was it his wife? I don't recall exactly."

"Inga?" The news took him by mild surprise. Inga had married Claude's son when he studied music in Berlin. Marc had been a boy then, living with his mother at the estate. He remembered that Aubert played the violin beautifully.

"I think Valli met Inga in Berlin a year or so ago, when traveling with the ballet company. Inga's always loved ballet. So their friendship naturally blossomed. When Valli mentioned the difficulty of living in Paris, Inga arranged things with her father-in-law, Claude."

Valli had gone to Berlin. She could have met Dietrich there. Perhaps that had motivated him to come to Paris.

"You know, don't you, that Valli and I are distantly related to Claude through Great-Aunt Calanthe?" Giselle said. "Calanthe's line crosses Claude's somewhere along the rambling family tree."

Marc's thoughts wandered again to Valli Chattaine. The sooner he talked with her, the better.

"When is she starring in the new ballet?"

"You're just in time. Saturday night."

That was tomorrow. "I want to speak with her about Gestler before we meet at the estate. Tell me, Giselle, do you think Valli holds mutual interest in Dietrich?"

She looked stricken. "Dietrich? Absolutely not."

He found her response curious. "But when it comes to a woman's heart—who can fully say?"

"I wouldn't think it's possible, I thought it was all one-sided." The idea appeared to agitate her. "She did see him in Berlin after Kraig." She frowned thoughtfully, then sighed. "But I just don't know."

That was the problem. Marc didn't know either, and until he did, he would remain cautious.

"Can you arrange a meeting backstage after the performance?"

"I suppose it's possible, but what if Dietrich shows on opening night as well? If he is romantically interested in her—"

"Did he tell you he was when you bumped into him at that party you mentioned?"

"No, he asked about the ballet."

"And about her return from Davide's place?"

Again, the mention of the mission station seemed to upset Giselle, and she changed the subject. "There's a few elite ballet enthusiasts who are permitted backstage after a performance. I can try to smuggle you in, but there's no guarantee I can do it. If I notify Valli, she may arrange it herself."

"I'd rather you said nothing to her yet. Our brief meeting near Bel-Abbes was not exactly what you'd call on warm and friendly terms." Davide had also arranged a dinner that Marc had been unable to attend.

"There's also a reception for the ballet company tomorrow night after the performance," she said. "British ambassador Hartley is hosting it. You could see her there if you care to wait."

"I'll try both," he said easily.

She retrieved her mink stole and handbag from the table, apparently willing to leave at last.

"Valli must have everything she wants here in Paris," he said. "Now that she landed the starring role in the ballet."

"Yes. If she's successful Saturday night, the theater critics will be falling all over themselves to write up the best reviews. I've watched her perform, I know what she can do. She's no ordinary ballerina. She dances with heart and soul. There is a special grace that she seems to have been born with, that if developed, will bring her to the very top." She sighed regretfully. "If only I had stayed and fought on. Ballet is her life now, not Kraig, nor anyone else for that matter."

"Meaning that no one is likely to break through her armor, is that it?" he smiled faintly. Even Dietrich?

"That, dear cousin, is about the sum of it. So if you have any plans, they'd better be good ones."

He tilted his head thoughtfully. He didn't doubt Valli's will to resist. Anyone who could go through what she did and come out dancing was a demoiselle to be reckoned with. No wonder she had rallied to Blystone, and stood up to his own questioning as well, not to mention Dietrich's at the mission station—if that discussion had been genuine. Determination ran in her blood. Well, he was determined to demolish Kraig from her memory. As for Dietrich, he intended to stop him as well—if he could.

He must make up his mind quickly as to whether he could trust Valli. Not until he did could the Surete use her to learn why Dietrich was here.

Marc was unsmiling. "The ballet Saturday night, what time does it start?"

"It begins at eight. It's a black tie affair with the reception following. Oh, I almost forgot..." She stood, walked to where she had left a small brown paper bag, and pulled out a book. "Another reason why I came by. Better read this."

He turned it over in his hand, looking at the title. "Ballet?"

"You ought to know something about the movements before you meet her, don't you think?"

He could see himself staying up late. Anything to please the Surete...and the ballerina with the blue-black hair.

He walked Giselle to the elevator and they went down to the lobby. He had called for a taxi and a few minutes later he led her out onto the wet street where the rain was falling in great drops. He noticed she glanced about uneasily. The taxi pulled up alongside the curb, the windshield wipers going steadily. Marc checked the driver's papers, who looked at him as if he thought him a wise guy. Satisfied, Marc passed him a French note, and the driver grinned, mollified.

"Take good care of her."

"Oui, monsieur!"

"Good night, Marc," she called, rushing to get inside from the rain. "I'll come by for you tomorrow night at six."

Marc almost shut the door but left it open a crack. He reached inside his jacket for Sebastien's letter.

"You're getting drenched," she said, laughing.

"After Sidi-bel-Abbes? I'm loving every moment!"

"Then I'll see you tomorrow night."

"Here. From Sebastien. Don't read it until you're safe in your bedroom. Good night." He closed the door and stepped back to the sidewalk.

As the taxi was pulling away from the curb he could see her looking at the envelope. He watched until the red taillights faded.

Giselle was right about some things. One was the ballet. He would need to spend the evening studying the book she had brought him. It would not do to meet prima donna Valli Chattaine again and not at least have some knowledge of the dance she had given her heart to master.

As the chilling Paris rain fell on him, his mind returned to Dietrich Gestler. Giselle had been adamantly upset over the possibility of Valli's interest in the handsome, ruthless German. Why?

# 9

Marc, dressed in black evening attire, paid the taxi man and turned to Giselle, who stood beside him elegantly dressed in white satin.

"Everything's been arranged," Giselle had told him on the way. "I've spoken to the director, Maurice Pierre. He assures me we can slip backstage after the performance."

Giselle also bemoaned the letter from Sebastien telling her of the Tangier appointment. "But at least Sebastien is an ambassador," she said proudly.

They left the busy street and came toward the theater, which was an old ornate building glittering with chandelier light. They ascended the wide steps to the double doors that stood open. A doorman in professional black attire murmured his greeting and offered his classic French bow. Marc returned the typical response and passed through with the stately Giselle on his arm.

At once she began the introductions. This was Captaine Marc Louis Durell of the Sidi-bel-Abbes 1st Regiment Etranger in Algeria. He was in Paris for a short time to visit his ailing great-uncle, Monsieur Claude Ransier. The name Ransier was well approved of in France, and smiles greeted him, even if the curious once-overs later wondered why Monsieur Ransier's handsome great-nephew was in the notorious French Foreign Legion. "He's ailing, they say. Has the rich old widower changed his will to benefit the deceased Madame Josephine's only son? Ah, but he would not do that! What of his own son, Aubert?" But naturally Captaine Durell would come to the ballet tonight, they reasoned. The Chattaine prima donna must be a great-great "something-or-other" to Claude through Calanthe Malaret in Tangier.

There were polite smiles all around, the expected friendliness, the raised eyebrows behind his back— "Legionnaire! Rogue, to be sure!" Then Giselle was maneuvering them toward the theater entrance.

Inside the large salon came the sparkle and twinkle of still more crystal chandeliers. Marc felt the soft thickness of scarlet carpet beneath his feet. He was inundated with the glamour of ballet paintings on the cream walls framed in heavy, dark wood and dusted with gold. Carved marble vases were arranged along the walkway into the theater proper, displaying a bounty of spring roses the color of mauve.

Parisians in black evening dress and gowns that shimmered were clustered together like French wine grapes into elite little groups, talking in hushed tones as if they loitered in some sanctified cathedral. Marc ignored the masculine glances sent Giselle's way, just as he pretended to not notice the subtle glances women draped upon him. He paused in order to read the white and gold board with its theater announcement:

*Paris Opera Ballet Theater Presents:*

**GISELLE**

Cast of Characters:
Mlle. Valli Chattaine (Giselle)
M. Rodolphe Gaillard (Albrecht)
M. Maurice Renault (Hilarion)
Mlle. Joyeuse Marquet (Myrtha)

Choreography:
M. Charles Chardin and Mme. Ivonne Giles
Stages by M. Fabien

Music:
M. Raoul Montieth

The title of the ballet, *Giselle*, Marc found ironic. What did Valli think of her first starring performance bearing the name of her sister? Did women ever forget a betrayal? The pain must have been unbearable when she discovered the "other woman" was her dear, dear sister. He glanced at Giselle, but her white face was a theater mask all its own.

Marc had prepped himself last night and this afternoon in an attempt to become acquainted with the authentic dance terms for what his layman mind normally described as "whirls, jumps, and graceful landings on tiptoes." He still felt inadequate, but he understood enough to appreciate the difficulty of the moves that Valli must perform tonight if she were to be considered successful by the sophisticated dance critics of Paris. He was still holding the book Giselle had given him, and she would be at his side to fill him in as well.

They walked through the doors into the theater proper that smelled of rich, dusty brocade, leather, and antique carpet. He followed her up a narrow flight of carpeted steps to one of perhaps a dozen viewing boxes on the left-hand side of the room. Across the theater were a dozen more boxes that were beginning to fill with enthusiasts. A few heads were turning in their direction. Giselle pushed the curtain aside and stepped in, taking her seat and handing him a small pair of binoculars and the ballet program. Marc settled back in the plush velvet seat, looking down on the large stage with its dark curtain moving gently. He was interested in this display only because of one ballerina he had heard so much about from others. Although he had met her in the hot blowing sands of the Sahara, she remained a tantalizing mystery. It would surely help to see her in the environment that was her pride and joy.

Giselle was scanning the other boxes with her binoculars to see who was there.

"Aren't you ashamed of yourself?" he goaded lightly.

"On the contrary, I'm delighted. So! Madame Antoinette is in the company of Monsieur Vissard. While salient Lieutenant Leon is off fighting the Nazis." She swept the binoculars about.

"What if she turns her binoculars on you? *Who* is that scoundrel legionnaire sitting alone with Madame Ransier?"

"Word will get around anyway—" Her voice broke off.

"See anything interesting?" came his low question as he deliberately turned his glasses away from the direction she'd been looking.

"He's here," she said, her lips barely moving.

Marc managed a smile as though they were continuing their conversation. "Who is?"

"Dietrich."

"Certain?"

"I'd know him anywhere, even without his uniform."

"He's been promoted to the SS," Marc said. *No wonder he didn't have his uniform on,* he thought angrily. *There might be at least a few red-blooded Parisians who would go home and return with their weapons.*

"Behaves as if he's at home," she said.

"Why shouldn't he?" he said acidly. "Many in the government have made the Nazis feel comfortable here. He must think France will soon be under German occupation."

She tensed beside him. "He has seen us together now. He will never forget your face even if you left Paris for Tangier tonight."

Why should it matter that he was seen with Giselle? Marc had no intention of leaving without getting his job done. "Let him wonder about me. It may draw him out. Nothing like baiting a hungry wolf."

Marc's casual sweep of the boxes had made its full circuit and reached the box where Gestapo agent Dietrich Gestler sat. Marc was more curious about whose box he sat in and whose company befriended him.

"Who rents that box?" he asked.

"I don't know. I can find out tomorrow."

"Recognize anyone with him?"

"I was trying to. I've only been in Paris for a month. They're all strangers. British ambassador Hartley should be able to tell you. He is hosting the reception later. He's seated across from us in that other viewing stand to your left. I'm sure he's aware of everyone here tonight."

The lights were dimming. Marc had just enough time to locate Dietrich in his binoculars. As he adjusted the glass the handsome face of the German officer focused into view. Marc too would recognize his quarry anywhere. Dietrich Gestler: age thirty-seven, single, five feet ten inches tall, one hundred and seventy pounds. Light blond hair, gray eyes, a stubborn jawline. In his youth, in contrast to his ballet brother Kraig, he had been a boxer until banned from the ring in Frankfurt for continuing a fight with a visiting Norwegian after the referee had called a stop.

And yet, Marc thought, Gestler fell prey to the weaknesses of most other men. He was here because of a woman. But which woman? Valli? Giselle?

*He's seen us as well*, Marc thought. *He probably watched us come in together. Right now his calculating mind must be weighing the risks of involving himself with two rivaling sisters who had both been in love with his younger brother, Kraig, while at the same time wondering who the stranger is so cozily seated beside Giselle.*

Marc believed Dietrich must know of Giselle's marriage three years ago to Colonel Sebastien Ransier. He was certain Dietrich would be more determined now to learn what was happening with Valli and Giselle, as well as to find out everything he could on legionnaire Captain Marc Durell.

*Perfect*, Marc thought, watching him evenly through the binoculars. *That's just what I want you to do, Gestapo agent Gestler.*

"The curtain is going up," Giselle whispered with relief.

All eyes turned toward the brilliantly lighted stage. Darkness blurred the box in which Dietrich sat.

Marc turned his binoculars back to the stage and upon the woman whose loyalty he must determine, and whom the Surete hoped would aid them in discovering what was on Dietrich's mind.

Despite Marc's interest in Valli, he had to force his attention away from Dietrich and onto the performance. He remembered what he had read about the dance, declared to be the epitome of "the Romantic era of ballet," and popular for over one hundred years because of its drama. *Giselle* was called the Shakespearian *Hamlet* since it was one of the few performances where the ballerina with the starring role had to be both dancer and actress. The "Giselle" of the ballet would pass from innocence through madness, and finally, commit suicide—not exactly a pleasant ending, Marc thought.

"Valli has worried about her acting for weeks," Giselle whispered. "Rodolphe worked to make sure the choreography accommodates her character changes. It's difficult to say which most enhances the performance, the ballet steps or the acting. The performance will confirm her either as a prima donna or simply a good ballerina."

Marc rooted for her success but wondered if he would be able to convince her to leave Paris amid cheers and bouquets.

"There—it's beginning," Giselle said.

Valli Chattaine came on stage as "Giselle," dressed in the charming costume of a Rhineland peasant girl in a dirndl dress. He wished he could see Dietrich's face. His expression would reveal much of his true emotions regarding his brother's ex-fiancé.

As for Marc, he wasn't surprised to find Valli looking so beautiful. Even on the West Algerian train, enduring blazing temperatures, she had been memorable. *But, now!* Who could not admire her grace and dignity, the hard work of a charming demoiselle with the delicate movements of a swan? She was far more striking than he had remembered. He felt his heart sink as she moved like an angel without wings through the painted props of a Rhineland village. Her hair, blue-black and shiny, flowed down her back in one long curl. A smile formed at the corner of his mouth. Well, meeting her again would prove interesting.

Her footwork was light and elegant. The pace of the dancing was in half-time to the music, which allowed him, a novice, time to see and appreciate what was happening.

The corner of Giselle's mouth went down and she whispered: "Looks like Dietrich isn't her only admirer."

Marc said nothing and focused his binoculars.

Her simple steps required extreme concentration, and the half-time speed needed control that resulted only from long and disciplined training. Valli performed the classic steps and positions of the body, catching the mood and personality of "Giselle." She was innocent, fragile, and full of joy and satisfaction as Albrecht, a prince who pretended to be a peasant, hid behind some bushes watching her.

"Notice her slow, double *frappes* with *releve*. Very simple," Giselle said, "yet requiring tremendous control and strength at that speed. Next, Albrecht will declare his love."

Valli performed a sprightly dance to show her happiness. He noted that it was repeated throughout the ballet...

"Ah! Did you see? That was what we call a slow *grands jets*—from a standing position without any preparation to give her 'lift'—and she landed firmly in 'attitude,' holding position after the jump! Marvelous. You can be sure the critics noticed that one!"

Marc glanced at Giselle and saw her smiling to herself. *No jealousy there now*, he thought, secretly applauding her maturity.

Marc had only a faint notion of what a *frappe* was, but he certainly enjoyed watching Valli performing them. There were more, and what Giselle whispered excitedly as "big *temps de fleche*." That, Marc did understand. "Now she kicks high and to the front, followed by a bouncy *pas de basque* backward toward the rear of the stage." The lightness of execution was remarkable since it was performed slowly, requiring greater strength than if she was performing them at top speed.

Her dancing, though highly controlled, appeared like carefree skipping around the stage. He knew what looked to be effortlessness had demanded years of torturous practice.

Giselle went on now and then whispering explanations, speaking of the "strong preparation and finish, the holding positions, the introducing pauses, the sustaining movements" that lasted as long as possible.

Then, the Rhineland villagers returned from the fields and the other ballet dancers performed "fluid *developpes a la seconde*"—simultaneously rising up on the *pointe* of toes and slowly revolving into a back "attitude" turn.

Marc watched Albrecht join in, doing multiple *entrechats*, a step requiring great force, and then landing perfectly still in *plie*, without the slightest rebound off the floor, before pushing off again from a dead halt.

Valli ended the dance with perfect *pique* turns toward downstage center, her black hair falling over her shoulder. She finished with a fast triple-spin *pique* turn. Enchanting, Marc thought.

Now came the hunting party where Valli's love was betrayed. Marc noticed that Giselle moved uneasily on the seat.

Ironic, thought Marc. What was Valli thinking as she played the girl with her sister's name? And all the while her sister sat in attendance.

The hunting party arrived on stage. Valli danced "Giselle's" theme song again in a sweet little dance for the character named Bathilde, the beautiful lady of the ballet group. If Marc understood the theme correctly, Bathilde was a princess and the woman that Albrecht was obliged to marry.

The hunting party soon retired to Giselle's cottage to rest, while the village boys and girls leaped and twirled about the stage, eventually calling Valli out of the cottage to join them. Then Albrecht reappeared. He placed a crown of flowers on Valli's head. Again Valli was dancing brilliantly.

Marc lounged comfortably with his binoculars as she hopped across the stage on the tiptoes of her gilded slippers, all the while doing *frappes* with her free leg, then changing the position of the leg, and her body, with each delicate movement.

She doesn't need to worry about her shining hour in the sunlight of fame, he thought. The write-up tomorrow in the theater section of the Paris paper would be applauding the new prima donna Valli Chattaine.

After Valli's exhausting solo, Albrecht joined her again. In turn, they were joined by other ballerinas in an ensemble dance full of high spirit, the arms were wide open, welcoming, peasant-like, with hands on hips.

The happy moments came to an end, however. The jealous gamekeeper named Hilarion hurried off to identify Albrecht as a nobleman. The hunting party emerged from the cottage to bear witness and Valli learned that Albrecht couldn't marry her; he was engaged to Bathilde!

Another gentleman, Marc thought cynically. Kraig should have danced the part of Albrecht. Beside Marc, Giselle sat quietly. Marc watched as Valli performed the "going mad" scene. The music was her familiar haunting theme, except this time she performed with stumbling steps, careening.

Beside him, Giselle reached for a handkerchief.

The dancing was superb.

"It requires technical judgment to stumble through those steps like a dying person," Giselle whispered. "Yet she's maintaining enough of the 'real' for the audience to recognize the same steps she performed so gracefully earlier in the ballet."

Valli dramatized shock, then a heartbroken spirit. Marc wondered if she might not be remembering her own betrayal. She danced her way from anger to recognition that she'd been betrayed. She became sentimental, as if reminiscing about the short-lived love affair, then, mental confusion and fear took over, followed by crazed passion! She whirled her way to a startled Albrecht and grabbed his blade. And for a moment it looked as if she might plunge it into his heart, but then she ran it through her own heart, falling gently, slowly, softly as a petal in the breeze to the floor, while Albrecht stood in agony and regret staring down at her.

The curtain lowered. The applause broke like thunder. Giselle sat, pale, when Marc looked at her. He reached over and patted her hand, then stood with the others, clapping toward the stage.

A minute later Valli came out and bowed, followed by Rodolphe. They turned toward each other and bowed, then left the stage.

Giselle was standing now and laid a hand on his arm, her eyes bright with enthusiasm. "Wasn't she wonderful?"

Marc was thinking: *Yes. Too charming. She'll never give up Paris and this kind of success for the sands of the Sahara...or for a French legionnaire.* But he refused to allow that thought to lodge in his mind for very long.

He glanced toward the box where Dietrich Gestler had sat and saw him standing, his head golden beneath the chandelier light. He applauded energetically, his eyes fixed on the stage. He did not look at Giselle.

*Then the woman on his mind is Valli,* Marc decided with certainty.

Giselle gestured to the box exit. "I'll take you backstage, Marc."

He wondered, *An introduction to end it all? Or is it just the beginning?*

# 10

Valli ran backstage exhilarated and breathless, her ears filled with thunderous applause. In the hall leading to her dressing room she stopped. Laughing, she jumped up and down, exchanging hugs and kisses with the other members of the ballet troupe. "We did it," she cried, "we did it! Listen to the applause!"

Ballet star Rodolphe Gaillard entered the fray, laughing, lifting her in the air, then brushing his lips on one cheek, then the other. "Magnifique, Valli! You could not have done better, ma chere! The reviews in tomorrow's paper, ah, you will be crowned the new star of ballet!"

"You were at your very best, monsieur!" she said with a laugh. "Oh—your lift before my twirl away—and I was so afraid I'd miss it, but I could sense your confidence."

"Ah, practice makes perfect. It is good we spent so many evenings going over it, oui?" He was smiling down at her, his face glistening with sweat, his hair stuck to his forehead.

"Yes, monsieur!" And before the growing gleam of interest in his eyes could sprout to new heights, she turned away to her elderly maid, Mimi, who also waited to celebrate the happy moment. Mimi loitered, all smiles, hands clasped at her bosom.

"Mimi, what do you think?" she cried happily and drew her forward and kissed her wrinkled cheek. "I couldn't have done it without you, either. You and your prayers, Mimi, they have brought me before our heavenly Father's throne so many times."

Mimi beamed. "I watched through the curtain, ma petite, and you danced like an angel." She placed Valli's black cloak snugly around her, making little protective noises about the dangers of the chill draft. "You'll catch cold," she said, as though Valli were a stallion who had just run a race and needed covering. Valli laughed. At the moment everything seemed delightfully amusing, and Paris in the springtime was the most wonderful place in all the world.

*Nothing can ruin my joy right now,* Valli thought. *Even the Nazis could march in, and I'd throw mud in their eye!*

Rodolphe caught her hand and kissed it. "I will see you tonight at the reception, Valli," and he ran lightly down the hall to his cubicle to bathe and change. Before he could enter the door, he was swamped with well-wishers and members of the press.

Valli took advantage of the respite to escape to her own dressing room, which was brightly glowing with mirrored lights and a few comfortable pieces of furniture from her flat. Recently she'd spent so much time practicing that the room had almost become her living quarters.

Mimi closed and locked the door as Valli twirled again, arms hugging herself, eyes closed.

"I have thanked everyone but You, Father. You, who have given me a healthy body to dance, and the opportunity to learn and succeed. Through heartache You brought me into a relationship with Your Son, Jesus. How could I ever be bitter now? You had good plans for me all along. The disappointments of life have become Your appointments to learn and trust."

Mimi too had paused, head bowed, calmly accustomed to Valli's outbursts of conversation with God, which often took place in the most unusual moments, regardless of who might be present.

Her thanksgiving finished, Valli danced on toward her dressing divider. "I can't believe it, Mimi. I didn't make one mistake tonight." She went behind the white-enameled screen embossed with a twirling ballerina in scarlet chiffon. It was the one gift from Kraig that she'd kept after he had run off with Giselle and broken their engagement.

Valli had disposed of the other gifts Kraig had given her through the years they had dated, including the engagement ring which she'd sent to his Paris address, where his mail was forwarded to an aunt in Germany. The divider screen with the raven-haired twirling ballerina she had been unwilling to part with. She'd been Kraig's protégée when he made a present out of the dressing screen with the promise that one day she would be a leading performer. Tonight that had come true. In a silly gesture she kissed her fingers and touched the girl's red ballerina slippers.

Valli joyfully slipped behind the screen. Sitting down on the red stool she began to untie and loosen the white ribbons of her slippers from around her ankles, her long hair falling across her left shoulder.

Mimi went to answer the "code" knock on the door. It was the errand boy, Andre, bringing a large basket.

"More roses, orchids, chocolates, and cards galore for Mademoiselle Valli."

"Do you hear, chéri? You are loved," called Mimi from over her shoulder as the door closed and locked again.

"Ah, success!" Valli joked. "How Paris loves a star in her springtime years. But will the gay Parisians love me in my December?"

"December?" laughed Mimi. "Wait until you are my age before you speak of December."

Valli smiled. "Yes, Mimi dear, when rheumatism keeps me home before the fireplace, old and gray, who will love me then? The flowers and chocolates will cease," and for emphasis, Valli winced and massaged her toes and instep that actually were hurting. There had been a serious note to her voice as she joked with Mimi. She deliberately laughed at herself sometimes just to keep sane and sober, especially on a night like this beautiful evening, when despite the monotonous drizzle of rain outdoors, the stars seemed to shine in her little world. She remembered what Davide so often said: "Spring and summer are but two seasons of life, ma petite. So too, are fall and winter. Prepare for both. For then, you will not be so surprised by the sudden chill of life. And in every season, remember: our God is faithful."

With both ballet slippers off, she briskly rubbed the other foot. Thank God the mild pain hadn't kept her from dancing tonight, as she feared it might when going into the ballet. No one knew about it, least of all the ballet director! If he had, he wouldn't have permitted her to dance tonight. The honor would have gone to Bridgette. In some ways Bridgette was the more experienced dancer, but she was undisciplined and spoiled. Even though the pain hadn't interfered with her dancing, Valli was aware of an increased stiffness in her right ankle. Not even Mimi knew about it—she would have worried too much.

Still in her costume, she came from behind the screen, blotting her perspiring face, throat, and arms dry with a soft cream-colored towel until she could shower and dress for the reception at Ambassador Hartley's. Mimi had brought the basket across the room to a table and began arranging the flowers, cards, and candy.

"Looks like Christmas," Valli said cheerfully.

Mimi didn't answer. Her back was toward Valli and she stood there.

"Anything wrong?" Valli called.

Mimi turned with a smile and came toward her. "Now what could be wrong on a night like this?"

Mimi was a widow who'd been with Valli from the first year of her ballet training. Mimi had been the cook at the school, but Valli had gotten on so well with her that Mimi had wanted to work for her after she graduated, so Valli had hired her as a personal maid. She wouldn't admit it to herself, but in many ways Mimi made up for the loneliness Valli felt over losing Great-Aunt Calanthe. Mimi stood just five feet tall, and her feet were swathed in low-heeled black leather shoes. She wore a plain black skirt and cotton peasant blouse, and over that, an apron with two huge pockets usually stuffed with odds and ends she would pick up to put back in their rightful place, though she often forgot where she put things. Her gray hair was pulled back and pinned into a heavy round knot, and she wore a floppy black dustcap with loops of gray-white burgess lace that looked like a limp cobweb.

Several knocks sounded on the door. Mimi glanced at her questioningly.

It was a tradition to receive a small group of enthusiasts backstage after a performance. "I expect Giselle to come by for a few minutes," Valli said. "Better let them in."

Mimi scowled her dislike. "Giselle, humph. She has the nerve."

"Now Mimi," Valli urged gently. "She asked my forgiveness three years ago when she married Colonel Sebastien. She's still my sister."

"Anyone can see you've given her more than what's fair. If you want my opinion, chére enfant, she hasn't changed so much, though she has married a noble man." She went to answer the knocking, and Valli worried to herself that Mimi was more right than wrong.

She set aside the disturbing consideration as cheerful voices reached her ears from outside in the corridor. She recognized one of the voices as her sister's.

Mimi looked over her shoulder and whispered: "Madame Giselle has someone to introduce." She rolled her eyes toward the ceiling with appreciation. "Wait till you see him."

Valli smoothed her damp hair away from her face and straightened her costume. She nodded to Mimi. "Let them in. I'm all smiles."

A moment later Giselle swept into the room, pretty and talented in ways that only Giselle could be. "Valli, you were superb." She was joined by an elite group of well-wishers from the Paris theater culture and journalism crowd, and some that she had never seen before. The charged room burst with congratulatory remarks and laughter, and Valli was soon chattering happily with her admirers.

During a moment of reprieve, Giselle drew her aside. Valli noticed the dark circles under her eyes carefully concealed with makeup. Had some anxiety been interfering with her sleep? Valli hoped Sebastien would arrive soon.

Giselle said in a low voice: "I hope you won't mind, but I've brought…a friend of Sebastien's along."

Valli smiled at her sister and said, "I'd be glad to speak with him." She expected he would be an older man who might want her to autograph the ballet program. Visitors often did so, and she felt honored to make someone happy.

"He prefers to wait in the corridor until he can speak with you alone," Giselle told her.

So he was in the hall. He must be shy.

"Keep everyone talking, will you? I'll be back in a few minutes." She picked up a ballet program and signed her name across the front. Giselle, looking pleased to be the center of attention, walked over to a huddle of well-wishers who were leaving corsages and cards on the table. Giselle began greeting them, sounding very much like Valli's agent, and Valli was able to slip out the front door.

The corridor was nearly empty now, since the guard on duty was by the stairway refusing to allow anyone to come up. She glanced around and saw Sebastien's friend waiting by the little table where a coffeepot and cups sat.

She cast him a smile and walked toward him—

She stopped.

Marc stood waiting, his appreciative glance warming her. As his gaze came to hers, a vibrant awareness, each of the other, brought what seemed to Valli an intense silence.

He was, as she remembered, rather extraordinary in appearance, which made the moment all the more difficult to handle. Tonight he did not fit the interesting mode of mercenary soldier but looked instead the suave Parisian, dressed in an immaculate white shirt and black evening clothes that matched his hair and brought out the best in his light blue eyes. He walked toward her.

Valli tried to hide her surprise. *Am I supposed to remember him? Or was that incident on the West Algerian train meant to be kept a secret? Is this supposed to be our first public meeting?*

"Welcome to Paris, Captain Durell," she said simply, waiting for a cue from him.

But he gave no clue. "A pleasure, mademoiselle. Your performance tonight made the visit worthwhile. It was breathtaking."

The compliment was no more than what the others had said, but when Marc suggested that she had been breathtaking it brought a flutter.

"Why thank you, monsieur."

They lapsed into silence again, and his steady gaze caused her to glance away toward the coffeepot. "Would you, um, care for some coffee?"

He smiled. "No thank you, demoiselle."

She said for lack of anything better: "Do you know much about ballet, Captain?"

His smile remained. "Very little," he confessed.

She had known that, of course.

"Giselle brought a book on ballet to my hotel last night. If she hadn't, I would have been totally lost at her explanation of the terms."

"I hope it wasn't too dreadful." Valli was pleased to think he'd taken the time and effort. Even the idea that Giselle had gone to his hotel didn't trouble her after Davide's hearty endorsement of Marc's character. Not that she completely trusted Giselle's motives!

"Even a novice can appreciate the beauty of ballet," Marc said. "I hope to see you perform again some time."

"You are too kind, Captain Durell."

"Not at all." He looked at the program she held.

Embarrassed, realizing he wasn't the devotee she had thought wanted her autograph, she started to place it behind her back but he saw and asked, "Is that for me?"

"Well—no, I thought you would be someone much older, with a daughter. Sometimes visitors who attend a ballet ask the dancer to sign the program."

His smile was disarming. "What a charming idea. May I?" he reached for it.

"Oh, but surely you wouldn't want..."

"Why wouldn't I?" his eyes danced. "But I'd prefer you put my name on it...and maybe something personal..." He took a pen from his pocket, still smiling, and handed it to her. "Let's see—what would be appropriate do you think? 'To Marc, still thinking of our intriguing moments together beneath the Sahara date palms!' What do you think? A little too much perhaps?"

His eyes flickered with amusement and she smiled. The formality between them eased, and she plucked the pen from his fingers. "Strange...I don't recall being beneath any date palms, Captain, only the broiling sun."

"We'll need to do better next time."

She paused.

"Here in Paris, maybe?" he asked softly.

She hesitated, her heart beginning to pound. "Maybe."

"Just, 'maybe'?"

She finished writing the message and handed him the program and pen. His eyes held hers. Her lashes lowered. "All right, yes."

He folded the program and placed it inside his jacket, watching her. "When?"

"Tonight, if you like."

She was amused when a subdued look of surprise showed in his eyes. He must have thought she would lead him on a merry chase before relenting. Little did he know how pleased she was that he was here in Paris. She wanted to ask him about Blystone. Had the Surete heard from the Englishman yet?

"Tonight suits me well," he said.

"The British ambassador is giving a reception for the ballet company tonight. We can meet there if you like. I'm to be there in an hour. I'd prefer not to attend, but one just doesn't snub the British."

He smiled. "No, one doesn't, and expect to get away with it, that is."

"The ballet director would also expect me to show up," she explained. "Some journalists and theater critics will be there. We can talk afterwards."

"Then I'll wait for you here in the hall." He glanced at his watch. "Is there a telephone I can use?"

"If you're not disturbed by the noise, there's one in my dressing room. You can use it for a few minutes, if you like."

Valli walked down to her door and he reached over and opened it for her. She smiled and entered, with Marc behind her.

The laughter and chatter were loud enough to conceal her voice. "This way." She brought him to a small wardrobe room. She switched on the overhead light, displaying numerous ballerina costumes. There was also a small desk and telephone.

"Don't mind the clutter," she apologized. "I've been working night and day with my dance partner ever since I returned from Davide's."

"Your partner, Rodolphe?"

"He's probably the finest ballet dancer in Europe after—" she caught herself from saying Kraig. If he noticed the awkward hesitance, he ignored it.

The black telephone sat on a cosmetic counter. She pushed bottles of perfume out of the way and turned, handing him the receiver.

He took it, and as she turned to leave, his faint smile toyed with her. "You're sure that I can trust you? This phone isn't tapped, is it?"

"Wouldn't you be surprised if it was, Captain?" she closed the door, seeing his smile deepen as he dialed.

Valli stood outside the door a moment. *What an intriguing man.* What had he said back at Bel-Abbes about his reason for coming to Paris? He had already been told about Monsieur Claude's illness, and now there may also be the secret business surrounding Blystone, and Dietrich Gestler. She was uneasy as she remembered how he had asked her about recognizing Dietrich at the train junction, and how she had said no. That made for some difficulty. Her thoughts were interrupted as Giselle came up with mink stole and handbag in hand. Valli noticed her taut, pale face at once. "What is it, Giselle?"

"Oh, nothing." She smiled tightly, slipping her stole about her bare shoulders. "I can't stay is all. Would you explain to Marc that something popped up and I've got to run?"

"You can tell him yourself if you like. He should be off the telephone in a few moments."

"You tell him for me, won't you? Merci." She was walking toward the front door.

Valli went after her. "What about the reception at Ambassador Hartley's? They're expecting you. Are you going to call and explain?"

"Oh—yes, that."

"With Sebastien's new post in Reynaud's government you told me you wanted to become friendly with foreign dignitaries," Valli protested, feeling a rise of impatience with her ability to shrug it off.

"It doesn't matter now. Sebastien won't be coming to Paris. He's the new ambassador to Tangier."

It took Valli a moment to recover from her surprise. Ambassador?

"Marc can tell you all about it," Giselle said. "He's the one who delivered Sebastien's news to me last night in a letter. I'm to leave with Marc in a few weeks." She glanced at Valli with that sly, amused look she wore so often. "You too will come with us if he has his way."

Just the hint coming from Giselle that she noticed Marc's interest caused Valli's emotions to draw back. Her sister had made those same innuendoes about Kraig.

"I've no intention of returning to Tangier," Valli said calmly. "Especially now, after tonight."

"I'm not surprised, but Sebastien mentioned in his letter that Marc will try to convince you to leave Paris before the war makes escape impossible."

Valli remembered Dietrich's boast about the Germans entering Paris, and it brought a shiver. What if France did find itself being trampled over by the Nazis? If they marched into Paris—no. It was unthinkable. She saw the same unpleasant look in Giselle's eyes.

But leave Paris! "I can't leave now," Valli repeated. And why would Sebastien even expect her to? Not with Great-Aunt Calanthe so cool and distant. Valli started to ask more questions about why Marc would think she would return with him, but Giselle laid a hand on her arm. "Look, I've got to run. See you at Monsieur Claude's tomorrow. You are coming out to the estate, aren't you?"

"Yes, I suppose." Valli was still thinking of Tangier. If she returned she could see Davide and help at the mission station, but how could she walk away from her career now, after her success tonight? God had enabled her to achieve the success of her dreams. He wouldn't be asking her to uproot so soon and leave it all, would He? It didn't make any sense!

Giselle was in a hurry, looking anxious. "Tell Marc that Great-Uncle Claude is expecting him to arrive in the morning." She dug into her handbag. "Here are the keys to my car. Marc can pick you up at your flat as well."

"What of you? How will you get there?"

"I have another ride for tonight," she said stiffly.

Valli watched her, wondering at the sudden change that had come over her in so short a time.

"I've got to run," Giselle said. "Explain to Marc for me, will you?"

"I'll try."

Giselle shut the door behind her and Valli was left staring at it.

Valli fought the rising tide of irritation that Giselle seemed to almost always provoke. Again, her sister raised more questions than answers. Again, she was dropping everything, including her responsibilities for the night, and dashing off on some impulsive errand that she felt no obligation to explain, leaving Valli and others to clean up after her and make excuses for her at the reception.

A few minutes later Valli said her last good night to those who had stopped by with congratulatory remarks. The dressing room was now deserted and the laughter had ceased, producing in her mind a heavy, portending silence.

What had come over Giselle? she wondered again. When Valli had left her to speak with Marc in the hall she had appeared to be in animated spirits. She recalled how Giselle had walked over to speak to a group of a dozen or so fans that had squeezed into a corner of the room and were laying corsages and cards on the guest table. Tonight had been unusual with so many people coming and going. Except for a few familiar faces, even Valli couldn't name all those who had dropped by.

She glanced around the now silent room, wondering. Was it her imagination or had some exchange ensued between Giselle and one of those nameless guests? Valli turned and looked over at the table where Giselle had stood filling in for her while she had talked to Marc in the hall. The table was laden with lovely flowers and cards. But perhaps something unpleasant had occurred there, something that had altered Giselle's plans for the evening.

Valli stood thoughtfully. She couldn't be positive, but it seemed that something must have happened in the ten-minute period between the time she had left the dressing room to meet Marc and when she returned to bring him to the telephone, something that made her totally disregard the reception at Ambassador Hartley's. Giselle flourished on parties. She wouldn't have avoided this one unless there was a strong reason. It couldn't have been because of disappointment over Sebastien's new position in Tangier, she hadn't appeared that bothered by the news, which was also rather strange.

As Valli waited for Marc to finish using the telephone, trying to make sense of it all, an eerie silence walled her in. Except for those few people she trusted—Mimi, Marc, and Giselle—someone might have managed to slip into the dressing room posing as one of the theater critics. She dimly recalled a man with a benign, "smiling face" whom she had never seen before in the usual crowd of ballet goers. She had thought he was a friend of one of the foreign journalists who wrote theater news for home newspapers and had paid scant attention to him.

*Come to think of it, I don't remember seeing him with the others as they left just now,* she thought, rubbing her arms as though she felt a cold draft. He must have left when I brought Marc to the telephone, just a few minutes before Giselle.

She walked over to the table and looked at the flowers, piles of cards, and small white envelopes, as though one of them might hold the clue. The people had been very gracious to her tonight, but the warm golden glow from the spotlight of success had faded, leaving her with a sense of apprehension.

Valli looked down at the cards again. She would ask Mimi to gather them all up and put them in a box for later, when she could read them at her leisure. There was no more time to waste worrying now; she still had to bathe and dress for the reception.

She turned. What was keeping Marc so long on the phone?

Still holding the keys to Giselle's automobile, Valli walked to the back room. Marc was just hanging up the phone. She stood there thoughtfully.

Marc took one look at her and a slight frown formed between his eyes, and he said quietly, "What's wrong?"

She stirred herself awake. "Am I that readable?"

"You look as if you've just stumbled over Blystone's body."

Valli's hand went to her throat. "Oh no. They found the poor Englishman. He's—?"

Marc's frown deepened. "Yes. I was just told."

"By the Surete?" she whispered.

He looked at her. "Yes," he admitted reluctantly.

"Where did they find him, near Sidi-bel-Abbes?"

"No, Lisbon. He sent an SOS. But when our man arrived, it was too late."

Poor Blystone. She shuddered, remembering how she had carried his canvas bag around for two days before she had gotten rid of it. And thinking of the bag reminded her of Dietrich.

Marc was watching her, and as if guessing the direction of her thoughts, his slight scowl returned. He took her arm and led her from the room. "I shouldn't have told you. A dead Englishman and Nazi agents aren't good company for a young woman who has just danced her way to stardom."

"No, I wanted to know. I've thought of Sir Blystone many times since Algeria," she admitted in a low voice. "I was cheering him on in my mind, hoping he'd make it safely to London."

He didn't look pleased with her emotional involvement. "I rather thought you would. You'd have hidden him here in Paris if you had the chance and tried to smuggle him out. Right?"

She smiled crookedly. "What's wrong with a little patriotism, Captain Durell?"

"Not a thing. In fact, I admire the trait in you very highly."

She scanned him. "You're rather involved in the struggle against the Nazis yourself, if I recall."

"You'll make the Surete very happy."

When she lifted a questioning brow, he added, "I need to talk to you about that, but not here."

"Very mysterious."

"Let's hope so." He looked at his watch. "I'd better leave and allow you to get ready for that party at Ambassador Hartley's." He noticed the keys. "Are those for me?"

"Yes, how did you know?" She handed them to him.

"Giselle said she would leave her car." He glanced about. "She's waiting downstairs?"

"No. She had to leave suddenly." Valli tried to hide her impatience with her sister's perceived antics. "Something important came up, she said. She asked me to tell you."

Marc looked concerned. "Is that what she said, 'something came up'? Did she explain what the urgency was about?"

"I'm afraid not. Giselle is rather, shall we say, impulsive?"

"So I've noted."

"She did say that Monsieur Claude is anxious to see you and asked that you drive out to the Ransier estate tomorrow."

The front door opened and Mimi came in carrying two dozen scarlet roses with dewy petals, spicy with fragrance.

"Oh, how lovely," Valli said, but Mimi did not smile and looked at the velvet richness as though it contained poison ivy.

Valli took the armful of extravagant beauty and inhaled the fragrance. Delicious! "Don't tell me it was that nice American journalist again?"

"No, it was not the American."

Valli noted the vague hesitancy in Mimi's tone, and it alerted her. "Who, then?"

"Monsieur Kraig sent them," Mimi admitted. "They arrived while you were performing."

Valli's mind whirled back to the mission station. Dietrich had said that Kraig attended her performance of the

*Black Swan.* Was he here now? *I don't want to see him. I can't see him.* A whiff of fragrance assailed her with sentimental nausea.

With a brief start she realized she was not alone in the room with Mimi, and Valli's gaze reluctantly went across the room to Marc. As she might expect, he was watching her alertly, weighing her response to Kraig.

Mimi too must have recognized the dread she felt because she winced and came to her, taking hold of her as though Valli were a child who had fallen down and skinned her knee.

"Oh chere enfant. It is my fault, yes mine! I should never have brought them here."

Embarrassed because Marc was looking on, Valli managed a brief laugh. "Don't be silly, Mimi. I never turn down roses. Here, put them in a vase, will you?"

But Mimi was entangled within her own distraught emotions and continued as though she hadn't even heard. "I should have sent the roses back marked 'refused.'"

Marc, who only moments ago had spoken of departing, evidently changed his mind and leaned his shoulder into the wall, watching her.

*He's found sunken treasure,* Valli thought, nettled, feeling as though she were performing on stage again. Why was he so interested in analyzing her response to Kraig?

"No, Mimi, You mustn't keep things from me. Everything is quite all right."

Mimi looked doubtful, but dug into her big apron pocket. "There was this card with the roses. And a letter came earlier," she confessed guiltily.

"A letter?" Valli took the card from Mimi.

"Yes, a letter from Monsieur Kraig. It came in the noon mail. I feared to give it to you before the performance tonight," she apologized, her eyes worried. "It was so important for you to have a free mind. Who knows what it would contain? Something to upset you so badly you could not dance. So I put the letter under the box of chocolates."

Seeing the woman's face fall, Valli hastened: "It's all right. Don't worry so."

Nevertheless, it was with uncertainty that Valli turned her back to Marc and walked over to the small table where the other flowers, cards, and chocolates were piled in tribute. She read the small white card that Mimi had given her.

> *Congratulations, Valli. You deserve every happy moment of your success. I wish I could have been in the audience to cheer what I know will be your most stunning performance, but I am in Madrid. I have written you a letter in which I explain the danger we are both in.*
>
> *Always, Kraig G.*

Valli read the message for the second time with a furrowed brow. *Danger? Which we are both in?*

She turned slowly and looked over at Marc. She knew she could trust him, but was it fair to Kraig to share his concerns with someone from the Surete?

*Fair?* she scolded herself. *Was he fair with you? Remember the wedding dress two weeks before the ceremony? It's still hanging in your closet at the flat. But I'm not to treat others the way they treat me,* she argued with herself. *I'm not to retaliate—*

Marc walked over to her, looked at the note in her hand, then scanned her face in a wordless invitation to turn it over to him. Valli found emotional saneness in the intensity of his gaze and in his steady strength. When she looked into those blue eyes beneath dark lashes she seemed to forget all about Kraig...

Marc said gently: "Are you all right, demoiselle?"

She nodded, and to prove it, slowly handed him the card.

He read it thoughtfully, but surprisingly he made little comment. "May I keep this for awhile?"

Again, she merely nodded, and he placed it in his jacket pocket. He looked down at the table, and the box of chocolates caught his interest. It was open, and he lifted it up and looked down at the table.

"What's wrong?" she whispered.

"Did you open this?"

"No, why?"

"Where's the letter?"

Mimi had walked to the small white dressing table to place the roses in a vase of water, still releasing her emotional upset by mumbling her irritation with Kraig.

"Mimi, do you have Kraig's letter?" Valli asked her.

"Yes, it's right there, under the chocolates." She pointed to the long, low table where Valli and Marc stood.

"It's not here," Valli stated, trying to keep alarm out of her voice.

"Oh, but it must be." And Mimi scuttled across the room to prove her wrong. She searched, then more frantically. "I put it right here—"

"Are you sure, Mimi?"

"But yes, I set it down. Right here—" she tapped the table with her finger—"beneath the bonbons to show you after the ballet."

"Someone opened the box," Marc said.

*Yes*, Valli thought, meeting his eyes. *And when they lifted the box they might have seen the envelope and taken it. But why?*

Mimi's face puzzled. "But—it is odd. I know I set it there."

"Check your pockets, Mimi," Marc suggested. She did so, emptying out a comb, a handkerchief, and an odd assortment of bric-a-brac, but no envelope.

An uneasy premonition caused Valli's spine to twinge. Someone had taken Kraig's letter. Danger, he had said. Kraig couldn't be involved in the matter about Blystone could he? She wanted to ask Marc, but not in front of Mimi. Then, what danger could he have alluded to?

"Are these all the cards?" he asked Mimi.

"Yes, I put everything there with the flowers."

Marc turned to Valli. "Mind if I look through these? Someone might have thought the letter got covered up by the box of chocolates by mistake and simply moved it into the pile of cards."

"No, go ahead and look. But it does seem odd someone would be rude enough to open a box of chocolates that were meant as a gift." She drew up two chairs.

Somehow Valli was not surprised by all this. From the moment she had arrived back in France, over a month ago, and entered ballet practice, the West Algerian train incident had continued to trouble her. It was as though it had all been a nightmare from which she had yet to awaken. Now, tonight, with the news that Blystone was dead and the mention of danger in Kraig's note, merely reinforced her concerns. If there was danger, it had followed them to Paris from the hot, blowing sands of Algeria.

"I just don't know what could have happened to the letter," Mimi mumbled, hovering behind them.

"You're sure you didn't just think you put it on the table?" Valli asked, sorting through cards with familiar names written on the envelopes.

"Oh but no, I remember so well." Mimi groaned, using the back of the chair to stoop to the floor. She began lifting the dust ruffles on the chairs and small divan. "I don't forget a thing, ma enfante."

Valli caught Marc's eyes and smiled.

Valli tried to soothe her. "Oh well. I'm sure it will turn up."

Mimi touched her forehead. "But now I remember. I *did* leave the room for a few minutes just before the ballet ended. When I got back, I was sure the letter was still there, but now I cannot know." She walked to the other side of the room, still searching.

Valli laid aside her pile of cards. "Nothing," she sighed to Marc. "Find anything interesting?"

Marc was engrossed in reading the names on the envelopes. "No." He lowered his voice. "When does Mimi leave here?"

Valli glanced at her. She was still puttering about, searching. "She usually leaves by now. Why?"

"I'd like to speak with you about this alone. Can I send her home in a taxi?"

She smiled. "Yes, if you can convince her. She's awfully worried about the letter now, and stubborn."

Marc stood. "I'll manage. Why don't you change for the reception?"

Valli hurried from the little room to run her bath water, leaving the missing letter and Mimi for Marc to handle. She was glad he had arrived tonight. His presence made her feel safe, and his concerns were flattering.

It must have been five minutes later when she heard the door to the outside hall open and shut. She smiled. He must have soothed Mimi enough to get her to go home. Sending her off safely in a taxi would also win her approval, since she often walked to save money.

Except for the rain falling outside her little window all was silent in the dressing room. Now and then she could hear traffic passing by in the street below, tires splashing water to the curb.

Valli struggled out of the dirndl dress used in her performance, musing over the night's events. Odd how Giselle had rushed off that way, and also that Kraig's letter should evaporate into thin air. Had Giselle taken it? Or the man with the smiling face? Valli preferred to think that Mimi must have mislaid it. In the rush of details leading up to the ballet performance tonight, she and Mimi both had been flying about. The simplest solution was that the letter had gotten misplaced. If not, it seemed the only other explanation was that someone had taken it. She must remember to tell Marc about the smiling stranger.

Kraig spoke of danger in the note. What might he have said in the letter?

Twenty minutes later Valli turned to the wardrobe to choose the gown she wished to wear. Mimi had proudly displayed a new low-cut crimson tulle with silver thread woven throughout.

Valli gasped, hand at forehead. "*Where* did she get *that*?" A note was pinned to it: "A gift from the ballet lovers at Le Shoppe."

*No, no, that will never do. Not for me.* Giselle would swoon to own it, but! Valli would thank Le Shoppe, but send it back. She chose instead a deceptively simple evening dress of soft, smooth blue velvet and a pair of matching Betty Grable high heels. A few small diamonds and she would be ready for the gala reception honoring her and the ballet company—and ready for Marc Durell. She smoothed her sleek hair into place, added some discreet color to her lips, and went out to meet Marc—to find that he had left. There was a note propped against the ticking clock. Valli snatched it and read:

> *Sorry I had to run off, but it was important. When I brought Mimi to the taxi I met an old friend on the street who plays a harmonica. I'll catch up with you at Hartley's.*
>
> *Marc*

A friend with a harmonica? Valli felt a rush of irritation and disappointment. It looked as if Giselle wasn't the only one who darted off with strange explanations. She crumpled the note and tossed it in the trash, then went to call herself a taxi.

# 11

As Valli arrived, the reception at the British ambassador's residence was well underway, and the throng of dance and theater enthusiasts extended into the garden area. There was food galore, and lots of good things to drink, as well as a large assortment of alcoholic beverages that she typically avoided—disguised in sleek bottles with French and Italian names. She sipped a Coca-Cola that seemed to harmonize with the recorded music by the popular American orchestras of Tommy Dorsey and Glenn Miller. Valli glanced at the clock between her smiles and "thank yous" to those swarming around her with congratulatory remarks.

After an hour passed she began to think Marc wouldn't come after all. Very puzzling after his insistence that he needed to meet her alone tonight. His old friend the harmonica player must have had plenty to talk about, she thought ruefully.

A late arrival was being admitted as she looked toward the double doors at the entranceway. Her heart wanted to stop. What was Dietrich doing here in Paris? She thought of Blystone, found dead in Lisbon, and her emotions recoiled. She glanced at Ambassador Hartley, but the silver-haired dignitary was deep in conversation with a guest and didn't appear to notice him. Neither did anyone else in the room appear troubled. Evidently no one seemed to know his true identity. His presence was more than Valli needed to challenge her dwindling resources.

Dietrich's gaze swept the room. Valli calmly attempted an escape, making her way toward the stairway leading to the ladies' powder room. He intercepted her with a sharp bow and a cool smile.

"Ah, Demoiselle Valli. How good to see you again. You were breathtaking tonight."

There was that word again, but this time it left her cold.

"I had hoped to meet you after your performance but ran into an old friend from Berlin. Though the encounter became extended, he was able to get me an invitation to your reception."

He? Valli looked into the smiling, self-assured face with the dueling scar on the chin. What friend from Berlin could possibly arrange an invitation to the British Ambassador's residence?

"I can't believe you came all the way to Paris to see me perform," she said, adding a smile to soften her words.

He laughed. "I wish I could say yes, fraulein, but I am traveling with an entourage from Herr Hitler in order to deliver a letter to reasonable officials in your Reynaud government."

Your Reynaud. A cryptic way to speak of the French republic. She read the smug lines of superiority on his smiling face.

"Reynaud is being offered a fair and just peace. Let us hope France is wise enough to accept it.

Ah, the mighty German nation, the new Aryan masters of Europe! "And if they are not 'wise' enough to accept surrender?" she asked boldly.

He gestured sadly. "All out war, fraulein. What else can be done if France continues to meddle on behalf of Belgium?"

"France and England have commitments to friendly nations who may be attacked without cause. If France doesn't fight to stop aggression against our neighbors, where will we meet the Nazis next?"

His smile was chilling. "Paris, perhaps. But before you burst into outrage at that, my dear fraulein, consider the fairness of Herr Hitler's offer."

"You mean France can depend upon the 'good will' of the benevolent fuhrer."

His contained smile remained, but his eyes reflected anger. "I assure you he can be quite benevolent when his objectives are met with cooperation, though understandably that is little comfort to you at this turbulent time. Let us speak of other things...do you plan to return with Giselle to Tangier?"

She hid her surprise. How could he possibly know about Sebastien's new position? "I've no immediate plans of leaving," she said wearily, still upset over the idea of Nazi soldiers coming to Paris. "Have you spoken to Giselle since your arrival?"

He smiled. "As a matter of fact, I have seen her tonight. She was leaving the theater when I called to her."

Valli wondered if Dietrich was the one Giselle had rushed off to meet.

"It was unfortunate we only had time for a brief exchange. She was in a hurry to catch a taxi to keep an appointment."

Was he telling the truth? Valli wondered. If it was Dietrich that she had rushed off to meet, Giselle could still have come to the reception, even if late. She remembered his boast of working in the German embassy in Tangier and wondered if it might have been a lie.

"What of you? At Davide's, you mentioned a job at the German embassy in Tangier. Do you still have plans?"

"It may be my work in Paris will keep me here longer than I first anticipated."

She pretended to underestimate him, thinking him vain enough to want to impress her. "But it shouldn't take you very long just to finish your errands for Berlin." She yawned and glanced about.

It worked. She saw his mouth tighten as his gaze dropped. "Not mere errands, Valli. I work for the Reichstag."

The Reichstag, of course, housed the main German government in Berlin. "Oh, is that important?"

He laughed. "I should like to see your expression when you find out just how crucial my assignment is in Berlin."

It was all she could do to force a smile and appear interested and friendly. "Then I suppose you would know some of the Nazi politicians."

"Politicians? What if I told you that there are instances when I dine alone with von Ribbentrop?"

She had heard the name, but what did von Ribbentrop do? She raised both brows, as though surprised, though not too impressed. He well knew that she disapproved of the Nazis.

"Perhaps I have underrated you a little."

He looked satisfied that she would admit it. "I believe you have." He laughed impatiently. "It is satisfying after five years to see you realize you were wrong about me. Nothing frustrated me more than to tag along with you and Kraig to Paris cafés, while you admired his ballet skills yet dismissed my involvement in the Nazi party political meetings. Now look at us. Kraig has proven himself a fool. He has nothing, living in the hills of Greece, working futilely in the underground against the Nazis. Whereas I hold a position in the Reichstag."

*Kraig—in the underground...*

"Perhaps it is merely my hope, fraulein, but I anticipate you may change your mind about me as well as the Nazi Party," he said unexpectedly, a new confidence in his tone. "While I've plans to return to Tangier, my main interest now abides in Paris. You, of course, will want to stay on, now that you've danced your way to spectacular success tonight. In the future, I may be able to help you more than you realize." He looked smug.

She didn't like the way it sounded. What made him think she would ever cooperate with him?

"Naturally Giselle will go back to Tangier," he went on. "Now that Colonel Sebastien—or should I now say Ambassador Sebastien Ransier—holds a strategic position. One that Giselle finds intimidating," he said, with a twitch of a smile.

"Why do you say that?" Valli asked coolly. "She wasn't intimidated over the possibility of Sebastien serving in Reynaud's government."

"Oh come!" he scoffed. "There is no need to rush to her defense around me. I happen to know what kind of woman your sister is, the way she and Kraig ran off to Madrid together like two foolish children."

"I suppose your brother was an innocent lamb, deceitfully lured away by her overpowering charms," she said.

"I have nothing but contempt for her, a simple-minded Jezebel."

Valli flushed and struggled with her temper.

"That you would defend either of them amazes me, fraulein."

"I am not defending their behavior, but if anyone has a justifiable cause to be morally outraged, it is I. I don't see that you're in any self-righteous position to—"

"Perhaps," Dietrich cut in coolly, "you are still so foolishly enamored with my simpleton brother that you are willing to take him back even after he shamed you."

Humiliated by his blunt words, she had a strong desire to slap him.

"You needn't concern yourself."

"Ah, but dear sister Giselle is concerned."

"What do you mean?"

Dietrich smiled unpleasantly. "She knows that her folly in running off with Kraig could jeopardize the state of her husband's suitability as ambassador. If French wives are anything like German wives, they won't like her around thier husbands. Those in Tangier married to governmental officials will be watching her like a bunch of mother hens when a fox prowls the coop. Scandal always has a way of coming unmasked."

Was he suggesting he might unmask it? Valli realized she couldn't defend her sister because the accusations were true. Like a sinner before a holy God, the stain of sin was real. Giselle might try to hide the facts, but her deeds were indefensible. Having never come to the one and only Savior, she had no covering for her folly. Even before a hypocrite like Dietrich Gestler. Valli remained mute, embarrassed for her sister.

There was a malicious glint of humor in his eyes. "I have offended you. My apology." He bowed. "I am sure we will have opportunity to talk again more congenially, tomorrow at the Ransier estate, perhaps?"

"You are going there?" she asked, surprised.

"I was invited tonight during the ballet." But he didn't explain by whom. The news was disturbing. Why would anyone in the Ransier family invite Dietrich Gestler to the estate?

"What luck, Valli, that you will be there as well. Since I am staying in Paris tonight perhaps I can drive you there in the morning?"

As if she would! "I have a ride with Monsieur Claude's nephew."

He smirked. "Yes, I was told about his arrival."

She found Dietrich's insinuation unclear, as was his source of information.

Dietrich looked a trifle scornful. "He is a brave soldier in the renowned French army no doubt."

"Yes, very brave," she quipped. Dietrich's pride nettled her. "He is a legionnaire." *And an agent in French Security*, she would have added, but naturally didn't.

"Then, he was the one I saw tonight at the theater, seated in a box with Giselle. What is his name, Durell?"

"Yes," Marc interjected cheerfully. "Captain Marc Durell, North Africa. And you are Dietrich Gestler?"

Both Valli and Dietrich turned to see a suave, smiling Marc who revealed nothing about his true feelings.

"Welcome to Paris, Herr Gestler. I take it that you also were impressed with Mademoiselle Chattaine's performance tonight?"

Valli was surprised by Marc's congenial manner, and her glance at Dietrich showed his quizzical expression. Even so, she could sense that both men were measuring each other.

Dietrich had also revived a masquerade of charm, giving a little click with his heels while gesturing with his blond head. "Captain Durell. Yes, I was just telling the mademoiselle how much I enjoyed it."

"Dietrich said that he knows Monsieur Claude, your great-uncle," Valli said.

If Marc found the news surprising he kept it to himself. "Then maybe we'll have time to meet again. Will you be here for long?"

"Perhaps longer than I once expected, Captain Durell."

"Then we'll need to get together one evening and exchange news. It's been some time since I've visited Germany. Maybe you can help me understand your new fuhrer."

Dietrich smiled amiably. "Herr Hitler is a complex man to explain, but I would be remiss if I did not try. And perhaps you can help me understand the complexities of North Africa. I was there, only recently, as Valli can tell you." He turned toward her. "How is your brother's mission work coming along?"

"I wish I could tell you. I haven't heard from him since my return over a month ago."

Dietrich turned to Marc. "I can't help thinking I have seen you there."

"You may have. Davide and I are friends."

"Oh?"

"I'm stationed at Sidi-bel-Abbes, or was. When I return, I'll have a new post in Tangier."

"Then perhaps I will see you there, as well."

"I'm sure we'll have occasion to meet again," Marc said with a smile.

Dietrich made his goodbye and left. Valli watched him go.

Marc turned toward her a moment later. His brief overview told her she had made the right choice in choosing her gown. "You were friendly with him," she said.

He noticed the surprise in her voice. "That's one way to learn what he thinks and hopefully what he's about. Remember that."

"What?" she looked at him, wondering why he would say that.

Marc explained. "I saw you across the room. You were angry when I entered."

"Oh, did you notice?" she asked dismayed.

"You'd do a little better keeping a tighter rein on your dislike of the Nazis."

"Yes, I know. But they're so intolerably arrogant."

"That's why they're Nazis," Marc said dryly.

"I didn't think you expected me to act friendly with him."

His gaze came to hers, and he was about to say something, then apparently changed his mind.

Valli had begun to recover from Dietrich and began to notice Marc. His blue eyes were guarded, as though critically analyzing her. *Why, he's wondering if I may have enjoyed seeing Dietrich again*, she thought. The idea was so preposterous that it provoked a smile. *He's still trying to understand me. Well, that goes both ways.*

Amusement showed in her smile. "I trust you enjoyed your tête-à-tête with the harmonica player?"

"Not as much as I would have enjoyed our discussion. Sorry I had to run off. I took a chance that you might still be here. Does that invitation to talk still hold?"

She would have expected a man of his merit and rank in the Surete to be overly confident, even vain, but he was so unlike Dietrich that his decorum made him interesting.

"I wouldn't expect you to ignore your duty just to favor me."

"Mademoiselle, it is I who am favored...by your company. Let us be accommodating and forget everything unpleasant—at least for a while. You deserve to enjoy the party given in your honor. Would you care to dance?" he asked.

Artie Shaw's popular "Begin the Beguine" had finished and the next recording was Tommy Dorsey's "I'm Getting Sentimental Over You."

Somehow she wouldn't have expected him to know how to dance, and again he pleasantly surprised her. He wasn't fitting into the mold she had imagined.

"I'd love to dance."

"Good."

They moved out onto the dance floor and he drew her into his arms. Valli smiled demurely and succumbed to her favorite instrumental. Romantically stirred for the first time in four years, she wondered what else might be beginning in her life. She must be careful. There was no guarantee that Marc would be around for very long. "An armful of paradise," he whispered into her hair.

She lowered her long lashes. "You surprise me, Captain Durell."

"Do I? I've waited much too long for this dance. It was interrupted in Tangier by an interval of years. At Saint Cyr I used to think about you and wonder how you were doing."

"I'm flattered...I'm surprised you remembered our brief but volatile meeting in Tangier."

"I remembered you very well, and I was disappointed that you didn't answer my two letters."

She looked into his warm blue eyes. "I wish I had."

"Do you? You're not just—what's the word—flirting? I'm vulnerable to your charms, you know."

She laughed. "You're making me very curious."

"Do you remember that military ball you came to once when you were in ballet school?"

Yes, she remembered that Marc had been there, across the room, but that he'd been summoned away.

"You came with Kraig Gestler."

Her eyes lifted to his again. Now why did he bring up Kraig, and of all times! She sensed that he watched for her reaction.

"Why mention him?"

He raised a brow over her bluntness. "Why not? He's been between us for years, and still is. I was always jealous of his good fortune."

Her eyes searched his. Had his compliments been planned to lead her into a discussion of Kraig? What was he trying to find out? Maybe Marc's so-called "vulnerability to her charms" was just an act to get her to talk. She'd better watch his flattery, this man seemed to be a more dangerous entity than even Kraig had been, if that were possible. She did know that she was finding herself drawn to Marc much too quickly.

"Your eyes have lost their romantic glow," he said, his mouth curving.

The instrumental had finished, and the music went right into another Dorsey hit, this one a rousing swing.

"If you're not too tired?" he asked.

Valli laughed, thinking that he wasn't quite comfortable with the faster pace. She was surprised, however, as she whirled her way in and out of his arms as comfortably as with the professionals in the ballet company. When it ended, only slightly out of breath, she applauded him. "I guess I have a great deal to learn about you," she said. "Where did you learn to dance?"

"The blowing sands of Bel-Abbes don't offer much in the line of ballroom dancing, but believe it or not, dancing is a requirement for French soldiers to graduate officer's school. It is called 'style.'"

She laughed. "Did you enjoy it?"

"I hated it. But then—practicing my 'style' with a tough, hundred and ninety pound Sergeant just wasn't quite the same as with the most graceful of ballerinas. I survived by telling myself that if I were ever to impress the dancing princess, I'd better be as serious about my footwork as I was at hitting the bull's eye at the gunnery range."

"Can you?" she asked. "Hit the bull's eye, I mean?"

"Seldom miss it."

"Since I'm to be so friendly to Dietrich, I'd better warn him," she whispered.

"Better not," he whispered back. "I want him to think I'm amiable, unsophisticated, and just a little bit naive."

"I think you'll have a hard time convincing him...and I thought we weren't going to discuss unpleasant things. Let's pretend there's no such thing as German soldiers on the outskirts of France. Right now all I want to do is dance with you."

"You won't find me in a mood to resist."

As Marc held her, to the tune of Glenn Miller's lovely "Moonlight Serenade," it seemed natural to find herself in his arms. She might awaken tomorrow morning and wonder, but at the moment this was exactly where she wanted to stay.

# 12

"With you in my arms, I wouldn't mind dancing into the wee hours of the Paris dawn," he whispered, "but this isn't getting my job done; it's making it more difficult."

She smiled. "So you're one of those inexhaustible Surete loyalists for whom nothing interferes with duty."

"You're not supposed to know that."

"Davide told me."

"I thought so. He's trying to lay the groundwork."

"For what?"

He smiled. "For your explicit trust in me."

She looked into his eyes. "I think it is your trust in me that is lacking, Captain."

"I'm willing to change my mind...and don't you think it's time we called each other by first names?"

"Now seems as good a time as any."

A new song started up that kindled thoughts of her past relationship with Kraig. She tensed, trying to shut off the spigot of memories flooding her mind, but it was too late, her feet missed a beat, and she went rigid. They stopped dancing and Marc looked at her then glanced down to her strappy heels. She avoided his gaze.

"Your ankle's bothering you, isn't it?"

Valli had been trying all evening to hide it and thought she was succeeding.

Surprised, she said: "You noticed?"

"You're limping a little."

"I thought I'd disguised it. It's nothing, really."

"I think we've had enough dancing for one evening. I'd like to bring you outside and talk."

She nodded, and trying to forget the song and what it had once represented, she walked beside him toward the garden door.

"Mon Cousin Marc, how good to see you in Paris. I understand my father has called for you." Aubert Ransier bowed lightly in Valli's direction. "Your performance was noteworthy, Valli."

Valli smiled her thanks and looked at Marc, noting there was little resemblance between them. Aubert Ransier was of medium height with a small, tight mouth below a chestnut-colored mustache. Valli knew that he was a man of some importance in the Reynaud government and she often saw both him and his wife Inga in attendance at the ballet theater. Marc's countenance defied understanding. Was he pleased to see his cousin after so long a time? She couldn't tell. It piqued her curiosity thinking that Marc wasn't the only one who held back emotionally. Aubert too, appeared dignified but distant, as though he were little more than a government official greeting any of the guests here tonight at Ambassador Hartley's. He wore a polite, perpetual smile, and his eyes watched Marc incessantly.

"Hello, Aubert. I didn't know you were here. Did Inga come?"

"No. She wasn't feeling well tonight. The dampness, you know." He looked at Valli. "She was dismayed to miss your performance. This is the first time she had not been able to attend in months, and the one she had most cared to see."

"Oh, I'm sorry she missed it, perhaps another time," she said, still smiling.

"I didn't know you were avid ballet goers," Marc said.

"We enjoy both music and ballet. I saw you there tonight with Giselle, but after the performance you were gone before I could locate you. Does my father know you've arrived? He's anxious to see you."

"I thought I'd drive out to the estate tomorrow."

Aubert smiled thinly. "We will look forward to seeing you there." He turned to Valli. "You will of course visit us this weekend. Inga would love to talk with you. She could not have been more excited about your lead role in *Giselle* if you were her own daughter."

"Merci, Monsieur Aubert. I look forward to visiting with her. I hope she will soon be feeling better."

"Thank you. Now, Cousin Marc, you must not allow dear Claude to upset you with his exaggerations of coming 'German atrocities' in our beloved France. He isn't well, you know. A man suffering from insomnia at his age is prone to imagine a great many erroneous things."

Valli glanced at Marc to see his response. He merely smiled and looked completely at ease. "Perhaps Great-Uncle Claude has been listening too much to the BBC," Marc said.

Aubert appeared momentarily bewildered.

"There was a bulletin just tonight about the German invasion of Denmark and Norway," Marc said. "Coming so soon after Finland's surrender to Russia and news about the Nazis building a new concentration camp for Jews, I can understand Great-Uncle's concerns."

Valli looked down at the polished floor as Aubert's thin smile melted away.

"Yes," said Aubert. "But one needs to be cautious about British journalists. They are somewhat sensational. Well, Marc, I must be running. I wouldn't have left Inga alone tonight except she wanted me to see the ballet and report back to her about Valli's achievement." He held out a pale hand. "We will see you both tomorrow at the estate. Enjoy your evening. Au revoir."

Valli watched him walk away through the perimeter of party guests and disappear into the next room. Odd greeting, she thought. She would have expected a little more warmth between the two cousins.

"Rather than discussing Finland's armistice with Russia, I thought we'd been transported there," she murmured. "That was a very 'chilly' greeting from your cousin."

"Yes," Marc said, his tone untroubled, "but not surprising. That was exactly what I expected. Louis was considered an outsider."

"Louis, your father?" she studied his face curiously, wondering about the family difficulties.

"Captain Durell was a 'no-account scamp' who met my mother in a field hospital near Verdun. From what I've been told by Sebastien, she had just lost the man she really loved in the fighting. She nursed my father back to health and married him before returning to Uncle Claude's estate. He never really accepted their marriage."

"I see." She thought for a moment about Marc's childhood and how he had ended up in the legion in Algeria. Marc, however, was now interested in Aubert.

"That theater box," he said. "Do they use it as often as he suggested?"

"Oh yes. Inga is one of our most enthusiastic supporters."

"I found out that Dietrich was sitting in the Ransier box tonight," he said thoughtfully, still looking after his cousin Aubert. "I find that strange and interesting. Especially now that Aubert is in Reynaud's government."

Valli found the news puzzling as well, even a little frightening. "What business would Monsieur Aubert have with Dietrich, do you suppose?" she asked in a low voice.

"That's what I expect to learn from Claude. I have an idea I'd better get out to the estate first thing in the morning."

The music was playing again and the floor was filling with couples. Marc took her arm and led her out the door and into the lighted garden.

The rain had stopped and the cool spring air smelled pleasantly of early roses and violets. There were guests gathered in small cliques talking in low tones or sitting and laughing over glasses of wine. Marc led her away from the others toward a Victorian gazebo, where climbing roses entwined the lattice railing.

"At least the seats are dry," he said, glancing at the fringed canopy.

Stepping up, he placed her in a cushioned white wicker chair, and Valli loosened the strap of her shoe and slipped it off her foot.

"It appears a little swollen," he said, stooping to look at her ankle. "Did you hurt it during the ballet tonight?"

She wavered before admitting she'd actually danced with an injury. "It happened yesterday. The bulb burned out in the outside lamp above the stairs to my flat. Both Mimi and I meant to replace it, but we've been so busy at the theater. I missed one of the steps coming home late last night. I barely twisted it, but it did feel sore this morning."

"And you still danced on it?"

She didn't sense criticism in his voice so much as curiosity, as if he was learning more about her personality.

"It was risky, I know. But if I hadn't danced—" she stopped.

"You would have missed the opportunity you've worked so hard for."

He understood, and it made her feel more comfortable.

"I won't know for a day or two if the performance stressed my ankle or not, but losing the starring role seemed unthinkable."

He stood and leaned back against the lattice rail, looking out into the dark, quiet garden with weeping willow and maiden hair ferns, as though his thoughts took a new path.

Valli sat in the shadows, massaging her ankle and resting. Thank goodness that other tune had ended. The ballroom double doors were open to let cool air into the house, and the strain of music glided on the breeze. Golden light was streaming out onto the brick terrace as guests were going back and forth carrying refreshments. It seemed to Valli that the evening's lighthearted mood had shifted as surely as though the bewitching hour had struck at midnight. Whether in her own heart only, or in Marc's as well, she was reminded that the coming war would end much that was now taken for granted. Multitudes were going into eternity, even at this moment, on the battlefields of Europe, and the war was drawing ever nearer to Paris.

She suspected that Marc wanted to discuss Dietrich, or even Blystone, and was waiting for the right moment. She was expecting to tell him about Dietrich's comments. If she spoke of Kraig's surprising involvement in the underground resistance movement in Greece, would he conclude that she had an ongoing interest in Kraig? Nor was she anxious to bring the Bel-Abbes encounter on the train back to the surface.

For the past weeks she'd been so involved with her ballet practice that she had tried to avoid thinking about the mysterious happenings on the West Algerian train. Now, the news of Blystone's death in Lisbon reminded her that the unpleasantness really hadn't dissipated, even here among spring roses and the stimulating company of Marc. The reality of these foreboding times heralded worse to come. And once again her mind rode the train through the hot, rippling sand. She heard again the stilted voice of Blystone asking for her help, heard the gun shots, the French policemen stating that the waterboy was dead—and the ominous roar of Dietrich's motorcycle in front of the mission station.

Now—Dietrich was here again in Paris. Kraig had said they both were in danger, yet his letter was missing.

Marc spoke in a low, detached tone: "You didn't see me tonight, but I was there when Dietrich arrived. You looked surprised to see him."

She looked up. The lantern light was behind him and she couldn't see his face, just his darkened silhouette leaning against the gazebo pillar. Now was her opportunity to set the record straight. From the hour she had first recognized Dietrich at Bel-Abbes, Marc seemed to have suspected her of harboring some personal reason for concealing his identity. After the pleasant evening dancing, did he still think so?

"I was surprised," she admitted. "I didn't think he would come to Paris."

"But didn't he contact you at the theater tonight?"

Whatever made him think that? "No, I didn't know he was in the audience until he congratulated me on the performance just now. Why do you ask?"

"And yet he promised you he'd look you up when he arrived here."

So, then..."Davide must have told you that Dietrich came to the mission station."

"Yes, he was worried about Gestler being overly enamored with your charms. So he warned me."

Valli smiled at his dry tone. She leaned forward in her chair. "Dietrich, enamored? He may have wanted to give that impression to Davide, but it was a lie. He didn't come to the mission station to see me."

Marc looked doubtful. "Interesting that you think it wasn't genuine, why? He did come to Paris after all, and I can see the way he looks at you."

She ignored the latter, and said, "I don't think it's genuine for several reasons. First, he didn't notice me on the train."

"He certainly noticed Blystone, who was next to you at the window. How could Dietrich miss you?"

"Well, I'm convinced he didn't notice me and I can tell you why."

"What makes you say so?" The vague allusion of hope in his voice caused her to wonder. Was it prompted by concern for her safety, or did his attentiveness tonight denote his own romantic interest?

"I'm almost sure he didn't notice me because he didn't come to Davide's for that purpose. He didn't know I was there until he walked in and found me. When he did, he was as surprised to see me as I was to see him."

"Hmm..." Marc tapped his chin. "I must admit your observation is intriguing. Because if Dietrich didn't go there to find you, the next question is even more curious. Why did he go if he's not one of Davide's friends?"

"He's not. Davide had never met him before."

"Yes, that's what he told me."

She frowned, remembering the strange incident that occurred just before Dietrich arrived on the motorcycle. She told him how the Berbers rushed to hide.

"One would think the German Wehrmacht was invading. They simply disappeared," she said. "At the time I wondered what gave them cause for alarm."

"Did you mention this to Davide?"

"He was as bewildered about it as I was. No one could give an explanation, not even Haroun. We asked him."

Marc lapsed into a speculative silence. Valli glanced about the gazebo, where the shadows were undisturbed by the dim garden lights.

"But when Dietrich saw me, he pretended I was the cause for his visit," she whispered. "And he maintained that impression even when we argued politics."

Marc must have known about the disagreement because he didn't ask her to explain. So she went on. "I doubt that he could ever truly be enamored with anything except his fuhrer."

Marc smoothly steered the conversation from Dietrich toward his brother Kraig, but no matter how casual his manner, she found herself tensing at the mere mention of his name.

"Those early days in Paris," Marc said, "when you and Kraig made the rounds of the cafés with dear old Dietrich tagging along—didn't Kraig resent his presence?"

Embarrassed, she shrugged. "He didn't seem to."

"Not even when he ruined a summer night by discussing his Nazi political meetings?"

The memories were disturbing and Valli leaned back into the shadows.

"My apology for prying. I don't like this anymore than you," Marc said.

She explained, "You have to understand that Kraig felt indebted to his older brother. He worked and supported them both while Kraig finished ballet school."

"By boxing?"

"Yes. I dreaded his going with us, but Kraig felt he couldn't refuse him, that he owed him."

"Even when he could see how Dietrich's politics upset you?"

"What was he to do?" she asked defensively.

"I could think of half a dozen things," Marc stated laconically.

"Well Kraig didn't," she conceded tiredly. "He would simply listen."

"And it was you who debated Dietrich?" There was a smile in his voice.

"Not every time. Kraig didn't want me to argue. He was always concerned we'd upset him. But there were times when I couldn't stand his rhetoric, and it was then we would debate."

"How did Dietrich react to your statements against Hitler?"

"He became angry sometimes, other times he seemed to enjoy the mental duel." She realized what Marc was hinting at. "You're wrong. He wasn't falling for me. Did Davide tell you how Dietrich and I were disagreeing again when he walked in on us at the mission station?"

Marc smiled briefly. "He did suggest you weren't very excited by the prospect of his visit to Paris."

"Dietrich became angry when I criticized his precious Reichstag."

"So I heard, but as for discouraging him, I doubt it very much. He did come to Paris just as he said he would. Men like Dietrich are apt to overlook a woman's rejection of their politics when they have more basic interests in mind."

She sat quite still, her gaze meeting his.

Marc walked over to the lattice railing and was looking toward the house, lost in his thoughts. She arose, slipped on her shoe and walked over to stand beside him. It was beginning to rain and the drops patted the gazebo awning.

"What will it take to convince you I have no interest in Dietrich?"

"I admit I was suspicious at Bel-Abbes. But now I can't see the gracious ballerina Valli Chattaine wanting a man like Gestler."

Afraid he would read her secret thoughts, her gaze lowered. She was surprised at herself for the way she was thinking of Marc. If she wasn't careful...

Valli's mind turned to Kraig. She had been both startled and pleased by what she had learned about him tonight.

In the lantern's light the raindrops glistened like tears on the intertwining roses.

"Whatever you think of Dietrich, Kraig has at last made the right decision. He's working with the underground movement in Athens."

Marc turned to look at her. He frowned. "Dietrich told you this?"

"Yes, tonight. I had the impression he hadn't meant to let it out. He became angry with me and felt the need to defend an injury to his perceived honor. He felt it necessary to attack Kraig for what he was doing."

"Yes, I noticed he reeks with pride. Look, Valli, regardless of your convictions that he doesn't care about you, I'm inclined to think otherwise. I think he's always been a little jealous of Kraig. So perhaps his news about his brother isn't as simple as he tried to make it appear. However, that doesn't mean Kraig can be taken at face value either."

She realized Marc had little cause to trust Kraig and would find it easy to doubt his genuineness. At the moment she didn't know what to think.

"I'll admit I was shocked when I heard. Kraig has always been a pacifist. But the war changes people. They often become more sacrificial, more serious about the things in life that matter."

He leaned against the rail watching her. "Some do," was all he said.

She knew what he was thinking, that she still carried the torch for Kraig. There was a pause. She turned away from his intense gaze.

"I'll admit that the Surete is aware of what Kraig's been doing in Athens," he said. "I heard about him from them tonight when I called. But that doesn't mean they accept him as genuine."

So Marc already knew. If Dietrich hadn't explained, would Marc have kept it from her? Probably.

"Why not accept him as genuine?" she asked. "Because his brother is a Nazi?"

"No, that isn't the reason, Valli. We're a little more fair than that," he countered.

"Then why?" she asked pointedly, her eyes searching his.

His jaw set as though he thought she was doubting his motives more than Kraig's. "Kraig's been conducting a ballet theater in Athens. He was there when the Germans marched in. We have an eyewitness that says he met secretly with Dietrich."

Valli looked away, watching the rain drip gently on the roses.

"Unfortunately, no one else was present when they talked. So we don't know if their views clashed or not. Since that meeting, Kraig's been involved in anti-Nazi rallies in Athens. We could say that he has excellent reasons to turn against Germany, but it's also true that his new anti-Nazi rhetoric could be diversionary. Under Dietrich's orders, Kraig could be attempting to gain favor with the underground in order to infiltrate them for a future German invasion."

"And you think Kraig is helping Dietrich?"

"I know what you want me to say, that he isn't helping him, but I don't know that for sure."

Marc's reasoning was logical, but she resisted. "Dietrich had no reason to tell me about Kraig. He didn't approve. In fact, his true colors showed tonight when he insulted him, along with my sister. He's contemptuous of Kraig and I don't think he was putting on for my benefit. He was actually angry when I refused to attack Giselle."

"You have a point," Marc said. "I watched you both from across the room before I joined you, and I could see he was angry at times. You both were. So if we make you happy by giving Kraig the benefit of the doubt—"

"It's not a matter of making me happy," she murmured stiffly.

"The answer to the next question may explain why Dietrich knew about Kraig's new allegiance," Marc went on. "He may have read it in the missing letter. And if he did, then maybe you're right about Kraig. He has chosen sides in the conflict, and it looks as if he's finally made a wise decision."

Her breath caught. "Of course! The letter. Marc! You are brilliant."

His mouth curved. "I'm glad you think so."

"Dietrich could have stolen it. That would explain everything—well, almost."

"It could explain what Kraig meant in the note about both of you being in danger," he said soberly.

"Yes, and if Dietrich passes on what he found out about Kraig to the Nazis in Athens—" she stopped, her eyes searching his for confirmation. She could see he agreed. Kraig, even at this minute, could be in mortal danger.

"Yes," he said quietly. "If Dietrich betrays his own brother, and they locate him, it will mean his arrest. But that doesn't explain why Kraig included you in the danger. And that's what worries me." He looked off toward the house. "That letter might have explained."

"Then you think Dietrich stole it?" she whispered.

"No, not Dietrich," he said lazily. "Dietrich didn't enter your dressing room." He looked at her evenly. "Unless you're keeping that fact from me."

"Why would I do so?" she asked, nettled. "I've told you everything I know. Except there is one other thing—Dietrich dines alone with von Ribbentrop. He told me so."

Marc's brow lifted. "You've been busy. So he told you that, did he? My, he *is* trying to impress you."

"Let's not jump into that mess."

He laughed, but sobered quickly. "I don't think I'm going to enjoy having you in dangerous games with Dietrich."

She looked at him quizzically, but he didn't explain. "It wasn't Dietrich who stole the letter. Someone was sent there for that purpose who must have known a letter was coming and managed to get in to your room. Don't be offended by this, but how well do you trust Mimi?"

"With my life," she stated.

"Then we'll eliminate her. I admit she was genuinely upset tonight when she thought she'd misplaced it. Did you know the others who showed up?"

"There was someone I wondered about," she began uneasily, telling him about the man with the smiling face loitering on the fringe of the group near the table.

"He never spoke to me; he just smiled and kept in the background. I didn't think much of it and thought he was brought along by one of the journalists."

"And that was when you came into the hall to speak to me."

"Yes. And then you came inside to use the telephone. I spent several moments with Giselle, greeted the guests for perhaps ten minutes, then everyone drifted out. That was when Mimi came in with the roses and mentioned the letter from Kraig that came that morning."

"And I take it you never spoke to the smiling stranger?"

"No. I don't recall seeing him after that. He must have left when I brought you to the telephone. Marc, do you think he was a Nazi agent?"

"Maybe." He looked at her thoughtfully. "Giselle also left soon afterward, didn't she?"

"Yes. But surely you don't think she'd take it?" she said incredulously. "Why would she assist Dietrich?"

"If she did, the answer to that question could be very important. You did say she behaved tensely tonight."

"Yes," she said worriedly. "But after the way Dietrich spoke about her, I can't see them working together. He called her a Jezebel."

"The Nazis aren't known for generating warm feelings for those they manipulate," he said. "There's a possibility she's cooperating with Dietrich because he's given her no choice."

The word manipulate stirred an unpleasant memory. She was remembering something else Dietrich had said.

"He did allude to manipulation in some of the bizarre things he said tonight."

"Did he?"

"He also brought up Sebastien. He called his new position 'strategic.' And he said Giselle may find herself intimidated by her past."

"He said that? Those were his exact words?"

"Yes, and when I asked him why, he implied Giselle wouldn't like her shady past to jeopardize Sebastien's position. 'Scandal always has a way of coming unmasked,' was the way he put it."

"Blackmail, I wonder. I should have known where it was all leading when she came to my room last night and mentioned being followed. It could have been the man you saw tonight in your dressing room. Somehow it didn't register that Dietrich might use her past with Kraig to get to Sebastien."

The very thought was upsetting. She absently plucked a thorny rose which stuck her finger. She winced and looked down at her hand.

Marc reached over, removed the wet rose, and his warm hand closed over hers. "Get stuck?"

"A little," she murmured, aware of his vibrant touch. She looked at him, and for a moment their gaze held as Kraig receded from her mind like a fading sunset.

The rain tinkled pleasantly on the gazebo roof and dripped soothingly from the fringe into the rose bushes.

Valli felt herself being drawn like a magnet into the intense awareness that had been developing steadily between them ever since their meeting at the Bel-Abbes train junction. She removed herself from its force by dragging her eyes away and pulling her hand loose.

"She said she was being followed?" she reminded him. "Then what?"

"Maybe he made contact."

"You think Giselle may have been asked to bring Dietrich's friend to the dressing room tonight?"

"Either that, or Dietrich's friend got himself in and confronted her there at the table. She went off to meet someone, didn't she?"

"Yes, even Dietrich admitted she had another appointment. He saw her for a moment in the theater lobby."

"So he says. *He* may have been the appointment."

"But he arrived soon after I did."

"He didn't need long with her. Giselle could have passed him the letter in the lobby and went on her way. Where she went afterward is anyone's guess. But what troubles me most is Dietrich's power over her. Next time he may want her to get something far more important to the German cause than Kraig's letter."

Valli's mind ran riot, imaging all sorts of situations that not only endangered Giselle, but Sebastien, and even France.

"But she wouldn't go that far," she whispered.

Marc looked at her gravely. "Covering up one sin often leads to others. Like King David. He allowed one of his most loyal soldiers to be killed in battle to hide the shame of his adultery with Bathsheba. Unlike David, Giselle has no commitment to God. Who knows what she might do if pressured?"

Yes, who knew...Valli lapsed into troubled silence, preferring not to think about it.

He turned her toward the lantern light, and after scanning her expression, frowned. "We still have important issues to discuss and this isn't the time or place. You look exhausted. I think you've had enough of everything for one day, including the Surete. And that ankle needs to be rested. Why don't I take you home?"

"Yes...I think I'd like to go now."

"Giselle's car is parked just down the street. Where do you want to go, your flat or the estate?"

"My flat. I need to meet with my ballet director tomorrow." She glanced about at the shadows and vines. Although they had kept their voices low and had given the impression of having a romantic interlude, the darkness did offer opportunity for eavesdropping.

As he led her from the gazebo Valli appreciated having someone to shield her from the stormy blast, someone like Marc who didn't appear to want anything in return. Concern seemed to be part of his personality, as well as valor, and if she weren't careful she could easily find herself forgetting all the hard and bitter lessons learned over Kraig.

When they arrived at her flat, Marc insisted on seeing her safely to the front door, advising her to remind the landlady to have a new light bulb put in above the stairway. He took her key and unlocked the door for her. Mimi had left a small lamp burning on the table.

She loitered, looking at him. "Are you driving out to the estate tomorrow?"

He leaned in the doorway. "I've got to see Claude. If you like, I can drive back into Paris in the evening and pick you up."

"I wouldn't want to trouble you. I can hire a taxi to bring me there. I usually do."

"No trouble."

"If you're sure..."

"What about dinner after the ballet performance? Someplace quiet. We still need to talk about a lot of things."

"Yes...around eight?"

"All right."

As their eyes held, she wanted to break the spell, or did she?

He said with a brief smile: "Do you think that you'll ever be able to give me a chance?"

She looked at him, wondering what he meant.

"Kraig," he explained softly. "He's always in the shadows. His presence is annoying."

She was surprised he thought that. Was it true? She didn't think so. It wasn't the memory of Kraig that was bidding her to be cautious, but Marc himself, and the way he had affected her feelings so quickly.

"I've wanted to get serious with you from the moment I saw you in Tangier, when Davide planned to introduce us. It's been years since Kraig," he reminded her. "Are you going to let him control your future indefinitely?"

His frankness surprised and embarrassed her, and she had no answer yet. Could Marc have nurtured an interest in her all these years? The thought was flattering. She didn't love Kraig anymore, she told herself, but neither did she have the courage to allow herself to fall in love again, even if Marc was the one man who had proved he could rekindle the fires she had imagined were forever dead.

She felt she owed him an honest response. "There was a reason why I stayed away from you in Tangier and when you attended War College. Your father was a legionnaire, with quite a reputation with the ladies, and after I saw you with Giselle I thought you were just the same. I can see I was wrong. I was sincere when I said tonight that I wished I'd answered your letters. But back then, well, I thought you were a rogue."

"A rogue...because you walked up on the lawn and found Giselle kissing me?"

"Yes, something like that." The memory still troubled her, even though Davide had nothing but praise for Marc. "I was wrong. It was Kraig who proved false."

"You blamed me for something I didn't instigate. I was behaving myself, knowing you were there. I'd already been cautioned by Davide to display my most gallant conduct. I was half asleep when Giselle came up. The next thing I knew, your older sister—well, you know the rest."

"Yes," she said wryly. "It does sound more like Giselle's tactics. After all these years we should bury the past and be friends."

"Friends is a good place to begin. There's still Kraig between us—until I can make you forget him and we're 'alone' at last, I suppose that's as much as I can hope for. But before I venture on the slippery slopes of emotional involvement, I'd like to know how hard and how far I'm apt to fall if he shows back up in your life."

If Marc was cautious of slippery slopes, then what of her? After all, she had been the one who took the long fall to the bottom. She imagined that falling in love with Marc could be just as down-spiraling.

His question was closing in upon her. At the same time she knew she didn't want to discourage his interest in her. She must delay, she needed time to think.

"It's getting late," she whispered, but Valli looked at him tenderly to let him know she was on the threshold of emotional involvement with him. "I'm afraid our voices might awaken Mimi."

"I have a notion a stuka bomber wouldn't awaken her, but your point is well taken. Good night, chere demoiselle." He stepped back, then appeared to remember something. "I nearly forgot. I have something for you." He reached inside his jacket and handed her an envelope. "Sebastien asked me to deliver this. It's from Calanthe."

"Calanthe?" she repeated, shocked, looking at the older woman's shaky handwriting. For a moment she held it as though Marc had delivered a Christmas present.

"I thought it best to give it to you when you could read it alone, in the privacy of your flat," he said, as if he understood the possible emotional impact. "She wants you to come back to Tangier. That makes two of us, but for different reasons. You'll need to make up your mind soon, Valli. Even now, escape by sea or land poses risks." His eyes held hers. "It won't be long before all routes out of Paris will be closed."

She looked back at Calanthe's letter and felt an agonizing pull in two separate directions. "I can't leave Paris now, Marc. Not—not after tonight."

"Before all this is over," he articulated in a low voice, "you may need to, regardless. Unless you want Nazis filling the audience of the Opera Ballet Theater. It isn't going to be a pleasant place to be for the duration of this war. Stay, and you may end up performing ballet for Goering, as well as Dietrich."

The thought turned her cold. "I'd die first."

"That may not be far from the truth." He took hold of her, lifting her chin, his eyes caressing her face. "But I intend to see that doesn't happen. I have selfish reasons of my own. I've already waited years while Kraig Gestler stood between us. I may be a patient man, but I'm not unwise enough to leave you here for Dietrich. Remember, once Paris is in German hands, *they* will become the law. That will make it instantly easier for Dietrich to get what he wants."

Valli was drawn between opposing emotions. She needed to stay in Paris to perform at the theater, but Marc's interest was exciting, and Dietrich and the German army taking Paris left her frightened. "They won't take Paris," she insisted. "The Maginot Line on our border with Germany will hold just as it did in the Great War. There are miles and miles of underground bunkers, machine guns, artillery and—" she stopped, seeing the look in his eyes.

"Yes, I know," he said. "And brave French soldiers. But I'll simply ask you what I wish our generals of genius would ask themselves: What if the Germans come through the Belgium border?"

She stared at him. "But that's impossible. Belgium is our friend, a fighting ally."

"Ma chere, even a determined ally is not likely to hold off thousands of panzer divisions and stuka bombers. Can Belgium hold out? Today, Germany invaded Denmark and Norway. Next, Belgium. If Belgium falls, thousands of French and British troops will have to retreat to the vulnerable beaches of Dunkirk!"

Valli had no answer, and envisioning division after division of armored tanks invading France sent her heart into a sickening dive.

Marc was watching her, and her expression brought a slight frown. "Still determined to stay?"

"I—don't know. I need to dance tomorrow, and there's always a possibility you are wrong..."

"I'm not wrong about this." Valli was already standing close to him, with his hand on her arm, and it took only a moment to find herself drawn into his embrace, his lips warm on hers. Aware of little else, and hearing her heart thumping in her ears, her world was in flux. It was several moments more before he released her, and Valli drew away, breathless. For a time they stood looking at each other.

"I'm sorry," he said too gravely. "I took advantage of the moment."

In looking at him, Valli didn't think he was sorry at all; he seemed pleased her emotions had melted in his arms.

"Good night," he said with a smile. "Now, let me hear you lock your door."

Valli lifted her chin with dignity and turned her back, going inside. She closed the door gently, and locked it, noting that her fingers trembled. She heard him turn and go down the stairs.

# 13

Jacquette had not been heard from since last night. Marc had left him out front at the Paris Opera Ballet Theater with orders to watch Dietrich, but a call to Danjou at the Surete informed him that Jacquette was still unaccounted for.

Marc had arisen early and rang down to the hotel office for coffee. To get his mind off Jacquette he turned on the radio while showering and dressing to keep track of the war bulletins.

Denmark had surrendered to the brute force of the German army and was now under Nazi control. Norway fought on, her soldiers taking to the ski slopes where they outsmarted the Germans at every turn. German paratroopers were reported to have landed in the mountains.

Meanwhile, the Parisians were complaining about ration cards issued back in February, while certain pacifists in Reynaud's government complained equally about the agreement signed between France and Britain prohibiting either country from making a separate peace with Berlin.

"Monsieur Aubert Ransier has suggested the agreement favors Britain and is a noose around the neck of France."

Marc caught his own reflection in the mirror. He was scowling as he slipped into his blue jacket. He switched off the radio, glanced at his watch, then at the telephone. He had reported in to the Surete late last night on a public telephone, but he'd better talk to Danjou again about Jacquette and Aubert. It was a nuisance to have to stop on the way to use a phone, but he'd wager that Dietrich had this one tapped by now. And by now, the Gestapo would have contacted agents in and out of Paris to find out everything they could about his past and present. His record at Saint Cyr was an open book, and so was his service to General Nouges of the Foreign Legion, although the work he'd done was not. Dietrich would know of course that he was related to Sebastien, but there was no easily attainable record of his working with him in the Surete. If Dietrich discovered anything it would be his record at Sidi-bel-Abbes, but it too revealed nothing of his true work and emphasized his gallantry as a legionnaire in infantry. Still, Marc was quite sure that by now Dietrich had a sharp, curious eye on him. And after his meeting last night with Aubert, both men must be curious about what he would say to Claude.

Marc left his hotel by 8:30 A.M. and drove Giselle's Renault down the bustling Rue Royale through the heart of Paris toward the lush pasturelands and vineyards making up the countryside where the Ransier estate was built.

When he arrived an hour later, the estate looked as impressive as he remembered it from his last visit when he was a student in Saint Cyr, France's West Point.

It was an immense, triple-story house of classic eighteenth century style, sitting back among hawthorn and chestnut trees, its many windows catching the mid-morning sunlight.

Memories of his boyhood came rushing to meet him on the wind, stirring to life the day above all others that brought the depths of grief. He had been nine years old. His mother Josephine's funeral had taken place in a cold cathedral where his boyish footsteps had echoed on the stone, where candles had not penetrated the gloom, and where the religious ceremony in Latin had not chased away his sorrow.

Afterward, Marc had climbed these same stairs when he'd been called to his great-uncle's suite of rooms. Marc had entered that imposing bedroom with Louis XIV furnishings and heavy brocade drapery to find Claude pacing in a maroon smoking jacket. Off to one side, standing near the large bed had stood his only child, his son Aubert. Aubert had come home from Berlin, where he had been studying music by the great German composers, and he had brought with him his new bride, Inga, a violinist.

Claude had welcomed the boy Marc into his room, then sat down in a tall, wingbacked chair, looking morose and emotionally defensive.

"Now that your mother is dead," he had remarked, "the family and I have come to the sober conclusion that your destiny is bound up in French Algeria. As Aubert has reminded me—" and he gestured toward his son, "it was against my wishes for Josephine to have ever married Louis Durell. It was out of kindness that I took her back into this house when she returned without him. Kindness, because she was without money and carrying you in her arms, a child of just two years. Your father, as I have told you before, was a sergeant under my command at Verdun in the Great War." His eyes took on a reminiscent glow. "We both served under the great soldier, Petain. So, my boy, out of respect for Louis' bravery at the time, and your boyhood enchantment with a father you have never seen, I will say no more about him." He frowned and cleared his throat. "Are you listening to me?"

"Oh yes, Great-Uncle Claude."

Claude had smiled. "I have enjoyed having you here at the estate—er, to play chess and checkers with me." He glanced at Aubert. Aubert, a passionless-looking young man with a shock of light chestnut hair falling across his pale forehead, and blue eyes, wore an appropriately gloomy expression as he gazed down at Marc, hands behind his back. "Yes," he echoed, "yes." However, Marc knew that his cousin was pleased to see him being sent away. Aubert had then looked at his heavy gold pocket watch that caught the light and glimmered.

"Sebastien is due in an hour, Father."

"I don't need any prodding, Aubert."

"Of course not, Father dear."

Claude had resettled his lanky frame back into the chair and proceeded to fix Marc with a look of regret. "I told you many times why your father is not here in France." He cleared his throat again. "I used my influence to help him er—'leave' Paris before the gendarme apprehended him for—untoward behavior—"

A sound, something like a snicker, came from Cousin Aubert.

"Not that I ever believed Louis was guilty of scurrilous behavior, you understand," continued Claude. "However, he could never visit France again, and your mother could never go to him, and so! Time rushed on. Louis kept his word that he would never return, although his absence caused your mother grief. Now, however, with Josephine's untimely death, the family has decided your future rests with Louis, a mercenary soldier in the Foreign Legion. While, out of affection for your mother, I am willing to see that you do acquire a military education at Saint Cyr, I cannot, because of my own son—" and he gestured to Cousin Aubert—"grant you any sizable inheritance in the Ransier fortune."

At nine years of age, the last thing Marc had been concerned about was a family fortune, but the idea of being sent to live with his father sent excitement surging through his heart.

"Yes, Great-Uncle Claude."

"And so." He sighed. "Your father will take over your future."

Marc had been careful to hold back his enthusiasm, his hands interlaced behind him. Inside he laughed. *At last! At last! I'm going to be with my father! A great soldier.*

He did not regret leaving France at all. He wanted to be with Louis more than anything that the Ransiers could offer him. Contemplations of a far away place of mystery called Sidi-bel-Abbes sent his boyish imagination soaring. He would become a great soldier too; for he did not believe his father could be anything less than a man of infinite valor, a hero fighting for the glory of France!

"I am sorry, Marc, if this causes you unhappiness. Naturally, you may come back each year and visit us."

"Yes, Monsieur Claude," he said politely, as taught. He feared if he showed too much pleasure over meeting his notorious father in the blowing sands of the Sahara that the family might reconsider. He could see that leaving the estate was expected to be a somber ordeal.

In the years he had lived here, isolated emotionally from everyone except his mother and Claude, he had little time to develop warm feelings for Aubert, who had spent most of his formative years in school in Germany. Now and then Marc would be allowed to play checkers with Claude, and when that happened, Henri had brought up large mugs of hot chocolate and sweet biscuits dipped in a very rich Belgium chocolate. But Aubert had remained a dull stranger pining over his practice with a violin.

Marc said regretfully: "I am sorry too, my Uncle, that I have not pleased you."

"Now, now, it is not that you have not pleased me, it is only—"

Aubert leaned toward his father and said with a soft voice, "Father, you need not trouble your health with long explanations."

"My health is fine. I shall be returning to the government soon to carry on my duties."

"Marc just doesn't understand the reasons for sending him to his father. Why try to explain?"

*Oh yes I do, Aubert,* thought Marc. *It's you who doesn't want me here, not Claude. Because you are jealous that your father enjoys my company. But that's well enough with me.*

Cousin Aubert handed Claude a letter. "From Sebastien. I spoke to him of Josephine's boy after the funeral. He has volunteered his assistance in the matter of taking him to Algeria."

Monsieur Claude did not look surprised as he took the letter and the pair of spectacles Aubert handed him. "Yes, I was expecting this."

"Josephine's boy." Aubert had always called him that.

Of the younger Ransier men, Marc liked Sebastien the best because he was a military officer in North Africa and knew his father.

"Very well, then. It looks as if everything is arranged," Claude had said a moment later, folding the message. "Fortune has it that Sebastien will be leaving in a month for Tangier. He'll bring you on the voyage with him. Once there, he will make arrangements to turn you over to your father in Algeria."

"Yes, Great-Uncle Claude," Marc said, anxious to leave. "Shall I go pack now?"

Claude scowled, and Marc heard him and Aubert whispering. "I'd swear the little rogue looks pleased about this!"

Aubert smiled grimly. "He takes after his father. What do we expect but his pleasure over getting away from genteel civility and restraints?"

"Yes, yes, but it isn't decent. The handsome little imp looks like a canary that's found the cage door open! He does not know what he is in for. The Foreign Legion! A company of scoundrels! I have half a mind to change my plans and keep him here."

"A mistake, Father. He has the troublesome, adventurous ways of Louis. When he does enter Saint Cyr, he's likely to be dismissed. He'll cause us all less problems in the future if we deal with the matter now. Let him go with Sebastien."

Claude sighed. "Still, the boy is Josephine's son. And he has a good wit. He beat me at checkers last week."

Marc pretended he hadn't heard and stood looking from Aubert to Great-Uncle Claude.

"Very well," Claude addressed Marc. "Yes, you may pack."

Marc had bowed his dark head sadly and felt the stiff white ruffle scratching his chin. He doubted his father wore ruffles. Photographs of French soldiers fighting the Germans at Verdun did not show frilly shirts. Marc wanted to be like one of those soldiers who never cried, even though old Henri had told him otherwise. They wept when no one was there to see, he had told Marc. Then, Marc would make certain no one ever saw him cry, the way he had heard his mother's soft weeping late in the night when she thought no one heard her in the room next to his own. He had vowed he would grow up to make her happy, to make her laugh and sing, but that vow, like the flowers on her grave, must yield to the laws that governed mere mortals.

"Au revoir, Great-Uncle Claude." He had turned toward Aubert and bowed again as taught. "Au revoir, Great-Cousin Aubert." And he had thought, *I like you least of all.* He backed from the imposing bedroom and out the door that old Henri held open for him. Once in the hall, with the door shut behind them, Henri had laid a hand on his shoulder and said, "Well, now you have your wish, young Marc. You will be Louis Durell's son."

Yes...he had been his father's son.

And now, in the spring of 1940, sixteen years later, Marc was back, prepared to reopen the door into Claude's imposing bedroom at his special request.

Marc left the car parked in the drive and walked in the sweet springtime air to a wide sweep of stairs and up toward a solid double door. The door opened before he rang the chimes and the old butler, Henri, smiled, and stepped back with a small bow.

"Bonjour, Monsieur Marc. Monsieur Claude is waiting for you now, in his suite."

"Merci. Is Madame Giselle Ransier here?"

"No, monsieur. She drove into Paris yesterday to attend her sister's ballet and Ambassador Hartley's reception, but she has not yet returned."

Marc knew she had missed the reception. The news that she hadn't returned to the estate was troubling, and he thought of Jacquette. Both had last been seen outside the ballet theater.

"What about Monsieur Aubert?"

"He is in Paris in a meeting with Prime Minister Reynaud."

That accounted for Aubert's terse statement earlier that morning opposing the agreement with Britain. Marc glanced up the stairway. "Is Madame Inga feeling stronger this morning?"

Henri lifted two skimpy gray brows showing his surprise. "Oui, Monsieur Marc, she is well. She is out riding this morning."

Marc showed no surprise. "She is not ill?"

"Oh no, monsieur."

Interesting. "No need to show me up, Henri."

"Very well, monsieur."

Marc walked across the wide, glossy floor where shadows clung to the spacious corners of the hall and the towering ceiling. A double staircase gleamed and its burgundy carpet silenced his footsteps as he went up. Monet paintings looked down with isolated splendor. He tapped on the thick door.

"Come in!"

Marc smiled and opened the door.

His Great-Uncle Claude Ransier was sitting in his wing-backed chair before a table spread with his favorite chess pieces. His hair was whiter, but still thick and well groomed, and his deep-set blue eyes were a little more sunken, but the gaze was observant beneath dignified brows. He pushed himself up with his heavy walking stick and beckoned him to the table.

"Hello, Marc. Wonderful to see you. Wonderful. Close that door—and bolt it. Then come, sit down. No need to ask whether or not Sebastien gave you my message."

Marc did so and pulled out a chair opposite the chessboard. "Sebastien thought it might be important so I came at once. You're looking well, Uncle. I expected to see you in bed."

"Bah. I wouldn't give that traitorous son of mine the satisfaction. He and Inga think I don't know what's happening behind my back, but I'm well aware. I'm aware too of the tragedy facing France by these weak-kneed, softheaded pacifists. They ignore the BBC." He gestured toward a large radio and another shortwave set. "Bless the British."

So he disapproved of Aubert's politics. Marc said to draw him out, "Traitorous? Dear Cousin Aubert? That's a severe indictment, Uncle Claude."

Claude gave him a level look from under his brows as if he wondered if he were serious. He waved a hand of dismissal. "Come, come, let's have no masquerading before me, young man. I know as well as you that you and Aubert never got along. The blame lies with Aubert and me as an uncle."

"Now I wouldn't say that. You arranged through Sebastien to send me to Saint Cyr. I'm indebted to you for that."

"Things could have been better between us, I know that as well. About Aubert, he is a *mous*," he explained, disappointment written on his face. "A traitor to all that France stands for."

A *mous* was a dove. Marc waited to respond, believing he would receive more explanation if he didn't push for it. For Claude to label his own son as traitorous was surprising. Even so, he was credible. Sebastien would not have taken his request seriously if Claude hadn't been a loyalist toward France. Marc had known little of Aubert's politics until recently. He had assumed Aubert was as much of a hawk and loyalist to his government as Claude had been in the years he had served Prime Minister Daladier before Reynaud had taken over.

His great-uncle saw his caution and shook his head. "You're a gentlemen I see. You wouldn't have labeled Aubert for what he is if I hadn't unmasked him first. Well, don't squirm. It's a fact. It hurts me to say this of my own son, but it is so."

"Evidently you think Reynaud will soon appoint Petain second in command."

"The pacifists in his government give him little choice. Aubert would force Reynaud to resign, if he could, allowing Petain full power. The first thing Petain will do if placed at the head of the government is set up a meeting with Hitler and negotiate an armistice," Claude said with disgust. "And sadly, a large percentage of the French people support this treachery. Oh yes, I know they speak of 'peace with honor,' but Hitler does not know honor. He knows only collaborators." He lowered his voice. "And Aubert is not only a mouthpiece for this defeatism in the name of peace. He would overthrow Reynaud by force if he could."

Petain, who was now ambassador to Spain, was considered a national war hero who had served with distinction in the Great War at Verdun. Although in his eighties, he was extremely popular with the French people. While they thought Reynaud a hawk and a supporter of England's Churchill, they believed Petain could bring about peace with Germany.

"Defeat runs like a hidden reef throughout France, on which the ship of state will run aground," Claude complained.

National pride and honor may have gone out of style, Marc thought gravely, but if so, some of the reasons led back to the bloody battle of Verdun in the Great War. The last war had crushed something inside the French soldier that had not yet healed.

"Yes Uncle, Petain has been inclined toward caution even since 1917, and he is sensitive to useless human suffering. He must gaze out on Hitler's war machine and wonder if France will again be left with nothing but a great sacrifice of French soldiers in a vain attempt to halt the Panzer divisions," Marc said thoughtfully.

Claude looked at him crossly. "Is that your view as well? You mean I've called you here to listen to more syrupy prose poured on Petain? Bah! I thought you at least would have a backbone. Peace at any price!" His shaking hand went to sweep the chess pieces off the board, but Marc quickly caught his wrist, his gaze even.

"It is not how I feel, Uncle. I thought you knew me better. When a nation yields to evil, whatever the reason, there can be no true peace. There is only compromise and shame. My observation of General Petain was just that, an observation."

Claude looked at him for a long moment, then satisfied, he smiled cryptically. "Well, you had me frightened there for a moment. I thought you had spoken your own heart. It is refreshing to know he has not galvanized the thinking of all true Frenchmen. There must be a soldier left in the Ransier family after all."

"There are many who feel as we do," said Marc. "Prime Minister Reynaud himself is committed to fighting with

England as an ally. 'The stake in this "total" war is total. To conquer is to save everything. To succumb is to lose everything.' Those are the words of Reynaud."

"Yes, and thank God there are yet strong voices in France, and men like de Gaulle who will fight, who will lead the resistance," Claude said. "Yet the majority..." he shook his head. "They are not angry enough over the evil of Germany. Instead, they are afraid to oppose it."

Marc looked at his great-uncle. "Did Aubert tell you he was working toward armistice?"

"No. He knows how I feel about it. I overheard him discussing the matter with members of a political group that meets downstairs once a week."

Marc looked at him. "Aubert heads a political group?"

"That, young man, is one of the reasons I wanted to see you." He looked toward the bolted door. All was quiet.

"They don't think I'm paying attention to the late night gatherings going on in my own house," he said resentfully. "They expect an old man in his dotage to be fast asleep when the Nazi collaborators arrive in their motorcars and stay until after midnight."

"Are you telling me Aubert is a Nazi?"

"Naturally he doesn't call himself that. In his own mind he is a good Frenchman doing what is best for France. So do the others. Perhaps a dozen in all, they call themselves 'Friends for Peace.' 'Compromisers' for shame and failure is what I call them. Collaborators! You can use any label you want, it comes out the same. They're pro-Nazi, and Aubert is likely to be in touch with von Ribbentrop himself." His eyes gleamed with internal rage. "*My son.* Those early years in Berlin in the 1930s did more to change Aubert than merely turn him into a violinist. I learned he attended Nazi rallies while there. It was at one of the Hitler Youth meetings that he met Inga, a true Nazi loyalist."

The angry tears in Claude's eyes convinced Marc he was sharing information that had earlier broken his heart.

"He and the others are willing to sell France to German control to spare us war. Isn't that generous of them? Appeasement is to be embraced rather than sending our young French lads off to spill their blood. They are doing us a 'kindness.' They would rather see a nation of subservients fawning at the fuhrer's boots!"

"I'm afraid life isn't that simple," Marc said flatly. "Sometimes a nation has no choice. Either we fight, or we bow before an evil master and carry out his orders. What will France do when Adolf Eichmann demands we give up French Jews?"

Claude said in a hushed voice, "Do not say such a thing."

"It's happened in Poland, Czechoslovakia, Austria— why not France?"

"Because we are civilized people."

"But civilized people do not surrender to Hitler because it is easier than fighting him."

Claude frowned at the chess pieces on the giant board.

"If we welcome darkness into our government," Marc said, "then we cannot expect a nation based on righteous principles, but a haven for demons. It's our choice. To do nothing is to accept our future as fate. Our destiny is not inevitable. God will raise up those to lead the fight if we turn to Him in humility while there is time."

Claude shook his head wearily. "Yes, Marc, if it is not already too late. Even my own son is cooperating with Berlin." Claude trembled with emotion. "His beliefs speak louder than his denials. He and Inga are both collaborators.

They have pro-German contacts in Spain as well, where Monsieur Petain is now ambassador."

Spain...Marc's thoughts traveled to Kraig Gestler. Was he really in the underground?

"Have you confronted Aubert about his beliefs?"

"I wanted to talk to you and Sebastien first."

"A wise decision. We don't want them to think they're being watched. We need to know who the contact is for von Ribbentrop."

Claude's face turned a sickish pallor. He looked toward the door again and spoke in a hushed voice. "You won't need to go far to find him."

Marc turned and looked at him sharply.

Claude lifted an ivory pawn and stared at it. "What if I told you the Gestler family in Berlin is related to us by marriage?"

Silence descended like a curtain. Marc stared at him.

"Yes," Claude murmured, "I know what you're thinking. I was shocked too when I found out. I overheard Inga on the telephone with her nephew." His gaze swerved to Marc's. "Gestapo agent Dietrich Gestler."

The news refused to sink in. Marc thought back to Aubert's bride brought home one summer from Berlin. "Inga Gestler? You're certain, Uncle Claude?"

"Yes. A little unnerving isn't it? I found out only recently. I'd been under the impression her maiden name was Schroeder. Then you do remember Aubert's marriage?"

"I remember that Aubert studied music at one of the great schools in Germany. He came home with a bride, but I never knew her last name."

Now he thought he understood what Captain Zimmer meant that night near Oran when he spoke of a family member who had come to Paris after the Great War to find work. "Did Inga have a sister?"

"Yes, her older sister is Dietrich and Kraig's mother. She died when they were children. Until her death, she worked as a maid here in Paris. I had Henri check the old house-keeping records. Inga hired a German maid when you were a boy. She was here for about two years. Do you remember her?"

"No, nor do I remember seeing Dietrich and Kraig Gestler about the estate."

"They were here, but at the woman's bungalow about a twenty-minute walk away."

As Marc considered all that Claude told him, he worried most about Aubert's contact man with von Ribbentrop. He examined the black bishop chess piece. Who else could it be but Dietrich? Marc recalled what Valli had told him last night. Dietrich had boasted about having private meetings with von Ribbentrop. It made sense now why Dietrich would risk coming to Paris. He had several excuses of course, including a romantic interest in Valli or Giselle. But now, there was even more reason. Inga Gestler Ransier was his blood aunt. And what better agent could the Nazis have in Paris than his Uncle Aubert, a member of Prime Minister Reynaud's government? Especially when Aubert wanted France to have an armistice with Hitler?

Marc looked up at Claude. "What do we know about von Ribbentrop, Uncle?"

Claude took the chess piece from Marc's hand and scowled at it. "He's typical of the rest of Hitler's cabinet. A thug at heart. Hitler sent him to the London foreign office and to Paris to negotiate new terms allowing Germany to rearm after the Great War. It was said later that von Ribbentrop hadn't negotiated at all, but arrogantly laid down ultimatums. To the shame of both Paris and London, they capitulated. Even von Ribbentrop was surprised at his success." He frowned.

"Dietrich is now in Paris," Marc said. "I saw him last night at the ballet."

"Is he?" Claude stood, using his cane, his face flushed with anger. "The effrontery of Aubert bringing a member of the Gestapo into my house—"

"Uncle, stay calm. We don't want him to suspect we know he's an SS officer. We play his visit his way. We let him carry out his plan to visit dear Aunt Inga and Uncle Aubert before this *tragic* war separates close family members."

Great-Uncle Claude's mouth twisted into a grim smile. Marc recalled how Sebastien had told him at Bel-Abbes how he could trust Claude, that he had friends in the Surete. Marc said quietly, "The Surete would like to know what it is Dietrich expects to learn while here. We may also uncover names of other collaborators that will help us in the future should France succumb to the Germans."

"Yes, I know the way it works," he said unhappily, sitting back down with a groan. "That's why I contacted Sebastien. Nevertheless, I don't appreciate a Nazi walking about my house."

Neither did Marc, and it was all he could do to be civil to Dietrich. "We need to remind ourselves that before this war is over, German soldiers may be as thick as termites in Paris and billeted on this estate."

Claude looked disgusted. "Swallow our national pride and play the subservient race," he said bitterly. "And to think Dietrich is getting information from my own son and daughter-in-law."

"What better masquerade than to come to visit 'family' as a civilian? However, two can play at that game. He doesn't suspect me either—yet. But there's more that troubles me about Dietrich than his visit here with Inga and Aubert. I've reasons to suspect he's watching Sebastien."

Claude looked worried rather than angry. "Sebastien? But he's in Tangier."

"But Giselle is here," Marc said quietly, meeting his gaze evenly.

"You think Dietrich has discovered he is in the Surete?"

"The SS has very nefarious means to discover such things," Marc said grimly. "If he does know, he may suspect some form of information is to be passed from Paris to Sebastien to the French military in North Africa."

Claude rubbed his chin thoughtfully. "Um...this changes things. If Aubert is aware of some ruling about to come from Reynaud..." his reason drifted.

"Or de Gaulle," offered Marc, "in agreement with London, for example."

"Yes, yes...I see what you mean. But what would Giselle have to do with that? Pardon my saying so, but I've often felt she was rather a flirt, and rather dim at that. I wondered what Sebastien saw in her."

Marc evaded the issue. "Tell me, Uncle, does Aubert have any idea what either Sebastien or I do?"

Claude shook his head, frowning. "He's never brought it up, and I've made certain I've kept your roles as illusive as the shifting Sahara sands. He seems to accept both of your military careers at face value, although he does know about Sebastien receiving the embassage at Tangier. He was against Sebastien serving in Reynaud's cabinet all along, even though de Gaulle recommended Sebastien."

"That may have been strictly based on rivalry."

"Yes, Aubert has always been a jealous one," Claude agreed sadly. "Too bad I listened to him when you were a boy and sent you to Algeria."

Marc appreciated the comment, but didn't pursue it. "Giselle didn't come back last night from Paris. Do you know if she has close friends there?"

"She's told me very little about herself since she arrived. Why do you ask? What does Sebastien's wife have to do with Dietrich?"

"Perhaps nothing, but the Nazis are never content to go after their primary victims, Uncle. I know how they work: terror and intimidation, riots and assassination. They like to start with the children and wives of an agent, just to soften him up a little. If Dietrich wants something from Sebastien, then he will first circle Giselle as his prey, looking for weakness. When he has found it, he'll move in for the kill."

"Not a pretty picture," Claude said soberly.

"No. Not pretty at all. But then, I've never thought we should try to make evil look like anything except what it is."

Claude looked old and tired. "I've come to the latter years of my life only to learn that everything I planned for Aubert has been squandered on a godless, evolutionary philosophy. I sent him to Berlin to study music, and he comes back a Nazi! Any son of mine who will collaborate with the enemy is no longer worthy of being a son." He had leaned forward, his face flushed with temper, and began a coughing spell. Marc went to him, easing him back into the chair, and handed him a small bottle of syrupy medicine that was nearby. Claude took a sip and his coughing slowly eased.

"You must stay calm, Uncle. We need you."

"Need me? That's the first time I've heard anyone in this family ever say they needed me. They need my house, my money, and my power in Paris politics. Ah yes, they can appreciate all of that. Aubert and Inga both...can't wait until my heart stops so they can inherit everything—but I've out-smarted 'em. I've changed my will. No, no, I won't hear any protests from either you or Sebastien. I've made up my mind and carried it through to completion before anyone even guessed what I was doing. Now, no matter what happens, my wishes will be carried out one day. Even if Germany occupies France—one day, everything will go equally to you and Sebastien."

"It isn't right I take anything from your firstborn son. Sebastien won't hear of it, either."

Claude laughed. "Well, you'd both better get used to the idea. It's done. And there's land elsewhere too, outside of France. But say nothing of all this to Aubert. Now, never mind that—it's Dietrich I'm worried about. I'm a sick, old man. I can't do much on my own to foil Dietrich. You'll have opportunity now, since you're here. It makes for an interesting gathering."

*Yes, one big happy family,* Marc thought grimly.

He needed to let Danjou know about all this. What it might mean was uncertain. Did it have anything to do with Blystone's death?

Marc laid a hand on his arm and squeezed it gently. "You'd best get some rest, Uncle. I have a meeting this afternoon with our friends at the Surete."

# 14

As Marc came down the stairs, he was thinking of Valli and his dinner date with her later that night. He wanted her out of Paris as soon as possible, but how could he convince her? If he drove back now, he would have time before dinner to arrange a brief meeting with Danjou and report his latest findings.

Marc stopped, hearing voices out in front of the house. The crisp tone of the man's voice convinced him it was Dietrich. Was the woman Giselle? He almost wished it was. At least he'd know she was alive. Before Marc had time to retreat, the door was flung open and Inga charged inside with Dietrich following. Inga, an attractive blond woman in her early forties, was in riding clothes, and she snapped her small whip across her gloved palm for emphasis to her words as she hissed at Dietrich: "I do not care what the orders may be in Athens. If anything happens to Kraig I'll go straight over your head to Himmler."

Himmler, the anemic little man with rimless glasses and a mustache, who might appear as a school master or bank clerk, was actually the ruthless head of the notorious SS. Marc, who had just overheard the critical information, would have given anything to be able to immediately vanish. Neither Inga nor Dietrich noticed him at first. Though the Renault was parked in the drive, they must have thought that Giselle had returned. Then Inga stopped dead in her tracks when she saw Marc on the stairway. What to do now? Marc wondered. Her eyes widened. Dietrich stopped in the doorway, looking up at him.

If he was going to bluff, he might as well go for it. He pretended as though he hadn't heard. Marc tossed them a disarming smile and came down.

"Ah, ma chere Inga, how wonderful to see you again!" He grabbed her, kissed both flushed cheeks, and looked down into her bewildered face with a laugh. "And Cousin Aubert told me you were ill. I didn't know the dour old fellow had developed a sense of humor at last. You look magnifique! Young enough to be his daughter." He turned to Dietrich. "Well hello there, Dietrich, I've just heard the astonishing news that we're cousins."

He hoped his absurd behavior unsettled them enough to think he had indeed not heard Inga's ugly slip of the tongue about Himmler. His announcement also appeared to give them just the pretext they needed to account for their shock. Inga looked as if she'd suddenly developed seasickness, and Dietrich struggled to steady himself.

"Cousins," Marc repeated, turning the screw tighter by emphasizing the word. "Who would have ever guessed?"

Dietrich, more experienced at deceit than Inga, recovered quickly. His guarded smile reflected cynicism.

"No one, unless they had been told. Who told you, Cousin Marc?"

"Ah, a good question. I see our little secret was not yet to have been released to the press. Sorry, Inga," he said easily. "However, it's safe enough with me. I was pleased enough to hear it. Maybe you'd better sit down...I hope I haven't upset you. Grab that chair, Cousin Dietrich."

Dietrich firmly shut the front door and stood staring at him, unsmiling. Marc drew up the hall chair, but Inga refused to sit. Marc knew he'd better shock them even more.

"To answer your question, Dietrich, your German cousin, Captain Zimmer, trusted me enough to tell me the news in Bel-Abbes."

That Marc knew Zimmer and would dare mention him brought a sharp, interested glance from Dietrich.

The lines around Inga's mouth tightened. "Zimmer told you that? I'm surprised he would."

Dietrich changed almost at once. He was now watching Marc with alert, nervous interest. Marc's open manner had him guessing what he was trying to accomplish. One thing was clear, they had momentarily forgotten that Inga had said she could contact the head of the Nazi SS.

"Marc has to know sometime, and it is late in coming, isn't it?" Dietrich said. "All the little skeletons must come out of the closet, as the British like to say."

"Then again," said Marc, lowering his voice and turning earnest, "why should our German cousins be hidden away in closets and treated so disrespectfully? That there is good German blood in the family will one day be a cause for pride. Perhaps sooner than anyone thinks."

Dietrich's hard blue eyes were genuinely puzzled now as they flicked over him.

Inga stepped in boldly. "France and Germany are at war. Naturally, there are those French who resent our ties to Berlin."

"It is too late to turn back," Marc said, "they'll soon change their minds. Many others now celebrate the union."

Clearly they didn't know what to make of him. Dietrich said bluntly: "And which type of French soldier are you, Cousin?"

Marc looked at him as if faintly surprised by the question, as if Dietrich was supposed to know. Marc answered casually: "Half of my legionnaire friends in Algeria are Germans. And it is no secret the legion prefers Aryans in positions of leadership, officers of superior astuteness—men who can fight, who can lead the rank and file recruits from lesser nations. I thought Cousin Zimmer would have made that clear to you."

Dietrich only became more unsettled. Throwing in Zimmer's name again took him off guard. Dietrich knew what he had wanted Zimmer to accomplish as a spy in the legion at Oran, and Marc could see that he wasn't sure just how much Zimmer had told him. Marc sensed he was gaining and continued.

"Captain Zimmer and I served together in the Sahara."

Dietrich hesitated, as though uncertain as to which way to proceed.

"You served with Zimmer?"

"I told him I'd do everything I could to cooperate with the family."

Dietrich looked at him, as if wondering what to say.

Marc waited, staring back deliberately as if he expected something more.

Inga had regained some of her composure and came to her nephew's aid. "Why would Zimmer tell you Dietrich and Kraig are my nephews?"

He had to bluff. "Zimmer was distressed over your sister's sad death here in Paris."

"He told you that?" She was becoming angry.

"He felt as if more should have been done for her. A servant's life...working herself to death to support her two boys." Marc too shook his head sadly, then shrugged, looking from Inga's tense face to Dietrich, who had lost his smile. The meaning was clear enough: Inga had not shared her good fortune of marrying Aubert Ransier with her widowed sister and two boys. And Zimmer felt it was unjust.

Dietrich remained silent and watchful, but Inga was clearly angry. "Zimmer talks too much," she clipped. "My sister was happier here than in postwar Germany."

Marc deliberately remained silent, thoughtfully tapping his chin as if not sure he was convinced.

"The Allies of France and Britain did little to ease any of the grievances of the German people," Dietrich added. "Life was better in Paris even if she did work as a maid."

Marc could have quipped his true feelings, saying that it wasn't the responsibility of France, England, and America to rebuild the cities and economies of their enemy, but that would have unmasked him.

"Greedy capitalists," he said. "France and England prefer to keep Germany weak."

If he had quoted one of Hitler's favorite charges, they seemed to lap it up. Dietrich looked interested and scanned him again. "So you are friends with my cousin, Captain Zimmer?"

"A brilliant tactician." In reality Zimmer was an average captain. If only Marc could discover what it was that Dietrich hoped to get from Zimmer.

"He too has been transferred away from Sidi-bel-Abbes," Dietrich offered. "The French Foreign Legion has been busy rearranging the posts of their best soldiers."

Meaning that Dietrich knew both he and Sebastien had also been given new posts at Tangier, thought Marc. "Then Zimmer told you about his new job?"

Dietrich shrugged. "He mentioned he was sick of the sand and heat and put in for a transfer to Tangier."

He was lying. Zimmer hadn't mentioned Morocco. Dietrich was trying to learn if Zimmer had actually trusted him. It struck Marc, then, that Zimmer's interest in Oran might be crucial.

"Morocco? You're mistaken. It was Oran."

Dietrich's eyes flickered from the shock, and his mouth tightened. "Oh. Was it?"

Marc affected calmness although his heart skipped a beat. *Oran*. That was it. That must be the location Dietrich was interested in and why he was watching Sebastien. The French fleet!

"Yes, Zimmer mentioned Oran when he called me to his command tent. It was the night Sebastien called me back to Bel-Abbes."

By now Nazi agents would have discovered as much about Marc's past as possible and reported it to Dietrich, but they had nothing on him. The less he tried to cover up, the more he might be able to convince Dietrich he agreed with Cousin Aubert's politics.

"You met with Sebastien before you came here to Paris?" Dietrich asked, taking out his cigarette case and a lighter.

Marc suspected he might be recording his answer. Dietrich offered him a cigarette. Marc declined, but Dietrich took one out and lit it.

Inga was clearly nervous now, glancing from one to the other. Dietrich looked at her, and Marc suspected he was telling her to leave them alone. She excused herself. "I'm so glad you're here, Marc. You'll be staying, naturally? I'll have

Henri open a room for you. Your old one has been redone. Henri!" she called, and the man appeared. "Monsieur Marc will need a room for a few weeks."

"Oui, madame, it is ready. Shall I bring your bags up, monsieur?"

"I'm afraid I left them in the motorcar," said Marc.

"No problem, monsieur. I'll send someone."

Inga walked toward the stairs. "I'd better see if Claude needs anything."

When both she and Henri had gone, Marc turned back to Dietrich. Nice little interlude, Marc thought. It had given Dietrich time to make up his mind about something. He must have done so, for Dietrich looked pensive as he drew on the cigarette. "How well do you know my cousin Zimmer?"

"Well enough to work together agreeably," Marc suggested. He could see that Dietrich was uncertain, wondering if he had mistaken Marc as an enemy when he might be working with Zimmer to aid the German cause. Marc was aware that he was taking a risk as he gestured toward the open door as though they might discuss more in a private walk. Dietrich stepped out with him into the weak May sunshine.

Marc walked toward the Renault, parked beneath some Hawthorn trees. Henri and a younger servant had collected his bags from the car and were carrying them toward the house.

"I've an appointment in Paris," Marc told Dietrich as they walked slowly toward the motorcar. "Perhaps we can continue our discussion tomorrow. I'll be bringing Valli back with me."

Dietrich finished his cigarette, his free hand stuffed into the tan riding trousers. He looked at the path thoughtfully as they walked.

For a moment neither spoke. Their shoes ground the pebbled path where blue violets were blooming amid heart-shaped leaves.

"Zimmer never mentioned you," Dietrich murmured.

There was much more to that simple statement than an ordinary listener would have surmised.

"When did you last see him?" Marc asked.

Dietrich appeared uncomfortable. Clearly he wanted to be the interrogator. But perhaps he too felt there was more to lose in covering up his presence at Bel-Abbes, since Valli had seen and talked with him at Davide's mission station and there was always the possibility she would mention the incident to Marc.

"Over a month ago. I was visiting some American friends in the area who run a plantation near Oran."

Marc was curious about this plantation in Oran but thought it wise not to pursue it now. He could ask Sebastien to check into it.

"Who sent you to Zimmer's regiment?" Dietrich asked. He had stopped on the cobbled walkway and turned on his polished boots to look at him.

"General Nouges. He wanted to learn if the German officers were loyal to France or leaned toward Berlin."

Dietrich laughed. "What! The French can't trust their own soldiers?"

"I question whether they can trust their own government."

Dietrich's eyes glinted under his light golden lashes. The wind rushed through the tree branches. Some clouds were blowing in from the Seine River.

Marc opened the car door. "I'll be passing through Oran on my way back to Tangier. If you have any message for Zimmer, I can easily deliver it."

"I will keep that in mind, Cousin Marc. But since I may be going back to Tangier myself, I should see to Zimmer. Perhaps we can journey together," he suggested. "The voyage will prove more pleasant with the company of Valli Chattaine and Madame Giselle Ransier."

"Yes," Marc said pleasantly. "As I told Uncle Claude a short time ago, just one big happy family." He got in behind the wheel and started the engine.

"Did Giselle lend you the automobile?"

"Yes, last night, but something must have come up because Henri says she didn't return."

Dietrich responded with a sharp, interested glance. "She is not here?"

"No. Any idea where she might be?"

"None."

As Marc drove from the estate, he glanced up at the house and saw Great-Uncle Claude's window. He was standing there, having watched him and Dietrich.

Dietrich's surprise when he learned that Giselle was not here had told Marc that he probably wasn't involved in her disappearance. Perhaps Jacquette too had avoided Dietrich. Had he followed Giselle from the ballet theater last night instead of Dietrich?

There may be a message waiting even now at his hotel or with the Surete. He would also arrange a meeting with Danjou about what he'd learned from Claude...and Dietrich.

The French fleet at Oran. He was sure now that whatever Dietrich hoped to accomplish concerned the warships.

# 15

As Marc's footsteps down the flight of stairs were dying away, Valli leaned against the door holding Great-Aunt Calanthe's letter. She lifted the envelope and stared at it in the dim lamplight. Did it hold more disappointment, or had the threat of war softened her great-aunt's stance against receiving her back into her heart?

Valli removed her coat and hat and laid them aside, then went to the sofa and switched on another lamp. She was intending to open the letter when the squeak of a floorboard startled her. The sound wasn't from Mimi's room, but her own. Heart in throat, she watched a darkened figure step forward.

Valli smiled warily. "Giselle, you frightened me."

"We're both frightened," Giselle said in a low voice.

Valli watched her walk to the small window and make sure the shade was still drawn, then check the bolt on the door. Satisfied, Giselle turned and faced her. "I heard Marc's voice. I'm glad you didn't let him in."

Valli watched her sister curiously.

"I didn't want him to know I was here," Giselle continued. "He'd be angry with me if he knew I was involving you." She smoothed the front of her gown with nervous fingers. "I wouldn't have come, except I've no one else but you to turn to. That is, no one I can really trust."

Valli might have felt vindicated, even flattered, but her emotions were dull. Trust, a strange word coming from Giselle, but she refused to dwell on that for long, afraid the old resentment might wrestle its way back to reign in her heart. *God is teaching me how to forgive,* she reminded herself. *I mustn't feel spiteful toward her. To love and ask for nothing in return is indeed a victory.*

"Is something wrong, Giselle?" Valli glanced toward the door to Mimi's room, but Giselle shook her head.

"She's not here. She gave me her bed and went off to spend the night with someone she knows." She walked toward Valli, and in the lamplight her face was pale and tight. "Just about everything is wrong since Dietrich showed up."

Although agreeing with Giselle, Valli remained cautious, not willing to share what she knew until her sister first explained what worried her. Marc seemed to think that Giselle had taken Kraig's letter, and she may have even turned it over to Dietrich. Could it be true? She obviously disliked him. Why would she do such a thing?

"I admit Dietrich isn't conducive to one's peace of mind. Are you being blackmailed?"

A flicker of shock crossed her face. "Yes, how did you know?"

"I saw him tonight at Ambassador Hartley's. He talked about you a little."

Giselle's eyes were distrustful. "Did he? He has the nerve."

Valli sat down on the sofa, still holding Great-Aunt Calanthe's letter. Giselle was too concerned with her own fears to notice, and Valli casually placed it with her unopened mail on the table. "It was something Dietrich said tonight."

"What was that?" Giselle persisted.

"In so many words, he said your reckless past has made you vulnerable, that you were a detriment to Sebastien."

"Well, he's not so far from the truth after all. I have been reckless and foolish. And it's only now when I fear losing Sebastien that I realize how desperately I want to keep him! And my marriage—Dietrich has something on me. He said he'll reveal the matter to Sebastien if I don't cooperate."

"Marc mentioned someone following you. Is Dietrich involved in that as well?"

She looked surprised. "Marc told you? Yes, I was followed again tonight, but I lost him before I got here." She stopped pacing, turned, and looked at her anxiously. "I've got to get back to Tangier right away. I've got to get to Sebastien before Dietrich does."

"Then...you did take Kraig's letter tonight, didn't you," Valli stated bluntly.

Her startled, pale face convinced Valli that she had. She walked slowly to the sofa and sank onto the cushion, dropping her head in both hands. "Yes," she said quietly. "I had to."

"Why? Dietrich?"

"Yes, he told me to bring it to him."

"Since when does Dietrich have such control over you to order you about?"

"I told you, since he has information that can destroy me and Sebastien."

Destroy her *and* Sebastien? "If he's blackmailing you, why deliver him more evidence, the letter for example?"

"Because I had no choice," she insisted. "You don't know Dietrich. He can be vicious."

Valli felt that she did know him, and that was why she worried about the letter. If Kraig worked in the underground the letter may have given information away. "Why did he want Kraig's letter? What was in it?"

Giselle avoided her eyes. "I don't know. I didn't open it."

"Weren't you curious?" Valli asked with disbelief. "If he wanted the letter so badly, it goes without saying there must have been something important in it."

She jumped to her feet. "For one thing, there wasn't time. He was waiting in the theater lobby. And besides that, someone else was following me to make certain I obeyed orders."

Valli thought of the smiling man standing on the outside of the group of well-wishers.

"I don't know who he was," Giselle said. "I've never seen him before. He followed me after I left Dietrich and stood to the side, but always where he could watch me. You were in the hall—with Marc."

Valli was quiet for a moment. At least she'd told her the truth about the man. "Why didn't he just take Kraig's letter himself and bring it to Dietrich? He was right there too."

"How do I know?" Giselle cried, frustrated. "Maybe Dietrich wanted to test me, to see if I would cooperate. Well, I did," she said bitterly and went to her handbag, digging out cigarettes and lighter. "Now he knows I'll follow his orders."

"Kraig sent a card with the roses. He said he was in danger...and that I was too."

Giselle looked at her with genuine fear. "Kraig told you that?"

Valli couldn't tell her about the underground, that information had come from Marc. If there was the slightest chance that Dietrich didn't know, she couldn't risk telling Giselle, not now.

"You've no idea what Kraig meant about me being in danger?"

"No...oh, I'm such a fool. I've gotten us both into a dilemma—and Sebastien too."

Valli believed there was much more she wasn't telling her, that she was only skimming the surface of a murky pool.

Valli looked at the telephone. Marc ought to be here, to hear all this. But she knew if she mentioned calling his hotel, Giselle would object. "Tell me everything, from the beginning."

"I can't explain everything, Sebastien wouldn't want me to. By a chance mistake, if you want to call it that, I happened to find out that both Sebastien and Marc work for the Surete."

Then she knew. Valli remained unreadable, saying nothing.

Giselle walked wearily to a chair and sat down on the edge. She lowered her voice and glanced at the door. "Dietrich thinks I have access to information the Nazis want."

"Do you?" whispered Valli.

Giselle glanced up. She snubbed out her cigarette. "Not yet. That is, I know what Dietrich wants me to find out. But he's waiting for word from someone here in Paris. As soon as the information is passed to Sebastien, I'm to relay it to Dietrich. By then, he should be in Tangier. Dietrich thinks I can gain the information in a roundabout way from Sebastien."

Valli stared at her. Indignation bubbled from her heart. "You mean spy on your own husband for the Nazis?" she whispered heatedly.

"Yes," she said dully. "I told you he was vicious."

"That fiend," Valli breathed.

"You don't think I'd do such a thing? Oh, I got Kraig's letter for him all right, but that's not the same thing. That's as far as I'll go. I'm ashamed I even did that. But I had to appease him long enough to throw him off my trail. Now that he thinks I'm going to cooperate, I've got to get back to Tangier. We both do, Valli. I need you to help me."

Information for the Nazis? Valli stood, distraught. "Let me call Marc."

Giselle jumped to her feet. "No, wait. Marc will go straight to Sebastien. I know he will. I need time to handle this in Tangier. Even if it's just a few weeks."

But did they have even that much time? "Giselle, if you have any idea what this information is, or why Dietrich wants it, you must tell me. You heard the news on the BBC. The Germans invaded Denmark and Norway. It may soon be too late! We can't afford to wait. We *must* tell Marc at once."

"There's something I must do first. Believe me, Valli, if I can get there ahead of Dietrich, I can foil him! Then," she smiled tightly, "we'll go to Sebastien and Marc. They can arrest Dietrich in Tangier."

Valli placed a nervous hand to her forehead, trying to think this through. She didn't like it. The information was too important to keep from Marc now. She pressed for more, to have as much as she could when she saw him tomorrow night at dinner. "Why Tangier?"

"Because that's where it will all happen."

"Not in Paris?"

Giselle shook her head.

"But why do you think you can foil Dietrich? How?"

"Because I will get something he intends to use to black-mail me with first, and I'm going to hide it. Once I do that there's nothing more he can threaten me with. But I can't do it all on my own. It will take the two of us. And you're the only other person I can trust with this besides Davide."

"And this *thing*?" Valli asked. "What does Dietrich know about it that has you in such a dilemma? Why not simply go to Sebastien, explain what it is, and what the Nazis are trying to do, and—"

"No, no. It isn't that simple. He has information to destroy my marriage."

Valli bleakly sat down. "Then you'd better tell me what it is. I won't help unless you do."

"You already know what it's about," Giselle said just as bleakly. "It's Kraig."

Valli sat motionless and quiet.

Giselle turned toward her, wringing her hands. "Diet-rich has photographs of us meeting at a café."

It seemed forever before Valli found her voice. "You mean Sebastian doesn't know anything about you running off to Spain with Kraig four years ago?"

"No. But it's worse than that. They are recent pho-tographs taken in Tangier."

Recent. Valli remained frozen in silence.

"It's not the way you think," Giselle said in a husky voice. "There's nothing between me and Kraig. I love Sebastien. I didn't realize how much until now," she said desperately. "It's all a mistake."

Valli stood and murmured, "I'll make some tea." She had to get away to muster her feelings. Giselle seemed to know what she was thinking and turned her back, head in hand. Valli walked into the little kitchen and numbly went about boiling water. She paced.

It was all a mistake all right, thought Valli, one that had destroyed any hope of her happiness for several dark and painful years. She had lost Kraig. She had been betrayed by both of them, and now Giselle had come back to ask for her help. Although nearly five years had taken away the sting and the wound had scarred over, thinking of her yellowing wedding dress still hanging at the back of her dark closet, the wedding invitations, the bewilderment, the whispers of friends—

Reliving the emotion again brought Valli a new rush of resentment, especially when she thought that Giselle had been seeing Kraig while married to Sebastien! But if sin had crouched at the door of Cain's heart ready to spring like a lion, then what about the dormant seed of bitterness that remained in hers? It could readily sprout again. In despair, Valli thought: *But if I truly meant it when I forgave Giselle, why do I still get angry? And I'm sure I don't love Kraig. And tonight, when Marc kissed me—*

Mimi had once told her that Valli had more grace to forgive Kraig than she did to forgive her sister. Was she right after all?

Yes, Kraig was to blame, but she blamed Giselle even more. Giselle had tempted him away—and now she was back in her life, again asking that Valli show grace and mercy to help her out of her most recent dilemma. She'd been untrue to Sebastien.

Valli felt a renewed surge of anger sweep over her. "Dear God, Giselle ruined everything for me by leaving her fingerprints on my white wedding dress. And why should I do anything to help her now? Why, God? Why should I risk myself? What has she ever done for me, except bring pain and disappointment?"

Valli shut her eyes. "I wanted him to be all mine. Yet Giselle took him first!" Her jaw clamped. Giselle had always been self-centered, not caring whom she hurt as long as she got her way. It had always been like that, even in childhood growing up in Tangier at Great-Aunt Calanthe's house. Giselle often lied to cover her tracks, and she had lied again to Sebastien—

Valli caught hold of her runaway emotions. She groaned, sinking into the kitchen chair, face in her hands. "Lord Jesus, forgive me," she prayed desperately. "Help me to stop feeling like a victim, when I can be confident in Your good plans for me. You have shown me grace. Help me to be gracious to my sister. She needs my support right now, not my condemnation. She has come to me because she trusts me. That says much about You, Lord, and how You've worked in my life. Give me the courage to let go of the past once for all. I want to trust Your goodness where loss and pain have left their scars."

As Valli sat there, the minutes slipped by. She became aware of the water boiling in the pan. The words of Scripture, read only that morning in Philippians chapter 3 came to mind with crystal clarity: "...forgetting those things which are behind, and reaching forth unto those things which are before, I press toward the mark for the prize of the high calling of God in Christ Jesus."

Forget what was behind, press toward the future and what God had in store. Accept the trial, believing that God's wisdom and goodness had allowed it, not to punish her, but to bring good.

Marc came to mind again, and to her heart...

"All things work together for good to them who love God."

Did she love God? Loving God meant obedience to His will. It meant trusting Him with altered plans, unrealized hopes, foiled goals. She could prove that love by trusting God through disappointment. Nevertheless, after the trial, divine chastening yielded the peaceable fruit of righteousness to those who submitted to the sculpting hand of God.

Fifteen minutes later Valli came from the kitchen carrying a tray of hot tea. Without a word she filled the cups and added sugar cubes. "Remember how Great-Aunt Calanthe used to let us pour honey in our tea, and how we used to fight over who got to lick the spoon?" she called.

She straightened and turned around, looking toward the bathroom. The light was on, but silence greeted her. Valli went to the door and looked in, but Giselle was not there. She came back to the living room. "Giselle?" Her eyes dropped to the chair. A note had been scribbled and pinned there. Quickly, Valli read it:

> *Valli, I'm sorry to have come to you like this. I should have realized I was being selfish to ask you to involve yourself in a matter dealing with my sin and Kraig's. I could see by your reaction that I've dug up old wounds. That was the last thing I wanted to do. Please don't worry. It's time I handled this on my own.*
>
> *Love, Giselle*

Valli stood staring at the words. A new and far different pain now pricked at her heart.

She rushed to the front door and went out on the stairs, but the late night contained nothing but rain and bleakness. For the first time she sensed what a shepherd must feel like when a lamb is lost and on its own in a dark, stormy night.

*Oh, Giselle!*

# 16

Valli awoke late the next morning to the sounds of the BBC news drifting in from the next room and the tantalizing aroma of percolating coffee. She realized Mimi was moving about in the kitchenette. Mimi always insisted on making a hearty breakfast before cleaning the flat.

Valli glanced at the clock on her bedstand and saw that it was 9:30 A.M. By now Marc would be on his way to see Monsieur Claude at the Ransier estate. Should she call about Giselle or wait until she saw him at dinner?

She threw aside the covers and sat up, remembering to stand cautiously to test her ankle. With relief she noticed there was no swelling, and when she placed her weight on it, there was only minor discomfort. She caught up her robe and slipped into it, then went to the mirror and picked up her hairbrush.

Mimi must have heard her moving about and looked in. Seeing that Valli was up, she returned a moment later carrying a cup of coffee.

"Good morning, ma petite. You rested well, oui? Le Captaine Durell called very early but did not want to wake you. He asks if you will meet him tonight at the Quai des Ormes."

That night Valli took a taxi to a romantic little restaurant on the Seine. Seated on the first-floor flowered terrace overlooking Notre Dame, the elegant outdoor lighting cast reflections upon the quiet rain pools left undisturbed by the busy wheels of automobiles. The Seine sparkled with dancing diamonds beneath a rose-tinted skyline.

Along the sidewalk there were dozens of small cafés with awnings over white-clothed tables, beckoning a refuge to passersby from the mizzling rain. Here, on the terrace, Valli smiled at Marc, who had just sat down across from her after apologizing for arriving late by lavishing her with fresh, sweet violets and nonpareil chocolates. He told her he'd gotten away from a long meeting with the Surete just in time to change for their dinner date. He looked, of course, the most handsome Frenchman in the place, and she wondered if she would be able to forget those light-blue eyes watching her so intensely once he returned to Bel-Abbes.

Valli made much over the violets and was rather surprised that Marc was such a romantic man, having come from the rugged background of the Foreign Legion. Marc too might have noted that she had taken special care to dress for the dinner, despite the subdued look of worry in her velvet-brown eyes. Her wavy blue-black hair fell smoothly down her back, and according to the fashion of 1940, it was drawn up away from her ears and held in place with diamond-sprinkled combs. Teardrop diamonds winked at her earlobes. She wore a white ermine stole and a sophisticated black evening dress designed by the famous Coco Chanel, and a dab of perfume from Guerlain.

She sipped from her glass as she watched him over the rim. Some romantic music drifted to them from one of the smaller cafés on the street. Though she had been finding it difficult to keep her mind off the problems at hand, she was now troubled by the thought that she didn't know how long it would be until she saw him again. What if something happened to Marc? While he was away would he know that she didn't care for Kraig anymore, that more and more she was finding her emotions drawn to him?

She envisioned him out in the hot Sahara and wondered if he ever felt the disturbing isolation of heart that she knew while sitting here by the wet streets of Paris listening to a refrain from a French tune on an accordion.

He looked at her and the warmth in his eyes told her he guessed what she was thinking, and as if to prove it, he leaned toward her attentively, taking her hand into his and bringing her fingers to his lips. She felt her cheeks warm.

"I'm pleased that I am not competing with Kraig for your attention tonight," he said.

So he could read her thoughts—and heart. "You make too much of him."

"Do I?"

"That was years ago."

"Why do you still keep the wedding dress and wedding invitations in your bedroom closet?"

"How did you know that!"

"I spoke with Mimi this morning while you were fast asleep. She cries easily and worries about you. She confessed her great distress over her chere enfant." He smiled. "It doesn't take much encouragement to get her to tell me anything about you I want to know."

"Is that fair?" Irritated with Mimi she pulled her hand away and placed it on her lap. Her lashes squinted as his brow went up.

"Well, I would like to know if I'm in competition with a wilting wedding bouquet."

She realized how ridiculous the idea sounded and smiled. "I'm not taking them with me to Tangier. If the Germans do come, they can have the old invitations."

"That's the first encouraging word I've gotten from you."

She laughed softly. "Really? And I was thinking it was all going rather too quickly. We've only just met again a month ago, and what do you call what happened last night at my front door?"

"A good beginning," he said with a slight smile, and his gaze drifted to her lips.

Valli lifted the violets and played with the heart-shaped leaves. For the first time in years she could thank God she hadn't married Kraig. Her eyes lifted to Marc's. I'm already falling in love with him...

"What's that song they're playing, do you know?" he asked.

"Tommy Dorsey's 'I'll Be Seeing You,'" she said in a quiet voice.

He was looking off toward the Seine, and despite his attempt to keep the dinner pleasant she could see he was troubled. With the Nazi dragon blowing flames of destruction across the Western Front, an uncertain summer cast its pall of death toward France and Britain. "Did you learn much at the Ransier estate?" she inquired, wondering.

"Enough to raise more questions," he said.

She hoped the reunion with his Great-Uncle Claude had gone well. She didn't want to pry and considered instead how to bring up her own meeting with Giselle the night before.

"I don't want to ruin the evening, since it's likely to be the last one we'll enjoy for some time to come," he said quietly. "But we have a good deal to talk about, much of it unpleasant."

She understood. Fear and sadness seemed to ripple the water on the Seine, as well as the violets on the white table.

"Yes," she murmured, gently touching the purple flowers, so delicate, so easily crushed. "I know. I have much to tell you as well. I heard the radio bulletin on the way."

German troops were seen moving toward Belgium. French troops were poised and waiting...

Marc was fiddling with his napkin. She felt sorry for him. For a soldier of valor, the talk of France suing for armistice was especially painful.

"You must leave Paris," he told her again.

The anxiety tightened in her chest. She couldn't leave yet. "I spoke to the director of the ballet today. I have two weeks more of performances to fill. As soon as they're over, I'll consider going to Tangier."

"Two weeks will be too late, Valli. We're lucky if we have a week before Germany hits us with everything in their arsenal. Regardless of my feelings, or respect for the French soldiers, they won't be able to hold the line. They don't have the armored divisions for a formidable fight, nor do they have an adequate strategy."

"I can't forsake the ballet troupe now, Marc! Bridgette has left for Vichy and there's no one else able to perform *Giselle*."

His intense gaze held hers. "How can I make you see it doesn't matter now?"

"It matters to me."

"In two weeks there will be officers from the German High Command filling those theater boxes. Will it still matter?"

"You told me that before," she said a little stiffly. "I won't perform for German officers."

"Yes, I told you last night. Now I'm more convinced than ever. You're not likely to be given much of a choice. I don't say things to exaggerate or frighten you. Nor do I want to spoil your opportunity to dance."

Her eyes faltered. She should be flattered that he even cared. She also knew he had information about the German army that she did not.

"I know you don't," she admitted softly.

He reached into his jacket and removed a small white envelope and laid it on the table by her hand. "For you."

"What is it?" she whispered.

A brief smile formed on his mouth. "A train ticket to Marseille. You may not know it, but they'll soon be worth a gold mine in Australia."

Valli smiled in spite of herself, and their eyes held. "And what of you?" she whispered. "Will you be on the train with me?"

He looked away. "There are a few more things I need to handle first." He lifted his glass and toasted her. "To Tangier. We'll meet there again."

She didn't think so, but lifted her glass, her eyes watching him. She had to swallow hard to hold back the sense of loss and sadness. She looked away. It was beginning to rain, lightly at first, tinkling on the roof of the terrace. She had lost all appetite. Her eyes blurred as she looked out on Paris, Notre Dame, the Seine—

Marc's hand reached over and enclosed hers, warm, strong, and reassuring, saying more than words could ever do. Valli looked at the violets through her tears.

The waiter came in spotless white, and Marc ordered in a low voice.

Valli used the small reprieve to take out her lace handkerchief and dry the corners of her eyes.

"Have you any idea when Dietrich will leave?" she asked.

"If anything, he'll be here to meet the Germans. Paris is not a passing thing, but a destination."

"But he once said he had a job at the German embassy in Tangier. He told Davide as well."

"There's new information from Sebastien that he's lying about that. He's a Gestapo agent, not a diplomat. He may be interested in Tangier for smuggling operations, but Paris is his goal. He's after something else," he mused, glancing off toward the lighted Notre Dame. "Maybe more than one something. That doesn't rule out Tangier, though. I think he has plans to be there, but not to officiate at the embassy."

She lowered her voice and leaned toward him. "Marc, I think I know one of those things he's after. Giselle came to my flat last night. In fact, she was there when you brought me home from Ambassador Hartley's."

"Yes, I know."

"You know?"

"I've heard from my friend the harmonica player. His name is Jacquette, by the way, should you ever meet him in some unexpected situation."

Unexpected? She wondered what he meant.

"Jacquette followed Giselle to your flat last night after the ballet, and again when she left before dawn. She has her own little flat in Paris, did you know that?"

She shook her head, feeling a little better. She had felt terribly guilty last night when her sister had left. But Marc didn't know any of this, and she had to explain. She handed him the note Giselle had pinned to the chair. "I'll explain after you read this."

A moment later, he frowned. "All right, go ahead."

"She asked for my help with Dietrich, and at first I hesitated, but after I'd thought it through I knew I must help her. But when I returned from the kitchen where I went to make tea, she'd left this note. I felt dreadful, and still do, but I consoled myself thinking she'd gone to the estate, and that perhaps she'd also gone to you about Dietrich as well. Now I know she hasn't, and I'm worried. Marc, I've got to see her tonight. Will you take me to her flat? She can explain everything to you there. She won't want to, she asked me to say nothing, but if Sebastien is in danger and—"

"Wait a minute," he breathed, hand on her wrist, his eyes searching hers. "She came to you about Dietrich? And Sebastien? You'd better explain."

"You were right about the letter. She admitted she took it, but said she had to because she claims Dietrich is blackmailing her about Kraig. Sebastien doesn't know. And somehow Dietrich also managed to get some photographs of her with Kraig at an outdoor café in Tangier recently. Evidently they look rather cozy and she's afraid Sebastien will misunderstand."

"Did she tell you why she met Kraig?"

"No. There was so much being said, I didn't find that out. I'm afraid I was upset with her, thinking she'd been untrue again, this time to Sebastien. That's when I went to make tea. When I came back, she was gone. I may have been wrong about her being untrue to Sebastien."

"It wasn't your fault. With her lifestyle what else would you think?"

Valli glanced at him and wondered if he might have experienced her sister's flirtations.

"Regardless, she was desperate. She came to me for help and I've got to rally to her."

"I'll call her now. Do you have her telephone number?"

"No, I didn't even know she had a Paris flat. I thought she'd been living at the estate all this time except for her visits to Paris."

"Evidently there's quite a lot about Giselle we don't know. If you don't have her number, we'll need to go there after dinner. In the meantime, can you tell me everything she said about Dietrich and Sebastien? It could be very important, just the right puzzle piece the Surete needs. The trail apparently is leading back to Tangier, and Giselle may lead the way."

Valli did so, taking her time to make it as clear as possible, but after explaining everything to Marc she realized that Giselle really hadn't revealed that much.

"It's all still in the murky shadows, isn't it? If only I'd told her I would help, we'd know now what it's all about," she said with a note of self-incrimination.

"I've a suspicion she still wouldn't have explained everything. That's Giselle. She'll need to do more explaining tonight. Aside from the photographs she says Dietrich has, did she tell you what it is he wants from her and Sebastien?"

"No, but from her behavior and some things she said, I gathered that there was something more important than the photographs. She needed to get back to Tangier and wanted me to go with her. 'I've got to get back to Sebastien before Dietrich does,' she kept repeating."

"Then she expects Dietrich to contact Sebastien himself. That's important," he mused.

"I asked her, why Tangier—? And she said, 'Because that's where it will all happen.'"

Marc pondered. "I'll get more out of her tonight. She'll have to explain." He looked at his watch.

Valli too pondered as a chill breeze blew off the Seine where it had been raining minutes ago. She saw Marc looking off down the narrow street curving toward some trees. The rain clouds were drifting and the twilight sky was glinting lavender-gold above the river. She knew he disliked ruining the moment with talk about Dietrich. She thought about his concern for her—purchasing the train ticket to keep her out of a dangerous situation. Kraig wouldn't have paid that much attention. She could see the difference now, how one man appeared to cherish her, while the other had been willing to leave her with a wedding dress and a handful of invitations to a ceremony he had already been untrue to. No, Marc would never do that to a woman. He was the kind who would never get seriously involved unless he was willing to make a commitment that he wouldn't break.

"Have you met Inga and Aubert Ransier?"

Startled back to the moment, she looked at him curiously, wondering why he brought them up now. "Yes, many times. Why?"

"Ever notice anything familiar about Inga?"

Her brow furrowed. "Familiar? In what way? Why do you ask?"

His mouth turned wryly. "I mean her appearance. She's Dietrich's and Kraig's blood aunt. I found out this morning from my great-uncle. He's quite upset about it."

Her eyes widened and her long lashes blinked.

His dark brow lifted with amusement. "I can see your brain at work scrutinizing me. Not a chance of resemblance between me and the Gestler brothers. They're from Berlin. My cousin Aubert met Inga there years ago."

She remembered some mention of that. "Yes, while studying music. Inga told me. But this is shocking news," she whispered. "Who would ever have thought there was a connection between your mother's family and Dietrich?"

"Yes, unpleasant, isn't it? I never thought I'd be exchanging the cozy word of 'cousin' with a Gestapo agent. Claude is worried about more than ties to Germany. There's evidence Aubert is a Nazi at heart. He's collaborating with German agents, Dietrich being one of them. So is Inga."

"Monsieur Aubert?" she gasped.

Marc quickly laid a hand on hers, warning her to keep her voice low. There was distance between the tables, but voices could carry.

"But Monsieur Aubert is a member of the Prime Minister's cabinet," she said, still shocked.

"So he is. Except for General de Gaulle and some others, the Prime Minister had little choice except to appoint a bunch of spineless pacifists that are anxious to sign a surrender pact. We've heard that Petain has arrived as well. He's the ambassador to Spain, but he'll soon be Prime Minister."

Valli remembered the leaflets circulating on the streets with Petain's photograph. Beneath was written: *Yesterday, a great soldier!...Today, a great diplomat!...Tomorrow?...*

"Petain's presence is a disaster," Marc said. "He's now the rallying point for the doves who seek an armistice with Hitler."

"And your Cousin Aubert will stay on with Petain if he becomes Prime Minister?"

"He's working toward that. Inga is behind him. They'll both fit in well with a compromising Vichy government."

"What does Aubert do?"

"Interesting you should ask. Especially since Dietrich has arrived—and Giselle is talking about things wrapping up in Tangier. Aubert works with the French admiral, Darlan."

Her lashes narrowed thoughtfully. She knew little about the navy admiral, or why it would interest Marc.

"The French fleet," he cautioned. "It all has something to do with it, I'm almost certain."

"If only we knew what Kraig wrote me in that letter, it might tell us something."

"Maybe. If Giselle was truthful when she said she didn't read it, there's little chance we'll end up knowing what he wrote. Anyway," Marc said, "I can't help wondering if Giselle had some reason for not wanting you to see it."

She looked at him, surprised. "What would make her not want me to read it?"

"It may have mentioned something Giselle didn't want you to know about. She may have had her own reasons for cooperating with Dietrich. Perhaps the photographs aren't the main thing Dietrich has on her. Anyway, if Kraig wrote that you were in danger he may have been referring to Dietrich's intentions toward you. He may have known his brother was coming here. The Surete has been trying to get in touch with Kraig to find out. I'm afraid he's disappeared."

She wondered at his frown. Did he know something more about Kraig? If so, he wasn't anxious to explain. Neither did she want to hear the details. Kraig may well have been arrested by now. The idea brought a shudder. The Nazis in Athens would, of course, try to make him talk.

"And there are still a few things you haven't explained about you and 'Cousin' Dietrich."

Her brows arched. "Do you think I'm keeping secrets from you, Captain Durell?"

He smiled. "I hope not, ma chere, at least not deliberately."

She leaned back in her chair. "All right. Ask your questions. I'll tell you everything I know, which isn't much. Until I saw Dietrich at Davide's, I hadn't seen him in four years."

"You're sure you didn't keep back part of the truth at Bel-Abbes?"

So they were back to that. She should have known that she would need to explain the apparent contradiction.

"You did recognize him at the train station when Blystone got off," Marc said.

She sighed. "Yes, I made a mistake when I said I didn't. It was an honest mistake, Marc, because at that time I didn't know you." She looked back defensively. "Your agent friend Blystone insisted I say nothing about what was happening. I didn't know then that I could trust you fully, or that you were a French agent."

"When did you become convinced that it was Dietrich who drove up in that truck?"

"I suppose I always thought so...but I only admitted the truth to myself at Davide's when I looked out the window and saw Dietrich outside the door. By then I understood that he and the two men with him must have killed the waterboy and were after Blystone."

"He really wasn't a waterboy," he said quietly. "His name was Ahmed, and he worked with us in the Surete. Nevertheless, go on. You were at Davide's when Dietrich showed up."

"Yes, and I tried to escape through the back door, but then I remembered the canvas bag. I was afraid Blystone's name might be on some of his books or magazines. If that were the case, then Dietrich would discover that I did have contact with him on the train. So I knew I had to go back for the bag."

"A smart move, considering. Though I would not have let you go off with the bag if I thought Blystone left anything important in it. I'm told the bag had nothing except some small pouches of Sahara sand."

"Sand!" She said, almost indignant. "I was carrying bags of sand in that heat?"

He laughed. "My apology."

"Sand," she repeated, thinking of the heart-stopping moment when she had run into her room, grabbed the bag, and hid it in Davide's kitchen.

"Anyway," she said, "when Dietrich arrived, I didn't have much time to plan, so I put the bag in the rice barrel. Later, I hid it again in my room, and before returning to Paris I buried it."

"Buried it?" Marc laughed.

"Well, how was I supposed to know there wasn't anything important inside?"

"You mean you didn't look?"

"Of course not. I promised Blystone I'd take care of it, not go around snooping."

He watched her, hiding a smile. "Looks as if I owe you an apology."

"What! You mean you trust me at last?" she asked teasingly.

"I'd better, hadn't I? You know too much." He settled back in his chair, the straight dark brows on his tanned face lowering. "Blast Surete," he breathed, "between them and Blystone, we've totally involved you."

"Smile," she whispered, offering him one of her own. "We may be under watch."

"I've little doubt," he said, but he managed a devastatingly charming grin.

"Do not worry about me, Marc."

"I'll try," he said dully. "But you might as well tell me to stop breathing."

The rain played a soft percussion on the awning. A minute later he asked: "Tell me about Calanthe. What was in her letter?"

"She fears Hitler is madman enough to invade France. She wants me in Tangier for the war."

"Her fears are not far-fetched at all."

"No, but even so, I'm surprised Calanthe would ask me to return."

"She raised you, didn't she?"

"Yes, but you may not know that Giselle has weaved so many fabrications about me that at seventy Calanthe's mind is rather confused when it comes to the truth," Valli said, disturbed. "She even disinherited me in favor of everything going to Giselle."

"That was unwise. She owes it for truth's sake to get to the bottom of things before allowing Giselle to manipulate her."

"Yes, well that would have been far better, but she didn't," Valli said wearily. She looked at him, wondering. "Isn't that the way it was with you and the Ransier family?"

"Something like that. Now, after discovering Aubert is a collaborator, Claude has changed his will. As for Giselle, it's typical of fallen human nature to hide one's guilt by lying. Like Cain pretending to the Lord that he didn't know where

Abel was after he'd murdered him in the field. 'Am I my brother's keeper?' he had replied flippantly, as though he could avoid responsibility."

"Yes, anyway, Great-Aunt Calanthe is somewhat eccentric," Valli explained. "I know she's wealthy, but in the end she's not expected to leave me anything. Once, she promised me the house in Tangier." She sighed. "I loved that big old house. It used to belong to an emir."

"Yes, Davide told me."

"Now she's likely to leave it to Giselle."

"Until a few years ago, weren't you Calanthe's pride and joy?"

"Yes, she always thought highly of the ballet. It was she who encouraged me and Giselle to study the dance."

"When Giselle eventually broke up with Kraig, did she return to Calanthe?"

"I don't really know...I think so. Why?"

"You don't know what she told her about you?"

"No. But it was soon afterward that I was disinherited. Some months later Giselle wrote me a letter asking me to forgive her. Since then, I've corresponded several times with our great-aunt, but needless to say we've never been close since."

"Has Giselle gone to Calanthe to make amends for her lies?"

"She told me she did, but Calanthe thinks Giselle is just trying to bring us together again."

"And you've never gone to Calanthe to try and straighten matters out?"

"I've tried, but Calanthe refused. So you see why I'm rather reluctant to take her up on the invitation in her letter now. She's asking me out of duty, for fear of the Germans."

The silence between them brought back the sound of the raindrops. People on the street were hurrying to their destinations. The white-coated waiter approached, wheeling the sparkling dinner cart full of delectables, and the conversation, by mutual consent, departed from the path of gloom. For an hour at least Paris became just Paris, and Valli enjoyed herself and pretended the night would never end, her sweet violets would never shrivel, and the young French captain sitting next to her would always be there.

# 17

Valli leaned back into the Renault's passenger seat confident that Marc knew the way to Giselle's flat as big spattering drops of rain hit the windshield.

"Who is Jacquette?"

"What?" he asked. "Oh. A friend. I've known him since we were boys at Bel-Abbes."

She glanced at his profile and saw him scowling at the road as if something far different than their conversation had his mind occupied.

"Is Jacquette in the Surete?"

"No, not actually, though he's known by everyone and trusted. Most of all, I trust him, and we work well together."

"I see. Then he's in the Foreign Legion?"

Marc turned his head and looked at her briefly. He smiled. "Why so curious?"

"You said back at the restaurant that I might meet him sometime and I wanted to know who he was. Where is he now?"

He looked at his watch. "Probably sleeping. He was up all night watching Giselle. This is her flat here." He pulled off the street into a small parking spot in a square protected by medium-sized trees. Marc came around and opened her door, helping her out. It was still raining and she felt the chilling drops on her face. Marc took her hand and they ran toward some stairs.

"The lights are out," she said tensely. "Maybe she's left for the estate after all. We may have passed her on the road."

"We'll soon find out." He lifted the doormat and snatched a key.

Valli cast him a curious glance. "How did you know it was there?"

"Jacquette."

"He's quite an ally," she said dryly.

"That's why we work together," he said smoothly. "I can depend on him to accomplish critical tasks, sometimes with unconventional means."

"Like the key," she said with a faint smile. "Do you have one to *my* flat as well?"

He remained silent. With a start, she realized that he probably did. She looked at him somewhat ironically.

"Yes. It was one of the first things I had Jacquette do. Should something have gone wrong and I needed to get inside quickly...well, I'm sure you get the idea." He smiled a little, then knocked on the door, paying no more attention to her stare. When no answer came after several more discreet knocks, he used the key and slowly opened the door, gesturing her to step to one side against the porch wall. Valli's heart jumped to her throat.

"Maybe she's asleep," she whispered. "We'll frighten her."

Marc reached in and switched on the light, and the little room sprang to life. Valli looked past him and saw a damask-covered sofa and chair, some wilted flowers, some pretty ballerina figurines on the table and—her heart lurched at the scene. Beside a porcelain ballerina was the glowing review she had received for her performance in *Giselle*. Her sister had cut it from the newspaper and set it beside the porcelain figure. Valli was emotionally affected, as though she now knew that Giselle did love her, and did take sisterly pride in her accomplishments. She had saved the review and placed it with the figure on her table where she thought no one else would see it except herself.

Perhaps it was the stress, or the late hour, but suddenly she felt an overwhelming desire to simply sit down and cry, but couldn't because of Marc's presence.

He was making a quick but cautious search, and was already in the little hall where the bedroom door was open. A light flickered on. Valli stood still, somehow she had already guessed the worst and was holding the back of her hand hard against her mouth, her eyes shut tightly, waiting...waiting for...

She heard his steps on the carpeted floor, heard a door open and shut, followed by dresser drawers, a closet.

Valli was still standing by the coffee table when she realized Marc had left the bedroom and stood in the hallway.

"Are you all right?" he asked.

Her eyes blinked open to see him holding an envelope. "She left this for the landlady to mail to you. Looks as if she's packed up and left for Tangier."

"You mean—she's not in there?" she said in a small, breathless voice. "I thought she was dea—" she stopped. The anxieties of the afternoon, together with the fears of the future, were momentarily too much to carry, and Valli dropped her face into her hands.

"Valli," he breathed softly, coming to her. She felt the side of her face against his shirt and his arms enclosed about her. She stood in the shelter of his embrace as he whispered comforting words into her hair, assuring her everything would be all right.

"We'd better take a look at that letter," he said a moment later.

She nodded, feeling a little foolish over having leaped to the worst conclusion. "You read it to me, Marc."

He opened the envelope and read: "Dear Valli, By the time you read this I'll be on my way to Tangier. You already know the reasons why. If you change your mind you will be able to find me through Great-Aunt Calanthe."

Marc frowned, then handed it to Valli.

"What if Dietrich follows her?" she said tensely.

"He will when he finds out. But he doesn't know yet unless he's having her watched. He was surprised today when I told him she wasn't at the estate. She may have slipped out of Paris undetected. Maybe he was so sure she wouldn't leave that he didn't keep an eye on her. In any case, she'll reach Tangier before any of us. That may be the best thing that could happen."

Valli's hopes revived. "Because she thinks she can foil Dietrich by getting there before him."

"Yes, which is curious to me," Marc said thoughtfully. "There must be something she's trying to keep from him of greater consequence than the photographs."

"What could it be?" she wondered.

A knock on the door sounded as Valli turned quickly, looking nervously from the door to Marc.

He motioned her to one side. She saw him slip his hand to a gun under his jacket. Heart in throat, she waited as he opened the door a few inches. There was a low voice speaking in French. Valli heaved a sigh of relief as two Frenchmen casually entered the room. Marc went off to the kitchen with the older one. The second man leaned against the door, arms folded. Glancing in her direction, he smiled and nodded.

Valli watched Marc and the older man huddle together talking. He glanced toward her and said something, and Marc scowled. The man shrugged, touching his shoulder in friendly solace, and they both came to her.

"This is Monsieur Danjou," Marc told her. "You can trust him." A brief smile flickered. "He's my boss. He wants to talk to you."

She remembered the name Danjou and nodded to him. He was a tall, slim man with dark, intelligent eyes, and some gray at the temples. He bowed his head lightly.

"Mademoiselle Chattaine, I apologize for troubling you, but if I could have a moment of your time?"

"Yes, of course, monsieur. What is it?"

Danjou gestured to the sofa. "Please, sit down."

She did so, glancing at Marc, who offered a brief but encouraging smile. He stood, arms folded, looking calm. Valli felt anything but calm and her eyes swerved back to Danjou.

"Your sister boarded a train this morning for Marseille, I understand?"

"Yes, how did you know?"

There was silence. She should have known better than to ask the head of the Surete how they got information. She also wondered how they knew to find her and Marc in the flat, but she remembered Marc had made a telephone call before they left the restaurant. She looked at him and his face was unreadable.

"Your sister is being blackmailed by the Nazi agent Gestler, that is so, mademoiselle?"

Again, she glanced at Marc. So he had informed them on the telephone. But what had she expected? Anything so serious must be passed on to the Surete. Sebastien himself might be at risk and would need to be careful.

"Yes," she said quietly. "Please, Monsieur Danjou, is there any way the unpleasant details can be kept from Colonel Ransier? At least until his wife can broach him on the subject herself?"

"We shall be as discreet as we can be, mademoiselle. Marc has already explained the complexities of the situation. About your sister, did she explain what it is Dietrich Gestler hopes to get from Colonel Ransier?"

"No. Only that she was asked to spy on him and pass on information to Dietrich in Tangier. Naturally my sister refused," she hastened.

"Of course," he said in a solacing voice. "But she did not suggest the kind of information she was expected to learn from her husband?"

"No. I'm not sure she even knows yet, nor Dietrich."

His brows lifted and he glanced at Marc. For some reason that interested them both. Danjou said: "What makes you come to that conclusion? Was it something she said?"

"Yes. She implied that Dietrich thought she could get the information he wanted, but that it hadn't come through yet. Dietrich was waiting for something to happen in Paris first."

Danjou looked at Marc, and some wordless message passed between them. Danjou said to Valli: "If you thought you could help France in this dire hour, mademoiselle, would you risk your safety?"

"No," Marc gritted.

"Yes," murmured Valli, avoiding Marc's heated gaze. "At least, monsieur, I think I would. But who knows if I could go through with it? It is always easy to promise when one is secure and comfortable. If I were at the mercy of the enemy, I—I just don't know."

Danjou smiled a little, sympathy in his large dark eyes. "You speak honestly. It is all any of us can do. There is something important you can do now for France."

"Danjou—" began Marc, but Danjou shot him a silencing glance.

Marc jammed his hands into his trouser pockets and strode over to the window.

Valli's troubled gaze faltered to the floor. How could any loyal Frenchman say no?

"Marc tells me Dietrich Gestler is, shall we say, romantically attracted to you." Valli saw Marc turn and look at her, but she avoided his smoldering gaze. She said nothing.

"Gestler has already let a few significant things slip in his last two conversations with you, is that so?"

She thought of what Dietrich had told her at the mission station in Bel-Abbes, and again last night at Ambassador Hartley's.

"Yes, you could say that. His pride is incessant, monsieur. He becomes furious when I belittle the Nazis, or if he thinks I question his superiority."

Danjou's mouth turned. He glanced over at Marc. Marc did not smile and turned his head away as if interested in something outside the window on the street.

"Would you be willing, mademoiselle, to place yourself in Gestler's company again to find out what he expects to learn from your sister?"

The silence closed her in. The room seemed to shrink. She was aware of her unease, of Marc's glance, of Danjou's sympathy, of the man at the door frowning at his shoes.

"Yes."

Danjou looked relieved. He said nothing for a moment and then slowly stood. "Your courage, mademoiselle, complements the honor and valor we stand for as Free French."

Valli felt her skin tingle with patriotism. "Merci, monsieur."

Danjou looked quietly across the room at Marc, who had lapsed into stony silence. "Marc will explain what you are to do. Be assured, one of our men will never be far away. There is Marc, and now you have met Jacquette. There are others you do not know, but all will do their utmost to see to your safety."

She nodded and remained seated, afraid that her knees would not hold her up if she tried to stand.

Danjou bowed his head, then walked over to Marc. Without a word they went together into the kitchen and once again spoke in indiscernible terms. Valli did not think at all, but heard the rain pelting against the window pane. After what seemed twenty minutes, but might have been only ten, Danjou left Marc and walked to the front door. Jacquette gestured goodbye to Marc, then the two Frenchmen went out, closing the door quietly behind them.

Valli sat tensely waiting for him to talk. The moments slipped by. She looked over her shoulder into the lighted kitchenette and saw him standing there consumed with his own thoughts, hands on his hips. She groaned silently, stood, and walked quietly into the bright kitchen.

He began opening cabinets, searching.

"What are you looking for?" she asked in a meek voice.

"Coffee," he said tonelessly.

Valli joined in the search, found the small pot, and filled it with water. Marc had discovered a small bag of grounds and a spoon. He lit the stove with a match and started the water heating. Valli placed two white porcelain cups on the kitchen counter and hunted down some sugar, but there was no cream as the icebox held only spoiled milk and a piece of moldy cheese.

Neither said anything while the coffee boiled. Marc was leaning against the counter, arms folded, watching her. She studiously avoided his confronting gaze.

When the coffee was done she poured it carefully and handed him the sugar.

"Just black."

"I had to say yes, Marc," she said at last.

"No, you didn't. He was prepared for a no. I told him you couldn't do it, that you were leaving in the morning on the train. I'd gotten you a ticket, remember?"

"Yes, but—"

"Now, there's no guarantee there'll be another ticket available."

"Then, when the time comes I'll—we'll get out some other way," she said lamely.

"You think so? As soon as the news hits the streets, Paris is going to be jammed with an exodus. You'll be lucky to travel as far as my uncle's estate."

"What do you mean? What news?"

"What Danjou couldn't tell you, but what I will, is that a secret bulletin reached us tonight. Tomorrow it will be all over the radio. Hitler has mounted an all-out offensive against Belgium and France. If you want my verdict, that brittle French line will snap and General von Brauchitsch will have the Wehrmacht crashing through the border."

She gripped her cup, but said nothing, though words were lodged within her throat.

She must have paled, for he frowned and looked suddenly sorry he had said anything. He set his cup down. "Danjou asks that you avoid going to the estate. Stay here in Paris and go through with your ballet performances for the foreseeable future."

"If he wants me to learn anything from Dietrich, isn't it easier to go to the estate where he is?"

"We want to frustrate him. Let him get in touch with you. He will when you don't show up at the estate, especially now that Giselle has fled from under his nose."

"And when he gets in touch with me?"

"And when he gets in touch with you, accept any invitations to parties and dinners that he may offer. Cooperate with one purpose in mind: information."

"You're angry with me," she said.

"No."

She set her cup down, frustrated. "You *are* angry." She went to him, her eyes searching his. "I can handle Dietrich."

He finished his coffee, then set the cup down and looked at his watch. "There are some things I need to take care of. Do you want me to take you back to your flat, or do you intend to stay here tonight?"

His brittle blue gaze stared back at her remotely, shutting her deliberately from his thoughts. *He is angry*, she thought. *He really wanted me on that train tomorrow morning.*

"I'll stay here," she said dully. "If you're busy I don't want to take more of your time."

She expected him to say she was no trouble, but his gaze remained even as he nodded briefly, turned, and went into the small living room. "I'll be in touch," he said simply, and started toward the door.

Upset, she went after him. "Marc!"

He stopped and looked at her, offering no encouragement.

"You're being unfair," she gritted. "Why shouldn't I help my country? We're at war!"

"No reason at all," he said. "Except you're naive if you think you can emerge out of this 'cooperation' with Gestler without finding yourself in his arms. You think you can handle him. Can you?"

"I've no intention of permitting a Gestapo agent to hold me in his arms!"

"Do you have a gun?"

She drew in a breath. "Yes, a nine millimeter. And if necessary, I'll use it."

Her seriousness affected him. He scanned her. "See that you do. If not, I will."

Their gaze held, and he turned away to open the door. "Make sure you lock this after me."

She wanted Marc to be convinced that her feelings were bound up with him. "Wait." She walked to the door, taking his arm. As he looked at her, her eyes warmly clung to his. She threw her arms around his neck and drew his head toward her. "Can't you see I'm in love with you?" she whispered. "Not Dietrich—not Kraig. But you!" With a little cry she pressed her lips to his.

His arms encircled her tightly and the intensity of his kiss matched hers.

"Valli...I love you. I can't stand thinking of him holding you the way I am now."

"He won't," she whispered. "I won't let him. I'll insist on not being alone with him."

"If you can, limit it to parties and dinners, places where there are other people. But be careful, will you?"

"Yes, I will."

"You can reach me at this number. Don't hesitate to call if anything goes wrong."

She nodded. He bent toward her again, then on second thought, drew away. With a look that said everything necessary, he went out into the rain.

# 18

Every ring of the telephone was like a time bomb going off in her heart, and today was no exception. Valli had returned to her own flat the next morning and by noon had gone with Mimi to the theater to practice before that night's performance. Mimi was checking over Valli's costume, freshly delivered from the dry cleaners, when the telephone blared its warning, sending Valli into palpitations. She ran to the small wardrobe room in back and lifted the receiver from its cradle.

"Hello?"

"Ah, Demoiselle Valli," Dietrich said.

Her heart hit bottom. "Oh. Dietrich, yes hello."

"We have worried about you at the estate. You and Giselle both. Uncle Aubert and Aunt Inga expected you both for the weekend and neither of you arrived. Even Cousin Marc has not been heard from since his visit with his Great-Uncle Claude."

She tried to calm herself. "Oh, Dietrich, you didn't know? Giselle returned to Tangier. Fear that the war might interfere with travel sent her home early to be with her husband."

"Perhaps that was wise after all."

His answer surprised her. *He wants Giselle in Tangier so he can blackmail Sebastien!*

"But you have stayed in Paris and that is even better. You must not fear all of the propaganda of the news journalists and radio bulletins. If the Paris government and the fuhrer sign an armistice, you need not be alarmed, fraulein. I will make sure you are treated well, and all the family at the Ransier estate. Even Cousin Marc," came the lightly mocking voice.

Her eyes narrowed, and her cold fingers clenched the receiver. "Yes, I have been quite concerned about the family. It is reassuring that you can do something to make things turn out well."

"Perhaps now you will begin to relax. Is Marc there?"

"No."

"I would like to see you." The interest in his voice was clear, and she steeled herself against the dislike she felt.

"I've a performance tonight."

"Then I must attend."

She forced herself forward. "I do hope you enjoy it."

There was a slight hesitation. "I am sure I will. There is someone I want you to meet tonight. There is a small dinner party at his house. Will you come?" A dinner party should have several other couples at least. "A dinner party? Yes...I'll come."

He sounded pleased. "Until later tonight then. Auf Wiedersehen."

"Yes, goodbye."

Valli replaced the receiver and turned with a frown to find Mimi watching her strangely.

"Was that Monsieur Marc?" Mimi asked.

"No. Dietrich."

Mimi looked at her with open disapproval. "You will have dinner with *him*? When the radio news tells us the Germans are fighting and killing the innocent in Luxembourg?"

"It is business, Mimi," she whispered. "Marc knows all about it. Everything will be all right."

Mimi did not look convinced. "How can anything be right again when the Nazis are conquering all of Europe?"

"That is why I intend to have dinner with Dietrich Gestler," Valli said gravely. "Because so much is wrong. We all must do our part, whether small or great."

Mimi's eyes were worried. "And what is your part, ma petite?"

Valli took her ballet costume from Mimi and gave her wrinkled hand a gentle pat. "To learn as much as I can about Dietrich's reason for being in Paris."

"I do not like it. One does not play with snakes and not get bitten."

"Stop worrying," Valli scolded gently. "And now, I must get ready." She hurried away to dress.

By six P.M. that evening, the Paris Opera Ballet Theater was packed. Valli, wearing her ballerina costume and satin shoes, stood in the corridor with the other dancers, going through their basic routines while introductory orchestra music played in the theater. Valli walked farther down the corridor behind the tall, heavy maroon curtain and parted the edge a little to peer past the front stage and out into the greater audience. She could make out the boxes, but not the people who sat in them. Was Marc out there? Or anyone from the Surete? She looked in the direction of Monsieur Aubert's box and imagined Dietrich seated there. How different tonight was than her stellar performance when joy had filled her heart. She was tense, even nervous, and not at her best.

The ballet director beckoned her to the front of the dance troupe and she ran forward lightly, trying to cover her concern when her ankle twinged. Rodolphe came up to her and kissed both sides of her face for what he called luck, then, grasping her hand they stood in form, ready to dance out on stage like two light-footed deer at the appropriate music signal. Her heart thumped, and she tried to concentrate on her performance now. Nazis, Dietrich, Marc, and the freedom of France must stand back and wait...As the signal for Giselle's solo sounded its familiar note, Valli danced out on stage in her dirndl costume, aware of bright light, of the familiar wood floor beneath her feet, of the loud but grandiose music filling her ears. She saw nothing else as she concentrated on the classic steps and body positions. She performed half-time to the music with arrant concentration and control. She did her slow, double *frappes* with arduous control and strength. Then Rodolphe appeared as Albrecht to declare his love. Valli sailed through the buoyant dance to show her heart. She started on her slow *grands jets*— starting from a standing position, landing firmly, holding after the jump—

It was then that the pain surged through her ankle like an explosion, turning her strength to ash. Before she knew what happened she heard a hard crash beneath her as her head struck the floor. The lights above her seemed to weave and spin, then recede—

The audience gasped in unison, and a murmur like a surging wave from the sea rolled from the back of the theater to the front to converge upon her. Giselle's theme song turned from joy to hesitancy, but then started back up again.

Valli lay there, vaguely aware of Rodolphe kneeling beside her, a look of heartbreak in his eyes.

"Valli!"

The curtain was closing. The lights inside the theater proper were flickering on. The orchestra broke into French ballroom dance music, and the audience turned to each other in whispered alarms.


"I tell you I'm quite all right," Valli said later that evening seated in her dressing room with her foot propped up and some of her ballet troupe gathered around gloomily. Rodolphe hovered beside Doctor Guion, who pronounced that she had injured a tendon. The ballet director paced pulling at his hair. "Now of all times! With Bridgette gone and no one to take your place! How could this happen!"

"Everyone please leave," Doctor Guion spoke with profound displeasure. Barely reaching five feet tall, he marched to the door, swung it open, and pointed with a raise of his black brows. "Out!"

Surprisingly, they slinked away into the hall. Valli had a last glimpse of Rodolphe throwing her a sympathetic kiss, then shaking his head sadly and leaving without a partner. The ballet would be called off for the rest of the season. Valli was told she must keep her ankle elevated to help the pain and swelling and have a good night's sleep. Doctor Guion didn't seem to pay attention to the man who entered the dressing room as everyone filed out. Dietrich brushed past Mimi, as if her small protest belonged to a fly, and came up to the sofa looking down at her.

"A tragedy no less, my dear Valli. But a few weeks rest and you will be as good as new. You'll be dancing in Berlin before you know it—for the fuhrer himself."

Doctor Guion turned to look up at him as if a madman had entered. "Who are you?" he demanded.

Dietrich scanned him coolly. "A close friend of the mademoiselle." He looked at Valli. "Don't worry. I shall soon have a German physician look at your ankle," he said, as if Doctor Guion's prognosis was untrustworthy.

"Monsieur," Doctor Guion said in a chilly voice, "Since I am Mademoiselle Chattaine's doctor—"

"You are no longer her doctor," he cut in. "I have checked your history and credentials. You are a Jew. Your medical knowledge is suspect. You may leave."

Doctor Guion looked shocked. Valli leaned forward prepared to order Dietrich out of her dressing room when she remembered her work for the Surete. She had to bite her tongue to keep from saying anything. Mimi came up and was about to speak but Valli caught her gaze and warned her to silence. "Mimi, I'd like some hot tea please. Now."

Mimi, flushed with anger, gave Dietrich a venomous glance and turned away. "Oui, at once."

Doctor Guion looked at Valli. There was more pain in her soul than her ankle as she dropped her eyes and said nothing in his defense. *God forgive me*, she thought with anguish. The Jewish physician picked up his bag and walked out.

Valli was left alone with Dietrich as the room was cloaked in strained silence. She felt sickened.

"You show more and more good sense, Valli," Dietrich stated. Dressed in black, he stood blond and ruthlessly handsome, taking out a cigarette and flicking a shimmering gold lighter.

Valli steadied her nerves. "Why did you say there would soon be a German physician in Paris?"

His fair brows lifted a fraction as his gaze moved over her. "My dear, you mean you haven't heard the blistering news?"

"No, what news?"

"Well, that is to be expected. You have had your mind totally occupied with getting ready for the ballet. And I suppose the peasants, which hang about you, like that old crow, Mimi, wouldn't know either."

"I resent you speaking so of those dear to me!"

He laughed confidently. Yes, something must have happened, she thought, worriedly. Dietrich was more cocky than usual, more odious, if that were possible.

"All right, my little beauty, don't get upset. Mimi can be endured if you must have her about, but she doesn't like me, so you'll need to tell her to learn some manners. She'll need to learn her place."

What was giving him such brazen confidence? Her alarms grew. The injury to her ankle only made her feel trapped. What had happened today? If only Marc would walk in now...but he wasn't likely to because it was already planned that she would befriend Dietrich. But that appeared to be getting unexpectedly out of hand. Dietrich was taking over. He had changed even since his noon telephone call.

"What news?" she repeated, sitting forward.

In a few steps he was beside her radio, switching it on, and turning the dial. Valli tensed as the brutal harangue of Adolf Hitler rang out, being translated into English by the BBC.

"They've been playing these bulletins every hour," he gloated.

She stood, and while the twinges in her ankle were uncomfortable, she could still walk. She stood silently as the voice of Hitler turned her cold:

> Soldiers of the West Front!
>
> The hour of the decisive fight for the future of the German nation has come.
>
> For three hundred years it has been the aim of English and French rulers to prevent any real consolidation of Europe and, above all, to keep Germany weak and impotent.
>
> For this reason, all my peace overtures have been rejected and war was declared against us.
>
> Soldiers of the West Front! The hour for *you* has now come. The fight beginning today decides the fate of the German nation for the next one thousand years.

Valli looked at Dietrich, trying to remain calm. "What fight beginning today?"

"The 'Lightning war,' the *Blitzkrieg*," he stated proudly. "There are now 2.5 million soldiers of the German Wehrmacht, formed into 102 divisions, 9 of them armored and 6 motorized, massed along the French, Belgian, and Dutch borders." He smiled tightly and looked at his watch. "At 3:30 A.M. on May 10, the world as we know it was changed forever."

She stared at him. On the border of France? "How do you know this?"

"Because I am an official in the *schutzstaffel*, the SS as you know it. By now swarms of screeching stuka bombers are finding ready targets in Belgium and the Netherlands.

German panzer divisions and infantry have crossed the Western Front. The end in view? To conquer the British Isles and smash France."

Valli could almost imagine the sound of the Luftwaffe and see the skies over Belgium and the Netherlands aflame with dropping bombs. And the skies of France? She made her way to the window and looked out, but the sky was merely overcast, yet the street was filling with Parisians looking tense.

Because war on this magnitude had been too horrible for the democracies to contemplate, they had looked the other way. Like children whistling in the dark, they had hoped the evil would just go away.

She whirled. "So you call this terror 'honorable' war, do you? Your fuhrer's greedy appetite has no end. It began with the theft of Austria."

"Theft! Austria is the birthplace of Hitler!"

"And the world stood by and allowed the brutal invasion of Czechoslovakia, because they feared their comfortable lives would be interrupted by war and suffering coming to their own back doors!" She limped toward him angrily. "By doing nothing, they allowed the monster to grow even stronger: the ruthless invasion of Poland, the arrest of Jews—then Denmark and Norway, Holland, Belgium, and now even the border of France."

"And after that, Britain," he scorned. "Like a chicken, we will wring their neck. And eventually the United States—a nation of 'mongrels' as the fuhrer calls them."

"Better a mongrel than a lover of cruelty and death! You Gestapo are all the same, like brutal, deceptive, gangsters."

Dietrich's eyes sparked. He reached over and switched off the radio, almost knocking it over.

"As Hitler has said—'The victor will not be asked afterward if he told the truth. In starting and waging a war, it is not right that matters, but victory.'"

"The devil would agree. It is my opinion you Nazis are his army of flesh and blood."

Dietrich stepped forward, grabbing her arms so tightly that his fingers bruised her flesh. He gave her a shake and muttered something in German. His eyes narrowed, then he released her. "You asked for it. You are deliberately trying to enrage me."

Valli sank weakly to the sofa, but glared up at him. "What is it you are here in Paris to find out? Or are you here to place Petain on the seat of a puppet government in Vichy, France?"

He smiled coolly. "I am here for a number of reasons." He scanned her. "One of them is to retrieve the information you received from that bungling Englishman, Blystone."

Totally surprised, she lost her anger and stared at him. "Information that *I* have! You jest."

"Don't behave the innocent demoiselle. Don't you think I know you are working with the Surete? You and Marc both. He was fool enough to think I believed him at the estate when he pretended sympathies for Berlin. You both work for Colonel Ransier. And it was to you that Blystone passed his canvas bag. I saw the white rose on your handbag. But we will not talk here," he said sharply. "I will get the information from you at a more 'convenient' place—you are coming with me."

She didn't move. Stunned, she watched him, wondering how things could change so quickly. "Before Paris becomes a seething mob of hysterical travelers, we'd better leave the theater. I'll call down to my driver to bring the motorcar around front."

Valli watched him walk over to her wardrobe, select the things he wanted, including her coat, and walk back. "Put this on. It's raining out." He crushed out his cigarette.

Valli held her long coat, looking at him. A terrible realization was crawling through her mind as she heard voices gathering out on the sidewalk. Dietrich heard them too and he strode to the lone window and drew aside the lace curtain to peer below. As he did, she glanced across the dressing room to her handbag. Inside was her gun.

"A crowd is gathering to pass the rumors along," he murmured. "Sheep. Stupid sheep. Fit for the slaughter."

She took a slow step in the direction of the table and her purse.

Dietrich turned around and looked at her with a subdued but gloating smile.

"Within hours Paris will be in our hands—and everything within it." He scanned her. "General Walthar von Brauchitsch has sent 40, then 60, then 120, and finally 150 divisions against France. Magnificent! Can you walk? Or do I need to carry you to the motorcar?"

"Are you mad? I won't go with you anywhere."

"You have no say in the matter. You'll either come calmly, or I'll need to give you an injection."

"Injection?"

"Nothing hostile you understand. Just a mild sedative. It will make it easier to get you in the motorcar and to the Ransier estate." Amusement showed in his eyes. "You want to be safe when the victorious German army enters Paris, mademoiselle. I cannot guarantee that unless you are with me."

He reached inside his pocket and took out a hypodermic needle and a small vial of solution. "Will you come calmly, or must I force it?"

She looked from the needle to his eyes, then toward the door. As she did, her gaze briefly skimmed her handbag. Why hadn't she kept it nearer?

"I've no choice so it seems," she said with dignity. "I can walk. My ankle is not broken, just swollen. But if you think I have information to give you, you are deceived. There was nothing in that canvas bag but some smaller pouches of Sahara sand."

He smiled cryptically. "Did you empty the bags? No, I can see by the enlightened look in your face that you did not, but that you now understand there is something important. Important to *me* that is, to my future in a German-occupied France. The best of everything will soon be at my control." He looked pleased with himself.

She tried to delay. If Mimi realized something was wrong, she may have gone for help. *Please, Lord, help her understand and go for help.*

He took her arm and turned her toward the door. "Make no resistance and nothing will happen to you. We will have a little talk, that is all. We are old friends, remember?" There was a light mockery in his voice. "I was to be your future brother-in-law."

Perhaps she could get him to talk? "You killed Blystone for nothing," she accused. "The bungling old Englishman foiled you, the brilliant Gestapo agent Dietrich."

"He deserved to die," he said with dismissal. "No, do not take your handbag. What do you have, a gun?"

Her heart sank.

He opened it, smirked, and removed the pistol, placing it inside his belt. "Come. Before the crowd makes traveling impossible."

"The information you say I have—you are wrong. Bly-stone foiled you," she repeated. She could see the word "foiled" upset his pride.

"You're lying," he said. "He placed those postcards in your handbag and you passed them to Captain Durell. But that no longer matters. It is the canvas bag that interests me, and it always has."

"Why don't the postcards matter? It is you who are lying."

"You might as well know," he boasted. "It was about the *Blitzkrieg*. That information was what Himmler's SS called 'Case Yellow,' or the 'Y' plan for short. A few months ago the tactical plan for the German offensive on the Western Front fell into the hands of the Belgian general staff when a Luftwaffe plane was forced down in Belgium because of bad weather. Spies working for the French had pilfered the documents that detailed the objectives for Case Yellow. And French and British air reconnaissance reported heavy concentrations of troops and panzers just behind the Reich frontier. Yet in a stunning failure to evaluate and respond to a mass of intelligence, the French high commands let it slip through their fingers. They did nothing. And now it no longer matters because the successful *Blitzkrieg* is presently in progress, and as you heard on the radio, France will soon surrender. The German offensive is only thirty miles from Paris."

Valli stared at him. "They knew?" she whispered.

"Someone did," he said with a cool smile, "and chose not to prepare."

"Collaborators!" she said in anger. "Traitors—"

"It's too late for such useless emotion. What I want remains in the canvas bag. You see, as much as I despised

Blystone and the British, he was more clever than I first thought. And you are going to tell me where the bag is."

Her heart wanted to stop, then pound so hard she was breathless. Information in the canvas bag? Did he know this for sure?

"You brought it to Paris," he said.

Keep him occupied, delay him. "And if I did?"

"You're going to give it to me."

"What if it no longer exists? I left it on the train. I didn't think it mattered and it was too heavy to carry around. Anyway, I think you are lying. If you thought I had the bag, why didn't you question me at Davide's mission station?"

"I didn't know then." He smiled. "You see, I caught Blystone in Lisbon. The poor dolt was alive for several hours after I captured him. He talked. He told me he'd given it to you, and he said the postcards were in your handbag. And that they went to Marc."

"What does Giselle have to do with all this?"

"Never mind that."

She struck out blindly, hoping against hope to discover the truth. "Blackmailing her will not get you the information. You'll have to deal with me. She told me everything. After all, we had our disagreement over Kraig, but we *are* sisters. She confided in me before she went back to Tangier."

"She wouldn't have told you everything. There is another matter that you can't help me on. Too bad. She'll have to get the information I want from Ambassador Ransier, or should I say Colonel Ransier of the Surete. His new position in the embassy fools no one. We have German agents in Tangier and Casablanca."

"What can Sebastien tell you?" she asked boldly. "What can Giselle get from him that you want? Information on the French fleet?"

His smile wiped clean and he looked at her, surprised. "So she did risk confiding in you. The little fool!"

*The French fleet. Then Marc's suspicion had been right.* "If you think the Nazi U-boats can blow them up in Oran you're mistaken," she said boldly, daring to push still further into blind waters. She had taken several small steps backward toward the table, but he was so enraged he paid little attention. "They are on to you. They'll move the ships to the Suez Canal."

His golden brows lifted. "The French navy need have no fears that the U-boats will sink them. The Suez? Absurd!"

"Not absurd at all. You'll see. Now that Germany has begun its invasion of the Western Front, the French fleet will leave Oran for the Suez."

He smirked. "I am well aware that French admiral Darlan promised Churchill he would sail them to Canada. Churchill believed him at first, but Aubert has discovered through collaborators in Reynaud's cabinet that England suspects that Admiral Darlan will not sail the French warships to Canada and has no intentions of donating the navy to Britain."

*Canada?*

"We have good reason to believe Churchill will devise some plan to use the British warships in North Africa to foil the Nazis. Sebastien will be one of the first to acquire knowledge of the plan, and it is I that will learn what Churchill's strategy is.

"As soon as Marshall Petain is placed in power, Germany will have a French puppet government under their control. We will seize the warships and turn them on England. Churchill fears the formation of a giant German navy. When we command the Atlantic, the fall of England will be certain. We could blockade her. Without food from her colonies and armaments from the United States, she will be forced to surrender!"

That was it! That's what Giselle is being blackmailed to learn—Churchill's plan to keep the French ships from being used against England. Valli said nothing. Her heart thudded. But how to get that information to Marc?

The *Blitzkrieg* was progressing in full strength at this very moment. If the German panzer divisions crashed through the French defense, they would come storming across France toward Paris—Petain would be swiftly placed in power and call for a surrender to Hitler. If so, Britain hoped Admiral Darlan would refuse to turn the warships over to Germany, but if he did not...?

Suddenly emotionally exhausted, Valli sank onto the sofa and simply looked up at him. "I'm not going anywhere, Dietrich. You'll have to shoot me here."

"Don't be absurd, Valli. Paris will soon be under Nazi control. Fortunately, I will be able to provide for your security, and not merely because I need information from you. I have generous plans for one so lovely. I will soon be a rich man." He looked again at his watch.

She hardly heard him as he walked back to the radio. "It is almost time for Petain's speech," he said smugly. He turned the radio back on. As he searched the dial, she wondered what he meant. Why would Petain give a speech? Reynaud was the Prime Minister...or was he?

"France has all but surrendered," Dietrich told her. "The French units are broken by superior force. By now they should be disjointed and out of touch. German armored units can penetrate at will. The French military machine can no longer function. Marshall Petain has accepted the charge to form a new cabinet dominated by military men to bring about the surrender. Here he is now—"

Valli stiffened as the quiet, sad voice came on the air:

French men and women:

It is with heavy heart that I tell you today that we must stop the fight. I sent a message to the enemy yesterday to ask him if he would meet with me, as between one soldier and another after the fight, and honorably seek a way to put an end to the hostilities.

Valli sat, sickened, unable to move.

A knock sounded on the door.

Dietrich turned down the radio and walked to answer it. "Ma chere," Mimi said, "it is I, Mimi. I have brought tea and sandwiches. You must keep up your strength."

"No," Valli called, afraid Mimi would get entangled in the ordeal, but Dietrich glanced impatiently toward Valli, then threw open the door. Mimi stood with a pot of tea and one of the theater boys wheeled a cart of sandwiches, cakes, and tea.

"Quickly, we haven't much time, mademoiselle can use some energy," Dietrich said curtly. "In fact, wrap up the food. We'll take it with us. We have a long drive."

Valli stood, trying to hold back her alarm, and Mimi shot him a glance. "Where are you going with mademoiselle?"

"That, woman, is none of your business. Just do as I say."

"Bosch!" Mimi hissed and threw the scalding tea in his face. Dietrich cried out, his hands flinging upward to his eyes as he stumbled backward.

"Quick, Valli, run!"

Valli's gaze darted to the theater boy...Jacquette!

He appeared surprised by Mimi's response, as though it were unplanned. "Both of you, run!"

Valli grabbed Mimi's arm and rushed toward the door. The loud crack of a gunshot ripped through her ears just as they crossed the threshold. Mimi staggered in the hall and fell.

*Mimi!*

Mimi crumpled to her knees. Valli, dazed, stared at the bullet wound through her back, straight toward her heart.

"Mimi," she wept, sinking to her knees beside her and gathering her into her arms, tried to pull her toward the stairs down to the theater lobby. Mimi looked at her blankly, and her head tipped forward against Valli's shoulder. She was already gone. Valli, in shock, slipped to the floor on her knees, still clutching the silent elderly figure. "Oh Mimi, Mimi—" she wept, holding onto her frail body as tightly as she could. "Don't leave me, Mimi—"

In the back of her mind she was aware of a struggle going on in the dressing room, the sound of the tea cart crashing over, the hard breathing of men in hand-to-hand combat.

From the street people were shouting, there were honking horns as the traffic out of Paris was jammed. The long rush was on to escape Paris before the Germans arrived.

Valli sat looking down at Mimi, and at that moment little else seemed to matter. The world had stopped. The reality of the awfulness of the moment invaded her heart. Dietrich had killed her. He could have shot Jacquette, even herself, but he had taken his vengeance out on Mimi—an elderly woman, a citizen with few political beliefs.

Mimi was just one of the many casualties from the Nazi invasion.

There was another gunshot—then silence.

Her heart thudded. She heard footsteps. "Valli?" gritted Dietrich.

She released Mimi and struggled to her feet. Turning, she limped toward the stage. She pushed through the heavy curtain, breathing hard, and found herself on the dance floor with the lights still glowing. She looked out at the empty theater, but through the high windows she could hear the noise of the mob on the street.

Dietrich was coming, she could hear his footsteps in the hallway behind the theater curtain. She knew there were some stairs on the other side of the dance floor leading down to seats in the lower auditorium. She struggled across the floor, trying not to put her full weight on her ankle.

Dietrich pushed aside the curtain and entered the dance floor. "Stop! It will do you no good, Valli!"

"You killed Mimi."

"She was to blame."

"Stay away from me, Dietrich!"

"Valli?" The voice came from below in the theater, followed by running footsteps. It was Monsieur Danjou. She saw three dim figures running through the aisles.

"Valli!" Marc shouted, "get down!"

She dropped to the floor as bullets flew, making deafening sounds, through the theater curtains and walls.

Dietrich flung himself through the curtain and rushed down the hallway. Danjou and another man jumped up onto the stage and ran after him. Valli felt Marc's arms gathering her into his tight embrace.

"Darling—"

"He killed Mimi," she wept. "He shot her in the back."

He whispered his comfort, stroking her damp hair from her face and kissing her tenderly. "My poor, brave darling."

"Jacquette, too," she choked. "He shot him—"

Marc's arms tightened around her, and he buried his face into her hair. She clung to him, thinking now of his sorrow as well. The fall of Paris and the grief of France would touch millions, but the deaths of Mimi and Jacquette drove home to her heart that the evil of human sin had touched individuals. It was not a million tearstained faces she saw as the Germans marched into Paris with the swastika, but the smiling wrinkled face of faithful, caring Mimi and the courage of young Jacquette.

Just thirty-eight days after the initiation of the *Blitzkrieg*, the Reich victory came to fulfillment. South of Paris, the armies of the French Republic laid down their arms, and the new government of France under Marshall Petain appealed to Hitler for an armistice.

The French armies broke southward, through and around the city, and Paris was deliberately left undefended, surrendered to German occupation so that it would not be destroyed. The cities of Le Harve and Montmedy, the northern anchor of the famous Maginot Line, also fell to the Reich, and impregnable Verdun was cracked.

In the last free days of Paris, Valli's light-colored clothes turned a depressing gray and her eyes smarted with smoke as the French people continued to try and escape ahead of the panzer tanks. The omnibuses were still running, as was the subway, though late and sometimes sporadic. More gloomy than even this were the radio stations broadcasting martial music, a tribute to the last glorious battles of France against her enemies in 1914-1918. The news bulletins and communiques were interspersed with the music, and she heard people talking about bomb damage in the outlying districts around the city caused by stuka bombers. The cafés remained opened, and so did the Bank of France, and she saw long lines of desperate Parisians hoping to withdraw their savings for the long, lean years ahead before the Gestapo arrived in full force to confiscate it all.

The same night the Germans neared Paris, Marc and Danjou buried Mimi and Jacquette in a hasty ceremony just outside Paris near an abbey. Marc had found an old minister from one of the cathedrals who had refused to leave in the face of coming terror, and the minister gravely but calmly committed their bodies to the ground until the Great Day when Christ would call them forth.

"Only the body sleeps. The real friends you have lost are alive forever. I trust that they knew Jesus Christ as their Savior from their sins and that they are now at peace in His presence. For to be absent from the body, is to be present with the Lord, so Saint Paul has written in his epistle to the Philippians.

"For the Lord himself shall descend from heaven with a shout, with the voice of the archangel, and with the trump of God, and the dead in Christ shall rise first. Then, we, which are alive and remain shall be caught up together with them in the clouds to meet the Lord in the air, and so shall we ever be with the Lord. Wherefore, beloved, comfort one another with these words."

"Amen," Valli and Marc repeated.

Valli's tears had dried and her heart, though sorrowing, was not so burdened that she could not look toward the future with hope and trust in God. She knew beyond any doubt that dear Mimi believed that Jesus' atoning sacrifice on the cross paid the penalty for her sin before a holy God. She knew she was safe with Him, and that she would see her again one day. One day...she looked up toward the dark sky but could not see the stars or the moon for the heavy pallor of smoke that hung over Paris. But she knew that the light continued to shine brightly just on the other side. Now she would walk by faith.

Marc had a personal ritual he had wished to perform for Jacquette, and the minister accompanied him to the grave. Marc removed some emblem he had carried on a chain honoring the fallen soldier of valor who served with distinction in the French Foreign Legion. Valli's heart knew a pang. Had it been given him as a boy when his father died victoriously for France in Tangier? She believed so. That he wished to lay it with Jacquette showed how deeply he felt about his boyhood friend. Marc also kept something that had belonged to Jacquette: she saw Marc place a harmonica in his jacket pocket.

A few minutes later Marc joined her, taking her elbow. He led her out the garden gate toward the others.

Dietrich, she had learned, had escaped; he was probably joining up with the brutal conquerors heading toward Paris.

Danjou said, "General de Gaulle has managed to slip away unnoticed on the British general Spears' plane for London. There are others in Reynaud's government who will board the ship *Massilia* for Casablanca."

Valli looked at Marc. *What about us?* she wondered. *How will we get out?*

Danjou handed him an envelope. "From Monsieur Claude. He refuses to leave France. He says he will die here if necessary. He wants you to give this letter to Sebastien. And he has given this to you." He handed him another thick envelope. Marc took them slowly and placed them inside his jacket. "I cannot leave him here."

"It is no use, Marc. I tried to get him to leave. He is very ill, in bed, and refuses. He has the Tricolor of France in his room and his medals from Verdun. It is best to leave him this last choice of dignity. A choice of freedom."

Valli squeezed Marc's arm, comfortingly. He nodded. "All right. What of you, monsieur?"

"I," said Danjou with his dour smile, "will join General de Gaulle in London as soon as possible. You are to go on to Tangier and report to Sebastien. We will be in touch with you as soon as possible."

Danjou looked at Valli. "I understand Gestapo agent Gestler shared important information with you. For your service to France, mademoiselle, you will be gratefully remembered as one of us in the Free French movement under General de Gaulle."

Valli's eyes prickled with tears. "Thank you, monsieur."

"Now, can you explain to Marc and myself what you learned tonight?"

There was little time. She was told that a plane waited outside of Paris in a deserted field ready to fly them to Marseille. While they rode there, seated between Marc and Danjou, Valli told all that Dietrich had boasted of.

"Traitors," Danjou murmured. "We made sure the information about Case Yellow reached our own government, but someone kept it from our military. Perhaps from Reynaud himself." He looked over at Marc. "Looks as if collaboration with the Germans began long before the Wehrmacht arrived tonight."

Marc and Danjou were still discussing the other bits of information when the motorcar drove over the bumpy field to the waiting aircraft. Marc took Valli's hand and they ran toward the plane as the motor started.

Danjou smiled briefly. "I will join you later in Tangier. Find Blystone's satchel just in case there is some truth to what Gestler boasted to Mademoiselle Chattaine."

They looked at each other, then quickly shook hands.

"'La France a perdu une bataille! Mais la France n'a pas perdu la guerre!'" Marc said.

France has lost a battle, but France has not lost the war! Valli reiterated the words to herself that Marc had spoken to Danjou, words attributed to France's heroine, Joan of Arc.

Danjou was grave. "Viva la France," he repeated.

A minute later she was in the plane with Marc, buckling her seat belt. They began moving along over the darkened field, gaining speed. A moment later she felt her seat tilt as the plane lifted toward the dark sky, leaving behind Nazi-occupied France.

"It's just the beginning," Marc said, as though he read her thoughts. "One day, if God wills, we will live to see France free again and the Third Reich destroyed."

*But oh! the long, torturous road to be traveled before that distant hour,* she thought. *Au revoir, beloved Mimi.*

On June 18, General Charles de Gaulle broadcast from London, calling for a continuation of French resistance. The British government had also recognized him as the leader of the Free French, the FFL.

"This capitulation was signed before all means of resistance had been exhausted," de Gaulle's voice crackled over the airwaves. "This capitulation delivers into the hand of the enemy, who will use them against our Allies, our arms, our warships, and our gold. There is no longer on the soil of France an independent government capable of upholding the interests of France and the French overseas."

*But the Free French will fight on,* Valli thought.

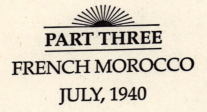

## PART THREE

### FRENCH MOROCCO
### JULY, 1940

# 19

The crescent-shaped harbor of Tangier Bay glittered a brilliant blue beneath a hot sky. Along the Ville Nouvelle, the European sector of Tangier, the stately chancellery of the French Legation glistened white amid the emerald green of palmeries. The International Zone consisted of the French section, the British, and the Spanish. The Europeans, called "Tangerinos" by the natives, sat in Petit Socco's thriving plazas amid deep shade, sipping sherry and reading the *Tangier Gazette* and appearing as far removed from the horrors going on in Europe as did the Americans.

Valli noticed that the bay was crowded with PT boats and subchasers and mentioned it to Marc.

"They're used by smugglers so they can dart across the Straits of Gibraltar," he said. "And we have as many international spies in Tangier as we now have Nazis in Paris."

They had taken a hackney from the harbor down the Boulevard Pasteur, toward Great-Aunt Calanthe's house, and past the Café de Paree, where men in white summer suits and Panama hats loitered, and parrots sat calmly in loops hanging from rings on the lattice-style cabana roof. Native Tanjawis were garbed in the hooded pristine white robes called *djellabas*. Suddenly Valli had an overwhelming desire to find refuge in Calanthe's home where she had grown up. Would she be waiting for her with open arms? She prayed that she would, that reconciliation might warm both of their hearts in the dark, tragic days that smothered the world.

"Are you sure you remember where you buried Blystone's bag?" Marc asked again, frowning against the sunlight that beat down upon them. He lowered his hat and watched her with the same alertness she had noticed on several occasions during the long journey from Marseille by boat.

"I can find the spot again," she repeated, trying to sound confident. "Unless Davide tore his house down and the sands have been at work."

He smiled wryly. "I'll take your word for it."

"Dietrich could be lying. Why would Blystone have kept something back from you?"

"It's too bad he's not around to tell us, but with all the turncoats recently, I don't think I'll be surprised if there isn't something to what Gestler boasted to you about. You're sure he didn't give you any hints?" he asked again.

"Well, only that he said it was something that could help him in his new job at the Paris Gestapo. Do you think Dietrich will dare show up here in Tangier?"

"I've every confidence he will. After all, he now represents the victorious Reich. He's probably as cocky as ever. The Germans have designs on North Africa as well. And now that the Vichy government in France is cooperating with Hitler, the colonies are as ripe for picking as the French fleet."

Valli opened her palmetto fan and glumly cooled her face and throat. "Well the heat tells me I'm home at last."

"I don't like rushing you, but within twenty-four hours I would like to head for Davide's. In the meantime, while you visit with Calanthe, I'll meet with colonel Sebastien at the embassy. I suppose Giselle will be with him. She can't have arrived much before we did. I'll send her over to speak with you tonight if she'll cooperate."

Valli wasn't looking forward to the trip to Algeria, but she knew it was urgent, and once she saw Calanthe she would know how well she was to be received back into the family.

Madame Calanthe Malaret's house was a grand specimen of flamingo pink with a white, heat-reflecting roof. There were cool palm gardens and terraces and a backdrop of blue water and sparkling sand, and now, many international ships of various sizes.

The hackney stopped at a bend in the drive and Marc got out and came around to help her down.

"You're sure you won't come in and rest awhile?" she asked him.

"I want to get straight over to the embassy. I'll be in touch tomorrow, or sooner if necessary. You know where you can find me."

"You can't come to dinner tonight? It will be wonderful on the lawn overlooking the bay."

His warm blue eyes flicked over her face and lingered on her lips. "Anywhere with you would be wonderful, but my personal wishes must be set aside until some other matters are attended to. Enjoy your evening—I'll be thinking of you." He leaned over and kissed her, his touch romantic and reassuring. "Au revoir," he said softly, turning to board the hackney for the French embassy.

Valli watched him go, shading her eyes with her hand, and then looked up toward the house. An elderly woman had come out the front door to meet her and stood on the sheltered porch surrounded by jasmine and other bright, warm-colored flowers. Her white hair brushed back into a smooth bun, Calanthe came down the steps wearing a long, cool flowered blue tunic.

Valli, heart thumping, took several steps, tossing aside her hurts, then ran to meet her.

Calanthe's slender arms opened to hold her, and they clung to each other with tears and words of apology and affection.

"Dear child, will you forgive a foolish old lady for her pride? I wanted to write you so many times!"

"Calanthe, of course I will."

"How wonderful you look, child, how blessed I am to have you back again. And this time *nothing* will be permitted to drive us apart."

Valli, brushing the tears from her cheeks, smiled happily, and kissed her great-aunt's pale cheeks. "I'm so glad to be back, even if it is under sorrowful circumstances."

"Yes, the news is filled with dreadful stories about the Germans. Oh Paris, how my heart breaks for the treachery done to her. But I have been listening to General de Gaulle's radio broadcasts and he will soon set up a government in Algeria to continue the resistance. Come, child, let's go inside, out of this heat. Lunch is ready and you look as if you could use something cool to drink. I saw Captain Durell just now." Her eyes sparkled. "I always did think him a fine and handsome young soldier, so different than those who have betrayed France."

*Yes,* thought Valli, pleased, *so very different, indeed.*

They entered the oblong sitting room she remembered

so well, with tall French windows which opened onto a terrace to a wide view of Tangier Bay. The lovely, familiar view drew her like a magnet. She had thought of this view so many times while schooling in Paris, and, later, working at the theater.

"You're limping a little," Calanthe noticed, surprised.

"A mild sprain. It will heal." She didn't trouble her with the dreadful details of her fall. "It will be some years before I ever get back to the Paris theater, anyway." A sadness seeped into her voice. How long would Germany occupy France? The realization was staggering. She blinked, as if to shut it from her thinking.

The colors in Tangier were always brighter than anything she remembered. She looked back out to the deep blue bay glinting like a jewel against hot white sand, the green and amber of squat date palms.

"I suppose you would like to see Nanette."

Valli turned. "Nanette?"

A small worried pucker formed between her aunt's silver brows as she opened the French double doors onto the terrace. A waft of warm saltwater air rustled the greenery on the white-gold table. "I admit I haven't seen her in two years."

"Nanette?" Valli repeated.

"You'll need to arrange matters with Giselle."

"Aunt Calanthe, *who* is Nanette?"

Calanthe looked at her, her frown deepening. "Do you mean to tell me you have not even bothered to learn her name?" she scolded.

Embarrassed, Valli shook her head. "Why...no, I'm sorry...I've not heard of her until now. Is she a relative of yours?"

Calanthe stared back, astounded, searching Valli's eyes. At last, she must have seen something that startled and overwhelmed her, for she paled, and a shocked breath escaped her lips. She reached to hold onto the terrace balustrade.

"Calanthe—" Valli took her arm. "Are you all right? Do you need anything?"

Calanthe closed her eyes, resting her forehead into her pale hand. "Need anything?" she murmured. "Only a good dose of reality...I think. How could I have just accepted—" she stopped, words failing her, and then gave up, shaking her head. "Oh dear, oh dear," was all she said.

Valli led her to the wrought-iron chair in the corner of the terrace and stood looking at her, concerned. "What is it, Aunt? Who is Nanette?"

Great-Aunt Calanthe took another moment before she straightened her shoulders and said sheepishly: "Your daughter."

Valli looked at her.

"That is what Giselle told me, several years ago."

"Giselle told you—" she gasped.

"Yes. You didn't know?"

"How could I have known what she told you? And why would anyone even think that? Both you and Giselle knew that Kraig had called off the marriage."

Calanthe sighed. "I see. You say Kraig called it off?"

"Did she tell you differently?"

"It appears as though she told me a great many things differently," Calanthe said tiredly. "The baby, the marriage. I was told you called it off because the idea of marriage no longer appealed to you. You insisted on putting your ballet career first, before everything, including Nanette. You didn't want the baby..."

Valli sat down, anger churning in her heart. Giselle!

"Needless to say Nanette is not yours—but Giselle's," Calanthe said quietly, "and I fell for her story...all these years. I believed that Paris and success in the theater had changed you, that you had told Kraig you were no longer interested in marriage...and that you didn't feel motivated to raise the child."

"So that's why you—" she stopped.

"Yes, that's why I was angry with you. You had so profoundly disappointed my expectations. There were times when I felt the need to write and tell you what I thought of your attitude, but Giselle said it would only make matters worse. I've made a dreadful mistake, child. Now I feel as responsible for this misunderstanding as Giselle. I should never have allowed her to control me as she has. I should have searched through all this for myself. I was hurt and angry, and my damaged pride demanded that I wall myself in. In the end, the silence between us produced even more misunderstanding, until the years themselves separated us even further."

Calanthe massaged her forehead as though it ached with confusion.

Valli, benumbed, could think of nothing to tell her. She sat looking at her, astounded by what she had heard. A child out of wedlock, that she had rejected in favor of her ballet career!

Giselle's lie certainly explained Calanthe's disappointment and why she had disinherited her. Did it also explain why Dietrich could blackmail her? Did he know about Nanette? He must. And that would explain the reason for Giselle rushing back to Tangier. What was it she had said in Paris—she had to return at once. She must do something before Dietrich could gain the upper hand. And when she had asked, "why Tangier?" Giselle had said, "Because that's where it will all happen."

"Not in Paris?"

Giselle had shaken her head, no.

Valli stood. "Aunt Calanthe, is there any way Sebastien might know about Nanette?"

"No, not at all. Giselle convinced me to help her raise and conceal Nanette all these years to protect your reputation. I thought I was being sacrificial for your benefit, in spite of your ungrateful attitude. Secretly I was furious with your recklessness. Now I can see it all so clearly—it was Giselle—all that time! I should have known. She's always been one to compromise standards, from the time she turned fourteen."

"Where is Nanette now?" she asked in a low voice.

Calanthe noted her urgency and looked at her curiously. "Truthfully, I don't know. She was being cared for by a French governess in Casablanca."

"Casablanca..."

Calanthe stood, suddenly indignant. "Now I know why she wouldn't let me see Nanette this past year. The child probably looks like her—" she stopped, her eyes averting, "and nothing at all like you."

At the moment none of this mattered to Valli. Nanette must be protected from Dietrich. She had to speak to Giselle, to make sure the child was safe. The matter of the lie and the pain it had caused could be handled later. The important thing was that Calanthe now understood the truth, and that in the end, God had mended their relationship.

"I suppose you're upset with me," Calanthe said, troubled. "I couldn't blame you if you left and never spoke to me again."

"Oh Calanthe, what you don't understand is that I have missed you terribly. Now that your arms are open to me again, why should I allow the pain from this past misunderstanding ruin the future? I love you and I forgive you, but God is the one who is the greatest forgiver. And is He in control of our lives? Does He have good plans for His children? The Scriptures tell us that He does."

Tears filled Calanthe's eyes. "You always did see the roses; I seem to have majored on the thorns. And Giselle—Giselle thinks all the flowers in the garden are for her enjoyment alone, selfish to the very end. She's to be pitied, not hated."

"I don't hate my sister at all," Valli said, her voice pained. "She's gone her own way, and in many ways she's suffering for it. I don't think she's been very happy with her lies. Now they're coming back to haunt her."

"You're right. But I'm not in a very good position to criticize her now, am I? I've not followed the Lord as closely as I should have. If I'd had a shepherd's heart I would have come seeking you when I thought you'd strayed. Instead, both Giselle and I have strayed. It was my lack of wisdom that permitted her lie to survive."

Valli took her hand. "But all of His children have times when they lack wisdom and suffer failure. God can use them as stepping stones. There is still time to follow the Shepherd. Sometimes He leads through valleys, sometimes to mountaintops, but we can have joy because we know He has good plans for us and not evil."

"Yes, where is that verse in the Scriptures about wisdom?"

"In Proverbs, 'The fear of the Lord is the beginning of wisdom.'"

"I should have remembered that. When I'm not trusting in God, I seem to have no way to even begin to know truth from error," Calanthe said thoughtfully. "And Giselle, maybe now, if I can show love for her after all that's happened, she'll be more inclined to listen."

"Where is she now, at the French embassy?"

"No, she and Sebastien left several days ago for the Foreign Legion military post. They also mentioned visiting Davide and trying to bring him here. Poor Davide! His health is troubling him again. What that boy needs is a long rest in one of my feather beds!"

Valli smiled. "We'll have to hog-tie him to accomplish that."

A servant came into the sitting room. "Monsieur Captain Durell is here."

"He must have been told that Sebastien is at Bel-Abbes," Valli said. Excusing herself from Calanthe, she hurried from the terrace and through the sitting room to the hall. Marc came toward her.

"How is it going with Calanthe?" he asked in a low voice.

"Very well. She told me about Giselle. I suppose this means we'll need to leave?"

"I'm afraid so, first thing in the morning. I'm anxious about Blystone's bag. The sooner you retrieve it, the less I'll need to worry about Gestler."

"You don't think he's here?" she asked in a hushed voice.

Marc's gaze became remote, as though he preferred to shield her. "I've learned never to underestimate a German agent. If we're here, and Giselle is here, you can be sure his superiors have sent him."

Valli hesitated. She must tell Marc about Nanette, but out of respect for her sister, she believed she should speak to her first.

"I'll be ready to leave when you are. Do come in. Calanthe will want to say hello. Would you like something cool to drink?"

Calanthe appeared in the sitting room doorway. "Captain Durell, how good you've come by. You've learned about the colonel being at the legionnaire fort?"

"Madame Malaret," he said with a small bow. "Yes, the aide de camp told me. I am afraid I must escort your niece there in the morning."

"Oh dear! So soon?"

"We have some important business to take care of with the colonel, but I promise to return her to you as soon as possible."

"Well, that is very good of you. Then if you needn't go until morning, you will stay the evening I hope? I'll have Banji ready a room for you."

"Yes, do stay, Marc," Valli encouraged. Her eyes laughed at him. "I must make up for that incident years ago on the lawn."

Marc smiled briefly, and Calanthe said curiously: "Oh? What incident was that, dear?"

"Marc was relaxing on the lawn and woke up to a big surprise."

"Well, I hope you didn't get a sunburn falling asleep in that dreadful heat."

"I got burnt all right."

Valli covered a laugh, looped her arm through his, and pulled him toward the stairs. "I'll see him to Davide's room. There's even fresh clothing there."

"Oh dear! He'd never fit into Davide's clothes," said Calanthe, coming up to the bottom of the stairway as they climbed up together. "He'll pull the buttons." Again, Valli covered a laugh. "We'll manage, Calanthe."

"I've my own baggage outside," he told her, amused.

"Banji! Bring up the captain's luggage, please," Valli called.

That evening, the scent of citrus blossoms, frangi-pani, and the Mediterranean air drifted to them on the lower terrace where they were having dinner in the garden overlooking the Bay. A white-robed servant waited on them, serving fresh fish that the locals had caught, a large salad with everything in it from black olives to the Tanjawi's staple, couscous, and a large supply of fruits and desserts. The conversation was pleasant and Marc appeared to steer clear of bringing up the war and the capitulation of France for fear it would disturb Calanthe. It was not until almost the end of the meal that Calanthe herself brought up the fall of France.

"I just can't understand it, Marc. How did the Germans ever manage to break through the Maginot Line?"

"Since 1933 the Nazis have been preparing for war. While they were rearming, building new, more powerful tanks and dive bombers, France was like a tired sleeping giant that had lost its will to fight. It was easier to roll over and play dead. When the moment came for the wills of the two nations to be tested, France was unprepared to oppose the Nazis."

"Oh dear," said Calanthe. "Yes, I see it now. Yes, I quite understand. Dear me." She shook her head, then looked at him, frowning. "You don't think they'll come here do you?"

Marc hesitated. "Eventually."

"Oh dear." She picked up a palmetto leaf and fanned her face. "Then perhaps I'll buy a pistol."

After dinner Marc walked with Valli down a flower-scented path and through a gate in the ancient wall first built by slaves of an emir. The path wound down to the shore.

"Did you ever see such a moon?" she whispered, gazing at the large silvery reflection on the bay. The water rippled like a school of silvery fish darting back and forth in frolic. The sand was still hot, and at this moment, the war seemed about as far away as Gestapo agent Gestler.

Marc didn't really answer, though he looked at the moon, and was silent for a long moment. The moonlight washed over them as the sea breeze sang through the date palms and stirred the dry sand against her ankles.

"I've heard from Danjou," he said in a voice that could only be heard by her. "He's safely in London. He's met with General de Gaulle and one of the British prime minister's top aides. Can you repeat to me again what Gestler told you about the fleet? What he knew about them?"

"The warships? Yes, I think so. He said Admiral Darlan promised the British prime minister he would sail them to Canada. But Darlan had no real intention of surrendering the French navy to Britain. Dietrich expected the Germans to seize the warships for their own use."

Marc looked out at the calm sea and she noted he was scowling.

"What is it? Can you tell me?"

"Gestler is right."

"But if that fleet goes to the Nazis, Britain doesn't stand a chance to hold out against the Wehrmacht. The only way England will remain a bastion of freedom in a swastika-draped Europe is by having access to the Atlantic. Now that

France has fallen, England has one hope: that eventually the United States will enter the war. But how long that will be, and what it will take to provoke President Roosevelt and the Americans to get involved, only God knows." Valli shivered in the warm wind. She looked at the moon, so peaceful, so undisturbed. She could understand why the United States so far across the ocean stood untouched by the sufferings of France, Holland, Poland, Czechoslovakia, and all of Europe—their lives were as pleasant as hers was now on this romantic beach walking beside Marc.

Yes...what would it take to get them to declare war on the Axis Powers?

"Prime Minister Churchill hopes to hold out as the Battle of Britain begins," Marc said quietly. "And our French fleet must *not* fall into the hands of the Germans."

"But—what if Admiral Darlan doesn't sail the fleet away?"

Marc looked as if his own words cut deep into his heart: "They've got to sink our own navy at Oran."

She gasped. "Fire on our own ships? Our own flesh and blood?"

"Yes. That's the order Churchill sent to the British admiral. They're on their way now from Gibraltar. Sebastien will present an offer to the French. They can sail to Canada, the United States, Martinique in the West Indies, or fight in the war with the Free French and Britain. If not, they will have to abandon ship."

"What do you think they'll do?" she whispered.

"If they're smart," he said with a trace of anger, "they'll sail at once to join de Gaulle in London and take to sea to fight. But Darlan is angry at de Gaulle. He is unlikely to aid Britain."

He didn't need to go on. She understood. If the French fleet did not cooperate, the British would open fire.

"They have to do it," he said. "I understand their reasoning, so do de Gaulle and the Free French. But if it happens, it will be agony, nevertheless."

They said no more, and after several minutes of walking in the wind with the sound of the water, he slipped an arm around her and turned her back toward the stone house.

"I've burdened you enough," he said. "But I wanted you to know what to expect. I'll need to send you on alone to Davide's station. Sebastien already knows and will meet me in Oran. Will you be able to handle the matter of Blystone's bag on your own?"

"Yes, of course I can, Marc. You've enough to worry about. As soon as I get it, I'll meet you at Oran, with Davide, if I can get him to come back with us."

"All right. But I wish I were going with you to Bel-Abbes."

She smiled. "There will be time enough for that later."

He looked down at her gravely, the breeze tugging at his dark hair. "Will there?"

"Now that my heart has found you, how can it ever let you go?" she whispered.

He held her tightly, as if afraid something could tear them apart forever.

# 20

This is how it had all begun. She had met Blystone on this train nearly two months ago. Valli imagined the Englishman in the hands of Gestler in Lisbon, at last confessing what he knew before his death. She shuddered and glanced about the train, noting that this time there were fewer passengers: a few locals and several disconsolate French men and women.

Valli gazed out the window as the sluggish West Algerian Company train followed the track through hot white sand freckled with dusky shadows. Marc had his duties to perform and had gone on to Oran to meet up with Colonel Sebastien and members of the FFL, the Free French under General de Gaulle.

At dusk, as the first evening star pulsated, the train pulled into the small depot at Sidi-bel-Abbes. A few minutes later she disembarked, surprised to see Giselle waiting for her. Her sister appeared tense as they got into an open military truck from the legionnaire fort.

"Marc sent a wire telling me you were due on the evening train from Oran," Giselle explained. "I'm glad you're here, Valli." She shot her a quick, searching glance. "Sorry I had to run off the way I did. It was necessary. Was it difficult to get out of Paris?"

"There were times when I didn't think we'd make it. The Germans were only miles from Paris when we flew out."

"It's only just beginning," Giselle said tensely. "There's no guarantee the resistance will prevail you know."

"We'll win," Valli stated firmly. "Eventually truth prevails, as long as God sits on the throne of His universe."

"You sound very confident," Giselle said tiredly. "I can only hope you're right."

The truck pulled through the gate of the fort. "Aren't we going to the mission station?" Valli asked, surprised.

"There's no one there right now. Davide is off holding meetings at some of the camps. The legionnaires are split over whether to swear allegiance to the Petain government in Vichy or fight on with de Gaulle with the Free French. There's been an upheaval, I'm told. The split is serious. Davide is with those who want to join de Gaulle."

The truck stopped in the fort yard. Giselle led her away from the common barracks toward a small area of rooms used for visiting dignitaries. "I thought we'd spend the night in the room they gave Sebastien. It's comfortable and safe."

Valli looked at her. Giselle looked grimly ahead.

The room had everything they needed, but was hot and airless.

"This is rather unusual for you, isn't it?" Valli asked, glancing about. "Couldn't you have gone with Sebastien to Oran?"

"I could have," she said, "but there is something important I had to take care of here. I wanted to see Davide, too,
but as luck would have it, he's away. He won't be back until
next week, so I decided to wait. It's not so bad, and it is
safe."

"That's the second time you used the word safe. You
don't think Dietrich is here, do you?" she asked quietly, but
bluntly.

"He can be anywhere by now," she answered nervously.

"Is he trying to find Nanette?"

Giselle turned, her eyes flaring slightly. They stared at
each other. "Calanthe told you."

"About *my* child?" she said wryly. "Yes. As you can
imagine, I was rather shocked to hear about her."

Giselle flushed and turned suddenly docile. "I'm sorry,
Valli, it was horrible of me."

"Yes, rather."

"I was desperate at the time. Kraig had just left me...and
I had Nanette. I knew Calanthe would never understand, so
I turned myself into a heroine, out to save the baby girl you
didn't want, that you had given up to pursue your ballet
career. I knew, that way, I'd be accepted into the Tangier
house. I was without money and without hope. Everything
calmed back down and went smoothly until recently. Then
Dietrich began hounding me."

Valli listened to Giselle confess while they sat across
from each other with a small table between them, with the
hot night air coming in through the open window.

"Is that when he threatened to use the photographs of
you and Kraig dining in Casablanca?"

"Yes. Naturally those pictures would suggest to
Sebastien that I was being untrue to him. Nanette was with
us. Kraig wanted to take her back to Athens, but I refused.

He hadn't done a thing to help me when I was in trouble. Why should he have Nanette now?" her eyes snapped. "He blamed me for everything. When he left me in Madrid, I waited by myself until she was born, then I hired a governess out of Casablanca, a little French woman who was good to Nanette. I went back home to Tangier after that, to Calanthe."

Valli said nothing. Calmly discussing the child of her sister by the man she had once thought she would marry was painful, but she realized with a sense of freedom that the one man she loved and wanted desperately was a man with character. Kraig had dimmed like the light from a lamp after the sun came up.

"As Kraig and I sat together with Nanette in the Casablanca café, he was warning me about what his brother, Dietrich, was up to. I'm sure that's what was in his letter. He told you about Nanette and how Dietrich intended to blackmail me, and he must have warned you of the danger. I think Kraig knew of Dietrich's interest in you. Naturally, Dietrich didn't want you to read about Nanette, and neither did I. So I took the letter as ordered."

"Ordered by the man in my dressing room? The one with the smile?"

"Yes...he was following me in Paris. He must still be there. Somehow Dietrich learned from a captured Surete agent that Sebastien was the head of the operation here in North Africa." Her eyes faltered to her cup.

"Go on," Valli said quietly.

"I worked hard after that to try and get my life straightened out. Davide was trying to help me. He still is. He keeps telling me God can forgive me through Christ and make something special out of my life. That's why I came here now—for help, but he's gone," she said with a catch in her voice. "Sebastien is very kind to me." She blinked hard. "I couldn't tell him about Kraig, or Nanette. I was afraid he wouldn't love me after he knew what I'd done. Then Dietrich contacted me. The Nazis seem to find out the worst about everyone. He contacted Kraig too and told him to threaten me to cooperate, but Kraig wouldn't do it. By then, Kraig was seeing life differently. He'd seen what the Germans were doing and he joined the underground." She lapsed wearily into silence, still avoiding Valli's eyes.

"Kraig has been arrested," Valli said quietly.

Giselle looked sickened and rested, forehead in her hand, her elbow on the little wood table. "Knowing Dietrich, he'll do nothing to help him."

"How did Dietrich contact you?"

"Through one of the serving girls at Calanthe's house." Giselle got up and paced. "And I do love Sebastien. It's ironic that I should find that out now, when there's a chance I'll lose him."

"You've got to tell all this to Sebastien," Valli urged her.

Giselle continued her pacing, hands shoved into her pockets, a grim but determined look on her face. "I'll tell him, but in time, and in my way, when it's safe to do so."

"And when will that be?"

"When Sebastien returns from Oran. Everything will be all right then. I can stop worrying at last."

Valli glanced at her, alert, but she pretended she hadn't noticed the mention of the harbor where the French fleet was anchored. Why would it be safer after Oran? Did Giselle know? Had Sebastien told her? Or had she secretly discovered the very information Dietrich wanted?

Valli watched her uneasily, trying to hide her feelings of sudden fear and distrust. Even if Giselle knew, she wouldn't give that information to Dietrich. She wouldn't betray the resistance movement, or Britain. Or would she?

"There is no end to blackmail," Valli said in a hushed voice. "If ever you cooperate with the Germans, do you think Dietrich would be satisfied?"

Giselle looked at her, making no comment. Her eyes averted to the clock on the wall.

Valli's fingers tightened. "What makes you think he wouldn't be back again in another month or so? You can't trust him. He could threaten you all over again for new information stolen from the Surete."

"I've got to take her away so Dietrich will never find her. London or New York may be the only safe places in the world."

"It will be difficult to find a ship out of Casablanca. And even if you could reach neutral Lisbon, the Atlantic is dangerous. With France fallen, the German battle for Britain will begin."

"It's a chance that must be taken."

Valli looked at her, surprised. "You're not thinking of going yourself? What of Sebastien?"

She wrung her hands. "If I confess to Sebastien," she began slowly, her words bringing pain, "then maybe he'll understand. He'll forgive me—and help me get on a ship for Lisbon, then England. Once Nanette is safe—I'll return."

Valli stood. "With the war, there's a chance you'll not be able to come back, Giselle. You could become separated from Sebastien."

"I won't think of that. It's depressing." She took a cigarette from her case and lit it. She glanced at the clock again. "Let's not talk about it anymore tonight." She ran her fingers across her forehead. "We're both mentally exhausted. Why don't you get ready for bed? I've been totally selfish talking your head off like this. There's a shower behind that door, and bunk beds."

Valli sensed that Giselle was more troubled than she was letting on. Why did she keep looking at the time?

"Yes, maybe you're right. We can talk about it again in the morning."

"Yes, that would be better." She reached for a fan and shook her hair out. "It's so dreadfully hot in here. While you shower and get ready for bed, I think I'll just sit outside on the steps and try to get a breath of air. The stars are beautiful out here. I like to sit and look at them and think what it would be like to escape far beyond."

Valli nodded and went to her small bag, carrying it toward the shower. "If you don't mind I'll lower these lights. They draw insects." Giselle didn't appear to even hear her as she opened the door and stepped outside. Valli left the bathroom light on, but turned the others off. She ran the water, then came back quietly to the window and peered out. As she had suspected, Giselle was walking toward the fort gate. Where was she going?

Valli ran and turned the water off, then inched the front door open. When Giselle was far enough away, Valli slipped out noiselessly into the hot night, glancing in both directions. Seeing no one, she followed her at a safe distance across the hot gravel, trying to walk quietly.

Valli neared the fort gate. It remained open until 9:00 P.M. and Giselle paused and glanced behind her. Valli had just enough time to step beside a shrub bush where the shadows were darker. Giselle went through the gate and Valli again followed.

Where could she possibly be going this time of the evening? To Davide's station? But their brother wasn't at the mission house.

Valli took the path and cut across the road that brought her to a flat, sandy field where more silhouetted date palms grew. She saw her sister walking ahead.

Within a brisk five-minute walk Valli had followed her to Davide's house, which was showing white in the bright moonlight. One lamp was burning in the lower front of the house, offering a protective glow.

Valli stopped. Giselle went up the front steps, removed something from her skirt pocket, glanced behind her, then unlocked the front door.

Valli sighed. So that was all there was to it. Maybe she had left some clothing there, or a book she wanted to read.

*Well, my little excursion wasn't in vain. This is the perfect time to retrieve Blystone's bag and take it back with me to the fort,* she thought. She didn't want to stay long in Bel-Abbes now that she knew Davide was gone. She could board the train tomorrow for Oran and bring the bag to Marc. Giselle would decide whether she wished to stay here or go with her to join Sebastien.

Valli went to the back of the house where the second structure, shaped like a horseshoe, was located, forming the living quarters for the Christian Berbers and their families.

She located a shovel and walked to the bougainvillea vines sprawling along the stone wall. The ground was still soft from where she had dug it up two months ago, and she went to work in the moonlight.

She was forced to use her left foot on the shovel. The process went slower than she had expected but within five minutes the shovel finally touched the canvas and she stooped and unearthed it, brushing away the loose, sandy dirt. She lifted it and carried it toward the main house, intending to bring it back to the fort with her. As she approached the Berbers' dwellings she heard voices, children fussing and women trying to hush them. She neared Davide's house and came to the side window. The light burned inside the room and she saw Giselle talking to someone who kept out of sight. Valli's heart began to beat faster. Who was with her?

Giselle's muffled voice sounded again, but whoever was with her spoke in a lower voice.

Valli gripped the canvas bag a little tighter and stepped to the side of the house to try to see inside. Giselle nodded, looking distraught.

Just then, Valli heard a child's voice crying again from one of the back rooms of the Berbers' quarters. A woman spoke in French and the child answered in French, continuing to cry: "Grandmere, where is my maman?'"

Valli's breath caught, and she turned from the window to look back toward the horseshoe of rooms. Nanette! So that's where Giselle was hiding her, masquerading her as a Berber child.

Valli's mind shot back to her visit at the station two months ago. The little girl hiding from Haroun's wife? Poor Nanette. She must have picked up the fear surrounding her here at the station when Dietrich arrived on the motorcycle. Haroun's wife, Saidah, had rushed away to hide her—

Yes, that was the reason the sound of his motorcycle had sent them all running to hide. And to think Dietrich had almost located Nanette that day. *He might have searched and found her even then if he hadn't been so surprised to see me here,* she thought. *I may have distracted him from pursuing his real goal.*

She could almost hear the sound of his motorcycle in her memory. Her spine tightened. Wait! What was that sound she was hearing now?

She turned, staring off toward the little town of Sidi-bel-Abbes, where lights in the taverns and gambling dens still glowed brightly. Across the flat, sandy field, the distant but growing sound of a motorcycle could be heard in the still, hot night.

She stood transfixed, clutching the bag. She looked back toward the window. She must warn Giselle, but would it not be safer just to take the child and escape while Dietrich confronted Giselle in the house? By the time he learned where Nanette was, Valli could have her at the fort. The most important thing was the child's safety. She was the daughter of Kraig and Giselle, two people who had betrayed her and hurt her so deeply. Even so, she must save their child. Once at the fort she could place an urgent call to Marc at Oran. He could then alert the authorities here at Bel-Abbes to search for Dietrich.

Valli shifted the heavy bag to her other shoulder and backed away from the window. Then she turned and rushed toward the horseshoe building.

The sound of a child's crying drew her to the right room. She knocked rapidly and spoke in French: "Open up! Hurry. Nanette is in danger. I'm Giselle's sister, Valli Chattaine. I think the Gestapo agent is coming on the motorcycle again."

Everything inside the room turned quiet, then the door opened a crack. An older French woman dressed as a Berber peasant peered at her anxiously. "You are Mademoiselle Valli?" she whispered.

"Yes, I'm here to help. We haven't much time. A motorcycle is coming. It could be Dietrich."

The old woman's hand went to her throat. She closed her eyes and whispered a prayer. Valli pushed past her into the room. "Where is Nanette?"

The little girl sat in bed in her nightclothes, with a tearstained face, her eyes wide. She clutched a rag doll and, in curiosity, ceased her crying and stared up at Valli.

Valli smiled and managed to speak calmly in French. "Hello, Nanette. I'm your Aunt Valli. I saw you below my window one morning. You were crying then, too. I spoke to you then, but you didn't understand because I talked to you in Berber. Come, we're going away. Maman will join us there."

Nanette's eyes brightened. "Maman?" she repeated.

Valli gave orders to the governess, who lifted the child into her sturdy arms. Valli locked the front door and rushed to the back. The governess followed, and Nanette grew perfectly quiet and clung to her doll.

Outside in the still night, Valli led the way, keeping to the side of the wall where the vines and thicker shadows clustered together, offering concealment. She had heard the motorcycle, but if it had been Dietrich he had cut the motor before nearing the house. The vehicle was nowhere in sight. Valli moved forward cautiously. Had she been mistaken?

She opened the gate and went through, with the governess just behind carrying Nanette. Valli stopped with a gasp. Dietrich stood there. He stepped into the moonlight, and his silhouette appeared massive within his dark clothing, his hair showing golden. She saw something in his right hand, a revolver.

"I see your ankle has healed," he said shortly. "You have walked straight to me, bringing Blystone's bag and the child. Well done, fraulein. You will be rewarded for this. Will a journey to Berlin be sufficient?"

Nanette let out a frightened wail. The front door was flung open and Giselle appeared, a German officer beside her.

"Captain Zimmer is with me," Giselle cried to Dietrich.

Valli floundered. Who was Zimmer?

Zimmer and Giselle walked through the shadows near the front door, and Giselle cried, "Nanette!"

"She's all right," Valli called back.

Zimmer spoke, "It's too late now, Dietrich," but it was Marc's voice! "Giselle is no longer threatened by you. Sebastien is already at Oran with the British admiral Sommerville. By tomorrow, if the French fleet doesn't yield, the British will sink the warships. There will be no swastika flying over the *Dunkerque*."

Marc!? Valli stood staring at him, as he came down the steps in German uniform with a revolver in hand.

Dietrich reached out and grasped Valli's arm, pulling her in front of him, shoving his luger into her spine. "One move, swine, and she will never dance again."

Valli blinked, ready for the blast that would either paralyze or kill her. When, suddenly, Dietrich's hold on her arm released...the revolver withdrew from her spine. She drew aside, wondering, dazed. She saw a dozen French legionnaires standing behind him, and a glowering Frenchman leveling his gun barrel against Dietrich's temple.

"Hello, Dietrich," he said curtly. "Remember me? Cousin Zimmer. Did you think I would actually betray the French Foreign Legion for the real swine?" he said of Adolf Hitler.

Dietrich's weapon was being snatched from his hand and Zimmer and the other legionnaires shoved him away and marched him toward the Bel-Abbes fort.

Giselle came running down the steps to Nanette, pausing to grab Valli first and kiss her cheek. "Merci, my sister," she whispered. "All is well, all is well." She took her daughter into her arms and walked away with her, the governess following.

Valli was still clutching the bag when Marc took it from her, set it on the ground, and pulled her into his fervent embrace. "Darling Valli," he whispered, kissing her.

"W-what are you doing here?" she asked a minute later, shaken. "And where did you get that uniform? Secrets of the Surete, I suppose?"

"We have many secrets, dear. Sebastien and I knew Dietrich was on his way here to Giselle."

"Sebastien knew?" she asked surprised.

"He knows everything," he said quietly, "even about Nanette. But he will pretend he doesn't when and if Giselle confesses to him. Let's hope she does. It will save their marriage. He'll know she means it."

"But Dietrich, how did you know he was coming here tonight?"

"A Surete agent followed Dietrich from Lisbon," he continued. "But I thought it best if you didn't know I was here until we trapped him. I arranged things carefully with Zimmer so you would be safe. Did you think I would leave you here alone while I stayed in Oran? I also arranged with Giselle to meet me here. I told her to say nothing to you. I knew you well enough to understand you would follow her. Dietrich was hiding in town. When he saw you follow Giselle, he thought he had what he wanted."

She clung to him. "I'll think about all that later...just hold me."

He did, telling her he loved her, then picking up the canvas bag he walked with her back into Davide's house where the light was shining once more.

# Epilogue

The long world war was only beginning. It was July 11, 1940. Although the battle of France was over, the French Resistance was just beginning, as was Hitler's battle of Britain. Soon Nazi bombers would cross the Channel and rain down a storm of terror.

When Davide returned to Tangier with Sebastien, he admitted to Great-Aunt Calanthe and to Valli that he had joined the Free French. Learning that the mission station must be closed for an indefinite period of time, Valli told Marc:

"Someone has to carry on the work at the station, so why not me? I can't return to the ballet theater, and my ankle may never be strong enough to dance professionally again."

"At least that would place you close to the Bel-Abbes fort," he agreed. "I'll continue to be stationed there for the next six months, as well as here at the embassy with Sebastien, but after that it's unclear where I'll be sent."

They lapsed into meditative silence as they strolled across the soft grass in the twilight.

"But by then," he added, turning her to face him, "you'll be Valli Durell, and I'll make sure you're as safe as the widening war will permit."

Valli held him, her cheek against his chest as they stood in the limpid breeze drifting in from across the warm blue water, the ripples reddening in the sunset. Her heart beat with his, and so too, her thoughts.

He had told her that the British had fired upon and sunk the French fleet at Meirs-el-Kebir. Admiral Darlan had refused to guarantee that the ships would not be turned over to the Nazis, nor would he give orders for them to sail to Canada or a neutral port. It was said that Prime Minister Churchill had tears in his eyes when he learned the fate of the French ships and of the deaths of the French sailors—until recently comrades in arms against the Nazis.

Marshall Petain had broken off diplomatic relations with London over the sinking of the ships. He had established a compromising pro-Nazi Vichy regime with headquarters not in occupied Paris but in Vichy, with himself as the Head of State. He had given a radio broadcast telling the French people to collaborate with the Germans.

Here in French Tangier matters had not yet come to a head with Germany. It was a lovely evening and Valli was with Marc, and for the moment that was all that mattered. The amber sun was setting above the Bay as she walked with him on the large lawn in front of Calanthe's house.

Valli wore a lovely pastel evening dress, and Marc was in the handsome uniform of the French Foreign Legion. Calanthe had given a *dejeuner* party in celebration of the diamond engagement ring now winking on Valli's finger. She smiled at Marc, who slipped an arm around her waist and held her.

They had much to be grateful for. Giselle had confessed all to Sebastien on his return, and as Valli had suspected, her brother-in-law was mature enough to forgive the broken past and ready to build the future on better promises. He loved his wife and Giselle, so it seemed, had realized how much she loved Sebastien. She had been so pleased that her husband still loved her that she had showed up at church on Sunday morning. Valli had real hope that one day Giselle might come to trust the Lord.

"Sebastien is adopting Nanette," she told Marc.

"I thought he would, now that the news about Kraig was dragged out of Dietrich."

She shook her head sadly. "I can hardly believe he would allow the SS to kill his own brother."

"He's not the first to kill his own brother," Marc said quietly.

No, the first man who was ever born was. "What will happen to Dietrich now?" she asked.

"He's been turned over to the Surete for further questioning. After that, he'll be transferred to a detention camp in the Sahara as a prisoner of war. As for my cousin Aubert and his wife, Inga, if they're alive after the war, they'll be tried as collaborators, along with all of the rest of the traitors in France, including Petain."

Yes, she thought, if the war ever ended...

"Are you going to tell me what Dietrich wanted from Blystone's bag?"

"It seems dear old Blystone wasn't the selfless patriot we thought he was."

"You mean he wasn't loyal to us?" she asked, disappointed.

"Oh, he was loyal to us all right," Marc said pensively. "He did fulfill the job of courier, getting our agent's information to us."

"And he lost his life for England and France," she said with a somber tribute.

"Maybe not."

She looked at him. "What do you mean?"

"It turns out Blystone was smuggling diamonds out of Dakar, and it was the diamonds that Dietrich really wanted."

"Diamonds," she repeated, shocked.

Marc looked at her with a lifted brow. "Now, aren't you pleased with yourself for so carefully hauling that heavy bag around for so long before you buried it beneath the rose bushes?"

"Bougainvillea vines," she corrected with a small smile.

"What if you had brought those bags of sand out to the Sahara and simply dumped them in a sand dune?" he teased. "You're to be commended for a duty well done."

She glanced at her diamond engagement ring, then met his gaze with a twinkle in her eyes. "You're sure this diamond isn't—"

He laughed, his embrace tightening. "Not on your life. That, my demoiselle, was bought by the hard-won wages of a poor legionnaire!"

"Not so poor from what Davide tells me. That thick envelope left to you by Great-Uncle Claude holds the deed to the Ransier estate."

"And, property in Greece. A villa."

Her eyes widened. His mouth turned into a brief smile. "Sure that isn't why you're marrying me?"

She slipped both arms around his neck, and her eyes spoke of her love. "How can I convince you otherwise?" Her lips turned into a tender smile.

"Like this," he whispered.

As the sun began to dip into a sea of red jewels, their silhouettes embraced as one, and the breeze gently swept the hem of her lace skirt against his boots. From inside the ballroom the music played, and the words drifted to them..."Yours, till the stars lose their glory..."

# Harvest House Publishers

*For the Best in Inspirational Fiction*

### *Linda Chaikin*
TRADE WINDS
Captive Heart
Silver Dreams
Island Bride

A DAY TO REMEMBER
Monday's Child

### *G. Roger Corey*
In A Mirror Dimly
Eden Springs

### *Melody Carlson*
A Place to Come Home to
Everything I Long For

---

## *Lori Wick*

A PLACE CALLED HOME
A Place Called Home
A Song for Silas
The Long Road Home
A Gathering of Memories

THE CALIFORNIANS
Whatever Tomorrow Brings
As Time Goes By
Sean Donovan
Donovan's Daughter

KENSINGTON CHRONICLES
The Hawk and the Jewel
Wings of the Morning
Who Brings Forth the Wind
The Knight and the Dove

ROCKY MOUNTAIN MEMORIES
Where the Wild Rose Blooms
Whispers of Moonlight
To Know Her by Name
Promise Me Tomorrow

THE YELLOW ROSE TRILOGY
Every Little Thing About You

CONTEMPORARY FICTION
Sophie's Heart
Beyond the Picket Fence
The Princess